THE

SYRINGA TREE

A Novel

. . . .

P A M E L A   G I E N

Published in the United States by
Random House, an imprint of The Random House Publishing Group,
a division of Random House, Inc., New York.

RANDOM HOUSE and colophon are
registered trademarks of Random House, Inc.

This novel is based on the author's
play of the same name.

Grateful acknowledgment is made to Jeremy Taylor and Gallo (Africa) Ltd. for permission to reprint lyrics from "Ballad of the Southern Suburbs," a.k.a. "Ag Pleez Deddy," copyright © 1962 by Jeremy Taylor. Reprinted by permission.

LIBRARY OF CONGRESS CATALOGING-IN-PUBLICATION DATA

Gien, Pamela.
The syringa tree: a novel/Pamela Gien.
p.   cm.
ISBN 0-375-50755-8
1. Apartheid—Fiction. 2. South Africa—Fiction. 3. Race relations—Fiction. I. Title.
PR9369.4.G54S97 2006   823'.92—dc22   2006041054

Printed in the United States of America on acid-free paper

www.atrandom.com

6 8 9 7

Book design by Barbara M. Bachman

For my father and mother,
with my love and gratitude

. . . .

PART ONE

. . . .

CHAPTER ONE

SOEKMEKAAR,

LOOKING FOR ONE ANOTHER

◎◎

*N*ewly *six, I lay* in the dark listening to the rattle of my shutters. The moon was gone from them.

Something moved in the passage outside my door. My heart banged up into my throat. I strained to listen, tried to be still. I must have called out. I felt warm fingers close my eyes. My father's hands smelled of long hours and antiseptic soap. "It's nearly midnight, Lizzy," he said, in the hope I would finally submit to sleep in my Johannesburg bed. In the dim light, I saw he was still in his creased shirtsleeves rolled up from the day, but without his polished brown shoes. Usually at night, he left them by the front door. He must have had to go out again after we fell asleep, on another call, someone sick on a farm at Fourways, maybe, or further out at Honeydew, a child bitten by a snake, someone trying to be born, someone stabbed. Newly qualified as a doctor, he was not yet thirty, with dark rims beneath his eyes.

"Is Mommy still in her bed?" I whispered.

"She's in her bed."

He closed my eyes again and turned to go. Still no moon.

"Tell of the wild dogs," I said.

He sat down around the middle of the bed where my feet ended under the blanket, and rested his head on his hands. He began rubbing his fingers against his scalp through his short-cut dark brown hair, slowly, like medicine for his head. "He loved the wild dogs," he began. "His black eyes, like newly lit coals, glowed within the small, flat plane of his features. He had never seen the face from which he peered, Elizabeth, never caught sight of the fire within him." He was the first, he said, the first to walk the African veld we now called our own.

The moon had not returned. In its place it had left only relentless night. Like the moon, I drifted away. It was the first of May, 1963, with the whipping dust of early winter already taunting the bleak Transvaal highveld with the promise of more drought. Evenings were starting to prick with cold. Veld grass blew flame-ready in dry whispers. Miles deep, men tunneled, dreaming of the beauty of the sky. Crickets kept the night awake, and outside, the city of gold lay quiet.

It must have been Salamina who lifted me in the dead of night from my sheets, her strong, brown Xhosa hands paper-dry from cleaning and washing. It must have been Salamina who wrapped my sleeping limbs tight within a musty blanket and heaved me, limp with dreams, up over her pregnant belly.

She must have carried me silently down the slate passage, through the kitchen door out to the waiting car, its headlights on, its hot breath steaming into the black highveld cold. It must have been her Xhosa tongue, clicking like soft rain on a tin roof, that kept me from crying out in my brief moment of waking, kept me from thinking it was the Tokolosh come to suck me away. "Tsht, Monkey . . . *thula baba*, jhe," I must have heard her whisper.

"Thank you, Salamina," my father said in the murmur of the house rustled into waking.

It must have been Salamina's sound and smell that lulled me back to the safety of sleep as she ran with me quickly to lay me in the backseat of the car. And it must have been Salamina who closed the gate behind us, watching as we drove away, her stomach swollen, ready, with a child who was not to be mentioned outside the walls of our house.

Before the first gleam of dawn began to light the Great North Road on the outskirts of the city, I woke in my blanket on the backseat. Peering out into the night, I saw the piling yellow sands of gold mines ghosting by like dark castles, their glimmer robbed, long gone. I knew, with a leap in my chest, this was the way to Clova.

It was the acrid odor of smoke that woke me—thousands of fires already fueling the daily life of the native townships, Soweto and Alexandra—the same smell that seeped from the pockets and folds of Salamina returning from her servant's day off each week—a black and sour smell. A smell I did not notice near my home, where electricity burned bright and there was no need of a fire except as a frippery on a chilly night. You are not allowed to go in there, not without a special paper, my sleeping head bossed me, into those townships. They lapped, silent as we passed, at the edges of Johannesburg.

Through the sweet, laden orange trees of Nylstroom we went, and out into the northern veld far from the lights of any city or town, where the sky was higher, blacker, and the early dawn deeper, quieter. It told you nothing. Only the swift rub of tires sounding their long, dark call.

My mother sat in the front seat, the promise of Clova in the distance ahead, her rough edges softened, calm again, with my father driving us further and further out into the veld. Too early for smoking but not finding a reason to wait, she lit a cigarette, filling the car with the scratching smell of a match. She opened the window, washing us in cool air, and rested her head back. From the backseat, I saw her eyes close down at the sides as she breathed out. The wet corners of her thick, black lashes wove top into bottom, like shongololo-worm legs folding together in the rain.

Not brushed or neat now, the soft curls of her Jacqueline Kennedy hair fell a bit over the neck of her green wool jersey, where the label stuck out. She managed to hold the cigarette and simultaneously finger her delicate pearl earring with the same hand, between her fourth finger and thumb—soothed, in her small cloud of smoke.

I did not risk tucking the label in for her, lest it scratch her skin, or aggravate her.

I thought, suddenly, of promising not to root in the sugar box when no one was looking. It was a promise I knew she would welcome, as it would cure the horrible, spiky condition called hyperactivity that routinely befell me soon after—prompting Salamina more than once to cry out, "Jheh, Miss Lizzy, you are jumping like a monkey!"

But on second thought, I decided to save the sugar box promise for later, if things got worse. For now, I would just be exceedingly quiet. I would say very little when we got to Clova, and would not appear like a pest too much in front of her, except maybe to stroke her feet as they peeped out of her blankets, if she napped there in the afternoons. Through sleeping eyes, she would not see me. I would smooth her feet, keeping my hand flat and gentle, the way she sometimes smoothed me.

As we drove, my head banged inside with the commotion of the day before. Usually, no one said anything about my mattress. Usually, Salamina and Iris, the newish nanny for baby John, carried it out to air in the sun. They'd lay it on the grass in the backyard for their lunch hour, then settle themselves, unbuttoning their cotton uniforms a bit under the powdery, yellow mimosa trees behind the house, eating doorstop-thick jam sandwiches and embroidering white pillowcases with jaunty flowers for their servants' rooms.

Late in the afternoon, my mother had come into my room to lie down next to me on my cured bed. In her yellow linen dress, creased and slept-in like a crushed lemon-cream biscuit, she lay with her face close to mine, loving me, her body grateful, like a boat that had drifted unexpectedly to safety after a terrible storm. She put her hand on my hair—chopped off in brown tufts to make it grow lustrously full in the future. One day I'd be jolly thankful for thick hair, she often told me. She kissed me, dozed with me a bit, and then said suddenly, getting up again, "Oh God, Elizabeth. You're doing this on purpose, aren't you? I just can't bloody cope with it. . . ."

It wasn't that I didn't remember to run if I felt it coming. I promise it happened without my noticing, creasing my khaki cotton *broeks* into burning, smelly folds. Mostly I waited for it to dry, hoping it would not stink and thereby alert someone. The sun helped a lot, if you were jolly clever and hared out there quickly enough. And rubbing the back of yourself in the dried-out flower bed helped, soaking it away in a sandy crust that stuck to the sopping broeks. If you were lucky and got the mixture exactly right, it would cake itself on to hide the chafing patch.

She must have smelled it in the mattress, smelled me, the bad stink of the dried sand. I had never heard her swear, or really even raise her voice. She held on to me again, and said she was very sorry, and again I was her harbor, wet with her tears.

By the time my father came home after dusk, her door had been closed for hours, and I had been quiet for just as long. I heard the tires on the dirt driveway. I heard his car door close, and waited in the passage until I saw him at the end of it. He was tall to me, with glinting, sad eyes, a quick temper, and, they had just said in the *Rand Daily Mail*, brilliant.

He put his black physician's bag down and covered his brow with his hand as if he had seen enough for one day.

"Mommy's sleeping," I whispered.

"Where's Salamina? Why are the lights off?" he asked. "Hello, my Lizzy . . ."

I leapt up to him. He had been at his consulting rooms all day, setting up his first practice at the top end of the stony hill that was Bell Street, where the buses came in from the black townships, and the dirt road was lined with tiny, sharp stones glinting like salt in the sun. Most of his new patients were going to be Afrikaans, some English like us, a whole lot black, and a few in between. He'd navigated with some skill and a bit of humor, he'd later say, the Afrikaans whispers

about the new doctor Isaac Grace being *"Jood,"* and more disgusting
even than that, his wife, Eugenie, *"Katoliek!"* He'd separated, as required now by the laws, the black consulting rooms from the white,
blacks going up the back stairs to their section, and whites up the front
to theirs—thinking all the while of time wasted walking between the
two. And there were other whispers he'd heard, surreptitious little
jokes, subtle questions from patients, meant as feelers to discover
where the new doctor stood in the ongoing problem of the native
question. Predictions were offered about the teeming, likely violent
masses. And now he had come home to find us in a heap, not coping
with ourselves.

He said nothing to me about the wet broeks. I might be in the
clear. Perhaps he'd already decided, before the broeks palaver, to take
my mother to Clova for a rest, and let her parents restore her. He
walked up the passage and went into her room.

Later, he let me ride on his shiny shoes, his feet under my bare
ones, around the darkening acre of our garden. He told me how proper
Mrs. Engelbrecht had mistakenly gone up the back stairs for Blacks
Only at the new doctor's rooms, and about the giggles and whispers in
his waiting room when, in her embarrassment, she sternly admon-
ished him to mark his stairs more clearly. "Why was she cross?" I
asked. "Don't know," he said, and then as if he wasn't really speaking
to me, "Afraid she'll catch something dire on the black stairs. Probably
leapt into her shower and scrubbed her bloody skin off."

At the tangled granadilla vines, we'd paused to search high above
for a tiny light in its unimaginable orbit. Four years before, in 1959, a
monkey peered out of his porthole as he soared through the heavens,
his eyes lit with tricks, doubts, and fears. I scanned the nocturnal sky
for him, his face glued to his window in the high silence above.

Suddenly, everything blurred.

"Brown pools . . . they think they're pools," my father said in the
bug-thick dark, licking his finger and digging a miggie or some flying
thing out of my eye.

The night smelled heavy-sweet with rotting moonflowers left over from summer. The throb of crickets drowned the din of my mother's quiet absence in my ears. Our house from outside was unlit, except for the passage so we could find our way to bed. *Oh no nothing will happen GOD won't let anything happen Oh nonothingwill happen,* droned in my night-head as we walked. The world inside our fence seemed suddenly as unpredictable as the world outside.

Bluer than English violets, my mother's eyes were already closed when we went back in—just her cool feet sticking out of the blanket she'd pulled over to cover herself away. My father splashed his face with water in the bathroom. I heard it drip on the floor. He did not put on the light in there.

I stood by her bed in the shuttered dark. Her room smelled of Blue Grass powder, skin, sweet tea, and sadness. I had crept in to soothe her, to pat her feet, to let her know that I would no longer wet the bed, or my khaki broeks, that I would not be impossible in *any* way, that I would wash myself jolly clean with Vinolia sandalwood soap (guaranteed to work, I knew, because it was by appointment only to Her Majesty the Queen, and you've never seen *her* filthy), that I would try to look pretty and to smell nice.

I patted my wishes into her soft skin, hoping they would melt into her sad understanding as she slept. I told her that I loved her. And not wanting to ever mention the words again, I hoped in my head that she had not meant it when she'd said earlier that she wanted to die, or run away.

Now in the morning, she seemed better—not saying much, and not minding anything around her. The wet worm-legs were still folded closed.

Clova would fix everything, we knew. It would be her refuge, her salvation—and mine. *Lucky fish us,* I sang on my breath in the backseat without making a sound.

John, not yet a year old, lay in his car crib next to me—sweet, oblivious, and allowed to be wet. I, on the other hand, had grown into a stick insect with "poo-tainted eyes," a fact announced with certitude last Friday morning by Loeska, the blue-eyed Afrikaans girl next door, at the fence of bushes dividing our houses, adding that *that's* why miggies fly into them—drawn to cesspools. Must be that I had some *Jewish* in me, or maybe even some *black*, she'd said across the fence.

"Rubbish," I'd managed, with a lump in my throat, scooting back inside like a rabbit with its tail shot off, declared deficient in both the looks and heritage departments. Peeping through the fence of bushes at every opportunity, I'd noticed that Loeska sported magnificent dresses, a different one every Sunday, with petticoats no less, huge *hoops* of eyelet-ribbon petticoats that put khaki shorts to shame. She had snow white hair that stuck straight out like a thatched roof. Sadly, all efforts to fatten her painful thinness with daily drinks of sweet Fortris had failed. Her father was the dominee of the Afrikaans church next door, a church we did not attend because, as my mother explained to me after a quick pause, we were too busy.

Longing to be Loeska's friend, longing to be anyone's friend, I realized now in the backseat with regret that I should have let her know I had *some* Afrikaans in me, by virtue of my father on his mother's side. I was no ordinary, rooinek English girl, our telltale necks burnt a shameful scarlet by the sun because we had no bloody business being in Africa. I just didn't think of it in time. All I needed was a plan. As soon as we returned from Clova, I would make a whole new beginning with Loeska.

Looking out now through sleep-caked eyes at the veld, I could smell the polish that smoothed the cracked leather seats of the old white Mercedes—it smelled sweet, like a new doll's head. It was ordinary out there, plain highveld winter, as we barreled along, so dry that our wool jerseys itched our thirsty skin to death. Anything that moved or tried to grow was stumped and hollow. There was not too much nice to look at, just brown, everywhere brown. And the sky through the car window growing brighter, and winter hard.

At first light, I saw wind curl the dust against scrubby bushes, coating everything that was momentarily green after only-joking rain with layer upon layer of dust. White tick birds rode still as statues on the rumps of cattle out early to graze on the barren veld. Native women balanced tin buckets of water on their heads, with brown babies tied in blanket slings heaved onto their backs. Their crusty feet slapped bare paths that cut through dead grass for miles and miles.

Curious, they stopped to stare, waving and smiling as if they knew us. They had missing teeth, ash skin, and dirty, ragged cloths wound on themselves for clothes. They had never ridden in a car. All around, the veld smelled of burning fires. Like the township fires on the outskirts of Johannesburg, a hollow smell of gathered twigs kindled under scraps of food and sour porridge.

Picaninns stood rose-brown as I stared out—beautiful, sinewy, seemingly right up out of the earth like miniature molded figures of clay. With ribs sharp as matches under their tight skin, they whistled and chased old tire rims with sticks. Like my Salamina, they knew special songs from long ago, jubilant songs, the songs of their kingdom. I stuck my head out of the window. The wind battered my ears as I strained to hear. You could try to learn those songs, but you would never know them as they did. I opened my eyes in the stinging air, and felt my father's hand tug me gently back. "Close that window a bit, Lizzy," he said, frightened perhaps that the wind would blow through my tufts and pull me right up into the sky to that waiting rocket.

"Look, Lizzy, a godly painting of the simplest landscape," he said. Our sky arched in height, width, and scope—the cradle of life, he told me, where the first man stood up out of this same arid dust and began to walk the land, mapping it out as his own. "From dust thou camest," my father loved to tease, full of Jewish-atheist (his self-appointed denomination) mischief, because where the hell else did we come from if there was no God?

No sign yet of the merciless heat that, even in winter, could punish the very life out of any man or beast daring to move in its scorching light.

Four hours deeper into miles and miles of nowhere, at Bandelierkop, a no-horse town with a train platform, a petrol pump, a fly-pestered dog, and a kafee selling cigarettes and yesterday's newspaper, we stopped for bananas, Joko Tea leaves, and Eet-Sum-More biscuits. My mother stayed in the car.

Stoffel, the Afrikaner behind the counter, was his normal, chatty self. He must have noticed the wilted look of us. "Hot for May, hey? Did you drove straight froo?" he asked, flanked at his till by hooked, hanging pieces of dry biltong meat peppered with stuck flies. He was so burnt you might have thought he shot up to the sun for his bath each morning.

He counted out a sixpence and two pennies' change with the precision of a banker, then slid a Chappies bubble gum in its brightly striped wax paper across the wooden counter to me. "No bloody rain, Isaac," he said. He always had something for me, and he always had something to say about the rain, usually that it had not come. And today he was worried sick about something else. "Can you bloody believe it," he said, holding up yesterday's Beeld newspaper for us to see. "Caught red-handed trying to blow up the railway line." We didn't need to buy the paper, my father said, we already had one. Actually, it was the *Rand Daily Mail* in the car, from a week ago, with us in it. Stoffel didn't get the *Mail*.

Back on the Great North Road for less than a minute, a dirt track turned off to the right. It looped for twenty-three miles through gentle, beige-dry hills, their fuzzy scrub stomachs tilted to the sun, exposing parched grasses, spiked aloes, and bearded, wind-frayed proteas, to bring us in a cloud of dust to a wire gate. I leapt up in the backseat. "Open the gate," I shouted, halfway out of my window. "*I* want to open the gate. We've arrived!"

Picaninns, eight, nine, then two more, swarmed like little black bees onto its wires to swing it open, welcoming us back with incessant chatter and wide smiles. Their cracked, bare feet pattered the dust to let us in. They were hoping we'd brought plasticine, toffees, comics.

Chief among them, almost fifteen now, her copper-tinged hair rough and tight like a coir-bristle mat, Meendli was there, with her wire mouth harp and a wriggling fistful of mopani tree worms. And Mphunie came running, Mphunie the cleverest, who could also spit the furthest. The soft whine of the gate opened to Clova.

There was nothing gorgeous about Clova—except the feeling you had when you were there. It was just a simple place, a beloved refuge in the looming, graceful shadow of the Soutpansberg Mountains, five hours north of Johannesburg. And in the opposite direction, almost but not quite by two days' driving, you would be as far south as you can go on the continent of Africa. Just a dusty farm, really, a quiet place to run wild with the picaninns by day, and when the sun gave up so did you, falling into exhausted sleep, scrubbed and smelling of violets and camphor cream for new-burnt patches. An old place, to run free as a monkey and filthy as you pleased.

Bursting barefoot from the car out into the rose-brown furrows, you knew for certain you were in a lucky place.

· ·

The farm lay over seventy-six morgen, south of the great Limpopo and Shashe rivers, their confluence marking South Africa's northern border into Rhodesia. The nearest small towns were Pietersburg, one hour to the south, and Louis Trichardt to the east, both named for Boer leaders who founded them at the end of the Great Trek.

Like a sleepy child in the arms of the mountain, Clova unfolded under changing skies from its lower foothills into a valley bedecked in isolated mopani and marula trees—the mopanis once teeming with protein-rich worms beloved of the natives, especially during the hard years of drought, the marulas providing endless merriment in the slapstick antics of baboons and elephants drunk silly on their berries.

Kudu, with gently spiraling horns, and waterbuck dawdled through the scrub, then leapt like an elegant dream, vanishing in the shimmering heat.

Flatty lizards peered out of every rock crevice, their flat-head eyes scanning for safe sun-drenching spots. By midday, the soil seared any living thing that set foot on it. Crackling leaves curled in on themselves like dried fetuses, longing for the morning mists already burned away. Bore holes gave water at their fickle whim.

My mother sat out on the cool, red-polished *stoep*, her quiet eyes staring into the purple folds of the Soutpansberg as though she were looking into the faraway life she had made for herself.

"Why don't you have a nice cup of tea, Eugenie," my grandmother Elizabeth asked. Tea with milk and sugar, the leftover British colonial answer to anything and everything. But my mother thanked her and said no, she would wait until later.

I was up and out like a shot with my grandfather, his boots tied up, his veld hat on, to plough the land before the midday scorch. In my filthy blue cotton hat, worn only under dire threat of the crows picking off my ears if I didn't, I rode with him on the rusty white tractor, sitting cross-legged between his long-sleeved, sinewy arms in the middle of the enormous, flat steering wheel. This way and that we veered, doglegging back at the ends of long, artful lines, giving me a spinning view. The African earth cracked open beneath us. Hard as a rock in some places, devoid of any visible life, sweetly giving in others. It would be rose-brown, he told me, as we racketed and jumbled along on the tractor. "Rose-brown, Lizzy, in the lucky places."

Jumping down into the furrows for a quick rest, I perched on my stick legs and heard for the first time from my grandfather the name of Mahila.

Hoek is "corner" in Afrikaans, a corner of land, usually, and Mahila was the old witch doctor who lived here on the land where we now stood. Black as the stenching folds of a bat's underbelly, he was said to cast spells into the wild, dry air with such skill that if you fell down crippled, you would never know who did it. Mahila's Hoek, Clova was called, but not by Mahila because he would not be stupid enough to think that land could be owned. This was his borrowed corner, a hundred years ago. And for about as long as that, the hoarse rattle of his seldom-used voice was mistaken for wind across the veld.

Some farmers said they'd heard Mahila was directly descended from the first human ever to set foot in this place. Whoever that was. No one seemed to know for sure, but my father had told me that prehistoric bones of a sleeping man, thought to be black, had been found nearby, curled in a pocket of the mountain. Scratched on the walls of his sanctuary were the faces of wild dogs, with beautiful ridges on their backs, ridges like pointed arrows pulling him to run alongside them. His bare feet mapped this pleasant place as his own. When he failed to wake from a dream, the hot winds covered his sleeping bones, his small, flat face. For thousands of years, the mountain had kept that man in its shroud, along with his watchful dogs.

Many blacks on the farm thought Mahila was the ghost of this first man, a moving shadow under solitary trees at night, keeping watch over the holy place he had found—waiting for his chance to return. By day, blacks and neighboring farmers alike hoped Mahila was nothing more than a lost dream blowing through the wild grass.

My grandfather's sun-cracked hands poured hot tea from the flask. We cooled ourselves in the small circle of shade cast by the tractor. In the soil running through my fingers, I suddenly noticed there was all manner of glinty stuff. "Gold!" I leapt up with the fervor of the first ever to see it.

It was not gold, he laughed, his watery-blue eyes twinkling under his veld hat as he looked out into the blazing sun. That I would find in the yellow heaps around the mines in Johannesburg, he said, his collar already pooling damp.

I lay in the furrow while he drank his tea, lifted his veld hat, and dabbed his head with a pressed, worn handkerchief. I was a worm in the brown under the vastest of blue. I burrowed in deeper, like the mopani caterpillars down at the kraals burying themselves to avoid being caught and eaten alive. I listened for Mahila, hoping I would never hear him.

Puff adders, my grandfather told me, dung beetles, and buck— glorious and abundant once—lay lifeless in Mahila's path, their joy sucked out and stored in his personal reservoir, the deep sockets of his hollow gums. For his own use. And just as suddenly as they fell there, they revived, staggering away, but only if Mahila willed it so. It could not be said if Mahila thought he used his power for good or evil. Good or evil lived in your heart, in what you decided about it. It could only be said for sure that he was swift, and unerring.

"*Vuilgoed* . . . filthy thief," rang out across the empty miles of Mahila's corner. Baffled, enraged tribesmen, drought-driven to seek a greener spring for their cattle, or the last shreds of stalwart Boers pushing through to the north in what was left of their ox wagons, all lost their livestock to Mahila's wiles. And in some cases, the weakest prey, their children. "Thief!" the tribesmen screamed right over these furrows into the mocking wind.

Mahila's good deeds went undocumented. They might have been countless. "No one knew," my grandfather said with a mind to fairness, folding the damp hankie back into his pocket.

Some thought Mahila retreated in his old age to the crevices of the mountain, stripping the trees of bark and worms, and screaming, like the Samango monkeys, his ferocious promise to return. Then he vanished into a night of ghosts. But the land where we now sat had remained empty. "No one would touch it," my grandfather said, flinging the last drops of tea from the plastic cup to the wind—my signal to climb back up.

From high on the steering wheel, I could see the farmhouse in the distance, a tiny, creamy oasis on the open veld, shaded by thorn trees and a few marulas standing around in an unusually dense and serious clump, as if they'd wandered over to take a look. We were too far to see if my mother was still out on the stoep. I knew she'd be in a deep sleep if she was, and my father would be keeping John quiet. I hoped my father had remembered to cover her with a light, not itchy blanket. She would be soothed in her dream by Clova, the way it soothed us all, the way it had soothed my grandfather when it first fell into his hands. His name was George Waltham, and I knew from my grandmother Elizabeth that he'd come to this hot African plain not because of his asthmatic lungs—although that was the given reason. He came for forgetting.

While he spoke to me of Mahila in and around the furrows, he never spoke of the forgetting. He'd sorted it out with my grandmother before they were to be married, and to anyone's knowledge had never mentioned it again. I knew not to, either. That's what forgetting meant.

About the time Mahila reigned, almost a century earlier, my grandfather was running on greener banks, the last child of a Victorian family, with the embarrassing distinction not only of being the last born of eleven, but born in France to boot. His father was a professor of languages. When not engaged in fiery debate with Charles Darwin in the British daily press on the subject of whence we really came, he occupied himself with the ins and outs of Sanskrit, and every syllable uttered since. However, he had not many words for his many children.

After a bravely borne term at the Sorbonne, he brought his vast family back home to England. Here he set the late lamb, four-year-old George, down on the banks of the river Thames to run, and run, and run, sailboat in hand, his white cotton collar folded neatly around his little neck—the only noticeable sign that anyone paid the slightest attention to him at all, being that he was the eleventh.

He had been told never to go to the water's edge alone. He had been told only dire consequence would follow—and dire consequence did.

Tearfully exhausted after a long search for someone to go down to the river with him, he quietly decided he'd jolly well go down there by himself.

After a few minutes, Marguerite, older by four years and number eight on the family rung, felt sorry for him and changed her mind. Like an angel of mercy she emerged from the house, floating behind him, her blue silk ribbon wrapping her dainty waist, her gossamer petticoats light as the first snows.

She saw him kneel at the water's edge. She saw his cotton-clad, boy's blue bum tilt up, his small hand free the sailboat on its voyage. She heard his cry as it sailed majestically away—forever. He never meant it to sail away forever. "Fetch it back," he cried out.

Marguerite plunged into the water behind the sailboat, her carefully set and beribboned morning locks bobbing about in the wet as she splashed after it. To George's delight, the little boat performed magnificently, carrying him with it in his wildest dreams as it floated away. He was so transported by its skillful dodging, its swift turns, its brave, billowing sail that he failed to hear the last cry from Marguerite. She sank like a stone, mute, wrapped in the sudden shroud of her dress.

By the time George reached the house, running from the thin film of tiny bubbles that rose where she sank, word rang out that a child was lost in the river. Men raced with ropes and oars. The river was high and dangerous. Finally, a sobering voice declared that there was no need to continue. A small, white cloud had appeared beneath the surface, as quietly as if it had fallen from the bright blue sky into the murky water below.

They lifted her from the river, a little flopped meringue, and carried her the two hundred long yards back to her house.

Shortly after that his lungs closed up. He sat for hours under a blanket, being steamed. He was frightened under there. The heat swirled like hellfire, where certainly he was headed. He hated the smell of menthol leaves floating in the tin bowl of steaming water. Sometimes Marguerite's face loomed smiling out of the steam. Mostly when she appeared, she looked just as she always had—jolly pretty. But sometimes she was blue and bloated, like a dressed-up rotten fish.

The drawing room filled with blaming eyes that looked nearly but not quite at him, before her casket was mercifully taken away. No one ever said it was his fault, that Marguerite was dead. No one ever said.

By the time he was grown, still struggling to breathe but managing all right in every other way, it was suggested he seek out "warmer climes" for his chest. His family would be sad to see him go, he knew. But they wouldn't really miss him. He was, after all, the eleventh.

From whence we had come was one question, but where we could go, quite another. The British Empire offered the choice of India, teeming, he feared, with people he knew, or Africa. And so, just as he had sailed in his dreams across the Thames on that fateful day, he decided he would set sail for Africa. He would find a quiet place where he would be a bother to no one, and where, he hoped, the warm air would open his lungs, and wash away the insistent damp in his heart.

Tall, straight as a dye and always a gentleman, my grandfather George arrived in Cape Town. He was instantly scorched bright pink by the sun, earning him the same epithet Loeska had bestowed on me—a rooinek. Dutch, French, and German settlers sported necks like tanned leather as their badge of longevity in this outpost.

Undaunted, he'd found his way to colonial ports with familiar names, East London, Port Elizabeth, and so on, where other blistered gentlemen walked the streets, and moist ladies, tenderly shaded by parasols, consumed thinly buttered anchovy toast with afternoon tea. Apart from the sweat and quiet melt of each afternoon, everyone simply did just as they did at home in England. It was both horribly familiar and horribly relieving.

After getting his bearings, along with a veld hat to protect his sun-ravaged cheeks and ears, he discovered to his astonishment that he had a good head for negotiating with the natives, and was fascinated by the evolving intricacies of colonial law. Going about his business for several years in a way that bothered no one, he heard quite by chance about a piece of land up north that no one wanted.

"Mahila's Hoek," the flushed farmer explained, sitting out in one of the cool evening gathering places on wooden benches under the Cape oaks. He licked Guinness froth, dispensed from the barrel, off his cracked Irish lips. His name was Thom. He would take George north with him, on the new coal-eating railroad, if George would not be persuaded that the dust-howled bowl of Mahila was worthless.

George wondered what terrible thing the land had done to be not wanted. It called him with the certitude of a kindred spirit, the familiarity of an old friend, perhaps just the way it had called Mahila. He put on his hat, walked down to the sea, and looked out at the blurred, faraway edge where sapphire deep water met the swirling Cape sky—the end of the world, curving down to the South Pole. The water's edge, he decided, had never been a good place for him anyway.

After four days ploughing north, in the early hours of morning, the train stopped for bitter railroad coffee on a tiny platform in the middle of the veld. Thom declared, "This town is Soekmekaar—Afrikaans, means 'looking for one another'!"

My grandfather could see nothing but the station, and in every direction the veld, vast and bleak. "Which town?" he asked.

This train ride, I remembered, feeling the tractor's steering wheel swivel beneath me, you *were* allowed to ask about. He would happily tell you if you did that he went looking for the land for four long hours farther to the north of Soekmekaar, and it would greet him with nothing more than a breeze feathering the dust.

Thom didn't want to stay long. "God help you" was all he said.

When my grandfather first set foot on this patch, he thought it had enough of a stretching shadow from the mountain in the late afternoon to keep him cool. To the great mirth of Thom, who owned Last Post, the neighboring farm, George paid the government for the land and began building a house. He fell off the roof, breaking his leg, but carried on regardless out in the middle of the veld.

"Dig some holes, put some sticks / *Fugga lo dugga* and put some bricks," he said was how he constructed it. And of course, *fugga lo dugga* is the black way to say "put some cement." Soon, smooth, creamy walls stood up, with only a few cracks from the sweltering sun, until it even had a stoep for sitting out and whipping cream into butter on a hot morning, and a cool floor to relieve boiling feet. In the hell dust of Mahila, he willed green patches of lucerne to feed cattle, and I, the luckiest fish alive, leapt down off the tractor to run through it. It was here at Clova that he married my grandmother, shy Elizabeth, after courting her in Pietersburg, where he went once a week to purchase teff for the animals and paraffin to light the farm at night. She was the pretty, plump daughter of Thom's friends there, German and English settlers. It was here at Clova that my mother, Eugenie, was born. And here, five hours north of the city lights of Johannesburg where I was born, that she brought me swaddled in a blanket, and put me into my grandfather's arms. "Elizabeth," she'd said, suddenly naming me after her mother.

My grandfather was already a bit deaf by then, being well over seventy. He picked me up now out of thick, knee-deep lucerne into his wiry arms. He never spoke of Marguerite, but from the dizzy height of the tractor his fading eyes seemed often to catch the last wisps of Mahila.

From Bandelierkop to Pietersburg, everyone knew he'd called the land Clova because in pockets and patches, it was surprisingly green, proving both Thom and the government wrong. In his hands, it transformed with an almost butterfly magic.

In the best exchange, I already knew, the spirit of men who walked the land would be graced by the spirit of the land. And the land, in turn, by those who walked it. Sometimes this was true, but like all hoped-for things, not always.

With my hat back on, I stretched my busy hands out far and wide from my perch on the steering wheel to pat the wild, dry air, pat it down and away as we went, making sure no crippling spells were riding the gusts, no evil spirits coming near. I busied myself with this secret job all day and every day—Mahila would not stare in at us from the outside dark at night, or finger my chopped tufts in my Clova bed. I would keep everyone alive.

Oh no nothing will happen
God won't God won't
Fall down crippled
Won't let anything happen

my never-quiet head sang inside.

We rumbled along, breaking the earth open behind us.

..

Lured by the gentle clatter of afternoon tea, the tinkling of spoons and cups, we revived and climbed out of our gossamer, mosquito-netting cots to gather in the promise of African night.

Long shadows melted across the red cement floor of the stoep. We came for hot tea that, strangely, would cool us, the comfort of ginger biscuits, lumps of brown sugar plopping into brimming porcelain cups—treasured Spode cups, and some made by Minton, brought all the way from England, chipped here and there, but with cheerful, painted green birds on them. And a few quiet words, out of consideration, because everyone had only just woken from naps, woken to the brilliant surprise of a few drops of rain in the dazzling sunlight, brazen as a handful of illicit diamonds. And like stolen wealth, it would last maybe three minutes, maybe four.

"Oh, a Monkey's Wedding!" My mother delighted in its fabled name, the oddity of rain in full sun. Rain at all, in fact. It brought smiles and a special sweetness to sleep-crumpled faces—George,

Gran Elizabeth, my mother, Eugenie, still quiet, and just for today, my father, Isaac.

From the kraal at the bottom of the farm, Sweetness and her sister Gladness, barefoot and black as the longed-for cool night, carefully carried trays from the kitchen with more cups, and warm buttermilk scones with bright strawberry jam, all covered with tulle netting to keep the flies away. Sweetness, like a sated bee, always slow—Gladness not.

Tea on the stoep was only for us. The servants would have theirs later, down at the kraal. Only those who worked inside ever came into the farmhouse. Picaninns were not encouraged to come up past the three steps of the stoep, unless, of course, they were sick or needed to bring a message. But Meendli, sitting slightly away on the last step, always remembered to come up from the huts. On her coffee brown neck, adoring the heat of her, a proudly displayed mopani caterpillar, fat, red, furry, stretched then lazed again, saved on her neck for later eating. In the many lengthy droughts over the past hundred years, the mopani trees had been scratched to bleeding by the natives trying desperately to find morsels of protein to feed their children. Now, the worms were a prized delicacy, with farm picaninns daring one another higher and higher to harvest them. Meendli crossed her thin legs—tall for a picaninn!—and in a lively chatter with herself smacked at flies with her yellow and green plastic flyswatter——hit one, miss one.

Echoing in the distance, sjambok whips cracked amid the whistle and cheer of the men driving the cows back into pens. They were of the Venda tribe, these natives—proud, wild, and blacker than licorice.

"Imbeciles," my father said, speaking of the government in its efforts to ship the labor off the farms, efforts that newly deemed blacks as being here illegally, when really they had nowhere else to go and would probably then, whole families of them, he said, bloody starve. A massive movement of the black population was imminent. In an inexplicable, illogical move, the government was speaking of transporting vast numbers of black people back, supposedly whence they'd come, designating tiny portions of the country for their resettlement. No one black was immune.

These rural areas were to be called homelands, a jolly nice-sounding place, I thought over my sugary scone, until my father's words revealed that there was nothing nice about them. They were barren, remote, and a sure ticket to isolation. The farm blacks were the least of the problem. Millions of urban blacks would now be removed from the cities, which, he said, spilling his tea as he set the cup back into its saucer, would now be inaccessible to them. But for the rare, rusted bicycle, most had no transport, in fact, no bloody shoes, he said, and would be trapped there.

He blotted up the messed tea with his serviette, which he started to fold, then just left on the table and leaned back in his chair. Reaching the cities and any hope of employment, he said to my grandfather, would now require these blacks to walk for hundreds of miles. In addition, stringent laws would remain in place, requiring black men and women to carry papers, within and outside the cities, so their movements could be both restricted and monitored.

What about Salamina? I suddenly wondered. What about Gladness? And clumsy Sweetness clattering the dishes in the kitchen. And Meendli, still cracking her flyswatter. Meendli would have to roll up the striped cloth she slept on like a flat mattress on the floor of her mud hut. Like her mother before her, Meendli had been born at Clova. Her small, rough feet would walk over the hills, never to be seen again.

"Most of them have been with me as long as I can remember." My grandfather touched the wall of the stoep, as if he could feel their hands in its smooth plaster. Many of them had appeared from nowhere out of the desolate veld, starving and in rags, to help him build the farmhouse. "As long as I can remember." He got up, walked to the end of the stoep, gave Meendli the bottom piece of his scone, the half that had the jam on it, then came to sit down again.

And then my father mentioned to him the whispers at his consulting rooms. A fat woman called Mrs. Visagie had asked him in hushed tones what he'd thought about that "cheeky kaffir" caught and arrested for his "blerrie subversive antics" in Rivonia. Rivonia was a suburb of Johannesburg, only fifteen minutes from where she sat talking with the good doctor on Bell Street, she noted. Could he believe it, she'd asked, that this Bantu was insisting on being called Mister, instead of just plain Nelson, his first name? My father lowered his voice, but I heard the rest of what she'd said . . . "A fucking native boy. Trying to cause terrible trouble." This "*Mister* Mandela!" had already affronted our courts by appearing in skins for his trial. "Animal," she'd hissed.

"Why does he dress himself in skins, like an animal?" I wanted to know, licking more jam.

"It's his tribal dress, Elizabeth. They use that to *call* him an animal."

"If he knows what's good for him," my grandfather said, getting up suddenly, "he'll wash his armpits, put on a suit, shut the hell up, and stay out of sight. They won't rest until they've bloody locked them all up, Isaac. Where the hell they're going to put them, I have no idea." He looked out across a bank of blue-green aloes rising like spears against the mountain, the closing sky above them already soaked in deep red streaks. "This bloody new government should just borrow Hitler's trains for the job, and be honest about what they're doing."

My grandfather wondered aloud if we hadn't been better off before. Two years earlier, Britain released its colonial hold on South Africa, and like a newborn colt up on trembling legs we stood for the first time as an independent republic. Although there were high hopes for uniting the nation, which in the mind of the new government, he said, meant healing the rift between Afrikaner and English, their century-old grievances still ran deep. For the most part, I gathered in bits and pieces from what he was saying, they were civil with one another, but there was an unspoken hatred in the eyes of many Afrikaners for the manner in which British troops annihilated and imprisoned their forbears. Their ancestors, they felt, had settled our land with unparalleled fortitude in long, dangerous treks to the north, where we now sat in comfort, drinking our tea. But English-speaking whites like us, a group that included a huge contingent of Brits, Russian and German Jews, as well as Portuguese and other colonialists, heard from their grandparents, like mine, a different story. The British had created concentration camps for the Afrikaners for the sole purpose of protecting their women and children during the Boer War. Marauding, starving blacks had been murdering them on their farms, and in corralling these Afrikaners into camps, British troops had done their best, under appalling circumstances, to protect the colony and have it thrive. In fact, many Afrikaans lives had been saved.

My father shifted his sun-frayed cane chair back into the receding shade.

"Move a bit this way, Isaac," Gran Elizabeth offered. Ever helpful, she pointed out that the brunfelsia, with its simultaneous show of blue, lavender, and white flowers in a massive shrub on the east side of the stoep, gave the most shade in the late afternoons. Because it had three colors of sweetly scented flowers all at once, she liked to call it her Yesterday, Today, and Tomorrow, but today she just said brunfelsia, its proper name. It was her favorite.

"With all due respect, George," my father said, shifting again to where she'd suggested, "my own grandfather told a different story."

I listened with all ears. This was about my father's Afrikaans grandfather on his mother's side—fodder for my new plan with Loeska. "Those Afrikaners were released from the camps to find their farms pillaged and burnt by the *British*, and all their cattle slaughtered," my father said, "leaving them in the direst poverty. And while the British troops claimed they'd imprisoned them in concentration camps for their own safety, it was really a wartime tactic to debilitate them, because the British suspected Afrikaans farmers were helping the Boer commandos under cover of night with food and sanctuary." My father said he'd visited his grandparents, as a small child, on what remained of their farm. He remembered asking for more to eat. After an embarrassed silence, his mother had whispered to him that the milk-soaked crust he'd been given was all they had. Many Afrikaners now could neither forget the starvation in those camps, my father said, nor the humiliating defeat of their brave Boer forbears at the hands of the British.

"Whatever the case, Isaac," my grandfather said, "they hate us. Even those with hearts of gold hate us." Like Hannes Botha, a neighboring farmer on the north side of the mountain, who always averted

his eyes and in fifty years had never greeted my grandfather in Bandelierkop, where they went for supplies. Furthermore, he said, none of
this was of any consequence now to the blacks, coloreds, and Indians
left disenfranchised once again by our new government. "We're
headed into a nightmare, Isaac," he said. The Afrikaners were intent
on wrestling their way back into power come hell or high water, and
the rest of us, English, Jewish, much less black, and anyone in between, were not part of their plan.

I knitted my grandfather's words with those of my father into a
simple wish that the world would right itself, and since no one was
looking, I emptied the sugar bowl upside down over my cup, turning
my tea into brown sludge.

My father got up. He walked over and stood next to my grandfather in the last, dappled bit of afternoon still holding on to the stoep.
He spoke quietly of black opposition, and opposition within that opposition, split factions shuddering the ranks of black groups, now
forced underground and trying to establish a path of survival. "They're
moving to violent measures, George," he said, "targeting railway lines,
power stations, anywhere they can debilitate without loss of life."

As if she no longer wanted to hear his words, my mother got up
and wandered out into the landscape, her delicate frame shimmering
in the heat. Gladness and Sweetness cleared the tea and wrapped the
leftover scones and jam into a white linen serviette to take down to
their kraal. And my grandfather George asked my father to please
help him translate legal documents he'd drafted into Afrikaans, which,
being British, he now spoke but had difficulty writing.

He was going to be allowed by the government to keep a small
number of documented servants, but not in the numbers, on families,
he now had on the farm. His petition might allow the Vendas to live
on the southwest corner at the base of the property, the way they always had, tilling a portion of land for themselves with the right to remain there in exchange for their labor. He'd found a loophole, he
explained: It might work if they continued to fashion their huts solely
out of mud and reeds. Only white people like us were legally allowed
to create dwellings out of brick. Bricks meant permanence.

"That's the way it's always worked," he said. "Fair exchange. We like it, they like it, everyone eats, everyone survives."

The last sjambok whip slapped in the distance. Meendli got up and sauntered away, licking red jam off her fingers. She spoke little English, mostly Venda, but could smile at you like nobody's business, and twang her mouth harp like a jiving devil. The sun was almost gone and the air pungent, sweet with the few drops of rain. Night crickets startled into sudden exuberance, the air thick with their racket.

Late that evening, I saw my father move slowly across the stoep with my mother in a quiet dance. Far from the lights of any city, the velvet night sky at Clova was high and impossibly jeweled with stars. The ink-black veld around us pulsed with unseen creatures.

My father looked into my mother's eyes as if he could see right into the sore place inside her, and she looked into his as if she might know how to calm it. "Have a good rest, little duck," he murmured to her. She hung in his embrace like a glittering fairy, lithe, elegant, the way she must have seemed to him the night they met. A farm girl with nothing, she had made her own dress for the dance in Pietersburg that evening. He had less than nothing of his own, but was on his way to the city of Johannesburg for his big chance, accepted to the prestigious medical school at the University of the Witwatersrand. He'd bought himself some new shoes so they'd allow him into the lectures, he'd joked. Only it was true. He often said he felt rough, coarse, from the wrong side of the tracks, and she helped him with some of the words he'd wanted to say. She seemed genteel to him, and the kindness of her gaze, her beautiful face, softened all that he found unacceptable in himself. They moved almost imperceptibly together.

A scaly lizard lay near on the red step, his soft throat beating. Like me, he knew his quiet place.

. .

The chain outside the kitchen door clinked as we hurried out into the night.

"Shoosh, be quiet," my mother whispered to me, my burning tears running.

Tarzan did not bark. He lay down again at the end of his chain.

The dank, sweet stink of the lav waited at the end of the long path lined with moonlit blue flowers of lush, high plumbago bushes, four hundred yards from the farmhouse.

Some people said if you felt anything on your skin out there it was probably Mahila with his hollow gums, wanting his land back but settling for you instead.

My pants pulled off, she picked me up and set me on the wooden seat.

"Carry me, uppy me," I whispered. "Hold me over it."

"I asked you before you went to sleep if you needed to go, you silly billy. I'll wait for you."

"No, wait inside."

Her face lit up, then disappeared in a smooth puff of smoke. She'd be right outside the door, she said.

Nothing will happen
nothing happen

The cold seat was worn smooth by everybody's bums. They warned you when you first came to Clova never to look down into the deep, black hole. *Psswswswsswss . . .* Make that noise, like water running, to make you wee. Through hot tears I watched her candle vanish from between the green wooden slats into the night. I couldn't smell her cigarette anymore, only the sweet stench coming up from the dark pit.

In Johannesburg, where only some people on the poorer plots of land still had to traipse out in the middle of the bloeming night like this to do their business, the *masimba* boys came early every morning with clean, clattering buckets from their donkey cart. "*Masimba,*" Salamina had warned me, was a swear word for shit, and saying that in either language would be a jolly good way to get a hiding.

Clova was too remote to be serviced every day, so a week of stink clumped twelve feet below. During the day, you could distract yourself with *Farmer's Weekly* pictures of giant tomatoes, jealously grown somewhere else. I could hear a scratching patter outside, Samango monkeys, maybe, hunting for the steaming banana stacks bought for the picaninns to prevent rickets. You'd never be able to grow a banana up here in the jawbone-dry northern Transvaal—unless you were an astonishingly lucky fish. Sweaty bunches of them arrived with my grandfather in the back of his green lorry, piled in with cans of paraffin to light the farm at dusk.

"Come back inside," I pleaded to the emptiness outside the lavatory door. My aching fingers gripped the seat. Rattlesnakes lived down there, gorging themselves. You knew to be quick or they'd sniff your skin, realize you were back, and slither up the slimy walls to feed on your flesh. No wee would come out. "Come back inside!"

"Silly billy, what's the matter, I'm right here."

"Take me *off* it, *off, off* it . . ." I leapt at her like a starving locust onto a *mielie* husk. She pulled my pants on again, the little red end of her cigarette making a magic swirl as she bent to pick up the candle, me in her other arm. Her voile nightie skimmed her body as she wisped us together out into the dark.

"Did you wipe? Shsh, stop crying." Bug-eyed, I clung to her neck, the smell of her face warm against mine. The door banged shut behind us, its green slats clattering against the rusty lock. "Shsh," she told it and me. "God," she whispered, "enough to wake the bloody dead."

We slipped through the night-smelling bushes, the swish of us disturbing the hush of leaves. The chain rattled. Tarzan was still awake. His glowing eyes stared like night fires on his relentless watch.

She set me down on the kitchen floor, cool under my hot feet, especially cooling at nighttime.

"Eugenie, is that you?" came a voice out of the dark. The scuttle of us had woken my grandmother. Usually, the passages at Clova were silent at night.

I fled by the light of my mother's candle down the tunnel of the passage back into bed, back under the eiderdown, safe from long fingers. "Good Lord, you don't need that—it's so hot," she whispered, but left it on me anyway, kissed me, blew out the candle, and floated away.

The gaping frogs had stopped. Only insects chipped at the night. Tarzan was out there, listening. He clinked his chain again, in the lazy, sour smell of smoke from the huts—fires long finished for the night—everyone safe in their beds.

Suddenly it started to run, the sweet, peaceful gush at last, with sleep coming quickly to fetch me before it got cold on the rubber wetting sheet. In the morning I would put on nice, clean underpants and cotton shorts from the generous pile packed for my holidays by Salamina. Waiting for sleep, I thought of her Xhosa hand on me, dry and warm. Usually she smelled of cleaning, love, onions, and the sweat of each day melting into her starched uniform. And sometimes, of sour porridge and soap. I missed her at Clova. She was most especially for me, I had decided, even though I was only one of her daily duties, albeit the most taxing. John wasn't even imagined when she first walked up the dirt driveway in Johannesburg, looking for work. "Ekschuse me, Medem, hez the Medem got enny wek?" she'd quietly asked, in respectful English, the neatly ironed, frayed collar of her dress wilted, wet with searching.

As if I had dropped from a tree right there in front of her, she smiled down at me. "Monkey?" she said, delighting me.

Her abundant brownness became my instant refuge. I claimed her. And she me. More than once I smeared myself in mud from head to toe, caking it on to be brown like her. More than once she'd laughed and said, "Jho! You are my little picaninni, Monkey." Which was not to say she was not strict, even frightening, if she deemed fit. She could rivet you to the ground with a look, and the thought of her anger was so potent I never dared tempt it. Black ladies, my father told me, from years of seeing it at the hospitals with his very own eyes, raised their children differently. *Their* children, he'd said, could misstep into a fire in the middle of their hut's mud floor or run out under the wheels of a car right by their front door. They had no lawn, like us, for running, in those black townships, and no special heaters. There was no room for error with black ladies, he said.

I lay thinking of Salamina's belly, greedily growing for months, and now pushing the buttons of her cotton uniform to an undignified limit. Her dire warnings echoed in my head—whatever it was that slept under her dark heart must never be told outside the walls of our house.

"You *go* to sleep, jhe," she said each night at my bed in Johannesburg, then sang our usual sleeping song. It told you not to worry—your mother would be there in the morning. "*Thula tu, thula baba, thula baba,*" she sang.

Now, in my Clova cot, I thought I heard her voice, deep as the brown of malt, soothing as the sour smell of your own pillow.

A farm fly, left over from the afternoon, stuck inside now, sulked in his lazy night flight from one side of the cot netting to the other, then sat in a blob on the tin pitcher of wash water set ready for the morning. Worn out with trying to escape, he had no more buzzing, and I, in my sopping river, was gone.

..

"*He wandered in* like a demented ghost," my grandfather said of Tarzan in the cold, predawn hour before we left for the station. "He was already old then, and that was a lifetime ago now, for a dog."

We were getting ready to take my father to the train at the tiny Bandelierkop station, with a flask of hot tea and some rusks in wax paper, for dipping. Unlike us, he had no time for resting, and would now begin a pattern of deathly long hours, making the tread of his feet at midnight a familiar sound. He'd walked the farm with my grandfather, examined any giggling picaninn that came near, and anyone else he could find, and concluded that everyone was in good health.

"Isaac, can't you stay?" my mother asked in the paraffin-lamp glow of the kitchen. "You're so tired, look at you—green around the gills!"

"Eugenie's right. Even in the newspaper—look at you there, you're exhausted, Isaac," my grandmother said.

On the dimly lit table, our faces stared out of the picture on the front page of the newspaper brought with us from Joburg. "Elizabeth six, baby John one, Eugenie, and Dr. Isaac Grace, magna cum laude at the University of the Witwatersrand, Surgeon of the Year"—photographed for my father's high accomplishment, and he slightly awkward in the public glare. "It has been a long road," he'd told the interviewer, "and I'm excited to begin." Buckets clattered and clinked the night awake in the distance down at the kraals, where milking had already begun. In an hour, when the sun came up, the farm would crack to life, and Tarzan would lie down to sleep after his solitary watch.

The newspaper photographer had arrived the week before our unexpected holiday, wearing a veld hat in a doe color. He'd removed the hat at the front door, and set up his camera with a flashbulb.

"Never mind green around the gills. Elizabeth looks shell-shocked," my mother said now, reexamining the front page already sold by hundreds of raggedy picaninns running barefoot in the early morning headlights at every red robot-light on Hendrik Verwoerd Drive, First Avenue Linden, right down Jan Smuts Avenue all the way to town, crisscrossing the streets of Johannesburg. "*Mail, Rund Delly Mail! Vaderland, Beeld,* or *Mail,*" they shouted as windows rolled down to pay shiny money for news.

My mother had washed me very early that day, scraped scraps of my hair with her brush into a tight, brown ball trying to make a bun. It sat like a small poo on my head. The more we tried to fix it, the odder it looked. Each swish of her brush sent us into fits of laughter until tears rolled down our faces. My mother pulled herself together, dabbed her cheeks, and said we needed to be serious now, the two of us, for the *Rand Daily Mail.* She buttoned me into my American colonial dress. Which just means the dress she felt looked like a dress from then, in a generous plaid of blue and purple under a white Peter Pan collar. "Yes, American colonial," she'd said, pleased with me.

"And Eugenie! Oh, Eugenie," my grandmother added, admiring the pillbox hat and the beautifully restrained day dress Eugenie had chosen for herself. If the photograph had been in color, you'd have seen it was subtle pink crepe with a delicate black binding around her young neck—startling elegance, my grandmother said—replete with gloves and gently pointed shoes—that might well have rivaled America's first lady. She hadn't smoked on that day, my mother confessed now, shy to be photographed, feeling queasy with nerves and afraid it might make her sick and spoil Isaac's proud day.

And right there, on the same page—although nothing to do with us, of course—a horrid thing about the new gold mines in Carletonville. They'd built houses for the black and white miners, my father explained in the dark kitchen, on unstable dolomite foundations. Suddenly the whole bloody lot, he said, sank away into huge holes. Like Pompeii, my mother said, you'd find people dead in their armchairs down there, smothered, their cigarettes and cups of tea perched exactly where they'd set them down before being swallowed into their graves. "The Sinkholes of Carletonville," she read again.

My grandmother lit another paraffin lamp, for the passage.

"Carletonville is hours west of us, silly billy," my mother said when I asked if the same might happen to us. Our house was in Ferndale, and even though the ground in Ferndale shuddered from time to time, it was nothing to do with Carletonville. Underground tremors, that's all.

At the station, as the train hissed and threatened, I heard ". . . despicable, illegal . . ." and ". . . too bloody bad" come from my father's mouth. "We'll hide it," he said, through the burning smell of coal.

"Hide what?" I jumped to say.

"Nothing," said my mother.

"Salamina's baby," my father said. I shrank back. Salamina's warning to not mention the child outside the walls of our house had been dire. There being no error with black ladies, I was shocked cold to hear him speak of it. But he smiled and said, "That will be Elizabeth's work."

Apart from the impending idea of school, I realized I was the likely candidate because I was available. Finally, I had a job, a secret, important thing to do. Finally, I'd been especially chosen. My father was the only other one with brown eyes, apart from native boys and Salamina and Iris and everyone, and for his company in that alone, I loved him. He handed baby John through the window back to my mother, rubbed my tufts, and reminded me of the "ten shillings" as the train spat, clanged, and pulled him away. "Nice to be a passenger!" he called out to my mother. She laughed and waved until we could no longer see him. He'd worked on the trains as a waiter, on the Rustenburg–Messina run, to pay for medical school.

Tomorrow we would be expecting the phone to sound the three rings of a trunk call, the signal for everyone else in the vicinity to immediately get off the common party line. Then the authoritative lady at the switchboard in the Louis Trichardt post office, in her bumpy, turquoise crimplene dress, would announce with great importance on the line in Afrikaans: "A trunk call for Clova from Johannesburg"—as if someone were phoning from the moon. To say he was home safely. But for now, he'd be doing some thinking on the train about how to keep the government from shipping the labor off the farm. Where were Hitler's trains? I wondered, looking around the platform.

We clambered back into Uncle Thom's old car. Suddenly I was wondering about Salamina's baby, and if my new job might be something to do with all of this. From what I'd gathered, I'd be responsible for hiding it away and for keeping it alive. That part I knew I'd be jolly good at, having so far kept my own mother alive by being exceedingly good.

Back from the station, I crawled under the Clova kitchen table to make lists in my head of secret Johannesburg hiding places: under the granadilla vines; inside my mulberry-leaf-lined shoe box amongst the silkworms; behind the Hulett's sugar in the food cupboard where usually only I went; under Salamina's bed; and high, high in the syringa tree way, way behind our house. I would position the infant on my back, instruct it to hold on and to remain silent. I would scale the ebony bark with my long, flat feet, more agile than any monkey, until I reached the highest perch, my sweet nest in the profusion of lilac flowers and golden berries. I would hide it in the syringa tree.

· ·

Tarzan barked hoarsely outside the kitchen door, then fell quiet again. He was on sixty feet of chain winding tight around the giant marula tree, and then back again, loosening it around and around—living in a circle. Sometimes he liked his life wide, and sometimes he liked it tiny. He was a very old dog, unpredictable, with sad, sparse fur worn thin in wiry patches, like coir fibers on the outside of a coconut—so rough it grated off human skin. In some spots, he was tanner than his usual brown.

"He's sort of a part-time leopard," said Uncle Thom, who'd insisted on driving us back from Bandelierkop station even though age now prevented him from seeing too well. Still hot and flushed, and still with an Irish wink, he squinted at Tarzan. "When you look at him *this* way, he's a leopard, but when you look at him *that* way, he's definitely a dog. A Ridgeback, maybe. That's why he's such a damn good watchdog."

Only my grandfather George dared touch him, in a quick pat-pat of scratching fur, and only when Tarzan was being more of a dog.

"That chain is driving me mad, George," my grandmother complained, busily stirring steaming breakfast porridge on the stove. My grandfather said she'd *kindly* married him, despite the upsetting silence that ensued upon his writing home to England to say he'd met his love in South Africa and was getting married. He'd thought his letter would be good news, since Francis, his eldest brother who'd gone to the Congo to teach everyone the Bible, had inexplicably disappeared. Put into a pot, eaten by natives, was the consensus. But my grandfather received only one terse line in reply: "Is she black?"

She'd married him anyway, and he never spoke to them again. Actually, she was quite pink, in a powdery, old-fashioned sort of way that belied her strength—hands that could tip a full, heavy bucket of udder-warm milk into the separator and churn it into butter in a heartbeat. She never forgot to cream her elbows at night, and some people made her shy when they said her eyes were as blue as English violets. As a matter of fact, she had mainly English in her, and no black at all, being directly related to King Charles's mistress, so she was even almost *royal*! But George Waltham never gave them *that* satisfaction. As far as he was concerned, they'd lost their chance.

Further, when the British royal family rode through the South African Commonwealth streets in 1947, the stuttering, uncertain King George and his Queen bravely got out of their car, gloved of course, but saying hello to everyone in the nicest way. And the thing everyone remembered about them was the startling blue of their eyes. That in itself was proof enough for me, with mine brown as a bug's, that in the blueness of her eyes alone my grandmother was indeed royal. I thought they'd have liked her quite a lot, those people in England. My grandfather was a George, and she an Elizabeth, just like the King and Queen.

"He's got to be on a chain, Elizabeth," my grandfather warned her. "He'll bite the picaninns and God knows who else. Won't you, Tarzan?"

Irritable from the station, we had been restored by the sight of porridge and fresh eggs bubbling in a butter bath.

"Let him just wander off the way he came. He doesn't belong here, George," she said.

"He came here, didn't he? He came here because he belongs here."

"That makes no sense at all, George." George always had a cheeky argument, she said of him, even though they never fought because he simply went voluntarily deaf. "It's the incessant rattling of that dreadful chain," she went on. "You're not *in* the kitchen all day, George, and besides, you're deaf. You don't hear it."

"Whaaaat?" he brayed.

"Stop it, that's not funny." She wiped her hands on the cheesecloth for the milk. "He's a frightening old ghost of a thing. Let him go, George."

My grandfather picked up the green block of Sunlight soap and washed his hands in the kitchen sink. "He doesn't *want* to go. He came here specially," he said. "Besides, it's good to have a wiry old ghost at the door."

He'd looked up one day, just sitting on his tractor, with "that open smell of earth, you know, and in the dust, I saw what I thought, in a sort of watery mirage, was a jackal—parched, staggering over the horizon. And then he just stood there for the longest time. God knows where he came from—his legs stiff, shaking, just staring out at me. But he was actually a dog, you know! With that beautiful ridge on his back. Poor bugger. He'd been on the roam forever, it seemed."

"Tell about when he followed you," I begged.

"Well, he followed me, yes, he did—surreptitiously—*all* the way back to the house. Your gran thought I'd brought home an old hyena."

"A hyena!" I said. "Maybe he'd eaten rotten meat along the way and that's why he stinks." With nothing to drink out there, he had dehydrated into a bristle brush.

"A terrible state he was in," he said, drying his hands at the open kitchen door. He looked out at the mountain already incandescent with heat. "I think he must have been strong, and very beautiful once." That's why he'd called him Tarzan.

Sweetness ambled in with tablecloths that had been spoiled by yesterday's lamb and mint sauce, all nicely clean again, to hang in the sun. "Sweetness," my Gran remembered, "ask Gladness to help you fold those. They're much simpler to iron when they don't get crumpled up in a heap. Then you can put them away in the cupboard."

"Yes, Meddem Grenny," said Sweetness in the dulcet tones that matched her name, as if my grandmother were hers also. Sweetness was already suffering in the heat, making it quite clear with a few well-placed moans, and it was only breakfast time. Run out without your shoes, and you'd get scorched to pieces.

My mother came into the kitchen, her skirt a flower field, trailing the delicate fragrance of Blue Grass powder.

My grandmother kissed her. "Eugenie, what was all that clattering last night?"

"I *asked* if she wanted to go, before we went to sleep, and she said," she looked at me under the table, very pretty, my mother, "no, no, no."

"We've got the potties, remember, under every bed."

"I wanted to have a cigarette anyway—nice, cool night, it's been so hot." She looked at me again, prettier than anything you can dream up even after you've been to the circus, the glistening half-moons of her immaculate young nails translucent, very much ladies' nails. Mine remained stubbornly lined with grime, no matter how much they scrubbed me. I'll never be a lady, I thought, with my mud nails and my secret sour smell. To make matters worse, someone in Bandelierkop, where we'd gone for cigarettes the day before, gasped upon seeing her—her feet, Romanesque, in clean white sandals, her tiny, broad-belted waist set on long, gamine legs that vanished up the yellow piqué Swiss-cotton swirl of her skirt. They turned to me and asked in utter disbelief, "Is that *your* mother?" They'd probably meant it as a compliment. I'd dug my soiled hands into my pockets and nodded in a confusion of pride and shame.

"Come, sit by me, little monkey," she whispered now, kissing my head. She smelled ever sweet, with her new cigarette—Rothman's because there were no Peter Stuyvesants. The cheek, she said, of that dirty Stoffel calling Bandelierkop a town, with its peeling paint, stale bread, sour milk, and no cigarettes—no excuse when you're right on the Great North Road like that.

Nestled under her arm, I thought how jolly lucky she and I were. Much more sophisticated in Johannesburg. We had toilets. Only infrequently now would you hear the bucket-dangling masimba boys whistling, cheering the donkeys, running down Flora Street and up behind the houses to the backyard lavatories. Mainly just for servants' lavs now. They came before the sun was up, those masimba boys—boys, even though they were men, being that they were black—because no one wanted to see them. Or *moentus* or kaffirs, some people called them, which Eugenie said never to say because it was very ugly indeed. In any event, you did not have to make an embarrassing din in Johannesburg at night, going outside.

"Oh, Elizabeth!" my mother suddenly said, sniffing me, sniffing my neck. "Did you wet again? Gladness?" she called out with that hopeless feeling. "Go and call Gladness."

Sweetness came running.

"Poofy," my mother continued, "you stinky monkey . . ." pulling my clothes off in the kitchen. "Into the bath . . ." She wasn't cross, just tired of the whole damned thing, which was sort of what I felt. "Sweetness, where's Gladness? Miss Elizabeth needs a bath."

Suddenly I was skidding, stark naked, this way and that on the red floor, the only cool place on a hot day . . .

"Jhe, Miss Lizzy!" Sweetness slid like a sugared doughnut off a plate and banged into the wall trying to catch me, but I was faster than a rocket to the outside tap in the blistering sand.

"She *said* I could have an *outside* bath," I said.

"*No!* Miss Lizzy, you come *inside,* jhe?" She swiveled on her squeaking bare heel. "Okay, I'm going to call Mummy, jhe?"

"No, she *said* I could!" Maddeningly, not everyone knew everything that was supposed to happen.

"Could what?" said my mother, appearing suddenly. "Elizabeth, did God give you ears that don't listen? Get inside this minute."

"Ah, no, you said I could."

"I said one day I'll give you a bath in the outside bath, but we're all waiting to have breakfast. Elizabeth, *get* in here this minute." She picked me up, funneled us down the passage, and landed us in the bathroom in the parachute of her skirt.

"I don't *want* the inside bath!"

"You're having the inside bath, and you're having it now. Come along, pants off—in you go." Splashing my bum down into the warm, soapy water already swishing around Gladness's hand, she said, "And wash that hair, Gladness, it's got sticks and things in it." The flower field floated up and away with her.

The inside bath was the pride of the farmhouse. Though it had no sewerage connection, it now had hot running water, relieving Sweetness and Gladness of the nightly task of boiling it on the flames of the black-iron kitchen stove in vast tin pots. Gladness kneeled on her ashy knees beside the smart porcelain bath on the stone floor to wash me. On the whitewashed windowsill, last night's burnt-out candle kept guard.

She smelled of special cream, Gladness, and didn't have to go far to get it because my grandfather George stocked it in the farm shop—a thatched *rondawel* not far from the orange trees. Everyone loved his shop because everything was free. He could not take any money, he informed me, because the till was broken.

Vanish whitening cream was only one of the marvels in there. They flatly refuse to use good old Nivea, he explained—Vanish whitening's what they want, to banish their brown and turn them all white.

Gladness could wash you until you squeaked. She, lucky bloeming fish, used her own outside bath down at the huts. I dreamed of her in it, washing her own such-a-nice wide chocolate face with pungent red Lifebuoy soap until it gleamed—a shiny brown light wrapped in a bright cotton doek, like a present coming over the hill in the morning, my grandmother always said.

"You sit still, Miss Elizabeth. You going to slip down the drainpipe and *drown*."

"Can you bath me in the outside bath tonight, Gladness?"

"Why you want the outside bath, Miss Lizzy? This one is tsooo nice," she said, looking with longing eyes around the bathroom. "The outside bath, it's a awld tin bukket! Come, uppy en out."

"Uppy and out . . ." we sang, in the special tune she made for it. To set the record straight, Gladness's outside bath was a jolly nice big tin, complete with dangling handles. You could drag it around and position it absolutely anywhere—next to your hut, or away from your hut. And fill it up to overflowing with bore-hole water in buckets.

Gladness suddenly turned into a big towel. She stuck her fingers like stiff, furry towel planks into my ears. *"OWWWWOWOW . . ."* I was screaming cross.

"Tsht, Miss Lizzy, tsht!" Such a nice face, but she never listened. "Come, your porrich. It's cawld now awready."

Clean shorts on, with a new chance, my bare feet slap-slapped down the passage to the waiting Maltabella porridge. It sat steaming brown in the white bowl, sprinkled with sugar, in a moat of cream.

"Do we have to have that on at the table, George?" My grandmother Elizabeth asked questions as if there were only one possible answer, and that would be the one she had thought of already.

In the scratch and prickle of the radio, words went missing. ". . . tuned . . . BBC, and here . . . news at seven A.M.," said the deep, round voice.

You were not allowed to speak when it was the news. So mostly it was porridge, toast, whisper-whisper with newly separated cream under the blue-beaded doily, eggs for everyone else because I, Elizabeth, did not *eat* eggs, whisper-whisper. And no making a racket with your spoon, either. Children should be seen and not heard, Eugenie reminded every day. The barefoot Sweetness, sister of Gladness but with *not* such a nice face, walked quietly because of the news.

Nothing had happened. Only business—and the Queen was off to Australia, which, like us, a loving colony, would be thrilled to receive her. Of course, they did not have Afrikaners in Australia, who did not think of England as home and who would be quite happy if the Queen buggered off and never visited South Africa again—ever.

" 'Aaauustralia? I'd rather die!' Algernon says to Jack," my mother chattered at a tangent, seeming to find that exceedingly funny. She'd heard it on the radio one afternoon, she divulged, while listening on her bed. Something to do with a wild man, I thought she said.

"You heard the news last night, George," my grandmother said, "and the night before, and every morning and every lunchtime. Do we really have to have it blaring at the breakfast table for the few days we have Eugenie here?"

He stood up, still wiry tall, stooping a little but remarkably straight for almost eighty. His khaki bush shirt looked on him the way it looked neatly ironed on the coat hanger each morning, and he never went out without his sleeves buttoned against the freckling sun. Picking up his veld hat, he said, "World war was declared between one news broadcast and the next. If you don't listen, you don't know what the hell's going on." He walked out into the heat, boots tied up, just the way it was, my grandmother Elizabeth said, the day he stormed off to fight Hitler. She dabbed her neck with her serviette. "Eugenie, pass the cream, would you?"

Tarzan snorted, and scuffled his chain to a quieter post in the shade. What they did not say on the radio was that just as the skies had grown ominous over Hitler, a change of weather behind closed Broederbond doors had already begun. *Broederbond* meant precisely that: band of brothers. Not everyone was invited, it being a highly sensitive matter. To be included, you would already have proven your loyalty, your undying bond to your Afrikaans heritage. This exclusive band was gathering in brotherhood, bound by necessity, by pride, and most important, by self-preservation. They would once and for all solve the plaguing native question, and thus preserve their own hard-earned rights.

I gathered from my father's words, and my grandfather's, spoken quietly here and there over dinner, breakfast, and walking the veld, that secret police were already banging people awake in the dead of night. They were already following, detaining, beating, and imprisoning those who would not conform. Black or white, they made no distinction. Just as the early settlers had done, they were drawing their wagons into a circle, sealing off their enclosed laager encampment with no sympathy toward the uninvited.

What they did not say on the radio was that a silent force was already brewing behind those closed doors. Only if you had ears that really listened would you have had any inkling at all of what was coming.

..

"*Is there a lucky fish* who wants to drive the cows?" My grandfather strode out like the Pied Piper followed by a noisy drove of picaninns. We'd been at Clova for seven days now, melting into the rhythm of the farm. It would be home tomorrow, my mother had decided—but for now, the luckiest fish alive shot out of the kitchen, down to the kraals, where farm natives tall as my father, black chests bare, smelling of sweat and fire smoke, and sporting lemon-peel-thick keloid scars from barbed-wire fences and tribal fights, wielded sjambok whips with the accuracy of lightning.

For hundreds of years, from far up north in the Congo, their ancestors had wandered down, filtering across the great Limpopo River to the rich, natural salt flats of the Soutpansberg Mountains, which they named Venda—"pleasant place." They had eaten wild figs in the presence of soaring eagles. They had painted with adoration, skill, and great beauty the shocking colors of narina and loerie birds on their round huts, dwellings made of the glorious mud that echoed the depths in their skin. Their high mountain lake held sacred water.

Their medicine men wielded unprecedented power, setting down the laws of the land. Their women bore great chiefs. Now, in rags, they drove the cows on borrowed land. And you'd never find them under a solitary tree where dead spirits loitered.

"*Sjihaaaaaaaah,*" they shouted, and me along with them, as massive Simmental heifers bashed and complained through the baptizing cattle dip, their branded rumps dripping out on the other side with chalk-white liquid to keep ticks at bay. Picaninns were next, sprayed down because those same ticks could make them scratch their thin legs bloody, and die, before one could say Jack Robinson. One tiny chap down at the kraals, Tletlie, had already perished in the spring, his fever so ravaging he could not be saved. Spraying was not negotiable, my grandfather announced. They lined up, ragged and giggling, squinting their eyes closed, their bare feet squirming in the dust, hating it.

"Why do you not wear your medals to work?" I asked my grandfather as he sprayed, thinking he'd look jolly nice in medals. No gentleman would *dream* of wearing them, he said. He said he did not need medals to gain the respect of the men driving his cows. And indeed, they spoke to him always with hushed tones, in deference to his age and his manner with them. And the fact that he spoke often to them in their own language, as much of it as he'd been able to glean in his years on the farm. They hid behind rough hands, embarrassed and amused when he spoke foolishly, but mindful always of his effort. Their eyes were frequently red from too much foaming beer brewed down at the kraal, their smiling breath usually sour. They were reed thin under frayed clothes. Many had been born at Clova and drove the cows as their fathers had. They were as proud as Zulus but gentler, as respectful as Xhosas but simpler, as poor, as primitive, and as beautiful as the surrounding hills. No, he told me, he did not need medals with these men.

Along with the reasons they'd been pinned to his chest, the medals were kept silent in the metal steamer trunk under the main bed— along with his life savings of forty pounds—in case of disaster. And a bundle of letters containing the raging debate between that amusing

Mr. Darwin and George's own father. Monkey stories, he'd wink, delighting me.

The only other special thing in that trunk was a rifle, of British Army issue, kindly allowed from his North African engagement with the Allies. Like the medals, of no use now, it lay quiet.

He walked ahead of my catch-up leaps into the lower cow pasture. We flapped through yellow buttercups so enormous you could wrap your whole face up in them like a hat. I tumbled behind him through the orange trees, and thorn trees with needle thorns longer than my bony thigh. And he promised to tell me a very important thing about being lucky.

That afternoon, I could not find my mother.

I ran, with my heart stopped and a vomit taste in the back of my throat, through the orange orchard, in between the rondawels, *Ohnonothingwill happen, Godwon'tlet anything* . . . all the way down to the kraals, where I knew sometimes, like me, she had hidden as a child.

She was not there.

I hurtled through the bottom fields of lucerne, all the way up toward the farmhouse, searching for her. Two hundred yards from the back of the house, I saw a small piece of her flowery skirt over the edge of a flat rock. She lay there, motionless, a filigreed shadow under the *doring-boom,* the spiky thorn tree. She must have gone there for what I thought she called "pieces and quiet," to the "only cool inch *in* this godforsaken heat."

Creeping closer, the only sound my quieting heart, I saw her white feet folded over each other in the shade of the leaves, in a bald patch where no thorns ever fell. Her straw hat covered her eyes and neck. "Come here by me," she suddenly whispered, thrilling me. Jolly clever. Eyes in the back of her ears. She patted the rock. "Come here by me, my darling."

I crept in and lay still with her on the patch blown slippery smooth by the wind. They'd found that Mrs. Ples lying on a rock like this, down near Krugersdorp, about three hours away. Plesianthropus was her real name, meaning *almost* human. Just her rather ladylike-for-a-monkey self, lying there. Mrs. Ples must have lain down for some pieces and quiet just like this. Her feet were not folded like my mother's. In fact, they found only her face. No one ever found her hat.

Mouse quiet, I told my mother, "Did you know you can tell how *lucky* you're going to be. . . ."

"Shhh," she said, like a small wave from the sea that could wash you away.

She did not want to hear the lucky thing.

"Swswssssswsw," I whispered, to let her know I knew to be quiet. No pest, me.

Then, "Grandpa George says you can tell how lucky—" I tried again in another kind of whisper.

"Just lie quietly by me," she said.

· ·

Hoisting me up onto the tractor, my grandfather pulled out the choke and with a terrible racket to start, got us going. Back on my steering wheel throne, he leaned me to the side for better visibility. "Hat on," he reminded, "or the crows will pick off your ears!" Winding the chewed elastic down under my chin so the wind could not find me, we were off into the faithful dust swirls.

I rode high with him—untouchable.

Down the sandy path we bumped to the lucerne fields with cheeky-faced, uninvited vygie flowers pushing through, down into a muddy, long patch, and down, down we rumbled in the lazy sun to the cow trough.

It sat in the far end of the lower pasture, a homemade pool of corrugated-tin sheets welded into a circle, and set on a small, round concrete floor. Filled with water from an irrigation line that had required months of digging from the bore-hole site, it was an oasis, filled with cud and anything else that hung from bovine lips.

"Don't tell your mother," he warned of the last-day, secret treat. Pants off, hat off, stark naked, I plunged into the lukewarm slime where thirsting cows lolled hot-spit tongues—splashing me soft and cool. Looking up through dripping eyelashes into the sun, I saw every color flying in the air over the Soutpansberg Mountains all the way to the end of the world, where Tarzan once stood, when he was wild, beautiful, and strong. And only Mahila knew his real name, and where he came from.

Suddenly, Meendli appeared damp with heat, and moments later, gap-tooth Mphunie peeped over the side of the trough. My grandfather said something to Meendli in Venda that I did not understand, then walked away to the tractor, turned his back, and lit his pipe. Meendli quickly unwound her batik cloth to just her ragged underpants, climbed up and over the rusting tin walls, and leapt into the green water, shrieking and flailing like a mad fish in a raucous explosion of joy. Mphunie slipped over the side like a small brown eel, and plunged in.

When I finally clambered back up onto the tractor, I saw Meendli wrap her dripping self back into her stripy cloth, and with Mphunie jumping on her heels, she jived and skipped away toward the smoke hanging over the kraals.

That night, there would be a million tears about going home to Johannesburg, me a sad sack climbing into my Clova bed, until my mother reminded me of Salamina's belly, with mysterious feet pounding on the inside to get out.

Luckily, no one but me heard her speak of it—not even the shadows pulling blue-black across the hills, waiting for someone to fall down crippled.

.. .

Soft, brushing kisses at dawn were always the last of Clova. My grandfather leaned into the back window to put his hand on my head.

"Last touch," he said.

The tires crunched on the tiny stones, through the wire gate to the lonely, dirt road now kicked up in pieces behind us. In my half sleep, I dreamed you could tell how lucky you were going to be.

Gifts, friends, foes,
Lovers to come, journeys to go . . .

I dreamed it, just the way he'd told it to me.

Hours later, I awoke to cigarette smoke, my mother driving.

"And who has just woken up?" she asked, spotting me in the rearview mirror. Quietly sad from sleeping, I reminded her that it was just me, Elizabeth.

"My Eeelizabeth," she said, seeming delighted. "Look, look over there, the storm coming."

"We need the lav," I responsibly realized.

"Can you hold on? Just a bit . . . look, look over there." Wide-open veld fell everywhere, with not even a few picaninns rolling their tire rims with sticks, and no native ladies balancing water in buckets. No one yet. But fast approaching, gloom in a perfect sky. "If we're very lucky fish, it'll stay over the road and we can drive right through it," she said.

Pit-pats echoed on the roof, on the front window and then all around, coming faster and faster till it poured down, thrilling my mother, "absolutely in buckets!" All of a sudden, the day was dark-feeling, drumming at us on the roof of the car with our windows quickly rolled up.

"Hold on, hold on," I instructed myself. We soared through splashing rain on the sucking-sponge veld, and then just as suddenly, out into the blue again. Glued to the back window, I saw that black shroud carrying on down the road to rain and rain as it went, but stingy, only where it hovered, teasing without mercy the surrounding veld where clumps of grass waited like limp tongues for a single drop.

My mother stopped the car, freeing me to run to a hidden patch. She appeared with clean tissues from her bag, and suddenly, brilliant, arching color striped above her from the clear blue to pockets of gold at the bottom, wet earth glowing bright in a bath of sun. She leaned against the car and scratched a match for her cigarette, stubborn, but then it lit. "God . . ." she sighed, breathing in the clean smell of rain. Her eyes, upside down from where I crouched, held the whole sky.

We rolled the windows down to let out the smell of egg saamies. Out of a clean blue dishcloth came a huge *koeksister* treat from Clova, that sugary thing with the Afrikaans name meaning "sister-of-cake," so sweet it made your gums curl. Syrupy drips ran down my face, flinging me right up into heaven, then back again to wash it down with hot tea from the flask. If you spilled on yourself, you'd be burnt to death.

My mother was ready to drive us again.

CHAPTER TWO

A SPECIAL, BROWN FACE

◎◎

Arriving home from Clova, we were met by municipality bulldozers at our gate. Instructed to park down there on the dirt road, we jumped over trenches ready for the new sewerage systems. Even servants' rooms would now have inside lavatories.

When my father decided on Ferndale, it had that in-between feeling. It was only just beginning to be a suburb, taking root after the Second World War when many were penniless and began building houses on cheap farmland well on the outskirts of Johannesburg. Out in the sticks, actually. We'd moved here from a flat near the university when Ferndale's open veld lay newly divided by dirt tracks and funnels of dust. Small stones clipped windshields, and the highveld wind painted reddish-brown sand up the sides of new, white walls. There were no streetlights, and even now, in 1963, streetlights would be the next hoped-for thing.

Delighting the monkey in me, trees for climbing were plentiful, a leftover of century-old, poorer farms now sliced into one- or two-acre stands—funny-podded acacias, and poplars with invasive, damaging roots that pushed right up through bathroom tiles to peer in at us. Golden mimosas sprinkled us with fine pollen mists all summer, and of course, jacarandas, their majestic purple blooms hinting that even in an empty place, life might one day be elegant and full.

There were no shops for miles around, except for the Portuguese Fish and Chips, conveniently also selling firecrackers for the English-speaking like us, who, still intrigued by Guy Fawkes, celebrated with a good blast every November. And on the corner of steep, stony Bell Street, the kafee where we'd go for cigarettes, cheaper brown bread for the blacks (cheaper before it was discovered to be more nutritious), white bread for the whites, newspapers, and a few American comics that no one could afford but everyone fingered, like *Casper the Friendly Ghost* and *Richie Rich*. The vegetable shop adjoined the kafee. Along with Vasco's Fish and Chips, they sat there in the veld, a little white-washed oasis, all run by the Portuguese.

They had conquered high seas for their kings and queens, and settled new lands. Now they ran the vegetable shop on our corner. Poor-whites. Their saving grace was that they were jolly nice and worked hard, separating them from the toothless, poverty-stricken *niksge-woonds*, used-to-nothing whites in veldskoens and filthy clothes down the road. English or Afrikaans who could neither read, write, nor speak properly, they lived in peeling houses with broken-down cars in neighboring Fountainblue—like the inbred Stinkfoot Venter family down there, whose feet stank because they'd been mired for so long in poverty. Inexcusable when you're white, everyone agreed.

It still sounded like a farm in places, the crow of a backyard rooster at disgruntled hens the first sign of daylight. With the prosperous division of farms, boxy houses were springing up, offering the "new life," a place to settle. The smell of bricks and wet cement cooled the prick-ling highveld dust. Each boxy house had a room at the very back of its acre, for the servants. One freestanding room, with a bath of sorts, running water, mostly just a cold tap, and if very new, a toilet.

An in-between place, for in-between people. Like a rude, higgledy-piggledy carpet of weeds, it was fast joining the tapestry of other similar areas, slowly becoming the greater, outlying, northern suburbs of Joburg.

My father said lightly to the estate agent in her white patent leather heels, mustard suit, and gold bullet-shaped earrings that if it were closer to Soweto, he might save more on petrol, given that he often spent the night there. By his account, her small eyes got even smaller, and her chin lowered into a disbelieving tilt. Some things were allowed, and some things were not, she knew full well. Whites have no business in Soweto, much less spending the night there. "And what are you doing in there?" she'd asked with a plastered smile.

"Baragwanath hospital," he'd said.

Our boxy new house had no streetlights and a threadbare lawn. Set well back from the street, it was kept in place by a three-foot-high chain-link fence, provided by the municipality to deter *tsotsis,* black criminals of no fixed abode. These tsotsis wandered the streets, sticking their hands through open windows at night to steal whatever they could. When residents grew wise and began to grab the invading hands until police arrived, the tsotsis fashioned long poles embedded with razor blades for their window-fishing. Even our blacks were afraid of the tsotsis.

Our acre sported a bony almond tree standing guard beside a dirt driveway, a barren orange tree, a bank of straggly mimosas, some old creepers that might be retrained, and leftover clumps of coarse, waist-high Kikuyu grass, tougher than weeds and almost impossible to destroy. Its erratic patches provided a home for the last of the wild snakes that for so long ruled the old farms. Salamina, Iris, and anyone black ran wild-eyed and terrified, screaming, *"Jhaw jhaw jhaaw!"* into the bush before even thinking to find a stick to kill them. And these same snakes thought nothing of creeping up shower drains to bask on bathroom floors.

My mother had been trying to make a garden for us, with roses, of course, and dreaming of some African jasmine for a verandah—if we could ever afford to add a verandah. But for now, bulldozers ploughed up our dirt street for sewerage pipes, and dust flames, not jasmine, licked at the white-plastered, three-bedroom house in Ferndale. It sat there, new and uncomfortable, but miraculously in the shaded grace of a massive old syringa tree. Part of the fragrant lilac family, someone told my mother, with dangerously poisonous berries. She would need to warn her children.

The syringa tree rose from the ground at the back of the property. Its golden berries followed syrup-sweet clusters of flowers exploding from its branches like suspended meteor showers to release their fragrance into the air—tiny star-shaped blooms, from palest lilac to the deepest purple, like the inside of someone's heart. Its shadow was generous, its roots black, gnarled, and deep.

I scrambled up the dirt path, hunting for my father. Salamina, waiting for hours for our return, and half asleep after her lunch nap under the mimosas, rustled into hurrying. She rapidly adjusted her not-quite-tied-on-properly *doek* on her head. She wouldn't be seen dead without it, a small kerchief that covered her crinkled black hair. Closing in on my heels, her belly loomed behind me down the slate passage.

My father was safe. I leapt up, stiff-happy to kiss his neck. "It was *dark* on the veld in the middle of the day. We drove right through the storm," I announced, "right through it, and Mommy said we've lived to tell the tale."

"I'm so glad you have, my Lizzy." He laughed, rubbing my wet hair into knots.

"Tell about the ten-shilling man," I said.

"God, Isaac," my mother said again, bringing in wet swimming costumes and towels, "you're *green* with tired."

"Later, my love," he said to me about the ten shillings. "Did you hit traffic, Eugenie? We were worried."

"Couldn't get her out of the water at Warmbaths."

"Did she behave?" he asked. They looked at me.

"Very good, actually. I didn't have to shout and she listened, and was *very* good!" She kissed the new knots on me. My father headed down the passage. "It's all right, darling." My mother stopped him. "Pietros is at the gate, he'll bring it all in." Pietros had run down from the servants' rooms when we parked, and had already carried baby John over the trench.

I tore through the laundry and back out behind the house, where brown grass made do on stingy, monitored watering, and dusty, disheveled sparrow-mossies, feathers frayed and desperate for a bath, scattered, startled, up into the wide, blue sky. I flew to the syringa tree, to my wooden place, the soft plank knotted on long ropes for soaring into the air, for disappearing into the sweet of high and higher. I climbed right up into the golden berry part, where cool, brown wood bent to fetch me, making spaces for the wind to blow through, for resting, thinking, and chatting. And where, if you were a lucky fish, you might find a thousand friends waiting for you.

"Miss Lizzy?" the rough voice crackled up through the leaves. "Is it you?" Zephyr, midnight black and ancient, Loeska's Zulu garden boy, some of his right-hand fingers long severed, stood next door rolling his pungent tobacco into a crumpled little square of newspaper to make a *zol,* "comfort," he called it, his homemade cigarette. He was close to eighty, with sunken black eyes, hollow cheeks, and crumbling yellow teeth that belied his physical strength. If you'd ever been at the fence, you knew it was the first two fingers missing and a big piece of the third on his right hand. They were no longer sore, healed over like rough potato skins—chopped off long before the rains stopped falling on the veld, Salamina once told me. He would never say what happened to him, but he'd worked in the mines years ago and clashed with police there during a violent outbreak. May have been an accident, my father said, or maybe not.

Zephyr leaned on his rusty rake, his cloud of smoke filling the air with its sour smell. "Aahw . . ." he said, "it is only you."

From a deep place within his chest, he had told me, when I first began to climb, that the spirits of our ancestors fly into the trees when they die, into the leaves and the berries and the bark. And that's why, when you carve your African mask out of a piece of wood, you can't choose the face you want, because the face is already there. You just open it out into the world to see who it is. Like being born.

"It's only me, Zephyr," I said. His raking continued behind the hedge and then disappeared behind Loeska's house.

I shot up to my highest perch in the lilac heaven. Did they know, I asked of the thousand friends, ancestors, and newborn leafy faces, that you could tell how lucky you were going to be? According to my grandfather George, life could be predicted after all: A small white spot on the nail of your thumb meant you were going to get a present. If it was just a little spot, it would, disappointingly, be just a little present. But if you awoke to a big white spot on the nail of your thumb, the present would be enormous.

"Gifts, friends, foes, lovers to come, journeys to go," I sang to the friends. One meaning for each nail of your five fingers. Navigating the high seas of unpredictability, I would now be able to tell my luckiness in advance, be ready for anything, and keep everyone alive at the same time.

The one to avoid was a spot on your middle finger's nail: sinister warning of a foe. A foe was someone who did not like you, my grandfather said. A foe wanted to hurt you. And sometimes, you did not even know why.

"Gifts, friends . . ." The newly appeared spot on my first finger's nail was quite obviously Loeska. A tiny spot might indicate a not-so-sure friend. But not Loeska, or she would never have manifested in so definite a spot, so big, so white. From up here, peeping over the tops of glossy hibiscus bushes, glimpses of her lit up the spaces between the leaves. She was a marvelous creature. The mere sight of her reignited my resolve.

Hurtling back to the brown world below, at least a few hundred syringa friends clambered down with me, duly warned that if you slipped, hanging upside down, you'd fall out and break your neck. We raced to the bushes that lined our dirt driveway, from where one could safely observe the new dominee next door, his house, his daughter, Loeska, and his proud, new church, like the others springing up across the veld, a triangular redbrick building with a needle-sharp steeple, his lightning rod to God.

Usually I heard her first: lovely shouts of "Rah rah rah!" followed by the miraculous sight of her stamping her delicate, bony foot on their cement driveway under luscious Chinese lantern flowers. Ignoring the thing she had said about cesspool eyes, I was poised to make a whole new start.

In her pale hands she held long sticks whose ends exploded into rustling fountains of glued-on crepe paper. In the dry, static air, her white hair stood on end. From the vigor of her stamps, I knew she was having an excellent day. They were so jolly glad to be living next door to the new doctor, Dominee Hattingh and his round wife, Marie, because Loeska needed special care. Her father's blood virulently allergic to her mother's, she, like all her siblings, had required a massive transfusion at birth to make her go pink again—followed by a desperate series of them to get the faltering pink exactly right. The borrowed blood must have filled each thin leg all the way up to her wispy neck.

"Rah rah rah!" she cheered to the ether, all punctuated with stamps. "*Ons* is *gouer, julle* is slower! Rah rah rah!" she screamed. By her fervor alone, you knew that it was so. She was indeed faster and better than anyone else.

Her important father, a tiny-eyed boat of a man, poured himself into seam-bursting black suits that, except for his ruddy, cherubic cheeks, concealed every part of him. With the highveld dust attaching itself to all that black, my mother said he was the visual equivalent of a dirge. Stringently Calvinistic, he was the dominee of the Dutch Reformed Church, which I first mistakenly heard as the Much Deformed Church. For months, they had been crusading to have me join them around the corner at the church on Hope Street, for *kinderkrans,* where every Wednesday afternoon, the children learned stories about their special selves and Afrikaans Jesus. That's when my mother explained that we were too busy.

I peeped louder, scratching about a bit in the hope Loeska would see me.

"Ag pleez deddy . . ." She chirped into a new song for my benefit!
CSH CSHHH, her sticks flew through the air. Frighteningly pale, she
cleverly remained in the shade of the Chinese lantern, choosing its
dreaded bees over shriveling up in the sun.

"Ag pleez deddy [she sang] won't you take us to the
drive-in
all six seven of us eight nine ten
we wanna see a flick about Tarzan and the ape men
And when the show's over you can bring us back again!"

She looked suddenly right at me. Thrilling to her nod, I leapt
through the fence of bushes—instantly sorry, the bushes being the
scratching, sore kind.

"Popcorn chewing gum [she roared on, allowing me to join,]
peanuts and bubble gum
ice cream candy floss . . ."

Desperate for her approval, I clasped my hands like the fat
Afrikaans ladies who sang in her father's church and tidied for meetings behind the wooden doors at night. Walking with Salamina to
Vasco's Fish and Chips on boiling Sunday mornings, we had seen
them from the street. Their voices shook with God, as if devout frogs
throbbed in their throats.

"Luhzza-biff!" she said suddenly, which ordinarily would have delighted me but made it clear she was still having trouble pronouncing
my name. Elizabeth is not a name they prefer in Afrikaans.

"It's Elizza-bith," I said with my new beginning in mind, trying to
simplify it for her, then in a moment of genius, "Like the Queen," I
proudly offered.

"The Queen should mind her own blerrie business, and go and live
in her own blerrie country," she promptly informed me. "We do *not*
belong to the Queen anymore." Then, upon further consideration, she

added, "Maybe the Queen should take all the blacks to go and live in England with *her*."

"... and Eskimo Pie [we sang on,]
ag deddy, how we miss ...
pepsi-cola ginger beer and Canada Dry."

In a final bravura display, the victorious cheerleading sticks swished and she vanished, engulfed by panicked calling from her house. "Loeska, *my skattie, kom binne!*" She was most beloved, and they wanted her inside.

The hundred leafy friends and I crept home through kinder bushes, and climbed again, branch by branch, up into the syringa berries, where we sat in silence.

"Only me, Zephyr ..." I called down, in case he was there, in case the rustle of us startled him. But he wasn't.

The few berries hanging tenuously through the winter like shriveled old gold would soon be obscured by a plethora of tiny lilac pods. And soon after that, as early as the beginning of August, perhaps, they would invite the spring and grow full to bursting, waiting to show their faces, waiting to be born.

. .

Late afternoon shaded the backyard granadilla vines into a hanging, hidden cave, safe and dark. It was musty and damp in there, rotting with overripe fruit fallen unseen.

Raiding my mother's cupboard for something fancier than my normally assigned khaki shorts, something with a petticoat maybe like Loeska's, something more ladylike, more persuasive, I burrowed in secret like a hedgehog through delicate sandals, sweet-smelling blouses, and pastel linen day dresses my mother had made herself to save money. Dashing into the granadilla cave to try on my chosen prize, I realized that you did not actually *need* a friend. You could shout out Loeska's song all by yourself, with your very own jumps. My skinny legs, in the rustle of my mother's only evening gown, rocketed me in green silk taffeta like a cricket right off the ground into the tangled ceiling of vines. "Popcorn, chewing gum," I roared.

Salamina's furious face appeared at the opening of the cave. "Houw, houw, houw, Miss Lizzy. What are you doing? I told you be *quiet*, jhe? The Madam, she is sleeping. She's got a *big* headache. . . ." She made a tall, imaginary pile of something on top of her doek. The headache was enormous. "*Jho! Batho ba Modimo*, Miss Lizzy," she said, calling on God. "What are you doing in the Madam's dress? Jhe? You be quiet. If you wake her up, the Master, he's going to give you a big, big hiding!" She stared at the green, thorn-shredded silk. "Come, help me to iron," she sighed, instructing me to follow.

"See, Salamina, I've got my baby on my back." I ran along behind, imitating the way she carried John, slung on her back in a blanket pinned with a nappy pin across the taut front of her belly. He was only up there on Iris's off-day, but it had been my special place, if ever I needed it, until she'd become so lumbering round.

"Oh, very good, Miss Lizzy," she said, paying no attention at all.

Tacked onto the kitchen, the laundry reeked of comfort: steam, wooden pegs, and the wispy fragrance of Sunlight soap on Salamina's skin. It had that newest of marvels, a washing machine, but it was a second-hand, rickety thing cursed every day by my mother when it jammed the sheets in a knot, or had to be filled up with water by hand using the garden hosepipe; or danced like a dervish across the floor.

A metal washboard hung over a white porcelain sink attached to the wall, with two rollers that invited you to stick your fingers into them. They squeezed water out of sopping washing before it was strung on the backyard line to sun-dry. Salamina's thick slices of white bread, spread with shiny dollops of Koo apricot jam, unfinished from lunch, sat on the blue vinyl counter above the soap cupboard, with her tin mug of tea, cold.

I tried again to engage her, trumpeting shouts with Scottish leaps, a trick I'd seen with my mother in Joubert Street in the center of Johannesburg, on a small stage out in the hot sun—the Eisteddfod com-

petition, where ladies performed kicks accompanied by a sweaty chap
with a bagpipe.

"Jho, Miss Lizzy." Salamina smiled, mystified. "Jumping like a
monkey."

"I'm hyperactive. . . ." I cried, and, yes, I had been in the sugar box.
I leapt into something of a knot. "That's ballet." Then in a newly fash-
ionable, tilting Twist, I challenged her to try it.

"Not with my big stomach, Miss Lizzy."

Was her baby ever going to be born? I asked her. She slid her hand
under her belly, already slung low. "Very soon," she said. "The Master,
he say, jhe, he say the baby, it's coming enny day now."

The magic of the baby so close, silenced me. I had long planned to
tell him hello, in his own language. I would say, *"Dumela, dumela
aghe?"* to him, just as Salamina greeted anyone who came to our gate.

"Dumela Aghe! Auw, Monkey." Salamina covered my head with her
delighted hand. "You are my little picaninni!"

"I'm not a picaninni, I am big. Sing me my wedding song."

"Oh, You are getting married Miss Lizzy?" she played along.

"Sing to me, oh maid of honor!" I commanded her to carry my
jewel-encrusted train.

"No, Monkey, I am too tired, jhe? I've got a big, big ironing to do,"
she said sternly.

"Aah, sing to me, Sally, I am a bride."

With sweat beading on her lip, she dunked her hand into the battered jam tin filled with water, and flicked the drops onto a carefully
folded sheet on the ironing board. And because singing takes less effort than arguing, her mouth opened in a deep melody. *"Iquira lendlela,
nguqonqo . . ."* Her tongue clicked, and I danced. Instantly, she chas-
tised my stiff legs. "Jhe, you move your hips, Miss Lizzy, you are a
bride." Her wide-spread, carrying hips began slowly to undulate. Her
voice rose like a queen's, deep and sweet. *"Nguqonqothwane,"* she sang.

Like a mountain of honey, her buttocks seemed to soften into the
teary cloud of steam. Pushing the black iron with her full weight,
she ironed and sang, ironed and sang—the longing song of the bride

she would never be. It was the song of the cowherd boys to the dung beetle trying to find its way home on the dusty path. And thus, she'd said, they taunt young brides. "Do you know your way home, Monkey?" she teased.

Her Xhosa clicks slapped at the roof of her mouth. "You don't tell anybody about the baby, Miss Lizzy?" she said, interrupting her melody. "The baby, it's not supposed to be here, jhe? The baby's got no pass, no paper. You don't tell Loeska next door, yhe? She will tell her father."

There it was—the riveting look. There would be no room for error with black ladies. She steamed the white cotton with unyielding precision. Her words hung in the humid air, a prayer that the haphazardness of me had listened, that I would remember her warning.

"The police will come and take the baby to live in the township, too, too far away. He will have to live with my mother," she said, "and she is too, too awld."

"Why can't he live with his dad?"

She wiped the damp from her face in a long silence. Finally, she said with sad lips, "With Mathias? Jjo, Lizzy, Mathias . . . is no good." She looked out of the laundry door past the horizon, further, it seemed, than hell. "No good."

She picked up the iron again. "So you don't tell anybody about the baby, yhe? The Master, he will get a big fine from the police, a lot of money. Yjo, yjo, yho, he will be very, *very* cross with you. He will give you a big hiding."

"I'm *not* getting a hiding!" I fell down tiny as I could on the blue-checked floor. I crept at her with mashing teeth and malevolent horns. ". . . because I am the Tokolosh!"

Salamina bashed her hands up in the air to protect the new life within her, flailing backwards into the wall. "Jyeh, Miss Lizzy!" she spat out—that pint-sized, shape-shifting demon a source of instant fear to anyone black. "You don't talk about the Tokolosh, yhe? The Tokolosh, it's a very bad spirit. . . ."

Victorious, I advanced, shooting up from my haunches to inquire, "Why is he so short?"

Caught between the kitchen wall and me, her eyes lit with ancient dread. *"Haaaaaah!"* I roared, delighting that the mere mention of the Tokolosh held such power, and that in my devilish incarnation, my own terror of him seemed momentarily to vanish.

"Yhe, Lizzy! You *don't* talk about the Tokolosh!" she yelled to no avail.

Relentlessly distracting her from ideas of hidings, I hissed the horrible legend in the hoarse rattle preferred by devils. "He's so short, he creeps his hairy self with his horns and his long thin tail, his face confusing you, looking exactly like someone you know—into your room in the night, up onto his toes he pulls his self up, up your sheets. You so scared of him," I declared, "you put your bed *up,* on bricks, so he can't come in the night and steal your spirit!" Indeed, Salamina's bed, Iris's bed, Zephyr's bed, and everybody black's bed in the whole country was up on brown builder's bricks, two at least under each leg, giving it height and safety. "Sucking your spirit right out . . . Thsloooooooooo!"

"Yjo, Lizzy!" She turned her stomach away, and fled with staring eyes right out of the house, past the orange tree that had never borne a single orange.

. .

That night, with no sliver of moon, icy fingers pulled the sheets of my bed open. My heart pounded out of my chest. My mind raced to the skeletal Mrs. Ples, dead for thousands of years, come to crush me in her jaws and return me to dust from whence I came; to the long fingers of the Tokolosh, peering over the lip of the bed in the dark to suck me away—*OhNonothingwillhappenGODwon'tletanythinghappen* . . . I flew up, standing high on the bed, screaming for my mother.

"Yes, silly billy, it's only me. Quickly, wake up," she whispered, and fell to her knees patting, hunting in the black space under me. He must have run under the bed with his hot breath. I felt the scratch of his taking fingers still on my skin, my throat banging.

"Is it school?" I asked, hardly daring to move.

"No, silly, it's dark outside," she whispered. "Come quickly . . .

where are your slippers?" She caught sight of me in the dim room. "Good Lord, what on earth are you doing sleeping in my dress? Honestly. Come quickly." She hauled the blanket right off the bed and wrapped me in it. Salamina had asked for me. The baby was coming.

"Her baby?" I shrieked in delight.

"Oh God, Elizabeth."

If you jump, wrapped in a blanket, you fall over.

"Quickly, *quietly*," she said anxiously, standing me back up and herding me down the cold passage. We hurried out into the cricket hum, past the washing line, through the everybody-sleeping night. The door of the servants' rooms glowed faintly like a slender ghost deep in the backyard. On the threshold, I peered in at the flickering dark.

"Come, come in," my mother said urgently, still whispering.

At the far end of the narrow passage stood Iris, not in her uniform, but in funny shorty pajamas, with her hair not hidden under her doek but naked and up like springs, her eyes wide. She had run like that, just after midnight, opened our kitchen door with the servants' key, run barefoot down our dark passage to knock with trembling hands at my father's bedroom door. "Come quickly, Mahstah," she had breathed in her high, thin voice. "Salamina is fallen down in the bathroom flaw." Now she stood silent, glued to the passage wall.

Iris's room was dark. The room of our sometime driver, Peter Mombadi, was dark. I'd smelled his Lucky cigarette out in the night when we came down the path. He must be out there, waiting.

As with our house, all the lights in the servants' quarters remained switched off. Even their small kitchen was dark, and their bathroom—dark. It always smelled sour in here, of *suurpap* porridge, of cheap, sweet, red hair oil, and foaming beer. And it smelled warm, of Salamina.

A half candle, melted-stuck onto a chipped saucer, burned on her table, lighting a few bottles of creams and a little pot of rouge I knew she smeared onto her cheeks for her off-days to Soweto. From my post at her door, I saw her legs, like stretched malt toffee, pulled high into the air. Up on my toes, I saw blood on the bed where she lay, and other yucky stuff also. She was drenched with sweat.

In the forbidden glow, my mother held Salamina's face on the pillow, and she held tight on to my mother's arms, her knuckles ash white. My father pushed against her bent knees, soaked through with perspiration himself. "Push, Salamina, *push,* goddamn you," he said, his voice harsh, his shoulder forceful against her foot. "Don't get lazy on me *now,* Sally. Push!"

The midnight moon had not pulled the child from Salamina as she had hoped, and now the moon had vanished. My mother stroked her arms and said quietly, as if for the hundredth time, "Come on, my girl, it's *one* more, Salamina, *one* more . . ." She wiped Salamina's cheeks, the tears and sweat that mingled there, and then suddenly, "The head!" my mother cried. "He's got the head! Come along, my girl, *one* more, Sally, it's *one* more."

"Push, Salamina . . . *push!*" my father demanded. Suddenly, Salamina shoved her head back into the pillow, buried her face into my mother's chest, and screamed her dripping mouth wide open, as a squelching river gushed from her body. And there, in my father's bloody hands, lay a slippery thing—a baby.

I felt my stomach turn. It was disgusting. It had no blue bonnet, no tiny rattle, no smile to which I might say "Dumela." It was covered in filthlike rotten yogurt—a crinkled, slimy mess—like a burnt chicken hanging in an endless, dead quiet.

My father raised it up into the air. "Oh God," he said, trying to catch his breath, "oh God, Eugenie . . ."

"Isaac, it's a little girl!"

"A little girl, a little *girl,* Salamina," he said, in exhausted, joyful victory. "You and Mathias have a little baby daughter."

He scratched something out of the back of its throat with his finger. It seemed to choke. And then, out of its muffled, long sleep, came a sudden sound. Life, indeed, lay within it.

"There we go," my father said, its bloodred screams now bright and full in its special, brown face.

Salamina's shivering hands slid under my father's—first around its shrunken bum, and then into the moist, crinkled place behind its neck. She brought it quickly to her face and, with searching eyes,

smelled it deeply, seeming to recognize it somehow. Like some ancient, knowing creature risen from the bottom of the sea, the hazy
membrane of time over its eyes, it stared across centuries, back at her.

She seemed to imprint its scent in her memory, then lay it on her
chest. Salamina's mouth dropped open, exhausted. "*Yjo, oh, yjho . . .* "
she uttered, falling back into the soaking pillow. "*Yjo . . .* " she said, a
sudden stream of tears.

My mother quietly gathered the blood-soaked towels that lay on
the floor next to the bed and walked down the dark passage to place
them in the bath. She asked Iris to quietly and quickly fetch soap
from the laundry room in our house *without,* she emphasized, switch-
ing the light on in there, and then to please run cold water over the
towels, letting them soak. Iris stood stock-still, nodding as if she
planned to do it, sometime, but did not move. So my mother opened
the tap herself, put in the plug of the servants' bath, and ran the cold
water until it turned the filling bath red.

My father threaded a needle at the foot of Salamina's bed. "I was
starting to think we'd made a terrible mistake, Eugenie," he said, when
she came back for more blood towels. "God only knows what we'd
have done." And then noticing me in the doorway, he said, "I think
take Elizabeth back in."

My mother covered the infant, still on Salamina, with a clean
cloth. I saw Salamina place her wide hand on its little sobbing back, as
if she meant to keep that hand there forever.

I watched her from the door. Her own picaninn had come.

. .

To my dizzying delight, Salamina called her baby after me. Well, actually, she gave her my name as her middle name. Her *real* name would
be Moliseng, like a soft song, Salamina said. And it meant, "protect
her, leave her alone." Moliseng Eleseebett—that was Elizabeth, the
black way. And her surname would be Salamina's, Mashlope—because
Mathias was no good.

Moliseng—soft song—Eleseebett Mashlope, not to be spoken
outside our house, ever. We had avoided a trip to the hospital and had

been graced with no complications. No one knew of her. Moliseng would remain hidden. My special job had begun.

Salamina did not come out for quite a few days. Six went by, then seven. "The Master insists, Salamina," my mother said, trying every trick, even tempting her with sweet tea and crisp, buttered Marie biscuits under the syringa tree, which now was a fluke heat wave–induced, premature profusion of tight, bruise purple dots between winter leaves that would soon become buds. And it was not yet July. He'd said it *twice,* my father, as he'd dashed out. He had made my mother promise.

"Eugenie, see that she gets up. *Make* her walk, even if it's just for a few minutes at a time. All we bloody need is for her to have a thrombosis," and he'd gone.

"You *must* walk, Sally, just a bit every day," my mother tried again, but Salamina turned her head into the pillow, away to the cold wall. "Come, the Master says you'll get a blood clot in your legs if you don't stand. It'll go to your heart. Come, up," my mother encouraged, lifting Salamina's shoulders from the bed.

The soft-song Moliseng peered like a new, smoothed-out moth from her cocoon, tightly wrapped in swaddling by my mother, so that after the safety of Salamina's womb she would not feel as though she were falling. No longer crinkled and dormant, her tiny brown fingers crept out, and out again, at every chance.

"She's trying to get out!" I warned, knowing that would be *tickets.*

"Shh, Elizabeth, it's all right. If she's not crying, she's fine. Come, Sally, *up,* my girl."

"Please, Madam . . ." Salamina hoisted herself up a little, and then lay back down.

"You've *got* to walk, Sally, come now."

She held on to my mother's arms, then, with a mighty effort, pulled herself up to stand, and leaned against her.

"There you are," my mother praised. "See, that's not too bad?"

Salamina left a sodden path of tears. I followed quietly as she walked, slowly, supported by my mother. She had dreamed of making a new house with Mathias. But none of that mattered now. Mathias was no good. Drops of sadness spattered down on the cement floor of her room—one here, one there, past the bathroom where the bloody towels lay over the bath to dry, and other bloodied cotton-wool pads lay in the dustbin. We passed through the servants' kitchen, where Iris—after being told for the umpteenth time to make it *laapa*, *outside*—kept a steaming pot of stinking suurpap porridge on their stove, seeping that sour smell into our every pore. Leaning heavily on my mother, Salamina made it to the small patch of sun shining on the concrete threshold. "Jyo, Madam, oh, Jyo jhe . . ." she breathed her heavy words.

"I know," my mother answered quietly. "Come, out a bit, there we go."

Salamina walked as if the bottom of her feet burned with the pain of living—and then no, she must go back, she said, she must go back in. "Please, Madam," she begged. She covered her face, shy, because she had no doek on her head. Her doek was a sign of her respect for you, but now, too tired to tie it on, her sorry head was bare, exposing tiny crinkled peppercorn black curls, of which I'd only ever seen the beginning row, where her face began. "*Please* to go bekk in," she said again.

They turned and followed her path of tears on the cement.

Other than her freestanding room at the back of our house, with its small kitchen, shared bathroom, a tiny room for Iris and one for Peter Mombadi, Salamina did not have a home. Her mother lived in one room made out of corrugated iron and cardboard boxes in Soweto, with no lights, no electricity, no running water, and no toilet. Sometimes she told us after her off-days that the highveld wind had ripped away her mother's tin pieces that made a roof, sending the loose stones and bricks placed to weight it down flying off into the dirt roads. Now Moliseng, according to new laws, must be sent to live in that Soweto shanty where she belonged, in the townships, with the rest of the natives. Salamina would send money each month for Moliseng's food, money she would earn looking after me as if I were her own—her picaninn.

For quite a while, Salamina wept at every little thing, and stayed, swollen-eyed, in her room. Some days, a few quiet songs to Moliseng filtered out of the servants' quarters. But only now and then, when her veil of sadness lifted.

Today, my mother found a patch of shade for resting, and looked up to see my father, doctor's bag in hand, racing out. "Isaac, where are you going?" she asked, thinking for a change he'd be home. But off he'd gone.

She settled herself under the awning at the side of the house, where the new leaves of the morning glory tumbled down in the silent thrum of nothing.

Nothing.

Except Salamina's heavy-sweet faraway song to the little black eyes that peeped out at her in the cool of her room.

"She's fighting," my mother said into the soft air. "That's good, she's fighting."

Eugenie's face, dappled with shade, slipped into a thousand pieces as I watched her, like a milky jigsaw puzzle, always moving. Now you could see it, and now it was gone.

In the morning she'd complained to my father that he was never there. And after breakfast, even though she never raised her voice, she shouted on the phone at the man from Nel's Dairy because *again* there were no bottles of silverfoil-capped milk by the front door when we woke up, with glistening rivulets running down their cold, morning sides. After she'd put down the phone, she said again she just wanted to run away.

"Oh . . . glorious" sighed out of her now in the lazy hum. Now and again the sweet pierce of an Indian myna bird, a cricket, or the crinkle of tiny, golden-yellow trumpet flowers still filled with syrup dropping to the ground where she sat reminded that nothing doesn't ever really mean nothing. Everything goes on, even when it seems to all ears to have stopped.

I watched. I pieced her together in the shade.

Suddenly, like the blazing sun in a clean orange doek, Salamina emerged—right up and out of her bed. The sweet-song Moliseng peered from behind the oozing, milk-swollen tieties that bulged Salamina's uniform. She was lodged there, in the grip of Salamina's arms.

"Does the Madam want some tea, Madam?" Salamina's almost-round-again voice offered.

My mother's heavy eyelids flickered and seemed to float, melting the moving shade to a new picture. Inspecting carefully, I realized her eyes were shut, not for escaping, but just against the glare. So not to worry, she was still alive. "No, I'm fine, thank you, Salamina," she murmured. She would probably be staying, I thought. She seemed to be coping much better since we'd come home. Clova had been just the thing.

The sun had shifted, but no one saw it move.

"Come, dance with Salamina, Miss Lizzy Monkey," Salamina suddenly invited.

Up we raced! Up the path by the washing line, away from all that had been so deathly asleep, to the bright green grass now growing like blazes in the untimely winter sunshine. Salamina dug her wide feet into it. Her body shook like fire rumbling loose, until a sound down deep within her rose up unashamed, to ring out over the tiny brown face. "Come, dance with Salamina, Miss Lizzy!" she called out to me.

Salamina sang, "Moliseeng! Moliseeeang Eleseebett . . ."

She looked at me, her Eleseebett, and then sang "Mashlope!" so every still and sleeping thing in our yard might know the naming of Moliseng Eleseebett Mashlope! Jubilant, we danced till we fell down, with swinging hips, Xhosa kicks, and fast, furious feet. We laughed until we could not breathe. Salamina had entwined me by name with her soft-song Mollie.

Salamina's smart orange doek had to be retied. She flopped down, exhausted, on the grass. Moliseng, whose name would never be spoken outside our walls, lay quiet beside her.

"Moliseng can stay for a while," my mother said that evening, kneeling to sweetly tickle her while Salamina dished up our supper, "because she's just a speck." Moliseng lay bundled like a tiny parcel with eyes in her basket on the kitchen floor. "Nothing more than a

speck! She's so teeny no one can possibly *see* her. Even someone looking with *big eyes* over the fence, they'll *never* see such a speck! Yes,
yees," she chirped into the new black eyes, "just a tiny speck."

Actually, you wouldn't want that speck. It could scream its head off
in the middle of the night, and Salamina more than once had to cover
its gaping, gummy mouth with a wool blanket to stifle the racket. We
did not need police banging down our door, my mother cautioned, as
they had done to the Van Stadens down the street—that Afrikaans
family found to be harboring God only knows who in their backyard.
"About *forty* kaffirs," the whispers said, because the Van Stadens were
too bloody lazy to go down to the pass office to register their servants.

My father had seen old Mr. Van Staden at his consulting rooms
soon after, suffering from chest pains, and saying these bloody arse-
hole police gave him a heart attack in the middle of the night—you'd
think he'd committed *treason,* he said. Kaffirs were kaffirs, he added,
and he didn't care *who* was in the back there, as long as they didn't
come over his doorstep, and didn't ask him for money. Where should
they sleep? And where should they piss? he'd asked my father in his
thick Afrikaans accent. The government hadn't put up houses for
them. And he hadn't noticed any public lavatories marked for blacks
along *his* street. How was he going to stop them? he'd asked those police. Buy a bloody gun?

Moliseng had no paper. The police would declare her illegal if they
ever found her on our property. And being a child, with no employment and thus no bloody business whatsoever being at this house, the
police would decide she would not be *given* any such special paper. *All*
children were now illegal on our properties. Black children. And for
good reason, for if they were allowed, *if* they were given a pass, the
thinking went, there'd soon be whole damn families of them living in
squalor in the back there. *Sies!* Unacceptable, was the growing consensus about that.

Most people would look the other way, my mother assured Salamina. Most people really would. Afrikaans and English alike. But
there could always be that one, English or Afrikaans, who might pick
up the phone to inform the police. A punishing fine would have to be

paid by the owners of the property, meaning us. Moliseng would be sent away to her aging grandmother in Soweto. Where God only knows what awaits her, my father said. Given my special job, if anything happened to her, I knew without question it would be my fault.

I called on every spell I knew. With busy hands I patted down anything coming near, silently relying on my chant several times a day— *Oh no nothing will happen . . .*

On guard, I was to make sure she was neither seen nor heard from the street. I was absolutely never to mention her at the house next door, and I was to make sure that she never, *ever,* when the illicit brownness of her climbed up and out of that blanket, ran by the fence.

CHAPTER THREE

. . . .

THE MONKEY

◎◎

There were two things I did not see at the end of August, nearly three months after Salamina came out of her room into the morning sun. One was late in the afternoon when the dominee's black Deutsche-Wagon made that terrible, petrol-mixed-with-oil exhaust stink as it drove funeral-slow up the driveway next door, carrying the red Mercurochromed body of Loeska.

Oh, she was still alive, but she'd had the most terrible day. Savagely bitten, unable even to be wrapped in a blanket, its wiry wool searing like knives into her bruised skin, she lay on the backseat in a moaning heap, dotted red from top to toe. The painted, red medicine ran all up one side of her body, up over her head, through the remaining scattered tufts of her white flossy hair, and down the other side: the neck, the shoulder, the arm, the thin, wishbone white thigh, down past the blue, bulby knee, down the skinny shin, into *and under* her foot. Red Mercurochrome mapped every puncture on her body.

I smelled the fumes of the Deutsche-Wagon, polished to shining every morning by Zephyr, from high in the syringa tree. I wanted to look, but did not, counting about four hundred berries all around me instead—new, greenish golden, and jolly poisonous. I counted them one at a time, trying to think, instead, of Loeska in her lace dress, with her snow-white hair sticking straight out. I thought of the Loeska I knew, rather—the one I loved and wanted for my friend. I thought of her fancy petticoat with the blue silk ribbons threaded evenly through the eyelets at the bottom, the same ribbon that lay in voluptuous rolls in that house next door where Loeska's mother, unlike mine, never napped. Instead she made homemade jams from pink guavas and figs, in tin-lidded glass bottles with special writing on them—jams consumed in vast quantities, it was rumored, by the delighted, portly dominee. And hats—she made all kinds of hats, with dotted-net veils like a measles-face, adorned with furry felt grapes, lettuce, and fruit salads on top. These were for Sundays only, and if somebody died—even if that was not on a Sunday.

And she made hats for the volkspele, of course, their breathtaking folk dances on summer nights, with smooth-fingered accordions and everyone weeping with remembrance of the terrible price they'd paid to settle our land. Loeska's volkspele frocks were respectfully long, in greens, blues, and pinks, and silky right down to the floor. Sporting floppy ox-wagon bonnets, they danced: clap, link arms, turn, and go the other way, *"tiekie-draai, tiekie-draai,"* turning on a tickey, only half the size of a sixpence—which, if you've ever had a sixpence, you'd know is a very tight turn.

I stared into my leaves and tried to think of Loeska in her volkspele dress, instead of *looking,* when they carried her nearly lifeless body into her silent house. Her tearful mother insisted that the police be called at once, and that the "people!" she said as sarcastically as she could muster in her grief, who owned these vile animals be punished. *Severely* punished.

I heard the words "Dirty outrage!" through the fence more than once, but in Afrikaans, hissing out as *"Vieslike skande!"* "Shame, man! These things just happen out of the blue," filtered up to my leafy perch in the syringa tree.

She'd been standing there, Loeska, at her gate, just like any other day, in her freshly starched lace, her blue-white skin responsibly shaded by a soft straw hat in palest green, they were saying. It was the green you see only in the newest leaves, which made it a very hard color to find, most especially in ribbons and fruits to match. Her bobby socks were neatly pulled up, making her delicate legs look more substantial with a clever ruffle of lace around the top of each sock. Balancing, visually, the hat, of course. As usual, she was doing everything right. And if you can believe it, I heard, she had been waiting not outside the gate at the bottom of her Flora Street driveway, but obediently *inside*, where she had been *told* to wait.

Out of nowhere, a vicious, raging little monkey with a blue arse had descended from the tree above her, sinking its razor-sharp teeth into her. "And yes! Let me tell you," babbled through the fence, "you are quite right in assuming there are no loose monkeys running around the suburbs of Johannesburg, for God's sake! I mean, pleeease!" they said. "This isn't some godforsaken farm out in the veld somewhere."

Down he raced from the acacia tree, through the bright bougainvillea, falling in a horrid little thud at the gate post, quickly recovering to leap *onto* her leg, where he bit, and bit, and bit all up one side of her, up over her thin-skinned head, piercing it from ear to ear, luckily avoiding her eyes, nose, and mouth because the hat tipped over them, miraculously protecting them, tore out a clump of her white hair, ripped into the lobe of the second ear, and down, down, down he went, leaving the last horrible bite in and *under* her right foot as she lay up-ended, dazed and screaming in the bright morning sunlight.

She had been waiting for the nice Breytenbach children two

houses down to come walking up the road with their plastic-covered prayer books and also-lacy socks. Those children were to join her for kinderkrans, in the shaded side room of the church, for very special stories about themselves and Afrikaans Jesus.

The visitors multiplied in strength and number as they gathered in shocked sympathy next door. "Aaagh, shame man!" one wailed. "Right at your very own gate these things can happen. When you are doing *just* as the Bible instructs! The unfairness of it all! Too much to bear."

These "people" would have to be prosecuted. They were the mangy, stunted Swanepoel family who lived five houses down from us across the street and had at one time, the whole lot of them, father, mother, and six children, been in the employ of a circus. A ramshackle outfit to begin with, that circus had long been disbanded, but these Swanepoels either didn't understand or just plain secretly kept some of the animals. They had been warned and warned but to no avail. And the evidence against their lawless keeping of monkeys, large and small, on their property in a caravan, for goodness sakes, had been mounting. Ever since Loeska's mother opened her door, three months ago, to that poor woman selling crocheted doilies from house to house.

On *that* awful day, there had been a frantic, gnawing scratching at the dominee's door, and upon opening it, Marie Hattingh, the dominee's round wife, found a woman pale as a ghost, her teeth chattering, almost unable to breathe, clutching a shuddering pile of beaded doilies.

"Goeie genade!" which means "Good grief!" (especially daunting when spoken in the high Afrikaans-Pretoria-seat-of-power sort of way,) Marie Hattingh had said. *"Kom binne . . . kom binne!"*

She'd called for Willery, who as usual didn't answer, to bring boiling tea to the lounge immediately. "Where *is* that native girl!" she'd had to say apologetically to her unexpected, shaken guest. Marie *knew* it would be all right to ask the stranger in, as the nice white lady wore a clean, ironed dress with a lace collar. And black shoes, sensible even though they *were* old and, Marie Hattingh noticed, needed a quick little polish. You never know, she was thinking, this lady might even have been interested in a lovely hat? But not right now, of course, Marie sensitively realized. The woman was in a ghastly state.

She had knocked on the door of "those people" down the road, and no one answered. ("Those people," to Marie, always meant people like us next door, people who were less-than. She, like her elongated High Dutch Afrikaans vowels, was a bit like blue cheese around ordinary cheese—inexplicably better-than.) The lady knocked again, and could hear someone sweeping inside, but still no one answered. Perhaps they hadn't heard her, she'd reasonably thought, and so wandered around the side of the house, chirped along by birds. She'd called out, with quiet good manners, of course, with her neat stack of beautiful doilies, wondering if anyone was home. And would anyone like to buy a lovely doily to keep the flies off their morning porridge? Hand-beaded, of course.

She could see the tip of a sweeping broom, that grass thatchy part on the bottom, moving back and forth through the leaves on the back porch—sweeping.

And of course, any reasonable person would think, Oh, good! They *are* home! And perhaps someone might like a doily.

When around the corner, at the back of the house, wearing an apron—she never said of what color that apron—stepped an enormous, staring, black-eyed ape, upright! Carrying his broom. No, *not* a kaffir, she'd blurted out, which she'd initially *assumed* out of just the corner of her eye—his shadow there, you know, big and black— expecting a garden boy or something when she heard the gentle swish of that broom.

No, not a native . . . An *actual* ape! He had been doing his sweeping, she'd stuttered.

They came from the circus, you know—the jibber-jabber, next-door visitors carried on through the fence—those animals, when it was shut down. And most of them were half mad and really vicious, because they hadn't had proper food in a very long time, and now were being kept, without a license, in the backyard, for crying in a bucket. "Cruel, cruel!" my mother had said, when *she'd* heard.

They *lived* there, the whole bloody lot of them, my father had said then, and they should be fined and cleaned up. It was about the only thing that he and Dominee Hattingh thought the same about, although they never *said* to each other they thought differently. However, on this they agreed. For the past three months, everyone thought it an utter disgrace, a disaster itching to happen. And now, Loeska lay in a bitten heap, with blocks of ice smeared on her every fifteen minutes to stop her crying.

The scattered doilies of that poor woman from three months ago sat in an honest pile waiting to be fetched. Blown here, there, and everywhere in the wind on that day, they had been gathered up in the road by Salamina and old Zephyr, after the woman had fled to the safety of the dominee's door. And they were there still, those same doilies, in the ticking-clock dining room of the dominee. Bathed in the silent smell of canned figs and molded straw for the hats, they waited to be claimed by the woman who had made them so tenderly, and who had set out with such high hopes that day. Unfortunately, she had never been seen again, not at the church, and not anywhere in Ferndale.

In the morning, my ears always attuned to commotion, I'd charged down to the dust cloud at the gate to see what was happening, along with several other neighbors, and Eugenie, who shrilled at me to get *back* into the house at once. She'd heard someone scream the word *monkey*, but did not know at that point about the bites. What startled her, startled the whole bloody street, actually, was Loeska's screaming . . . and the shocking sight of Paul de Kok, the Afrikaner who lived on the corner.

He had kindly, although no one realized at the time what he was doing, *kindly* run out into the street with his gun, firing it into the air several times, with his fierce dogs, who were trained to attack and kill anyone remotely black who set foot on his property. Except for his own servants, of course, whose scent they had been trained to accept. He ran shooting wildly up and down, and everyone else, including me, ran back into our houses.

Except for Zephyr, who despite his age and a hail of bullets scooped Loeska up in his black arms and ran with her, a bleeding, tangled ball of lace, up to their house.

My mother dashed from room to room locking our doors and windows, with Salamina fast on her heels doing the same. John and Moliseng lay safe and oblivious, asleep, in our kitchen.

Suddenly there was a frantic pounding on our door. My mother ran to open it, unafraid, I assumed, because she knew a monkey would not knock.

"Madam!" Willery appeared wild-eyed at the door.

Willery was *supposed* to look after Loeska. ("These *blerrie* native girls," I heard again now through the fence, "you just can't trust them.") "Madam, the Mahster Dr. Grace, kenn he come *quickly!*" Willery begged.

Unfortunately, he could not. He was bloeming miles away at Baragwanath hospital on Wednesdays, Eugenie told her. But before that news reached the house next door, their Deutsche-Wagon had been fired up. Loeska was already being driven hell for leather, bobbing in the backseat as their car careened down First Avenue, through Linden, hooting at everyone to get out of their path, all the way to Joburg General Hospital.

Still no one knew quite what had happened, until Paul de Kok, mercifully, calmed down.

"Stop *shooting!*" Eugenie had screamed out of our lounge window, and then unable to contain herself, scrambled back down to the gate.

He'd returned empty-handed. He reported that he "saw its fokken blue arse" swinging from tree to tree, and that he had it in his sights, but somehow, *somehow*, it had gotten away. Shifting his veld-skoened feet in the dust, beads of excited sweat dripping from his sunburned head, he vowed to shoot any bloody thing that came near. Which wasn't much different to how he lived his whole life, but this being a special day, he had a fresh excuse.

Apart from fears for Loeska, of course, now everyone, especially I, had to worry about where it was.

Long after midnight, my father was again called over to the dominee's house. Loeska lay in an agonized fever, sweating profusely, and by morning the dreaded word—no one could even bring themselves to say it, *rabies*—was on everyone's mind.

Even a fool knows there's no cure for rabies. You simply seize up, foam at the mouth, and die.

How could this happen, when you were doing just as you were supposed to do? Now the voices drifted up into the syringa tree, flaming with indignation and grave concern. I perched there, listening with all my might for Loeska's moans, for her thin, desperate wails of pain. I heard none. She was either already dead or in a deep, sedated sleep, mercifully numbed to the full horror of what had befallen her.

Through the branches I could see Marie Hattingh, dressed appropriately in navy blue. She personally greeted concerned visitors, who were now arriving in droves to bring custard milktart, for consumption, they clearly specified in supportive tones, after the stringy-salty venison pies they had baked. And of course, most important, they had come to pray.

"How many times do people have to be warned? And why do they not *listen*?" I heard Marie Hattingh say, dabbing her weepy nose with a soaking tissue in their driveway. And *they* said, the grieving visitors, "Shame, hey, to think she was doing *just* as the Bible *sayes*. So terribly, terribly unfair," adding, *"Hou moed"*—"hold your courage." And Marie did.

Because of all the prayers, of course, the fever broke in the morning. The relieving news rang out that Loeska would not start frothing at the mouth, rabid. She would indeed return to her normal sweet self, in time.

It had been quietly forgotten in my house, I gathered because of Loeska's terrible fate, that rumor had it that several dominees, some from as far west as Klerksdorp, attended a secret meeting of the Broederbond the previous month—the band of brothers intent on solving the native question. Some of the most illustrious Afrikaners had been present, but in secret. Plans were hatched that night. Resolve was strengthened. They would make our lives safer and better in every way.

Encroaching hordes of blacks walked our streets at night, drifts of them coming down from sure starvation in the homelands to look for work. They peed and shat in our roads, finding a quiet bush somewhere. You knew it was kaffir shit and not a dog, one irate patient told my father, because when have you seen a dog leave a pile of toilet paper next to his doings? They were climbing three, four, and five into one's servant's room at the back, like what had occurred at the dirty Van Staden house. And even if there had been buses or sufficient trains to return them someplace, many had nowhere to go.

The Broederbond was compelled to meet, the rumor said, because quite obviously, we were outnumbered. Eleven blacks to one white was their latest frightening count. Quite obviously they had no choice. Quite obviously there was not enough employment for everyone, and since kaffirs fornicated and multiplied with no care in the world for who might feed and house them, they needed to be controlled, they felt, with stringent measures. No more games. No more playing nice with the English *kaffir-boeties*, do-gooders who seemed to have about as little intelligence as the blacks. Soon it would be whole families, children, and God knows who else peeing, shitting, and living in the back of one's property.

Most blacks, of course, were all right, they conceded, but many of these natives were tsotsis, dangerous—as willing to slit your throat as they were one another's. And who could tell who was who? Once a kaffir, always a kaffir, they warned. We would all be murdered in our beds. Savages, with no respect for life, they decided. It was just part of their ways.

Standing in the post office line shortly after Loeska was bitten, my mother and I heard that scientifically speaking, they *were* different from us, you know, these blacks. This had been proven by, "Yes, I forget now the name of the man who did that testing," the knowledgeable lady in front of us admitted, her hair sprayed tight in a net like a helmet, as if she were going off to war. Their brains, under X ray, showed marked differences, and were, well, you know, smaller. "Complex," she'd said in hushed, purring tones, and even brilliant, she added magnanimously, next to the brain of an ape! But next to ours, "*definitely* smaller." Most people would not come out and say subhuman. But some actually *do* think and say that. "Less evolved, perhaps, is the better way of putting it," she'd decided.

We heard that one of these dominees, the honored guest speaker for that meeting behind closed doors, rose when he was introduced, his presence understandably a great comfort. He had explained, the rumor quietly informed, that blacks are the white man's *burden.* He'd reiterated to all present that it "sayes so, quite clearly" in the Bible. And he pointed to the exact passage in Genesis, God's own words regarding Ham and Canaan. "Cursed be Canaan. Slave of slaves shall he be to his brothers." Canaan and his offspring should be *houthakkers en waterdraers,* "bearers of wood and drawers of water," into eternity. He'd said it was our God-given "rrresponsibility to uplift them from their inferiority, but *not* our rrresponsibility to live among them."

His magnificent speech had cleared any doubt from the minds of those who had already begun to institute the new policy. Johannesburg would be White by Night, keeping us safe and sound in our beds—while all blacks, not registered by virtue of employment and carrying a pass to prove such employment, would be required at night to leave the city. And return the long distances to their designated townships of Alexandra and Soweto. Like a masimba bucket pouring out its slop at the end of each day, the city should empty of all undesirables each night. Now, how these natives would get to their townships was not our business, they felt. They would just have to get there. The law, after all, was the law.

Whites would now need a pass to go into the black townships, but of course, no one but the police would ever need or want to do that. I thought of my father at Baragwanath, a place that up till now had been a name in my head, the place to which my father raced out from time to time. Suddenly it seemed dangerous, a place for which he would need a special paper, and, probably, a conversation with the police. But these worries had to wait.

For now, we thought only of Loeska. Out of mortal danger, she lay shocked and crying in terrible pain, most especially from the bites on her head. She had to be tended day and night, and her wounds had to be painted, exactly as Dr. Isaac Grace from next door had instructed— painted in turns by all her family, exhausted now, as you might imagine. She had to be smeared with the terrible red Mercurochrome, which everyone knew burned like hell.

Unfortunately, if you were not adept with it, it ran everywhere— right through the dabbing cotton wool onto your fingers, streaming down the backs of your arms to your elbows if you lifted up your hands by mistake—bright but dark red, as if you had dipped your hands in blood.

And the whole family had to go to church like that.

"Unfortunate," they whispered in Dominee Hattingh's driveway.

The church next door was full for the impromptu morning service—giving thanks for the lucky rabies escape.

Embarrassing beads of sweat broke in the heat on the polite brows of fat ladies. Their thick, brocaded polyester to just below the knee rustled in counterpoint to the nylon swish of creamy thighs rubbing together as they sat. Their ample arms, from the door where I peeped in, looked like stuffed *boerewors* sausages. Many filed in with neatly folded lace hankies slipped under delicate, gold-bracelet wristwatches—in case they were moved to tears. Stiff, patent-leather heels and marvelous hats topped off each end of them.

When they were finally settled and hushed, I saw them raise their eyes to the pulpit, where Dominee Hattingh cleared his throat.

This glad morning, he said, he would speak of divine retribution— the payment that will be exacted by our Lord God Almighty for all malefactions. He said *payment* as if he were exacting it right then and there. And he had to give his sermon like that, his red, stained hands lifted up to beseech Almighty God, before his entire congregation.

The monkey was on everyone's mind.

..

The second thing I did not see, not because I was high in my tree not wanting to look but because I was already put to bed, and the shutters, sometimes left open on boiling nights, had been tightly closed.

No one was taking any chances at night, with monkeys, apes, or "anything of that ilk."

What I did not see, until dogs up and down the street howled the night awake, was Salamina walking by the garden wall in the comforting fall of darkness with the three-month-old speck, tearful but quieting, on her lulling back. *"Thula baba, thula, jhe . . ."* I heard her say, very low out there. She began to sing, rocking the speck, whose tears now were almost over. *"Thula tu thula baba thula baba,"* she sang, like a deep dream. The crying abated as the honey voice poured over the speck, humming deep and warm through Salamina's back as Moliseng lay bundled there, tied into the safety of her musty blanket. I heard her familiar chokes, her last sobs before sleep.

And impossibly—the searing lights of a police van blazed across the yard. Sniffing dogs ran alongside, searching the night. Flashlights careened up and down the dark street, lighting up my shutters, then vanishing from them again, deep into the yards, into every corner, glaring under every bush where it seemed something moved.

But not Salamina—stock-still, crouched to the ground in a heartbeat, the moon above her cruelly bright, and the speck startled, its cavernous mouth shrieking wide in fright until Salamina smothered the cries between her own back and the grass, as she lay hiding. "Sshht, Moliseng," I knew she would be whispering against her banging heart. *"Thula baba,* jhe, you don't cry, Moliseng, shhh sh . . ."

Boots, keys, more running, and chains, jangled the silence. Dogs with hollow throats barked. There'd be no fooling them, their scent-trained sniffing, their rasping voices sounding the alarm: Found! The smell of black skin out on the street. Most people heard nothing, because the shutters were so tightly closed. Anything could happen, we now knew, even when you were doing exactly as your Bible instructed.

I listened to the sudden silence outside the shutters.

Had someone phoned the police? Had someone seen or heard Moliseng, heard her first cry, the newborn life in her yelling out? Had someone seen the flicker of that candle, heard the muffled commotion in our backyard that night? Had someone reported her? Had they come for Mollie? I tried to stop my thoughts of Salamina lying on the ground in the dark. I pulled my pillow over my head, *not to worry, not to worry, nothing will happen.* I knew she would gather herself when the danger passed, dust the grass off the speck, off her blanket, and stand up. She would probably never walk by the fence with her again, not in daylight, and not after dark.

· ·

The next afternoon at half-past three, the police banged on our door.

I knew before the knock. I heard kicking boots run up our driveway. Glued to the dining room window, I saw the tall black policeman, who normally rode standing on the back of the police van, tear up past the house to the back of our property. I heard my mother's sandals on the slate in the lounge behind me, and the click of the front door as she opened it.

Two white policemen stood there, immaculate in caps and navy serge uniforms perfectly pressed, like cardboard cutouts against the bright sky behind them. I heard the kitchen door at the back slam shut—Iris, I knew, who a moment before had been standing at the kitchen sink washing lunch dishes. Iris must have run out.

"Checking on registrations, lady," one of the white policemen said to my mother.

"Oh," she said.

"Ja, we need to see all passes for this house, lady," he continued. "Are all your servants rregistidd?"

"Yes," said my mother politely. She turned to me. "Elizabeth, go and call Salamina, please, and tell her to bring her pass."

Frantic, I had no idea where Salamina was, and no idea where Moliseng was.

"Salamina's in my bedroom," my mother said quietly, seeing me stuck with fright.

I set off and ran headlong into Salamina coming down the passage with sheets and towels for the laundry. She set the bundle of linen down on the passage floor. "We need your pass, Salamina," I told her, terrified they would hear the name of Moliseng banging in my head. In a relieving moment, I imagined Mollie, lying peacefully next door on Zephyr's bed, already spirited away by clever, clever Iris! *That's* why Iris ran out, I thought.

Outside, the black policeman, his *knob-kierie* truncheon quiet in one hand, was questioning Peter Mombadi, and Pietros, our extra help for the garden. Isaac, our garden man, was off for the day in Alexandra township visiting his children.

Iris was nowhere to be seen.

Salamina showed her pass to the white policeman at the front door. He made notes on a grubby clipboard, its papers flapping in the wind while she stood there. She wiped her dry hands down the front of her dress.

"Elizabeth," my mother said again, leaning down to me, "won't you please fetch my cigarettes—from my bag."

I ran back down the passage. Her handbag was not next to her night table, as usual. It must be in her drawer, I thought. It was not. I flung open her cupboard and there among the shoes, two small, dark moons shone up at me—eyes. It was Moliseng, with dresses and coat hangers hastily thrown over her to conceal her. My mother had not needed cigarettes—she had sent me to Moliseng. I crept in to the bottom of the cupboard with her, closed its door as silently as a burglar, and prayed that she would not make a peep. Remembering how Salamina let her suck on her small finger, I put mine into Moliseng's mouth. I rubbed my other small finger through her tiny, dark peppercorn curls, and listened to her suck, and suck and suck through the banging in my chest in the dark.

After an eternity, the kicking boots walked away.

..

Some of my hundred friends from the high syringa leaves volunteered to stand guard in my room that night. It was rare that they would descend from the tree at all, and certainly I had not asked, but somehow they'd felt it might be useful. I chatted to keep them awake, to make certain they would be at their most watchful.

What if I needed to run out into the dark to fetch Moliseng inside? Why could she not live in her back servant's room in silence, instead of screaming when she should not? Why could she not go home to Soweto for good, where she would not need any paper, and her night screams would not stop our hearts? Why did she have to be born here at all? How and where would we hide her tomorrow, and the day after, and the miserable day after that, when she most certainly would peer out of her blanket sling on Salamina's back, as Salamina cleaned, polished, cooked, and ironed? If I had some of Gladness's Vanish whitening cream, I could smear it onto Moliseng—the whole bloeming jar—until she turned from her brown into white and completely disappeared. For a moment I almost hated her, thinking it would not be long before Salamina would leave us to go and look after this horrible brown thing that had invaded our house with the fear of her discovery. I no longer wanted my job.

I thought of my mother's closed eyes in the dappled shade. I promised the hundred friends that I would never, never let Eugenie run away. I promised I would not run by Loeska's peeping-bush fence, not wish I could live next door wearing Loeska's petticoats. I gave in, finally, on the sugar thing. I promised I would no longer feast in that box, causing my mother to cry out in despair, "Who has eaten my ingredients?" I would never again steal her green satin dress and wilt it in a pool of mud. I would scrub my nails until they gleamed like the moon, and smooth my tufts to look pretty. Of course, I would no longer wet and smell bad, and, most important, I would make *certain* that Moliseng stayed hidden, silent, and a problem to no one.

My sheets smelled of Salamina. With my hair slicked back after my bath at five o'clock, I lay in my bed, queenly, washed with Vinolia sandalwood soap—brown, but white people could also use it.

I listened to the passage—the sound of our night house, the sudden patter of that monkey . . . someone coming to slit our throats in our beds, the way Loeska warned.

Someone was in our house.

My heart stopped. Even if you listened with the skill of a fruit bat, you heard nothing. It was not possible for anyone to squeeze in from outside. The shutters were sealed. Painted white and peeling a bit but not missing any pieces, not gaping like those in the laundry room.

Everything was different now. We no longer safely belonged to the Queen. We even had new money. The found tickeys and shillings I prized in my grubby pockets lay discarded for shiny new rands and cents, and I was no longer measured in feet and inches but in brand-new, befuddling-to-all-adults increments called centimeters. I thought of the ten-shilling man my father had reminded me about on the train platform in Ramagoepa. I thought of how the man had run beside the open royal car bearing the stuttering King George and his Queen, startling them, refusing to let go of the side of their vehicle even after the Queen, fearing for her life, shattered his barbarian-black fingers with the handle of her umbrella to shoo him off. It turned out that he'd wanted to give her a present, his life savings of ten shiny shillings. What would he do with them now? What would he do with his ten shillings, I wondered, now that we no longer belonged to England?

What if Salamina preferred to go and live with the Queen, as Loeska had suggested? Even the Koelies, Loeska had said, those curry-stink Indians in Durban, were tired of the Queen.

The house spoke again into the night passage outside my door. Might I not hear if someone came into the house . . . ? Rigid, I listened with all my might.

Suddenly, like the first star in the sky, a tiny spark lit the gloom above me. No one had believed me—I pushed the sheets off and leapt down into the iridescent light, a billion stars falling around my bed. It seemed to be flying in where the moon soaked the shutters. No one else had ever been able to see it, except for Salamina, who admitted she *thought* she had seen some while singing our sleeping song. I knew perfectly well it was fairy light, shed when they dressed each morning, brushing their teeth, their hair, then dabbing on fairy powder—and it was floating right there, in full view. I jumped up and up to grasp it, satisfy my disbelievers with it, but to no avail. It danced above me, around me, fascinating me into forgetting. Someone coming to murder us . . . footsteps . . . the glinting light redeemed me again.

Perhaps it fell off the ears of Francesco the Clown, my father helpfully suggested when I first told him about it. Tickey was the beloved midget at Boswell Wilkie's Circus, who stepped into buckets and could never get out, but Francesco was the tall, sad, white-face clown, with his famously blue glitter ears. Sometimes the glitter got stuck inside his ear canals, necessitating a visit to my father's consulting rooms. My lucky fish father, right there with Francesco, would take an enormous syringe and suck the glitter out of his ears. And after, clouds of blue glitter trailed him all along Jan Smuts Avenue, all the way back to his circus. I called out in a panic—the feet were walking down the cold slate passage. . . . "Dad?" *God won'tletanythinghappen . . .* "Dad?"

"Shh, it's me, Elizabeth," my father said, leaning in at the darkened door. "Go to sleep now."

"Boy or girl?"

"Boy. Shhh, get back into your bed and go to sleep," he said, finally home from another night call.

"What was the name?"

"You go to sleep now."

His polished brown shoes faded away again. Sometimes he knew the name, and sometimes he didn't. Mrs. Dunkeld called her boy Bevrill. Poor thing, my mother had said. Just looking in his face, Mrs. Dunkeld knew he was Bevrill. Like a newborn mouse, his eyes were barely open.

I fled through the vanishing glitter bath back into my rumpled sheets, and was soon swallowed into the comfort of my pillow. The watchful friends had long flown back into their high berry place in the syringa tree. With my father home, every newborn mouse was safely in his bed after dark.

I tried to sleep. That bony-face Mrs. Ples, more of a monkey than a lady, and the deceitful Tokolosh took turns peering in from outside through the moonlit shutters.

Lying very still, I managed to drift away to a secret place. In his thick *Gray's Anatomy,* my father had shown me the breastplate. It hovered over the chest, a protected cavern for the heart. It closed our ribs, he'd said, just for that reason. If you put your hand there, you could feel—*boom-boom*—the double pound of your own heart underneath its armor. I'd listened to it many times through his stethoscope.

Outside, something darker, more magical even than the calming glitter light echoed in the same, ancient double-beat—Zephyr's drum—calling you without your consent.

Well, it would have been his drum if he'd had a drum. You'd be bloeming silly if you thought, like some people lying safely in their beds, that blacks had drums in the backs of people's gardens, in the middle of Johannesburg. It was just that battered, upside-down, empty paint tin, its metal pounded by dark, worn fists. It settled neatly into the dust at his feet by the fire, its hollow cry ringing out. To him, and all who could hear it—a drum.

Eyes barely open, I was already half ferried away to dreams. Suddenly my feet touched the cold floor. Zephyr's call sailed me in the billow of my white nightie down the dark passage—*boom-boom, boom-boom*—the first double rhythm of life, connecting me like a drifting moon to his drum.

I floated out through the kitchen door, down the step, and fell sharply on the path outside, scraping my knees. Suddenly they were burning sore, sand embedded under the skin. The moon had slipped away behind a dark mass gathering in the sky, giving cover to the night summons—*boom-boom*, it rang out, an affront to every Broeder who lay in his neat bed wondering where the hell it was coming from. Who had brought a fokken drum into someone's backyard? Savages, they'd be thinking—probably out there in fokken *skins*, dancing like animals. We should have told Zephyr to be quiet in the backyard. Where was he, I wondered, in Loeska's yard, or in ours, where he came sometimes to visit Salamina? My grazed legs stood me straight back up. Aghast, I was shockingly, illicitly outside. Who had left the kitchen door open? My heart skipped. My eyes peered through sore tears from my knees. "It's jolly dark out here!" I said to chase away whatever lurked. Where was the razor-toothed monkey? And the upright ape with his broom, where was *he* on a night like this? The drum pulled me deeper toward the back of the yard through bushes bathed in the liquid black of night. Scratching leaves hurried me through thicker black into a hidden warm patch, salvation. The hissing breath of fire spat crackled bits up into the air, and there, gathered in its flicker, dark figures huddled underneath the syringa tree.

Salamina—the sight of her glowed on my cheeks, dissipating my terror. I watched as one dark figure gave another a folded brown envelope and what looked like a tattered sheaf of papers. He tucked them quickly into his torn jacket, inside, into the pocket.

Iris was there, soft in the shadow—Iris with the biggest eyes you've ever seen—her pipe-cleaner-thin brown body straight off a farm somewhere, so she didn't know yet when to stop and when to go. Probably that "godforsaken homeland near the Transkei," my father had said when she couldn't quite explain where she'd come from. Or maybe didn't want to remember. She was extremely fetching in her uniform, everyone thought—the nice, clean spring pink my mother preferred. Now as I watched, she was taking off her doek, and her belt, and her shoes, undoing herself completely. She lay by the fire, scratching her head with her splitty nails.

Through the spirit faces enfolded in the leaves, I saw Isaac our garden man—tall, wiry like a darting black cat, talking with the two men who'd exchanged the envelope. Quite marvelously, Isaac had the same name as my father. Peter Mombadi, sometimes my driver, stood there also, right next to the fire, his cap still on. And midnight black Zephyr from next door, Zephyr whose fingers had long been severed. He dug the back of his callused fists into the bottom of the upside-down paint tin, pouring its deep belly cry out against the racing sky, BOOM BOOM . . . BOOM BOOM . . . a long thread of thunder without end, certain promise of a storm, but no telling when.

Suddenly, he sniffed the air. Without turning his head, like Mahila, who did not need to *look* to know, he buried his rapid fists into the drum. His cavernous gravel voice boomed, "FI FI FO FUMMM, I smell the blood of an Englishman! HAAAA, Salamina! I think we

have got a visitor! HIDIIING in the granadilla bushes . . ." Some of
the figures moved quickly away into the shadow of the tree. Salamina
straightened her back, fatigued even though the baby was no longer
on it. The speck lay naked, silent in the blanketing warmth of the fire.

"Could it be Miss Lizzy, Zephyr?" Salamina asked. She wiped her
forehead and laughed out loud with the loving despair of a day that
will not end. The figures drifted back into the firelight.

From my hiding nest, I saw her knees, her feet—the wide and special mud feet, bare like on the day we danced and named Moliseng in
the grass celebrations. They shifted slowly away from the fire, searching. Now if Salamina hadn't been so clever, she might have been
frightened, thinking it was the Tokolosh who lurked. "Monkey . . . ?"
She looked in under the dark leaf cave, and there, amidst the crinkly
granadillas, my shining eyes—gratefully discovered. "Auhw! Come sit
with us, Miss Lizzy," she said.

The missing Zephyr fingers flew in front of me through the drumming air as if they were still there. I stayed put, my own fingers
wrapped tight in my gauze nightie.

"Auw, *you* are *shy?*" Salamina tempted again.

I leapt out to the close safety of her thigh, where Zephyr could
not get me with the no-fingers hand. "Ask Zephyr to sing me
'Shosholoza,' " I asked her.

" 'Shosholoza,' Miss Lizzy?" She stared, astonished that I knew it,
"Yje Zephyr, 'Shosholoza'?"

I knew it jolly well, actually, from being driven by Peter Mombadi.
He would roll the windows down in the backseat of the old Mercedes,
letting the dust fly in to settle on my white Panama hat, so we could
hear the song of the road gangs digging up the road as we passed.

"Jho, Mombadi." Salamina was cross now. "It's for *you* we must
clean thet demn het every day!"

"Why do they sing it, Peter Mombadi?" I asked, hoping he'd tell
Salamina what he'd often said in the car as we drove on his errands.

He removed his cap and held it with both hands at the middle buttons on his pressed white shirt. Mombadi was formal and very still—
especially when he looked away, his sinewy face black as coal. In his

quiet voice, he said, "Oh, thett one, it's the wekking song, Miss Lizzy. It makes the wekk go fastah."

I dug my feet into the gnarled dirt under the syringa tree to show Salamina the road digging with the mesmerizing song. "HHHAAaaah!" Zephyr said. Suddenly his voice rang out like forty men slaving in the dust. "SHO . . . SHOLOZA . . ." He sang the part of the men at the rear of the gang, whose metal spades crashed into the earth, driven forward by the harmonic chant given by God in exchange for their chained place. I'd seen sweat gleam on their black heads, then spray out in a wave. Like a glistening adder they shuffled, caught in the roar of many having to move as one. With voices hot and deep, they held a low, steady rhythm that brought your heart right up into your throat. It told you deep down something was right, and something was wrong. Its repetitive drive moved them, step by step, closer to the end of day. It was the most beautiful thing I had ever heard.

"And then the ones in the front?" My stick legs leapt to Zephyr, begging him to sing like the men in the front.

"SHO . . . sholoza!" he cried out again, utterly delighting me.

"And then altogether!" I asked. I wanted the whole majesty of them, the joined-together sounds that welled up in me something for which I had no name. Zephyr's no-finger hand swooped down, a crusty, headless bird folding mine into its wing. Then crash-digging, shuffling inch by inch, he joined me with him into the glorious, sad chain that only some will know, and few will ever forget. He sang of Johannesburg, city of gold, city of pain, city that was not home, far from the wild Rhodesian hills. "Push forward, push forward," he roared, *"Kulezontaba, stimela, siphum' eRhodesia, SHO-sholoza,"* full, undaunted.

Iris scratched her cooling, itchy head as Zephyr and I carved an imaginary trough around the fire, opening the earth with rhythms that lived deep in his once powerful body.

Abruptly, he stopped. In the heat of the flames, he seemed suddenly old and tired. "HHHAAA!" He sighed. "We are not wekking now, Miss Lizzy." He beckoned for me to come. "We are eating now!"

I followed to the cast-iron pot, and looked in with him over its sulky, hot lip. Best made on the fire outside and famous for stinking up the place, suurpap bubbled in thick, lazy boils of acrid white stodge. Rich with sour milk, it shuddered you rotten with its smell—like boiled cabbage stench, only more sour, more starch. Next to it, in an empty jam bottle, the meat gravy left over from my supper.

Earlier in our dim-lit dining room, the quiet clatter of our own dinner had given way to the lull of Beethoven's adagio scratching a bit on the record player. My mother seemed to like it in the comfortless silence, with my father not yet home. She had looked around the table, the way she did every night. She'd asked Salamina to please put the Master's supper in the warming drawer. He would be late again, she said. Salamina and Iris, always shining clean at supper in pink or butter yellow uniforms with white doeks, had, as always, carefully brought in food and carried out empty plates. "Thank you, Salamina, thank you, Iris," my mother had said. "Oh, you can take what's left over as usual, but please"—unsure, she'd fingered her pearl earring—"leave a little bit of the meat for the children's lunch tomorrow."

Salamina had gently clapped the back of one hand into the palm of the other, twice. "Thank you, Madam," she'd said, lowering her eyes—the black way to say "thank you" or "I respect you," a quick *clap-clap* with eyes down.

And then, too late, my mother remembered. "Oh, and Iris . . ." Iris's pink had already disappeared, not knowing yet when to come, when to go. "Iris!" my mother called out, exasperated.

Iris jumped back into the room like a startled springbuck, her sudden reappearance softening my mother. Iris's big eyes looked out from under her boiling doek. "Iris," my mother said, smiling, reminding her yet again, "don't forget to lock the kitchen door behind you, and take the key *out, with* you. The Master found it still in the door this morning."

Iris hared off again, before we could say "good night." My mother twirled her pearl earring between thumb and finger. Her hand dawdled at her neck, her graceful neck, her throat. "Good night, thank you," she had called after them kindly as the kitchen door shut for the night.

Now at the fire, Zephyr took a wad of suurpap porridge and

swirled it in our leftover gravy. If I was a very lucky fish, he might sing the prayer song—the forbidden song. With a sudden hole in the pit of my stomach, I remembered Loeska's shriek when I'd tried to sing for her. "It's *forbidden,* you stewpitt!" she'd said.

Before she was half bitten to death, she had plucked the blood-trumpet flowers off the bignonia cherera in her backyard and slid her fingers into its crimson trumpets, making long red nails to point at me. She was able to sneer in those red nails, and say all sorts of clever things from under her snowy thatch. "You English," she'd jabbed, "you born here just like us Afrikaners, but you've got no bloody *respect* for yourselves. That's what my father sayes, and he knows." She gazed up into the heavens. "God tells him *everyfing.*"

She'd stared down at me. I'd wished more than anything that I lived next door with her, and had long red flower nails. "That's why we've got no rain, you know. It's because of you people making trouble with the blacks. They gunna come and kill you in your bed, hey!" She slid the red fingernail across the delicate white skin of her throat, as if carving a bloody grin.

I'd thought Loeska might very much like Zephyr's prayer song, but it had sent her into a bossy rage. Her weapon fingers flew like spears, her *r*'s thrummed like thunder. "That is *not* our national anthem," she'd said. "Our national anthem is wrritten by the *grrreat* Afrikaans poet C. J. Langenhoven, and you better stand up strrrraight if you want to sing it with me." Up she'd flounced onto the wall at the church, giving her a safe, hygienic distance. Slapping the back of my head to stand me to attention was the only thing she could think of right then to improve me. I'd willingly obeyed, and that, for her, was deeply satisfying.

Crouching at the fire now, watching Zephyr swish his sour porridge through thick gravy, I remembered how Loeska had grown with determination as she sang, the glowing conviction of those chosen by God to uplift the lesser. Her trumpet fingers blared in time to our *real* anthem, *"Uit die blou van onse hemel, uit die diepte van ons see . . ."* From the highest part of the sky, to the very depths of the sea—in other words, every nook and cranny in the place was ours. She'd belted out the finger-wagging words, "We will live, we will die, We for you, South Africa," and produced sudden marching to match, with a salute that looked just like the Hitler thing Uncle Thom showed me at Clova when I'd asked about the trains. I'd strutted behind her saluting, pleased to be in her backyard at all.

But that, of course, was before she had been nearly killed.

I wondered now if Loeska might hear Zephyr singing in the dead of night. Her room was way on the other side of the fence behind several rows of black-bug-infested hibiscus, behind the long trellis tables on which Marie Hattingh dried the guavas and peaches out in the sun for her jams. I wondered if all the way behind there, in the misery of her bites, she might hear Zephyr. She might like the song much better if she heard Zephyr sing it, even though it was forbidden. When I'd asked my father about it, he said that some black people were having secret meetings of their own. They were calling themselves the ANC, and closing their meetings with a prayer, the very same as Zephyr's song.

Zephyr stood. He slid his feet into worn, muddy boots left waiting by the fire. The bird-hand pulled a blanket up from the ground and swept it around his mighty, bent shoulders. He must also have been like Tarzan once, I thought, very beautiful.

Respectfully attired before God, he set his jaw against the dark landscape, for the forbidden prayer.

"*Nkosi, sikelel iAfrika,*" rose softly through his crinkled lips. "God bless Africa . . ." He many times had said the prayer song might bring God's blessings "on Aahfrika." They must be falling now from heaven like a glitter bath around us. My hands involuntarily patted them down into the earth as he sang,

"Maluphakamis'u phondo lwayo
Yizwa imithandazo yethu
Nkosi sikelela . . ."

Zephyr's song melted into the night, his deep and hidden prayer— for those who lived without water, without ways, without means, for those who walked miles and miles, whose children lay hidden in blankets at fires, and for those children; for those who tried to speak but who had been silenced. "Please, we are your children, please *help* us," he sang. *"Thina lusapho lwayo."*

His prayer was gentle but his voice raged. His blurred eyes scanned the horizon, praying for all he had witnessed. His mutilated black fist pounded his heart, on the armor of the breastplate. Then it rose up like a cannonball against the sky.

Iris, Peter Mombadi, Salamina, our garden man, Isaac, Willery from next door—and the strangers with no names, those who came for comfort through the dark leaves—gathered around Zephyr in the gleam of the fire. Together, in a soft, humming chorus, like something coming from far away, the words went out again, soaring up through the cathedral dome of the syringa tree, asking for God's blessings on Africa.

Loeska, as usual, had been quite correct. "That belligerent Nelson" asking to be addressed as Mr. Mandela ("a native boy!"), had been singing this song to close underground meetings. And while the words were indeed those of a prayer, according to the secret police and the watchful Broederbond, that savage's association with them had charged this prayer into a blatant call to arms, a war cry for black people. Just listen to the words, for Christ sakes, the Broeders were whispering: "Let the horn of Africa sound, rise up . . ." What the bloody hell else could that mean? "Hear us?" Naiveté would be the death of us all. The song was banned.

Suddenly, like magic, people flew before me, sucked up into the air, slip-spirits of what they were, standing a moment before around the coals. Swirling up like painted ghosts, they fled—under the granadilla bushes, up into the highest branches of the syringa tree, down, under Salamina's bed raised on bricks in the servants' rooms, forgetting the Tokolosh might be there, but with room for at least two more. *"Polisie,* police, pass . . . pass!" the certain, young white voice yelled above the beam of a careening flashlight. Police van wheels spun, skidded blindly in the loose sand out on the street, and then—nothing but panting silence.

Running boots gone, the flashlight's burning eye fell somewhere else, hunting for those who had no paper, those who were not supposed to be here.

A fugitive from my own bed, I blotted out the embers. "Pat it down, pat it down, *nothing will happen GOD won't let anything . . .*" battered like bullets inside my head. My breath was rapid, high in my throat, my hands stinging hot. The gauze moon of me, horribly lit white, paused in my forbidden orbit, stock-still, in the hiding leaves. All silent—except for that place under the breastplate, pounding.

Even the speck had mysteriously vanished, swooped up in her blanket, her mouth covered to be neither seen nor heard.

Some things were allowed, and some things were not.

CHAPTER FOUR

A VERY CLEVER BIKE

◎◎

Moliseng remained successfully hidden all through a sweltering, colonial Christmas. Tiny for almost eight months, she was easily concealed, mostly tucked in her blanket sling on Salamina's back, or propped up by herself on the laundry room floor while Salamina ironed sheets and tablecloths and occasionally meddled in my mother's cooking with too much salt. My job consisted of running like hell to warn Salamina if anyone in the house heard a police van, or boots, or dogs, and sometimes keeping Moliseng quiet in the back, way up behind the house under the syringa tree, well hidden from the street. Only twice, Salamina had been stopped by police as she returned from her off-day to Soweto, wanting to know where she was headed with a child. She was taking the "very sick baby" to see the doctor, she'd said both times, laughing when she told us about the "stupit polissman!"

We hunted for reindeer in the summer night skies, sprayed shaving-foam snow on the windows, glued blobs of white cotton wool on a small fir tree from Piet's Nursery, to make Africa look like England. We sweated through a roast turkey lunch at three in the afternoon, gorged on trifle loaded with cake soaked in Old Bristol Cream Sherry and hot custard, and pulled crepe-paper crackers into loud bangs, with riddles and toys popping out of them. Salamina got a pretty nightie from my mother, and so did Iris, who giggled when she opened it, and ran right out of the kitchen door, shy. And Moliseng got new nappies, and a white jersey secretly knitted by my mother as a surprise, with tiny rabbit buttons. She'd made me one in pink, with a brown collar to match my tufts, and John's was navy blue with a smart red boat on the front. My father's fancy lunch lay uneaten on the warming plate until late in the evening. One of the gold mine shafts had collapsed out on the Reef, and dozens of injured black miners, those lucky enough to be alive when the lifts finally raised them, their limbs crushed, lay at Baragwanath in Soweto.

The shaving snow stayed on the windows well into January, when in the raging summer heat, things seemed to happen in twos.

Monday: first, the day of the hot pants, and second, the permission letter; Tuesday, first, my mother's temper at the municipality, and second, "Yes, you *can* go." Friday was the day my grandfather phoned to say he was coming down from Clova. He was injured and needed my father's help. But that was a separate thing and only happened in a one.

On Monday, Prue came to explain about the velvet hot pants she'd borrowed from my mother going missing, and because she came on *that* Monday, ended up putting in her two cents about the permission letter for my upcoming new school. Prue was my father's sister, so he didn't need to be polite when she came at nap time and consequently was asleep in the bedroom. She was chubby and bubbly, a bit like cheap champagne, my mother once remarked—you get a bit of a headache if you've had too much of her. Her thick brown hair shaded round, shiny eyes, making her like a cheery owl intent on seeing the "whole damned world!" and preferring always to be *there,* rather than here. My mother said she *sounded* like a Prue, could *look* like a Prue (not today in tight, white stretch Helenca pants), but certainly did not *behave* like a Prue—Prue being short for Prudence.

While Prue sat in our lounge, my mother went into the bedroom to get a jersey, and in utter disbelief whispered to my napping father Prue's ridiculous excuse about the hot pants. "I mean, honestly, Isaac, she left them in a taxi!" my mother said.

"How the bloemin' hell did that happen?" he asked, trying for a sweet ten minutes to rest before his afternoon race to the consulting rooms. Standing at their door before dashing back to entertain Prue, I heard my mother say she'd kindly expressed only polite astonishment over the matter, telling Prue that it was quite all right, but *exactly!* she agreed with my father, how could that happen? My mother said it must have been a nice, warm hand that undid the zip in the back of the taxi. Putting on her jersey, she laughed, lit another cigarette, and said, "Imagine, slipping that chocolate velvet over Prue's ample thighs— how seductive! But I can't get over the practical matter of Prue having to get out of the taxi *without* the hot pants! Must have been bloeming drunk," she said, even though she liked Prue a lot. "Elizabeth, get back into the lounge this minute," she said, spotting me.

Prue was waiting to explain, but in the meantime wanted to busy me with her latest treats—circular, plastic Spirographs for sticking crayons into and twirling a million, varied shapes onto a page; and two cowrie shells, brown speckles gleaming on their glassy, round backs. Cowrie shells washed up on the boiling beaches of Durban in Natal— where Vasco da Gama, Prue babbled as we spiraled, landed in 1497 with rickety, scurvy-ridden sailors whose descendants later returned and kindly brought sugar to plant. He'd found it on Christmas Day, hence *Natal,* Portuguese for being born. Jolly glad, I was, that they planted sugar.

Prue was full of magical stories about the doings of others, and, I was gathering from the hot-pants saga, her own. Her special tricks for me that Monday included glass slippers with transparent high heels for clicking along the slate passage—and "breaking your neck!" Eugenie said, returning from the bedroom—and all the sorts of special things that usually only Loeska had. Prue just picked them up as she went. These were "Hong Kong."

Prue explained very well, *I* thought, about the missing hot *broeks,* which she was supposed to have returned to us a while ago. *I* understood completely, thinking she'd probably wet them, and feeling ashamed had rolled them in a ball and stuffed them under the taxi seat where no one would find them. But that was not the case.

She diligently scraped the clotted cream off her scone (too fat in the white Helenca pants), and when she finished explaining, she quietly ate the scraped-off cream until it was gone.

Eugenie wouldn't ever really have worn those hot pants. I mean, for goodness *sakes,* she'd said—even though the lady at Frock Heaven said she'd looked like Jean Shrimpton in them. Eugenie thought her legs were too skinny and too white, and the broeks, with a zip in the back, were a velvet chocolate brown, so they would have made her look even whiter. But she told Prue she had thought she might slip into the sun sometime . . . maybe put out just her pale legs, hoping they wouldn't freckle in their Englishness, and, you know, tan herself a bit. So she'd taken the bull by the horns and bought the broeks. She definitely would have looked better in them than Prue ever would, even though Prue was much more likely to wear such things. Regardless. Too fat or not. And that was Prue. Regardless!

"And I mean, you know," my mother would later ask my father, "who do you know without a car?" Anyone white, she meant. "Who takes taxis around Johannesburg in the first place? Bloody mad."

"It'll probably be fine," Prue said over her tea about the permission letter.

"I thought so too," my mother responded, "but Isaac's worried."

"Well, they wouldn't be doing it if it was too dangerous," said Prue. "They just wouldn't be doing it. The nuns wouldn't be taking a busload of children into Soweto if they weren't sure about it."

"Am I going in a bus to Soweto?" I asked, gleaning bits of this and that.

"Oh, it *knows,* does it?" said Prue—cream, cream, cream.

"We haven't decided," my mother said. She was talking about signing the letter sent by the nuns into whose care I was about to be entrusted at my new school. I was due to begin in a matter of weeks, at the end of January. They wanted to take new pupils to visit one of their township schools. The government was dead set against these irresponsible forays, but the nuns, my father said when the letter arrived, were cheerfully going forward as they always had. All they required was a letter of permission from the parents. The government could do as it wished.

The glistening brown and white cowrie shells sat on the Spirograph pattern. Like spotted turtles on a prehistoric rock map, they stared at one another.

And then my mother said something so quiet I almost didn't hear it, something to Prue: about someone who had been delivering babies in the Cape Province years ago, for years, actually, where holiday-Eugenie had run around Shelley Beach when she was small, burnt as brown as a berry. But right there, in that appalling township near Pyott's biscuit factory, someone helping the people there had been chopped, without mercy, into tiny pieces in the middle of the night.

I thought I heard something about nuns.

I quickly asked Prue did she know about Anne Boleyn, who'd gotten her head chopped off? It was in the "Did you know?" questions inside the Chappies bubble-gum wrapper read to me by Loeska—gloating, because Anne Boleyn was English.

Ignoring me, Prue said to my mother, "Well, going in a bus in the middle of the day, Eugenie, is very different to being out there night after night in the townships, delivering babies." Prue always had a good two cents to put in.

"That nun was *helping* them," my mother said, not so quietly, "devoted her whole bloody life to helping them. The natives just chopped her up."

Prue was demolishing the next glob of cream from a second scone and needing more sugary tea, being a second-cupper.

Speaking, as my mother now was with Prue, of hacking things to death, I wondered if anyone had seen me kill the chameleon. It happened right after Christmas, after two nights of police vans hunting up and down our street for tsotsis and anyone else who was not supposed to be here.

The chameleon crept into our backyard like a devil from long ago. It cleverly changed its yellowish-green leaf dress into clothes of the exact brownish sand I'd patted onto my mud cakes. I had used the round shoe polish lid as a baking tin to form them perfectly. Dry sand iced the top.

It stopped there, breathing, resplendent in its deceitful new suit. And then without warning, it jerked . . . sprinted splay-footed, swishing its swift, piercing tail shockingly right over the top of the cake, at me. I smashed the lid of the upside-down polish tin over its head, and with some involuntary, horrible force in my hands, I held the lid there. I pushed its sticking-out, flailing legs down, down to the center of the world, where the sinkhole houses were, where people who would never be seen or heard sat dead in armchairs. I felt suddenly much safer.

I held it horribly down until the legs stopped moving, until bulging out from under the polish tin lid, two watery eyes burst, running clear all the things they had ever seen back into the dust . . . *boomboom boom boom* leapt into my throat. I had run away very quickly, the smell of red-brown shoe polish on my hands following everywhere, and the quick pounding in my chest, in a big fright, not quiet for quite a while. Pietros carried on polishing, neatly tying up the laces of my father's shoes on the evening step. Then he asked Salamina for a *lappie* cloth to cover the polish when he had finished. The lid was missing, he said.

Would the new-school nuns into whose care I was to be placed, who could look right into your soul, see what I'd done? Now, as Prue licked the last of her cream and my mother said again about how the dismembered nun had just been trying to help, the cowrie shells sat on their complicated, patterned land, unblinking.

My father, rested a bit, kissed us all, and drove off to the hospital, where patients were waiting to be stitched. Mondays were busy, he said to Prue as he ran out, after the usual weekend bloodbath of tribal fighting in the townships. Prue also got up, to catch a boat to another somewhere, *without* the turquoise flowery skirt she hankered after because my mother *did* want to wear that now that summer was here.

By Monday evening, the permission letter lay unsigned on our kitchen table. Leftover curried eggs were going to do fine for supper, my mother decided, since it would be just her, me, and John. Too big for his high chair now, but stuck in there like in town square stocks, for his own good. Like a human cannon he spattered his eggs to high heaven. Such a *good* baby, my mother delightedly bragged to anyone who would listen. Salamina and Iris could take what was left over as usual, to put with their meat—off-cuts that came in brown paper and string with the rest of the shopping, with "Boys Meat" written on it by the butcher—for the servants' rooms. And after supper, Eugenie again reminded, "Don't forget to lock the kitchen door, Iris, and take the key out with you. The Master found it still *in* the door again this morning."

Iris was in disgrace. She had lied to my mother when she first arrived, saying yes, she did have a pass. Now when my mother asked her if it needed to be renewed, it was discovered that she did not have one at all. We would be fined, and she might be shipped off back to a homeland somewhere. And that wasn't the only worry. She was getting much better at understanding but still somehow failed each night to take the key out of the lock, leaving the kitchen door and our throats wide open to the night.

Monday ended with the question of permission for me to go into Soweto with the nuns undecided.

··

At the municipality the next morning, in front of everyone, the man with the stamp immediately and flatly refused to give Iris a pass.

We had sped down there early, before seven o'clock, concerned the line would already be crushing, with all the other Madams trying daily to get papers for their servants. Rigorously cautioned: I was *not* to tell about the speck.

We waited until almost midday in the endless snaky line on the cement out in the heat. Iris, if she did not get shipped off, would not be allowed to sleep in the servants' room, for even one more night, without a pass. She would need to travel back and forth to us every day from the township, and if found and questioned, would be arrested, fined, and hopefully not beaten. No one would know to phone us. She would just disappear, thrown into the back of a police van somewhere, and driven away.

When we got to the front of the line, the municipality man said she's not from the right place, and no, he could *not* give her the paper.

My mother banged her hand down on the counter, and asked him where he thought Iris should go and work. And why didn't he just lock Iris up right now? Didn't Iris look *exactly* like a murdering tsotsi? my mother shouted into the quiet room. And Iris looked with those biggest eyes away from the man. And even though she didn't usually know when to come or when to go, she knew that this was when to stand very still.

My mother's voice got loud, which happened only if she was extremely hot or tired, and was happening now because she'd been standing there in the blazing sun for hours—to be told no. For no bloody *reason,* she said. And who was supposed to look after John? And she couldn't cope, she said, and then some tears came out.

"There's no need to be aggrrressive, lady," the man responded, rolling his *r*'s like the metal wheels of a tank. "I don't make the law." He had an emphatic, thin, long face with slicked, oily brown hair, and a tight dot for a mouth at the bottom—like an exclamation mark.

"Well, what the hell am I supposed to do?" my mother asked, wishing that Isaac, or Prue, or *someone* had come down with her to tell this imbecile to get off his arse and stamp the bloody thing. And more tears came.

The man looked outside at the shifting line, black and winding like a trapped, human shongololo worm festering in the sun.

He looked at Iris, who said nothing.

On her thin, perched, ready-to-run legs, she looked very sorry that she'd ever left that nameless, godforsaken homeland. She twisted her skirt into a knot, making it seem a foot shorter above her ashy knees. Her shoes were too big, because they were Salamina's. She was not used to shoes. My mother had asked Salamina the day before to please make sure Iris was presentable that morning, with her doek on and her belt tied, and that crumpled, white, shredded tissue ever dangling from her bony hand put *away* in her pocket because it was the day of the pass office. And to tell Iris to please not scratch her head in front of the man. My mother had worried that Iris was teeming with lice when she first walked up our driveway hunting for work, but when my father looked, he said no, it's just dryness—scales from dryness. Like Tarzan wandering the veld with no water for so long, she'd dehydrated into a bristle brush. Now she had medicinal creams. And not to worry, it was not catchy, my father had said about her scales. Not catchy at all.

Iris's hands remained twisted into her skirt. She did not scratch. The pass office, with its green linoleum floor, was cool, made much better than outside by a whirring fan. To not blurt out by mistake about Moliseng, I bit my lips together like a sewn seam.

The man looked again at the itchy Iris—and again at the line. Then without looking at my mother's face (probably because of the tears) he stamped the paper, stamped it again, and then stamped and stamped some other papers, which he gave to the crimson-cheeked, fat lady in sweaty yellow crimplene behind the desk on the other side. Like a tire pumped to bursting, her cheeks swelled to purple as she took the papers.

Then the man slapped the first paper, stamped, down where my mother had banged her hand.

"Thank you," my mother said briskly, then murmured in a quiet, new voice, "Thank you."

The man did not answer, or say it was a pleasure or anything. He just turned his Brylcreemed head away to take out new papers. He looked at the person behind my mother, as if my mother were suddenly see-through or no longer there.

The fan made a nice wind to blow over the fat lady. Eugenie turned and walked away, with Iris and me following, neither of us quite sure what had happened. We followed her back down the line of Madams, and nannies in doeks, and garden boys old and young, squinting in the sun in the line of special papers. In the heat rising in waves from the cement, they shimmered like an army coming over a hill.

In the car, my mother crashed the keys into the ignition, ran her banging hand through her hot, limp hair, and said, "Okay. That's done."

Iris sat in the front seat, mute.

We drove out past the buses at the terminus, where more blacks sweltered in more wriggling lines. Women stood with babies, flies buzzing lazily around their streaming noses, tied on their backs, waiting for the bus to take them back home. Most still had no papers.

When my father got home that night, he signed "Dr. Isaac Grace" on the permission letter waiting on the red vinyl kitchen table. He was no longer so worried. He told my mother he had spoken to the nun at the new school, and that it seemed fine. It was only to the outer edge, they'd promised, and they did it all the time. Elizabeth will be going on the bus, he said.

The kitchen door closed. And for the first time, Iris remembered to lock it, and take the key out with her.

· ·

That night, no long fingers pulled at my sheets. Instead, the chameleon, made whole again, soared like a glittering bird high above my bed, his jeweled eyes lit with every color.

> *Nothing will happen,*
> *God won't let anything happen.*
> *Lucky, lucky, lucky fish, us.*

Iris lay in her newly allowed bed in the servants' rooms in the dark behind our house. The speck, full of Salamina's milk, lay quiet in her blanket, perfectly hidden. Salamina, and Peter Mombadi, and Zephyr from next door, and John—kissed good night by Eugenie and me—

safe in his cot, and lucky Willery, who *had* a paper, and Loeska behind the black-bug-infested hibiscus. Each lay in their bed.

Everyone quiet—except my father. I heard him bash open the shutters, and knew he must be standing there to cool himself, staring out into the highveld night.

..

The next Wednesday morning, Loeska called me a kaffir-boetie.

Brother of kaffirs.

For spending time up on Salamina's high bed.

I ran inside, Loeska's words smarting in my ears, only to have my ears really sting with my father's anger.

"Don't you *ever* use that word in this house," he said.

"Well, it's better than being Jewish!" I blurted at him.

My father picked up his bag, and for the first time in my life, did not answer me. He turned and walked out of the house, got into his car, and drove away, leaving me ashamed and thoroughly confused.

"Your dad, Isaac," my mother explained to me while trying to soothe my burning tears, had been brutalized at his predominantly Afrikaans school for being Jewish and English-speaking. Without question, it seemed, from every angle, we were the enemy.

It hadn't dawned on me that we *were* in-between people, from neither here nor there, but trying to be from here, rather than there. Just as Tarzan came to Clova, most of my family seemed to have wandered down to Africa like ghosts, in a misty swirl of unspoken dreams of a better life.

If you asked my father about his side of the family, he laughed and said they were really just a bunch of horse thieves—nothing even remotely royal about *them*! Of course, he didn't mean that at all. Even so, the news was not good.

Confirming Loeska's whispered suspicions that I might have Jewishness in me, accounting for the smell of my pants and my brown eyes, I'd discovered that not only was my father's grandfather Jewish, he was an escaped rabbi from Vilnius in Lithuania. He had swum across rivers with a chair and some money to escape the killing hand of the tsar, or worse, slow death in Siberia. I thought of him sitting on the safe side of the river, on his one chair. I marveled that he'd thought to bring a chair in the first place. Of anything else he might have grabbed. How jolly clever.

He'd fled to South Africa on the promise of finding more of his own people, and had in fact done so in a small town called Swartruggens, mercifully hidden from the taunting Afrikaners.

"Bloody fool," my father said of him. "Why didn't he swim the other way, to America?" Instead, this rabbi left his wife and two small children in Russia, and seemed to forget they were there. Undaunted, his determined wife, my father's grandmother, packed the children onto a boat and arrived penniless in Cape Town, speaking no English, uttering only the name of her lost rabbi husband until someone recognized it and pointed her north.

So my father's father, Edward, had no education, even though he had a lightning gift with numbers. A Jewish child of the streets searching for his father, he earned pennies selling soap made from horse fat. It seemed remarkable to me that you could get clean washing yourself with anything that came from a dead horse.

Starving and exhausted, they found him eventually, the missing rabbi, prayerful and scholarly as you might expect, deep in the shade of the shul. He was jubilant to see them, as if he expected nothing less than for them to show up in Swartruggens.

My father's maternal family were ghosts of another kind, that mixture of Afrikaans and Scottish he'd spoken about at Clova, who'd found themselves in the British concentration camps during the Boer War. Compromised on both sides, by the time my father's parents met, their union was indeed odd: a horse-fat-soap, no-education Jew with a lightning mind marrying a concentration-camp Scottish-Afrikaans shikse. He was turfed right out of the Jewish community for it.

"Why don't the Afrikaners like us to love Salamina?" I asked her, still distraught.

"It's not just Afrikaners, Elizabeth," my mother said. "There are plenty of English-speaking people who feel the same as many Afrikaners, and lots of blacks who don't like other blacks." She paused, and then picked me up in her arms and carried me down the passage to her room. "My goodness, you've grown into a giant!" she said. She hadn't picked me up in a while. We lay down on her bed together, in pieces and quiet. "And anyway, what does Loeska know? Salamina loves you," she said, "and I love you. And your dad loves you."

"No, he doesn't. He's cross about being Jewish." My mother laughed again. I was calmed by the pretty smell of her. We dozed off in each other's arms, tears all dried and finished.

We woke with the sun gone down, my father still out, John asleep in his cot, and a scrambled-eggs supper quietly left on the warming plate for us by Salamina, already gone to bed. The crickets had started their leg-rubbing racket out in the dark, and the air smelled excited, like rain coming, maybe. My mother closed the lounge windows but left the shutters open. We poured tomato sauce on our eggs, as if it were breakfast time, and ate them in the still, dark house.

My mind drifted again to Loeska's unconditional hatred. With bits and pieces of everything in us, I began to worry that we lacked enough of any one thing to really fit anywhere. We did not belong in England anymore. Lithuania was out of the question. Even Ferndale was beginning to feel as though it had no place for us. English-speaking, rooinek kaffir-boeties with not enough Afrikaans, a cruel British streak, and the foul taint of Jewish. We were a bit of everything the Afrikaners despised. "Kaffir-boetie!" she'd whispered, probably knowing very well it was not a nice thing to say. *She* would not, she'd declared, be caught *dead* in Willery's room. Some things were allowed, and some were not, and those that were not were becoming a lot clearer.

"Could you make me a dress with petticoats?" I asked my mother, who had drifted off into her own thoughts. Mercifully, unlike my father, I was about to be sent to an English-speaking school, run by Irish nuns. More than anything else, I looked forward to finding a friend who would fill the gap until I could persuade Loeska to like me.

Outside it had started to rain, a beautiful, clean, summer-night storm with raucous thunder that rattled the shutters with joy, lit up the black sky with streaks of lightning, and left rivers running down the dusty windowpanes. The air smelled cool, new again.

. .

The next thing about to become clear was that it was absolutely not all right to move someone's possessions and steal their place. It was not all right to displace someone. It was, in fact, a bloody cheek.

It happened on the first morning of the new school, which had deceptively started out as a magnificent summer day at the end of January, with the speck sitting up by herself on the bright patch of grass by the washing line behind the house. Like Moliseng, our garden was growing vigorously. Frangipani and even timid, heat-shy impatiens shot up defiantly into the blazing sun like delicate ladies thrust into a desert. With Moliseng carefully positioned there, Salamina could keep an eye on her through the laundry door and simultaneously scrub the kitchen floor. Because she had sucked Salamina dry as a prune, and now feasted on the same porridge as John, Mollie had grown heavy in her blanket sling on Salamina's back. But she was still more or less a speck, so even eyes-dying-of-curiosity from over the fence would never see her behind the house.

I was going to be exceedingly busy now. I would not be able to stand guard quite so much, or pat down and away anyone who came near. And quite honestly, I was relieved at the idea that if she was seen, now that she crawled off unpredictably in fits and starts, it would not be my fault.

Struggling with new laces in pinching, polished black shoes, and a navy thing called a girdle, which went around the outside of my winter uniform like a long, knitted belt, my new look required practice. Disappointingly, there was not a petticoat in sight, but topping me off, a navy blazer and a wide-brimmed straw hat rendered me clean and smart. I planned to keep the blazer on all day, to ensure the nuns would not see into my soul about the chameleon.

"She's been very busy with books and shoes and everything," my mother revealed when my father asked if I had eaten my breakfast. "No, of course not," she added, "the usual egg palaver. But it's the first day so I let it go." I was relieved about the egg being let go. After being chased around the yard with it, I finally took refuge in the syringa tree.

High in the flagrant, full summer dream of lilac flowers, I practiced answering questions the nuns might ask. My father had said not to take any notice of talk about God, that he was sending me there only because nuns were excellent teachers. But my mother thought it might be useful for me to have a few ready answers. "Who made me?" I drilled myself high in the berries hiding thick and green between the flowers. "God made me!" I shot back to myself. "Why did he make you?" I persisted. "He made me because he loves me!" These were some of the answers my mother remembered from her own convent days near Clova. I should be grateful, she said, that I was not being boarded as she was. Remembering her own sobbing at five when she was left at school to fend for herself, Clova being so far away, she wanted me in my own bed at night. I would be daily with the Sisters of Mercy.

"Can Prue come to that school?" I wanted to know in the morning as I was readied.

"Why wouldn't she be able to come?" my mother asked.

"Because Prue looks Jewishy, you said."

"Because she *is* sort of Jewishy. But not to worry. The whole family got thrown out," my mother said, tilting her lapsed-Catholic head mischievously, "because of the Scottish-Afrikaans shikse! So don't worry, you're probably not Jewish because he never went back there, to that shul," my mother said about my father's father. "There were two things he never liked, you know—one was Jewish food! And the other . . ." She never said what was the other, because a terrible screaming came from the back door, with Iris flailing wildly into the kitchen wall, scraping the skin right off her elbow.

She'd noticed the glint in the sun of the very polish-tin lid for which Salamina had been hunting, and understandably thought it would be jolly nice to return it to her. Luckily Iris's belt was *tied,* and her doek *on,* because she would have jumped clean out of her dress— seeing two colorless eyes hanging by rotting threads in the stench that flew up into her nostrils. The carcass stuck to the lid of the polish tin in her hand, its shocked legs electrified out on each side. Iris went flying right into the kitchen wall. Very loud I said the Tokolosh did it, which sent Iris flying again. "Jhwaaaaawh!" she exploded, right out of the kitchen door to her bed, safely up on bricks.

"Well, yes, it *was* a bloeming cheek," my mother said that night after my first day of school, about the moving of one's things and the taking of one's place. "But look, it's not the end of the world."

"What a cheek!" my father volunteered.

I felt slightly better after that. But, really, it had spoiled the whole day. And it wasn't the only disappointment either.

First there was no nun.

"They probably don't have enough nuns to teach every single class, Elizabeth," my mother explained when we were met at the classroom door by Mrs. Kloppers, who looked like a cross, hard line drawn on a page.

The nuns had to come all the way to South Africa from Ireland, with strict conditions given by our government in Pretoria about where they could and could not go, and what they could and could not say. My nun just hadn't gotten here yet, and probably by now, I thought, had rickets on her boat.

"Mrs. Kloppers has kindly invited us into the classroom," Eugenie said brightly. I now wished very much to be at home doing my Moliseng job, but followed my mother into the cool, shady room. Eugenie looked like a spring day, lime green leaves splashed all over her dress, and shoes with a little green button on the side, just for fun. She'd considered wearing her white gloves but thought that might be too much, even though it was an extremely special day, deserving of new for everyone.

And that's when it happened.

Mrs. Kloppers invited me to choose a desk in the empty classroom and then go outside to meet lovely children until the bell rang. I chose one, second from the front row, two away from the windows, bearing in mind that someone might climb in and chop the nun into pieces— if we ever got one.

Just as Mrs. Kloppers suggested, I left my new hat in my chosen place, along with my blazer, it being January and sizzling, and because everyone now knew about the chameleon, and went out into the morning playground hoping to find a friend.

Luckily, Eugenie, prettier than anyone could believe for someone's mother, was with me when we went back in. Because Wanda Richards (no relation, we subsequently found out, to the beautiful batsman Barry Richards, who dazzled everyone at Wanderer's Cricket Club on Sundays) had taken my new things and really rather dumped them in the desk at the very back, next to a Portuguese-looking girl. And Wanda was now sitting, with two interminable blond plaits flowing down the front of her blazer (still on, I noted, God only knows what *she's* killed), *at* my desk.

With my ears hot and my throat dry, we stood, lost, with the thin, hard line in front of the entire seated class.

"Well, what would you like to do, Elizabeth?" my mother asked, as if I would know the answer to such a horrid thing. Tears welled and ran down my cheeks.

"I'd like to go home," I said.

The whole class, including my mother and Mrs. Kloppers, laughed out loud. For some inexplicable reason my mother said good-bye, and told me to have a wonderful day.

And so the first days were spent sitting in the back next to the Portuguese girl, whose dad sold us Hubbard squash at his corner vegetable shop. And very kind he always was, smiling broadly with oily, black hair, his adding-up pencil stowed behind his ear, offering my mother "Banansh? Guavsh? What-lemoensh?" which everyone knew was watermelon. But they were poor, and I did not want to be sitting next to her. Actually, she turned out to be extremely nice although she smelled of sweet cabbage. She was Maria Manuelo.

And it turned out later that while nuns had vowed to be kind, Mrs. Kloppers (Afrikaans—you just knew by her name) had taken no such vow.

"Yes, what an absolute cheek," my father said loudly in front of me that night, "planting yourself in someone else's place."

"Plonking herself down, actually," added my mother. "The cheek of it, Isaac, moving someone's things and just taking their place."

It happened all over the world, my father said, looking at the larger picture, from which I deduced there were hundreds of girls like me all over the world, sitting in the back next to poor girls because of selfish girls like Wanda. It was human nature, he said. And it had been happening for ages. "Survival of the fittest, Elizabeth, that's all," he said.

Perhaps that rotten face-bone, Mrs. Ples, who had survived more hardship, more inclement weather, and more savagery than any of us could imagine, along with anyone *else* who'd jolly well gotten here first, would surface in the back there also, with me and the Portuguese girl.

"You have to rise up and reclaim your place. That's how it works." My father added, "If you want it back, that is."

But then you'd have to deal with Wanda. With my stalks of brown hair, her blond Viking plaits alone told me I'd lose.

When I got home from the third horrible day in the back, made bearable only by Maria Manuelo sharing her grapes with me, my grandfather George was sitting in the lounge ready for painful injections into the stringy shoulder of his right arm. Gran Elizabeth had remained up at Clova, holding the fort. He hardly ever left her there, but it was all right, he felt. The workers wouldn't shirk because he'd taken his neighboring farmer Wilmott's excellent advice and left a glass eye on the dining room windowsill, to "watch." With this all-seeing Master peering in every direction, she should not have to nag anyone to get things done. Wilmott discovered the clever trick after the war, when he accidentally left his newly cleaned eye on the kitchen table and mysteriously found the servants good as gold. Worked like a bomb! he declared.

My grandfather pulled his jaw tight around his teeth when the needle went into the shoulder joint, and didn't speak till it was out again. Tucking his arm back into his pressed shirt, he thanked my father. Being a gentleman, he usually thanked everyone. Except the officials who'd caused the goddamn problem in the first place. "They came on Sunday afternoon, Isaac," he said. "Sinister bastards, when no one expects them, and rounded up the whole bloody lot. Carted them off on the back of a lorry. It's taken us three weeks to find them all and bring them back to the farm."

He'd hurt his shoulder putting in new fences on his own, because the government had nothing better to do than to clear the labor off the farms. "They laughed at our documents, Isaac. We're now supposed to 'sell' them each a piece of land, I suppose where their mud *kyas* are—where their kyas have been for sixty bloody years."

My father closed his black bag.

"The crookery of it," said my grandfather George. "Those arrogant bastards in Pretoria decided we have to pay money for labor, and they shouldn't be allowed to live anywhere for free." He rolled down the sleeve of his khaki bush shirt, buttoning the wrist against the sun. "It's all a bloody joke to them," he said. "Seeming as though they're concerned about the rights of the farmworkers, but really they just want to get them the hell off the land and into the homelands, where they'll starve. I know Wilmott has no money to pay, and I don't. And nor the hell does Thom. We'll lose them all." He rubbed his arthritic hand down the side of his cheek.

There wasn't a single farmer up there who could make ends meet, with the desiccating winds that scorched their lands, and the sly rains that taunted but never came. They never made a farthing, but they'd found a way to put a roof over people's heads and make it work, and now it would all be destroyed.

"And good luck to you, the sergeant told me," George said, "getting them to grow anything. How many times have you shown them how to plant a row of *mielies* at their huts, he asked me, Isaac, and how to water them, and provide their *own* damn food, and how many times the next year do you come and find last year's one surviving mielie nearly dead? Pathetic, hey? Nothing planted, nothing watered, and they have to be told all over again!"

"Well," said my father, throwing away the sore-smelling piece of ethyl-alcohol-soaked cotton wool from the injection, "some of them *don't* seem to think that way. And they *do* have to be shown. You've had to do it yourself on the farm, George, show them over and over. But what are you going to do? That's Africa."

"He went on and on about how these Afs have been here all these millions of years," said George, "and hadn't even invented the wheel for themselves, and that's why they're bloody starving. And how they'd rather lie under the tree and wait for the banana to fall into their mouths than get up and pick it. And that all they really want is a bicycle! And a transistor radio." He rubbed his shoulder, and moved the arm slowly in its joint. "So," he said, "they loaded them up, bewildered, on the back of a government truck. Some of them took their picaninns, and some left them behind. The bastards just drove away, with them sitting up there in the back of the lorry in silence." He took out his hankie, wiped his forehead, his eyes. "N'zuni ran behind them and started screaming. He'd thought his picaninns had hidden in the kya, but there they were, up on the truck, being driven off to God knows where." He rubbed his cheek again and left his hand there, holding his head as if it were suddenly heavier than a melon. "The whole bloody idea's upside down, rotten," he said.

I wondered about Mphunie, and then Meendli. I thought about the twanging harp in her lips, her pretty, bony legs flicking up the dust. I felt suddenly worried, or angry, a new feeling in the pit of my stomach. Why *couldn't* they remember to plant their own mielies? What was wrong with them? Surely Mphunie, who could spit the furthest, could remember to plant his own mielies.

Weeks later, over our dinner table, my father asked Thaddeus, one of the anthropology professors at the university, why the bloody hell some blacks couldn't remember to plant their own mielies, and how that could be fixed. Thaddeus, who intimately knew their thinking, having spent years studying and living with them in their huts, said, "Some are hunters, Isaac, some are planters, and some are gatherers. Just like people in pinstriped suits in the most sophisticated cities in the world—some are hunters, some are planters, and some are gatherers. Those who are not planters have to be taught to plant. It's not their natural mentality, that's all. They've been hunters for thousands of years. And that's our responsibility. To help them."

It was quite simple, really.

Because the speck was not even born the last time my grandfather George came to Johannesburg, after Salamina brought the tea he went out to inspect Moliseng. She was luckily not yet too fat, so with his throbbing shoulder he managed to pick her up and make her gurgle like a fountain. Moliseng chirped and burped, her little black eyes shut tight, spurting with tickling tears.

"Most people turn a blind eye, Dad," my mother said.

Even so, he chose not to walk by the wall with her.

Well after midnight, the ground shuddered, and the little boxy house now nicely made a home with cool grass, tumbling white frangipani, and a new verandah, shuddered along with it, waking us all. For several minutes, the earth below reminded us with a lengthy and unmistakable tremor that we could all be displaced, forever.

Soon would be the day of going on the bus into Soweto. *You are not allowed to go in there,* banged in my chest. "Those kaffirs will kill you, if you go in there. You have to have a special paper to go in there." Loeska's dire prophesies rang in my head like her father's church bell through the night.

· ·

The rusty exhaust of a white Hi-Ace bus spewed steam like a small dragon into the dawn. Only some children had permission. The others would be staying behind at school to draw and do creative things with plasticine. Sisters Josinta and Miriam, in black-and-white habits, sat at opposite ends of the bus like bookends of mischief, ready with silly songs and limericks, Sister Miriam in the back, Sister Josinta at the wheel to drive.

We climbed up into the bus to choose seats. Wanda—recently demoted with another girl to the back of the classroom for "cheeky behavior," giving Maria Manuelo and me lovely desks near the front— wasn't coming. So I chose my bus seat in peace and quiet, pressing my face to the window where I could see my reflection, squint my eyes, and make myself disappear.

Mrs. Wilson plunged suddenly forward from the huddled mothers to bang on the bus as it reversed. She'd prefer Catherine to stay, she'd just decided—and do that nice plasticine. Catherine had to get out.

After an hour of lulling tunes and jokes, Sister Josinta turned off onto a long, dirt road heading into Soweto. Our wheels spat up stones in our wake at the tin houses lining the road. Well, not houses, actually. Just pieces of corrugated iron. Some people had found fancier, larger pieces than others, stacking them up with bits of flattened-out cardboard boxes, to make a home. I watched people walking with bundles carefully balanced on their heads—a stack of dry twigs for a fire, cloth bags of mielie meal knotted at the corners, sprinkling their black heads snowy with flour. Picaninns ran alongside our bus with no-teeth smiles. They waved and cheered us past broken-down cars that sat like rusty, discarded sardine tins at the side of the road. Useless. All useless, it looked like to me.

Picaninns ran and ran behind us as if we were the main event. A few had that green snot between nostril and lip, some just the clear kind but no tissues like Salamina put in my pockets every morning. Many had flies stuck like raisins on their faces and heads, bedeviling them, or flying alongside as they ran. And then I disappeared again.

The bus arrived in a little stony cloud and creaked open its door. The half-a-class poured out, confused, onto a sandy soccer field with no goals and clumps of defiant grass. A sudden tornado of cheering dust turned out to be a horde of picaninns running right at us. In the confusion of not knowing quite where to go, Sisters Josinta and Miriam shepherded us all into the hall next to the church.

It was not at all like Rosebank's church adjoining our school, where blue and white plaster-icing angels swam on the vaulted wedding-cake ceiling, punctuated with glowing candles at each end to remind God not to let anything happen. Instead, we found a concrete-floor hall smelling of tin buckets and strong soap. It looked to me exactly like the bus terminus down at the pass office but had been made pretty with an altar and some veld flowers for the unusual day of white children coming. No candles glowed, no smooth benches welcomed—just some squeaky, dark-slatted wooden chairs that echoed in the hollow space and looked as though they might leave sweaty patterns on the backs of your legs. A white ironed cloth bedecked the altar, embroidered with red flowers swirling in green leaves—just like the cloths that lay neatly arranged on Salamina's high bed on bricks, like her linen bedspread, stitched with a perfect circle of flowers—starched, straight, and smelling of steam and clean.

There were to be two surprises. The first happened after our half-a-class sang,

"Deep in thy wounds, Lord,
Hide and shelter me . . ."

After hours of practice enabling us to sing a three-part harmony, we stood with knitted girdles perfectly knotted over navy gym slips, shoes specially polished for the day, and gave our performance.

"Guard and defend me from the foe malign,
In death's dread moments, make me only thine . . ."

Then came some nice claps, some shifts, and a bit of a rustle bustle. Coughs.

After another short, shifting quiet, with us thinking the performance was over, we got the first surprise. The *other* children had a song. "JHEehh!" With the spontaneous eruption that must accompany trumpets in heaven, their voices soared in mighty harmony—unstudied perfection. *Smack!* their hands clapped in unison! And again *clap, clap!* "JHHEEhe . . . !" They did not have to stand nicely straight, we noticed, some still dogged with flies and that caked snot, some with shoes, some without, some with rags for shirts under tattered gym slips, some without. They clapped and stamped, their bodies melting into a tumult of glory that must have gone from the shreds of them straight up into the ears of God.

Our rehearsed choir stood silent, mouths open.

The priest stood up at the altar, in his green smock with a satin Eucharist stitched on the front, and his wire glasses slipping on his sweaty skin. When the last note sounded, he bowed his head, asked us to bow ours, and said a prayer for the "safe journeys of all men in this world."

He thanked the visitors—us. And then said, gesturing to the door, "Let everyone tumble out. And let them eat cake!"

Some of the grown-ups laughed. And he laughed, embarrassed, as if he had not meant to make a joke.

We did just that. A marvelous vanilla cake waited outside, with bitter-black, crunchy pips embedded in sweet, creamy granadilla icing. "Now, there's only one, one marvelicious cake," their thin, black teacher in her Sunday-best dress reminded them, so only the visitors could have some. But there *was* Fanta Orange for everyone. And in a careful circle on a paper plate, a nice packet of yellow-following-pink wafers. After a few tense moments, a bottle cap opener for the Fanta was found.

We ate the melty cake by their church door, silenced by its deliciousness. Since there was only one cake, kindly meant for us, their choir ran and cheered in the curious chaos of a million dust-field games. We licked our fingers, which you're allowed to do if there are no serviettes, and squinted out at them in the dazzling light.

The second surprise was a cardboard box pulled out from under the cake table with presents for us. I couldn't wait to tell Loeska. Not only had I not been murdered, I had been given a bicycle!

"They gave me a *bicycle,*" I might brag when I got home, even though I knew it was only a rusty coat hanger, bent into the shape of a bike.

. .

When I woke the next morning, the wire coat-hanger bike had still not turned into a real red bicycle like Loeska's. It wasn't even silver, like her old one. It lay in my sheets, rusted, waiting to transform itself into my very own bike—the way it had in its reflection, I remembered now, held up to the window of the little white bus as we drove out of

Soweto. Fly-ridden, ash-faced picaninns had shouted their good-byes, running alongside. They banged on our bus with their hands as it drove away, as if they wished for any small piece of us to remain. They disappeared in our dust. We had driven back on sand roads through floating streams of afternoon sun. We passed small spruits, now just drought-dried riverbeds with nothing more than a trickle, where animals and others had once found cool, sweet water.

All the way back we drove, through the fallen purple jacaranda carpets lining the lamp-lit elegance of Rosebank, back from Soweto, luckily before dark.

It had been only to the outer edge.

In my imagination I rode home on my own gleaming, red bike, made especially for me out of a rusty wire by a picaninn. I thought of him now, sitting in his corrugated tin hut around a small fire, wondering about the special day of the white children coming there—wondering, perhaps, about the cake. The delicious cake.

PART TWO

. . . .

CHAPTER FIVE

RUN, DONKEY, HERE COMES GOD

In the fleeting African spring, over before you can say Jack Robinson, rude August days of 1964 had already burned away the first blossoms, giving all things new and delicate no moment to shine. The syringa buds that survived this sudden heat burst in seconds into full clusters of shooting lilac stars, hanging heavy and fragrant too soon. In the blink of an eye, it was summer again. My mother hoped this one would bring rain in fantastic thunderstorms with displays of afternoon lightning that would send whimpering dogs scurrying under beds. Rain would relieve and settle us.

The brutal monkeys down the road had been shipped away and shot. Etched by Parliament, there were no longer secret parameters by which to live. We abided by them. The government's law of ninety-day detention for radicals caught undermining its policies had effectively driven dissenters underground. To increase its efficacy, this detention period was soon to be increased to 180 days of solitary confinement, the most productive method of police interrogation. Posting or writing antigovernment slogans was now raised in the Sabotage Act to the level of treason, punishable by five years imprisonment to a maximum penalty of death. Our streets were safer, emptier at night, many noted, due to police vigilance, and the pass law. Trips to the municipality pass office each time a new servant came or went were beginning, to many, to seem worthwhile. The police had everything under control.

My father slept with a gun under his pillow. Two houses away, someone was shot dead in his driveway for a few rands and an old car. In the mornings, my mother was to lock the gun in her top drawer. A job, I noticed as I brushed my growing tufts at her dressing table, that she never forgot.

Triumphantly, I'd had clean, dry shorts all day for months now. I was seven and I no longer stank. And even more victorious, I'd begun to conquer the night.

Moliseng, with a newly toothed grin as wide as the sky, careened in her tight black curls from one end of the slate floor to the other—inside, of course—driving us all bonkers. The speck had turned into a hurtling brown ball, with Salamina chasing her, morning to evening, making sure she did not crawl right out of the back door to the fence. Sputnik, my father called her, because, for all you knew she could already be on the moon.

School had become my morning refuge. In the event of police on the horizon, barking dogs, or even an unexpected visitor, Iris, Salamina, my mother, and even John sounded the silent alarm for Moliseng to be hidden, and each afternoon, I returned to resume my special job. It seemed to me in my limited understanding, in a silly spring moment of hope for relief of all and every kind, that the world had indeed righted itself. Of course, only if you had ears that really listened, and

eyes that read between the printed words of every now heavily censored newspaper, might you have known otherwise.

It would be hard to pinpoint an exact moment, but it must have
been around the time of that horrible shudder that things began to
unravel.

Broederbond meetings had gathered steam. Joining was still secret,
only now a proud one. Ladies at the kafee, at the Fish and Chips, in
the post office, and at elegant Ansteys department store in Rosebank
wore their smug membership like badges, flashed in knowing smiles
under pretty hats. In a silent coup, the Afrikaners, still humiliated by
their defeat at the hands of the British after the Boer War, were soothing their grudge with the goal of regaining their independence and
reestablishing their Boer republics. Not content with now holding a
white majority with their Nationalist Party, their work had to remain
secret if they were to successfully enrich themselves and reignite their
pride of religion, culture, and language. It was a pride already well
known to me, a pride that exuded from every pore of Loeska's blue-
white skin.

We were still not invited. They solicited only pure people. Pure
Afrikaans. And only those whose wives were vetted to be so also. We
heard on whispering winds of their meetings, still under cover of night
behind closed doors. But now, emboldened by silent agreement for
their doings, they had canvassed dominees, school principals, the
heads of statutory bodies, the law, the military, and the police. Every
high banking official, if qualified, was invited. Dr. Koos Viljoen, an
Afrikaner with a tanned, kind face, white hair, and green eyes, sat at
our dinner table one night and told us how he'd been quietly approached at the medical council. His wife, Lena, sat next to him in her
floral dress, crocheted collar, and perfect manners. She was pure
Afrikaans, with recipes she'd often shared with my mother from the
original Voortrekkers to prove it. Dr. Viljoen laughed and said,
"Shameless, hey?" My father said perhaps Koos should take them up
on their offer so we could know what the bloody hell they were up to.
And Koos said, "I'd sooner send you, Isaac!" They both knew that with

some, but not enough, Afrikaans in him, my father's Afrikaans patients would put their lives in his hands but couldn't look the other way with regard to his Jewishness. The Broederbond were so secretive that even many Afrikaners had no way of knowing who among them belonged. The tentacles of their brotherhood were as pervasive, as hidden as the blood vessels under their skin. In the end, they would wrest all control from the predominantly English-speaking United Party, and anywhere they'd failed to have legal power, they would be certain to have de facto authority.

In the meantime, they would plan. They would be the architects of the apartheid idea. So good, so necessary was this idea, it would be respectfully known as *Groot*—meaning high—apartheid—an imperative, high idea.

They would favor whites over all, most especially Afrikaans whites. Blacks, Indians, Catholics, and Jews were to be kept in place. English-speaking people were an evil with which they would have to live. Jews, constituting an integral part of these English speakers, controlled much of the country's economy—the gold mines, the diamond fields. They were despised but needed. The solution was simple. Afrikaners would entrench themselves in the powers-that-be at every level. Together, the Broederbond would preserve their anonymity to ensure the greatest success. They would quietly help one another. And like Mahila's crippling spells, no one would ever know who did it.

Dominees all over the land now comforted members at their high meetings with God's own words to substantiate their actions.

Within our boxy new house, in the seeming peace and quiet of full-blown summer, edges began to fray.

Moliseng ate her suppers in Salamina's room. As if the growing speck were an extremely polite visitor, Salamina schooled her meticulously never to sit on, or touch, our lounge furniture. The slate floor, Salamina decreed, was her limit. But often in the dining room, she climbed up to sit with us at the table, perched on someone's lap. Her little brown arms jumped and reached for anything she could lay her hands on. Even the tablecloth she loved, frequently stuffing spitty clumps of it into her mouth and rolling back in fits of giggles at John's furtive missile antics with peas, exposing her soft, chubby tummy over her nappy.

With Moliseng so distressingly mobile, luckily Loeska, hardly seen by anyone for months now, had been spotted only twice, both times under the Chinese lantern, wrapped in bite-soothing, ivory silk quilts, and lying on a special long chair. Taking quite a risk with the bees, I thought.

Peeking through the bushes, you couldn't actually see too much of her, except for her cheeks, now blown up like the errant monkey's blue bum—plied as she'd been with jellies and jams, about one thousand edible presents for each monkey bite. I'd counted them, marching up that driveway, in the hands of all the sympathetic ladies. Of course, she'd been through a hideous ordeal. But Eugenie declared Loeska had been better for months, and was just too damned spoiled to get up.

Fortunately, on this day of flaring tempers, Loeska was nowhere in sight. Salamina, with panicked, wet folds under her arms, her uniform clammy with endless vigilance, was hunting for me. "Monkeeey? Miss Lizzy? Monkey . . . ?"

The shock of her life, she got: billowing out of the top of the syringa tree, a snared parachute on the breeze. *"Jho!"* she exclaimed, at the long trail of flapping voile, and hanging under it, the white, usually stiff legs of me. I had flown into the purple sweetness, high into the glossy foliage, where everything that ever was a bird slept at night, and dangled myself by my knees under a tattered voile curtain attached with clips to my head and floating upward on the wind. (I would have worn my mother's veil, but she didn't have one. She had gotten married in courtly gray, because my father refused to set foot in a church.)

Dangling upside down was a jolly good position for forgetting the three things that had just happened. It was jolly good for forgetting that Wellington had threatened to kill Iris; that my mother refused to go to Baragwanath hospital; and that Mariko, who worked for gun-loving Paul de Kok across the street, had fallen into thorns.

In the early morning, with no school on Saturday, I'd found my father tying cotton thread fast and furious onto the legs of the dining room table, where he usually sat doing his thinking. "What are those knots?" I'd asked, mesmerized by his dexterity.

"Suture knots." He threaded them at the speed of light with one hand.

"Why are you tying them on the furniture legs?"

"Practice gives you fluency. You tie quickly with one hand, because you have the scalpel in the other."

"What would happen if you tied very slowly?"

"The person might bleed to death," he said. It was still dark, well before six, because Iris was nowhere in sight with the morning tea. At least thirty strings with hundreds of minuscule knots hung off the red vinyl table legs in the kitchen, off the orange tweed stick-leg chair in the lounge, off the coffee table legs, and even off John's retired high chair. Strings with tiny knots dangled from anything that had legs.

"I've done it enough, Isaac," my mother said, coming in in her nightie. She would no longer go to hell and gone every weekend to Bara, to help him stitch heads. "Why the bloody hell can't Steyn go in there with you, or Ned, or even Garber? They bloody *know* I'll go. They take advantage on Saturdays and stay home, while you do it all."

My father pushed his fist into the table, shouted very loud, and then banged the wall with the same fist.

I stood very still.

He shouted about "capacity," and "*all* have to do it," and "selfish," and some other things I thought I didn't hear. He shouted that ugly word "kaffirs" and "nightmare." I wished I could make myself deaf like my grandfather. I heard the front door slam. His old Mercedes revved and disappeared, kicking up gravel, toward Bell Street.

Salamina came through the kitchen door to start the day and found a broken glass on the floor, hurled at the wall by my mother after he'd raced away.

He had taught Eugenie how to suture, mostly head wounds, when he was still a student, because of the crushing weekend overload from Soweto at Baragwanath hospital and the shortage of doctors willing to be out there. Given that Bara, as it was otherwise known, was the finest teaching hospital in Africa, most of the time it was manned by housemen and students, while physicians in private practice moved on. Now that he'd set up on Bell Street, his inability to turn away from Bara over the weekends, and at night, frightened my mother. She'd continued to help when asked, but now she didn't want to go there anymore. And she didn't want him to go either. Things were changing. His driving through Soweto after dark some nights to get home from Baragwanath, she'd repeatedly said over the last few weeks, was just asking for trouble. He had John and me to think about, she'd said. He'd always just put his arms around her and said it wouldn't be for too much longer.

Payday, for most blacks, was Friday, and many headed straight for the Soweto shebeens, where they ended the nights with pungent, foamy pink beer and violent fights.

"It's about forgetting," my father had said.

I most especially wished I could forget my mother's sad eyes. When I went into her room to pat it all down, she pulled herself away on her bed and said, "Not now, Elizabeth." I crept away, with some soft beating in that sore place under the breastplate. She needed to sleep.

Luckily, because Wellington's threat could have been the last bloody straw for her, my mother was still asleep when the sun moved high and hot in the sky. Pietros had gone home the previous week for a funeral—another cousin had died, always a cousin (to get time off, we suspected). And always terribly *far*, the funeral, so by the time he'd get back, tough *eintjie* weeds peppered the lawn. My father had engaged the temporary assistance of Wellington—huge, Zulu, and blacker than tire rubber, with sour red eyes. He said he could weed very well.

On his first day, he'd diligently stabbed his spade into the ground until he was sweating bullets. My mother, with renewed spring hope, reported to my father that evening that Wellington had worked extremely well. He'd already dug an entire side of the house into open furrows ready for her roses. But then Wellington, Zulu, set his sour eyes on Iris, Sotho.

"But, Wellington, Iris works inside and you're working in the garden," my mother had said. His Zulu earlobes jiggled with the patterns

taken from the walls of the mud hut he grew up in. Like flat dough-
nuts with huge, pierced holes, their skin stretched thin around gigan-
tic, brightly painted discs. He'd refused to look at Iris as they ate their
suurpap supper. He hated her.

Now with my mother sleeping and not available to bring his lunch
out to the garden for him, and Salamina refusing to do so, he would
have to come into the kitchen to get his jam sandwiches and tin mug
of hot tea with his requisite five spoons of sugar. He swore if Iris was
there he would *not* enter. Then he raised his spade high in the air at
the kitchen door and cursed Iris for fierce battles lost and won. If she
came *near* him, he roared, "I will kieeel her!"

Iris was already under Salamina's bed, fled there with wild eyes,
preferring even the Tokolosh to Wellington's rage. The Zulus did not
like the Sothos, the Xhosas did not like the Tswanas, or was it the
Tswanas the Sothos? Trying to remember who hated whom, I heard
Wellington shout to the heavens in Zulu. Like the picture on the public library wall of ferocious, foot-stamping Zulu king Dingaan, who
invited the Boer settlers to supper, then massacred the lot of them as
they ate, Wellington kicked his massive, Zulu-*impi* feet high into the
air, and stormed down the driveway, gone. Never to be seen again, Iris
prayed. Thankfully, my mother was sleeping, with her tears well patted down in the dark nest I'd made for her, setting her pillows and
carefully closing her shutters.

The next day she would say with her elegant calm, "The Zulus are
a proud nation of warriors, and their impis were the finest of those
warriors. Wellington had to do what Wellington had to do." But now,
adding to the mess, Iris flatly refused to come into the kitchen because
the Wellington furrows lay gaping, ready to swallow into an early
grave anyone Sotho. And the Baragwanath hospital dilemma remained. Eugenie still did not want to go. Patients would arrive there
with knives still stuck in their wounds. "Heads bleed like stuck pigs,"
she remarked over breakfast, and said again she would not be going
back there. She finished her toast and tea, and went to lie down again.

And finally, because today was Saturday, there was always someone
at the gate, with mouthwatering peaches and cakes and things, in lieu

of payment for my father's doctoring. Sometimes, it was out of just plain gratitude for a life saved or advice given. On this day, further unraveling us, Esme de Kok, Paul-with-the-gun's wife, had to be told at the gate by Salamina that the Madam "is sleeping."

Esme de Kok, ruddy and round in her high-buttoned, flowery blouse with a diamante brooch highlighting her shelf of a bosom, her blond hair sprayed into place like that of a giant Goldilocks, put her softly baked venison pie, covered in an immaculate blue and white dishcloth, into Salamina's hands. Its golden pastry oozed juice from the stringy salt meat inside. This pie, she said, was for some sore throat thing they'd all had over there that Dr. Isaac Grace had kindly fixed. Then Esme de Kok laughed a silly, punched-out, high blood pressure laugh, exploding like little bullets firing out of her plump, red cheeks. She said how grateful they were for that throat thing being fixed, and she was so sorry, but she *had* to ask if Salamina's Master could *please* come to look at their servant, Mariko, no matter how late. Just to make sure.

And it turned out, the funny thing that had happened to Mariko, she said to my father when he finally got over there after operating very late, was that Paul de Kok had been out hunting with the *ouks* in the veld, his brave friends who had those lovely big guns that could shoot and kill "any fokken thing," I remembered from the day of the monkey. He must have been out there for days, under his khaki bush hat in the blazing sun, chewing salty strips of dried biltong meat, flushing his dazzled brain with warm beer, and killing anything that moved. He felt so blerrie good about himself when he turned back into his driveway—his *bakkie*-truck loaded with limp buck, flies already dipping into their eyes in the late, streaming sun—that just for the hell of it, he chased Mariko, who happened to be down at their gate fetching the de Kok post.

Paul de Kok aimed his vehicle at Mariko like a missile, and chased that "fokken kaffir!" . . . driving right at him. "It was so funny!" Esme said. Paul de Kok rolled down his dust-smeared window and shouted with reeking beer breath, *"Hardloop, jou fokken kaffir, ek sal jou morsdood ry!"* And Mariko did just that, running higgledy-piggledy all over the driveway to get out of the way, knowing full well *morsdood ry* meant "run down dead."

And hilariously, Esme chortled, he ran right into the patch of prickly pears! In fact, he *jumped* into them! And then Paul de Kok drove the truck *into* the prickly pears, and said the funny last line of that joke—"*Hardloop, donkie! Hier kom God!* Run, donkey, here comes God!"

Paul de Kok reversed and drove up to the house, revving his bakkie's engine for good measure, spinning those wheels until stinging dust and stones enveloped Mariko.

He shouted to Mariko to unload every buck. It was so funny, they said, to see Mariko, half blinded by sand, leaping through the prickly pears, covered in thorns from top to toe!

Even Mariko thought it was so funny! He just laughed, and said his usual answer of "Yes, my boss" to Paul de Kok, "Ja, my baas . . . Ja, ja . . . my baas," he'd said. Covered in those thorns. Because he knew, of course, that it was just a joke. Mariko had caught his breath, and unloaded the buck one by one. They had hung limply in his burning arms, their stiffness not yet come.

That night, when my father went over there to do the house call, he passed by the dead buck piled high by Mariko—a silent, stiffened mound of what hours earlier had leapt kingly through the veld. Even though he did not believe in God, he said later he'd found himself thinking their rigid bodies must have been the ecstasy they felt at their first glimpse of heaven.

He found Mariko in his dank servant's room at the back there, not saying much at all. And they were all *so* sorry it took the "very tired doctor" till midnight, with a torch! to tweeze out all those blerrie thorns, but God! it was funny.

My father, who usually loved the pies and all the peaches that frequently came from his patients, told Salamina the next morning to throw the venison pie in the dustbin and to return the dishcloth to that house. And Salamina did it. And also didn't say much.

Later, I stood at the door of my father's study. I watched him fold closed a light-brown envelope, with something in it, something thick like money. It was the same brown as the envelope I'd seen passed at the fire the night people vanished into the tree, and under Salamina's bed. The same brown as the small pile of envelopes in his desk drawer.

"What's in that?" I asked, startling him.

"It's nothing, Elizabeth," he said.

"Who is it for?"

"It's for Salamina," he said. He got up, and left it in the laundry. It had no name written on it. She would know it was hers, I supposed, because it was on her ironing board.

I ran out, and climbed to the very highest place in the syringa tree, tipped myself upside down to swing by my knees in the million purple stars, as if I were drunk on pink fermented beer from the shebeens. I did it for forgetting, just like everyone else.

I couldn't stop thinking of the spot on the fourth finger's nail. Gosh, you'd be lucky if somebody wanted to marry you, and take you somewhere, and keep you there forever.

. .

"Monkey!" Salamina yelled up to me. "The Master, he is looking for you." She laughed and called out, "The monkey . . . it's in the tree, Master."

"Thank you, Salamina," I heard him say.

"Dad!" I slipped down the smooth bark to land at his polished brown shoes. "Do you need me?"

"Yes," he said with a tired laugh, "I need you very, very much. Come, want to go for a walk?"

"Very much," I said, ready with leaps.

We went down the path in the last of the afternoon light. It smelled like heaven—that first falling of lilac flowers so heavy, so hot with their own sweet stink. My dirty feet rolled through berries, fallen much too early. Newly golden from green and too young to rot, but dropped by unexpected visitors whose scratched hands tore through them every now and then in darkness. The syringa tree had become a refuge. Its strong brown arms, filled with scoops and hiding places for me, reached into the sky by day, and by night held in their embrace those seeking safety from the police. Those exchanging words, plans, and assistance in its shadows around the night fires. Fallen berries in the early mornings told you something had happened. Now in the late afternoon light, they lay thick underfoot.

We passed the peeping fence where Loeska's blue-whiteness sometimes lay, still peeved, under the bees. We walked all the way around, through the granadilla bushes, under the frangipani flowers, full and holy white. Then back under the lilac stars in the miraculous softening of all that had been harsh in daylight.

"How many times have we walked on this path, Elizabeth?"

I racked my brains for my best estimate, and remembering that he was excellent with sums, decided on fifty million and sixty times.

He stopped in the half-light, looked over the bush-fence at Loeska's house, and way behind it, at her father's church. Was she lying there, under the Chinese lanterns? I wondered. "How many times have I told you that I love you?" he asked.

"Fifty million and seventy-eighty-five times!"

"I thought about you today," he said.

"Haaah." I jumped with astonishment, delighted. "What did you think about me?"

"I saw a little picaninni at my consulting rooms today. He had big eyes like you, soft little ears like you, and big, *long* feet like you!"

So there *was* someone like me, with the same big feet. "What was his name?"

"Matanzi," he answered.

"Matanzi . . ." Must be Zulu! I swished up the dust with proud, impi warrior kicks, one foot then the next, slapping down onto the earth. A friend at last! Matanzi of the big, long feet would be the last warrior standing on the world, and I with him, swirled in the burning glory of victory. His fire breath would frighten even the Tokolosh. "Yaaaaaa, Matanziiii!" I yelled.

My father laughed. "His mom brought him," he said. "He's eight. She carried him on her back, a long, long way, to see me. No bus, no nice old Mercedes for him." He looked at me. "And then all hell broke loose. Mrs. Bezuidenhout stormed out because we were seeing him in the same room as her little boy."

His eyes closed, remembering the chaos of the back stairs—Blacks Only—the white side, sixty people waiting, sick children coughing, crying, mothers smartly dressed for the visit to the doctor. And then the back stairs—the rush to find a table on which to examine Matanzi, whose journey to the consulting rooms had been so arduous his fever had burned his eyes into parched holes in his head; he was too exhausted to cry—the sudden push, his decision. He'd called to Bekka, his black nurse, to put him quickly on the first bed, which, stupidly, he forgot to look, was not a bed for the back stairs, but in the corridor on the white side. "Mrs. Bezuidenhout stormed out, followed by Mrs. Thompson, of all people . . . threatened to phone the police . . ."

He looked to the last light on the horizon, as if trying to obliterate the images of the day.

Like a rocket, I was up and at him. "Did the police come there?" I asked, my heart racing, my legs stricken stiff in the dust. Suddenly, I darted back toward the granadilla vine, with frantic hands trying to pat down the air, the path, anything that led to Salamina's room, to hide away the little brown secret that lived in our backyard. "Are the police going to come and fetch Moliseng?" I asked, my throat dry in my hot head. Would my father now be led away through the leaves, by the kicking boots and torches in the night, and never be seen again? Why was he so stupid? Why did he forget? Why did he do these wrong, wrong things?

"Moliseng will be safe here with us," he said. "Your special job, silly billy . . . We won't *let* anyone take Moliseng."

What he had not told me was that while English Mrs. Thompson had just plain driven off in a skidding huff, muttering, "Bloody woggery, wherever you go," Mrs. Bezuidenhout marched straight down to the pharmacy under his consulting rooms, where she loudly expressed her disgust. Marius, the Afrikaans chemist with his shining face in front of his medicines, was bemused by the goings-on. He told my father that Mrs. Bezuidenhout asked him if he, Marius, knew that the new doctor upstairs was *"Jood! En sy vrou, jy weet, Marius, is Katoliek! Ongelooflik!"* Then she'd added for good measure that she'd heard that a whole bloody *tribe* of kaffirs lived in our backyard.

Absolute nonsense, of course—except for the Jew and Catholic thing.

And Moliseng.

The disappearing place on the horizon was streaked with the loneliest red, a color known only to those who could bear to look, to those who read between printed lines—a color known to those who woke and slept under the heaving sky of Africa.

My father looked at me, at what must have been to him a small face catching the glow of the red, and he was able to say, not knowing how, but curiously, quietly able to say, "Don't ever make this place your home, Elizabeth."

In the grieving moment when day passes into night, lost forever to those who lived it, his polished brown shoes turned, and he walked away in the dusk. I followed, planting my long, berry brown feet in his prints, back to the house.

. .

That night, in my clean, white sheets, I dreamed of Mariko. He stood on Paul de Kok's roof, wrapped in the velvet robes of purple kings. In his thorns, he feasted. With broken teeth, he tore long, stringy pieces off the venison roof of that house.

Suddenly, the roof turned into a glorious buck, no longer lying dead. Its horns glowed. It folded Mariko into its winged flesh, rising up around him, a gleaming, muscle-twitching buck to fly him high into the night sky, then higher to where Mahila now reigned.

If I had not been asleep, I might have seen Mariko across the street, turning painfully in his narrow bed, his torn flesh pulsing in the cricketless night. If I had not been asleep, I might have known he was distracting himself with remembrance—his fifty-year-old feet running picaninn free, chasing an old tire wheel with a broken stick, turning it on the sweet-dust road of the highveld, the sun warm and kind on his back, rain coming maybe, drop by soothing drop, the wheel turning.

If I had crept out to Salamina's room, I might have seen her facing the wall next to her bed—the little speck hidden there, its tiny breaths in the in-and-out that make a life. I might have seen Salamina staring at the wall through tears that ran despite herself, the wall that could recede or advance, depending on how good you were in making tricks with your eyes. But the wall was no distraction. Just a punitive reminder of Mathias. Mathias of the no-good.

If I had been down the path in the dark—peeping in as I often did at her night door—I might have seen Salamina get up. I might have seen her stand like a hovering bird at the unwanted bed—forced to remember by the wall, the wall that was *not* the wall of the house Mathias promised—her own house, for when she would be old with him. This was not the wall that bound their lives in a promise.

Salamina must have been remembering the house as she stood there, the way it had risen up in her mind out of bare ground when Mathias spoke, in words as cajoling as treacle to a child—the walls, proud and strong, embracing her as he did when he arrived at the gate to see her, the rising heat of his body when he touched her. The promise of a house with running water, its own fence, a light! Even though she knew there was no electricity where they might be allowed to make such a house. But the magic of a light was there in the dream—the way he was. I might have seen her sink to the floor next to the bed, if Salamina had not refused when her legs crumpled, refused to allow herself to fall, her silenced tears smeared where they had shimmered, in a painful river run dry across her face. Instead, she crept back in, beside the small breaths of Moliseng. She put her hand on the tiny back, webbed with bones as fine as a sparrow's throat, the little pulsing heart underneath.

Salamina held on to her—the only remaining piece of what was to have been a house.

..

In the six months that blazed by, and February days too hot to know one from the next, we were graced with only one lightning storm, which ended in playful thunder—another Monkey's Wedding, with the flirtatious sun streaming through a veil of drizzle.

Moliseng remained neither seen nor heard. God, despite my father's protestations that he did not exist, had been listening. Nothing happened. Not to her, not to my mother, not to any of us.

Moliseng was growing. Her top lip curled daintily, her eyes were dark and moist, shaded by a small forest of black lashes, and she looked up at us with all the naughtiness of the prettiest imp alive. Best of all, she seemed finally to understand that the laundry door was her limit. Prompted by a mere look from Salamina if she ventured out too far, she cleverly babbled her version of "Hide away, hide away, Moliseng hide away!"

I had been cautiously good, most especially in the new nun school. I had become invisible to ensure that I did not end up like Leon de Vos, who had straight sticks of uncombed hair. "And no brain underneath that mess," said the thin, hard line. Unfortunately, my nun had still not arrived, and Mrs. Kloppers would rule for another year.

At first, I was the only one in my class privy to what had really happened. My father began inspecting my earlobes each night, the piece where they join on to your head. He'd had to stitch Leon's back on, after the thin, hard line had picked him up by his ears, dangled the full weight of his body by them, torn the one off by a quarter of an inch, and then started another crusty tear on the other. Some people's ears were apparently not strong enough to hold them up.

A terrible fuss ensued when my father arrived at the school, furious. No one knew why, except Leon and I, and, of course, the thin, hard line herself, who came back blistering cross from the principal's office.

Leon had gotten his ears torn standing up at the blackboard, trying to divide. With stitches now, and a bandage that made him look like a half-pint Egyptian mummy, he had special permission to leave or shout for help if Mrs. Kloppers ever touched his ears again. She never did, I noticed, watching on behalf of my father. Instead she made him repeat a poem for the whole class each morning, about a boy called Danie van Dam, whose hair was *"nooit gekam."* Not only was it never combed, there were rats living in it. Just making him say it aroused suspicion, causing him to be scrupulously avoided.

One morning, Leon suddenly declared that he had his own poem to say. She was an Afrikaans cow-dung, and her husband was an Afrikaans ape, he orated.

God only knows where he went after that. His bloodied ears and his poem vanished from us.

My father said it was never about Leon's ears, but because Leon had challenged the thin, hard line on the correct English pronunciation of the words *circumference* and *diameter.* She'd said it in the Afrikaans-trying-to-speak-English way, like inter-*fearence.* And *diameter* she'd said as in dia-rrhea. Leon had kindly informed her of her error. With the certitude of those who know best, and blaming it on the long division, she'd publicly hanged him by his ears. Some Afrikaners would not be told by anyone how to do anything, and that, my father said, included the rest of the world, whose opinions about what was happening in our country were of no bloody interest to them.

Speaking of certitude, Loeska was back at the fence again in glorious form. She handed me pieces of her orange. She let me run around the back of the church, where bosomy ladies heaped themselves up the steps for prayers. She even allowed me into the sanctuary of her room, now a sickbed shrine to the god-awful bites. It groaned with paper dolls, sprayed blue carnations in stiff, triangular arrangements, and every treat imaginable. Petticoat creations floated like parasols on frilly hangers across the azure ceiling of her room. Staring up at that blue, she must go straight to heaven, I assumed, for a quick visit, instead of sleeping like other people.

Delicious smells seeped from every corner of their house—banana slices, mango and spicy curry brought up to Joburg from the Koelie Indian market in Durban (nice to eat their food, Marie Hattingh often delighted, but that doesn't mean you have to let them live on top of you), swollen raisins, pawpaw and cinnamon-custard milktart. Inhaling the juicy air, I prayed that I could stay forever.

Loeska flounced onto her sailing-boat bed, directing me to sit in the lowly waves on the wooden floor, glossed to perfection each morning by the now almost-forgiven Willery.

"I had special permission," I said, about my visit to Soweto.

"Only the police can give you permission, and you gunna get killed, hey? Your whole family's gunna get murdered."

I often wished I had never told her anything about anything. She'd insisted on the same thing earlier, allowing me to ride on her old silver bike while she'd streamed through the bright ranunculi on her gleaming red one. Now in her room, she said, "Impossible, impossible, impossible!" until I had to forcefully say, "Listen, hey? I got special permission."

"From the government?"

"No! From my dad. Our choir was invited."

"Rubbish! Who took you?" Her eyes narrowed into suspicious slits.

"The *nuns* took me," I said, feeling enormously important, "and we came home before it got dark." I added the part about the dark because I thought she would be as pleased about that as I'd been.

"Those nuns are stupid," she said, "and they get hacked to death because they won't listen."

Her words thudded in my ears. That was the horrible thing Eugenie had said in the very quiet voice to Prue.

"They gave me a *bicycle*," I bragged, thinking it would soften her and at least render me equal in her eyes.

"A bicycle!?" Her eyes went Chinese again, but pale, watery blue like runny ice. "Rrrubbish!"

I noticed my voice got sometimes shaky and a bit loud, and felt rickety in my ears. "They gave me a bicycle—made from a wire coat hanger bent into the shape of a bike, with wheels and *everything*." Then I said, very loud, "My dad said it's a very clever bike."

She looked so Chinese now that her eyes completely disappeared into her cheeks. The white thatch of her hair quivered over those disbelieving slits so frighteningly that I actually wished she'd be stung by *all* the Chinese lantern bees for *pretending* to be Chinese whenever she didn't like what you were saying, and luckily—or unluckily, as it turned out—I heard Salamina's big, round voice calling, "Muuuuhn-keey?"

That word turned Loeska into a squinting Popsicle, frozen to the spot. I, instantly deaf, fled through the sore-scraping bushes before Salamina could say it again.

"Auw, Monkey! Auw, my Monkey, I thought you are in your tree, but . . . thje," she welcomed me home to her. "*Here* you are, jhe? Come uppy, uppy, Monkey." She leaned down to me.

I knew a jolly good refuge when I saw one. I clambered with big, long feet like a frightened kangaroo up onto Salamina's warm back, most especially comfy when Moliseng or John were not on it. And most especially nice to be carried through the granadilla vines, through sugar-sweet high frangipani flowers, clasping Salamina's brown neck with both arms.

I heard the dominee get out of his Deutsche-Wagon in the drive-way next door. He shouted for Loeska to come immediately. He had to call her again. And *again*, because now she thought there was a monkey outside and refused to come out.

And bloody cross he was. "*Liewe Vader!*" He said that normally to his dear Father God when he needed him the most. "What are you doing churning up the flower beds? Have you no respect?" If the old silver bike was out with the red bike, it meant only one thing, "that dirty Elizabeth" had been there. He said the "*Liewe Vader,*" and the "Have you no respect?" very prominently, right over the fence at us, hoping, it seemed, that somebody else, in addition to God, might hear.

When Loeska finally peeped out, assured that no monkey had come there, he tucked his gleaming black Bible under his sweaty arm. Bursting out of his suit with fat, heat, and crossness, "Get into the house," he now commanded. The house sucked Loeska back in.

High on Salamina's back, I could see their garden the way my fa-ther saw it. I saw the ranunculus petals, flaming red, orange, and jeal-ous, jealous yellow, floating like flopped-out, popped balloons all over the neat lawn. Rude bicycle tracks ploughed through their once perfect, sleeping beds.

"Salamina?" I asked, filled with horrible worries but riding queenhigh back to the kitchen.

"EeYees my Monkey?" said Salamina, like warm honey to a lost and found bee.

"Do you think Willery might murder Loeska in her bed?"

"Jho! Monkey! What? Are you *shlana? Whena shlana?*"

And in case you didn't know it, *shlana* means *mad.*

CHAPTER SIX

EVERYONE MAKES MISTAKES

◎◎

*P*ostcards arrived—*Prue in Capri,* adorned in fake-jeweled Cleopatra sandals with blue eye shadow to match; Prue in Alice Springs, Australia. Exactly where Jack wanted to send Algernon, my mother said, quoting her favorite radio story with that earnest wild man, "somewhere between this world, the next world, and Australia." From the picture, it was also a dust hole.

"Elizabeth, if I've told you once, I've told you a hundred and fifty times. But God gave you ears that don't listen." My mother moved below me under the syringa tree in a tired circle, trying to catch sight of me. "You will come down and *eat that egg!*" She fidgeted with her earring, her other hand crossed around her waist, like a small bird in a self-made cage. "If you do not, it will be on your plate for lunch, and then for supper. And you will not go to ballet."

Ignoring my vomit-gagging threats, she floated like a gossamer dandelion to the edge of the shade. "I can see exactly why Mrs. Stryck suffocated her five children," she said. "She was driven to distraction by children who will not *listen*."

I was already deaf. Because I'd seen about the pillows in the *Sunday Times*. That Mrs. Stryck must have walked down her passage in the middle of the night. I thought of the gun, safely put away in the top drawer each morning.

"She went quite mad," my mother warned. And then she made a joke for me. She rolled her eyes far back until, from where I was perched, I could see only ice white, and said, in a demented voice, "Quite maaaad!" I stayed very still. She drifted back into the house like an empty bottle on the sea.

She was only joking. However, Mrs. Stryck, I knew, was not in Australia, but right around the corner, right here in Ferndale somewhere. She'd done it in the middle of the night, smothered them while they were sleeping. *Oh no oh God oh* . . . Maybe Tarzan could wander down from Clova and rustle his chains, warn if anyone came near. Once, I thought he *had* come to me. But in the morning, there was no sign of him, no ghost marks from his chain in the dust outside my window.

And in the middle of this, Moliseng made the first mistake.

"Miss Lizzy Monkey, come down! I've got a very bad news for you!" Salamina came running, with Moliseng close behind. I slithered down the tree faster than snakes before the rain comes. Salamina looked at Moliseng with eyes of fire. "Monkey . . ." she said, "she *washed* it. It shrank very, very much." In Moliseng's hands lay shreds of shrunken, matted voile that had once been a dream of white, the dress of my bride doll. The news fell into my ears like thunder. My legs jittered in disbelief. That was my best doll, the one who held all my dreams of being taken somewhere else, by someone who would like me and want to be my friend, someone new who would not ever have seen or smelled me stinky. I squeaked in pain.

Salamina's frantic hands stitched the air as if she had needle and thread right there. She could make a new one for me, she offered. But I was marching away, my crying face bloodred. "I'm going to tell my mother what you've done!"

Salamina moved faster than she had in a long time, running after me. "We are *so* sorry, Miss Lizzy, jhe? . . . Please, Monkey?"

Moliseng ran behind, holding up the tattered remains.

"Nice and clean." She grinned. "Nice and clean!" Like a gleeful ant on a newfound pile of sugar, she asked me the way Salamina often did to help her to iron. She would be the ironing girl, like her mother.

"She's a baby, Miss Lizzy," Salamina implored. "She doesn't know."

I saw something in Salamina's eyes—a desperation I did not understand, a well of feeling, and a willingness to stoop, to ask me, a small white child, for something. Perhaps she suddenly remembered her long, painful search for work. Perhaps the cold wall by her bed seemed suddenly wonderful to her—a small somewhere-to-be at the back of the Grace house, with Pietros, with Iris, and Zephyr from next door—Zephyr, whose songs comforted her and allowed her tears to run freely at night into the fire under the syringa tree.

"She's a baby, Miss Lizzy." She cupped her hand over Moliseng (palm up, never down, or the child would not grow). "She doesn't *know*, jhe?" She touched her own head as she said it, touched the place where knowing lives, and I, who didn't quite understand, stood staring back at her.

"If we make a new one, could we make it with petticoats?" I dared to ask.

"We can try, Miss Lizzy!" she said, relieved, robust again. And then that awful speck had the cheek to laugh.

"Moliseng, come here! You are extremely naughty." I grasped her little arm. Quick as a flash, she grabbed a fistful of my hair, yanked me down into the sand, and climbed on top of me in an all-consuming feast of kisses. "She's covering me in kisses," I howled, buckled down at her mercy. I threatened to tickle her, but she held on to the clump of hair, delighting in her captive. "Let go, Moliseng," I warned again. "Kielie-kielie-kielie!" I tickled, until she opened her fist and squeaked deliriously down the driveway. "Moliseng . . . don't run by the fence!" My heart sank.

Nothing stopped her. Like mercury from a smashed thermometer, she spilled all over the front lawn by the street until Salamina shouted, "*Djo*, Moliseng!" ordering her to her side.

Moliseng stopped still, her hands raised up over her eyes to hide herself away. "Hide away, hide away, Moliseng hide away . . ." she whispered. And then, with no understanding at all, she ran away again, chiming out the words like a funny game.

"Hide away, Moliseng," I yelled after her. "The police are going to come and fetch you and send you far, far away!"

"*Poliesie*, Miss Lizzy?" Moliseng froze, covered her eyes again and asked me, "Miss Lizzy Monkey hide Moliseng? *Away!*"

"It's White by Night here! *You* are not *allowed.* You've got no paper."

"No paper, Miss Lizzy!" she said, finding that hilarious. Like a carefree, rollicking brown ball, she chanted "no-paper, no-paper" all over the front lawn.

"Salamina's got a paper, but you've got no paper! Hide *away!*" I shouted, chasing her, then gave up, ran into the backyard, and flew up into my forgetting tree. Salamina picked her up and disappeared with her around the back.

Most people had indeed turned a blind eye. Mrs. Visagie had seen Moliseng darting at the back when she came for church lunch next door and parked in front of our gate. And Mrs. Wilson, who was Catherine's mother, who'd preferred that Catherine stay and do plasticine instead of going to Soweto with our choir that day, and who worked in the Braamfontein mission, also saw her when she came to fetch a cardboard box of old clothes. Even those chubby Afrikaans aunties, Tannie Hester and Tannie Esme, the leaders of the other tannies, and very kind, really, with hearts of gold, my mother said, saw Moliseng momentarily in our driveway.

"So what, so what, so what!" I moaned, climbing through the branches to reach the moon. Moliseng just didn't think.

That afternoon, BANGBANGBANGBANG! boomed through

our front door. Minutes before it happened, my father, as if by instinct, shoelaces still undone, grabbed his medical bag in one hand and the car keys in the other, the sandwich he'd been peacefully eating abandoned. Actually, he'd seen them from our verandah, readying for their assault.

"Where are you going?" my mother asked.

"Emergency . . ."

"Oh, I didn't hear the phone ring," she said.

It hadn't. Gathering outside the dominee's front door in a buzzing of hat veils above the hedge leaves was the prayer brigade, preparing to strike.

"Aahg, no man darling, I'm not lying to the dominee again," my mother said, fearing the repeat of a previous Sunday where she'd had to make an excuse for my father's absence. My father kissed her, that brushing, sorry-I'll-see-you-later kiss, then, checking to see if there was enough of a gap for his escape, he even had time for fun, made devil horns on his head and said, *"Jy moet oppas, die Duiwel kom!"* which even ordinary Afrikaners know is a serious warning to be careful. Slicker than oil he fled, jumped into his car and was gone, leaving my mother on the verandah in a hopeless trail of dust. She opened her mouth to call after him, but nothing came out. She could hear the natter of the little swarm about to ascend our driveway, marching down behind the bush-fence, closer and closer to our gate.

I raced up onto the verandah. Sometimes, I was quick enough to jump into the front seat and leave with him, but not today. "What did Daddy say?"

"He said the devil's coming to get us," she said, in that matter-of-fact voice of disbelief and desperation in equal measure.

For a horrible moment, I thought it *was* the very devil coming. I leapt this way and that, what to do, where to go, how to pat him down . . . when I was stopped in my tracks by my mother's cry. "Good Lord, look at you! You're covered in mud from head to toe. Under the water this minute."

As ordered, I headed straight for the front door, to be halted by another sharp shriek. *"No!* Go around the back. And get Iris to wash you.

Tell her to hose you down," she said, "outside the kitchen door. And hurry up. They'll be here any minute!"

I understood suddenly that the very devil meant the very dominee coming. And I had only one second in my proud mud coat to inform my mother, "Iris says I look like a picaninni!" And that, from Iris, was a high compliment.

Sometimes my mother leaned her head against the trails of jasmine on the verandah. Like slow, leaden doors, her eyelids closed away the blue seeing part. "Oh God!" her soft cry went up, lonely, like someone's last exhale.

I raced off around the house, a white-eyed mud ball. I was Mphunie, I was Meendli.

> *"Emergency, emergency* [I called,]
> *Irissy, come and wash me!*
> *Emergency . . ."*

Where *is* that bloody Iris? my mother must have wondered, in the one quick space that allowed a thought into her jasmine oblivion.

Iris, who was gaining in both experience and skill, was already hurtling across the grass unrolling the hot, snaky-green hosepipe that dripped by the kitchen door in a shady little pool—already unrolling it like Hercules to get me clean. I shouted to her to hurry—the devil was coming! We pulled with all our might at the mud-caked shorts. Stuck to my skin, they had to be scraped off. I wished I'd escaped with my father. I'd be in the front seat with him now, listening to his car radio. Iris might like the Beethoven his radio played, I thought as she puffed and pulled at me, because it started with a drum—she'd often scratch her head and lie back in sweet dreams at the fire. Sometimes when Zephyr drummed, she was all of a sudden up, kicking and dancing like a dervish. "Listen to the whispering drum," my father often told me, beetling along through the veld. With the muddy shorts off, I sang out that drum to Iris, who was running to switch on the tap. Iris could balance water in a bucket on her head, and should have been doing so now. God help us if anyone saw us using the hosepipe! In searing drought now, already April and not a drop, we were cautioned daily to only spray the flowers after half past five, and only for ten minutes, but at least we didn't have to carry our baths in buckets on our heads, like the ladies who walk in the long, hot, dusty veld. The fine for wasting water was punitive. But with the dominee on his way over, this was an emergency. Iris was allowed to hose me down outside the kitchen door, to wash me clean.

Like a small spaghetti in a sea of green grass, I stood stark naked, ready. With Iris aiming jolly well, a volcanic jolt of sun-baked water erupted out of the hose and reeled me back. I furiously washed off my mud coat. The dissolved little brown shadow melted back into the secret earth under the grass. All my brown ran down in rivers into the ground again, to make me shiny and clean, and white again. Purified, I flew through prisms of light in the watery sun of my backyard baptism.

"They're knocking at the door!" I yelled, dripping naked, as if no one else had heard the pounding. Propelled by a mixture of excitement and dread, I shot like a snowy bullet into the laundry to find a clean, ironed, white shift dress waiting there, with Humpty Dumpty, before he fell, printed on the front. I yanked it on, like sticking toffee over wet skin, and ran smack into my mother in the kitchen. "Elizabeth, where is Moliseng?"

And of course, that bloeming speck was nowhere.

"You go and tell her to hide away," she said, with that pointed finger that meant a certain smack if you didn't listen.

BANGBANGBANG! blared out of the front door again.

"Oh God, oh God . . ." my mother murmured through gritted teeth, dabbing her neck. She opened the door. "Hello, Dominee." She smiled, suddenly radiant, like a perfect cake coming out of the oven.

There they stood on our verandah, the little swarm, in single file, poised for stinging—and led by the bursting-out-of-his-suit-with-goodness dominee. Like a giant bulldozer moving a hillside, he parted the air in front of him, plastered my mother to the door, and squeezed by. Without waiting to be asked, because he was "so frrrendly, you know," he barreled through the tight hallway into our lounge, followed by his four perfect ducks in new petticoat dresses: Roelien, sixteen, almost-a-lady so could now wear peach, with pointy little high heels; identical twins Elsabe and Mitzi, nearly fifteen, who just like the dominee were bursting with goodness, and maybe too much jam. And Loeska, the last lamb to enter, dressed in the pure white angels wear when they pop in from heaven. All very creamy, with matching hats and salads on top. I drip-dried in my pulled-on wrinkled dress. Some errant streams ran in secret places, there having been no time to properly dry. Marie (Mevrou die Dominee, they call her, Mrs. the Dominee) must have stayed home, resting from making all those hats and jams.

My mother, who sometimes couldn't resist, waited for them to file in and then said, "Please, do come in."

"How kind of you, Mrs. Grrrace," the dominee said, rolling his *r*'s like a farm tractor starting up after you've pulled the choke out, "and will we have the *puhleasure* of the good doctor's kumpanee today?"

"Please, have a seat, Dominee," my mother said, trapped and jittery but so polite she could have given lessons.

"Yes, thank you. I see my little ladies have already made themselves quite comfortable."

They had indeed, in a neat froth on the couch. I crouched on the slate floor by my mother's chair. Dominee Hattingh sat where he always sat, in my father's chair—"wedging himself *in*," my mother noted after, like a bus reversing into our garage. Now quite settled, his red cheeks parted to reveal all forty-two gleaming white teeth. His Bible lay tucked in some other folds of himself.

My mother began, apologetic and hopeful that this might curtail the visit. "Unfortunately, Dr. Grace had to rush out on an emergency."

The white teeth vanished and reappeared just as suddenly again under his little eyes, grown large with disappointment. "*Again!* But the poor doctor never has a moment's rest!" he marveled. "Yet, when these babies come, they come. There's no stopping them. Whose turn is it today?" he inquired, eager with anticipation at the prospect of a new lamb for his flock.

"Well, actually, he said something about a snake bite as he ran out."

My mother's gaze went longingly through the front door as if my father were running out right then. "Labuschagne, I think he said," she volunteered brightly, saying exactly what Isaac had said to say.

"Labuschagne?" His fat cheeks shook in confusion. He knew everyone, of course, but no, no Labuschagne. Then in a flash, pumped full of the godly light of knowledge, he remembered. "Oh, ja, Labuschagne! That's that huge family that lives on that farm theeehhre!" He pointed very far away, and with exactitude. "By Fourways!"

A ring of tiny wet beads had gathered on my mother's forehead.

"Was it one of the children? Do you know?" he asked, riveted with concern.

"Actually," said my mother, putting her hand to her head as if to slow her racing mind, "I think he said it was . . . the *old* man."

"Good Lord!" burst the dominee. And then with jubilation, he pronounced that that particular person had passed on! He quietly leered at Eugenie, taking careful note of the uncontrollable flush in her deceitful cheeks. And then he added, with a very nice smile, kindly, you know, but just for her full information, that not only had that particular person passed on, he'd passed on *last year*!

The perfect icing of Eugenie slipped into droplets staining the back of her eyelet blouse. If she'd had my skills of disappearing, she might have done so then. Instead she seemed to be relying on some faint, flyaway voice inside that this would soon be over.

The dominee leaned in to her, his stomach gushing into the arm of the chair. "Ja, we have to be very careful of these snakes, you know? The serpent of hell can creep up and *nip* at you, at any moment. . . ." Oh, he laced his speaking with abundant kindness. And with his eyes pulled tight into his redder-than-ever face, he warned, "We all know what happened to Eve. . . ." He said *Eve* with full knowledge of her sin, and the terrible, terrible consequence to all men weighted in his words. "Now don't we, Mrs. Grace?" And for good measure, he stood.

They each had their very own Bible, with a lush, silky, white ribbon to mark exactly where they'd paused in their talks with Afrikaans God. And you were absolutely *not* to tell them any jokes! They only came to pray, for rain.

In a brilliant flash of what was needed—chat about rain—I rushed to the dominee's side to tell him something serious I'd heard, hoping it might be helpful.

"Africa . . . has *no* fucking water," I offered, exactly as I'd heard it.

My mother gasped. "Eeeelizabeth!" she sputtered, as though she might choke on her own spit. She swayed a little on her feet, but no words came to explain. Then drawing herself up to her full height, she smiled weakly and said, "May I offer you some tea, Dominee?"

In the thudding silence that followed, the dominee pulled himself up to *his* widest boat shape and squeezed out, "Ag, no thank you, Mrs. Grace. We were just now blessed wiff tea, scones wiff kreeem, and homemade jam. You know, Marie always sayes, when she bottles the jam in the service of the *Lord*," his voice rose up, "it always comes out better." Looking down now in more ways than one, he lowered his jiggling chin onto his chest. "Let us bow our heads and *pray!*"

Shockingly, without warning, into this reverence careened a horrible brown ball, all arms and legs blown in on a silly song. Moliseng didn't think. I wished she'd evaporate, but with a gleaming and expectant face, the blot smiled up at the dominee. *"Imithi goba kahle, ithi, ithi!"* it blurted out. *"Ithi . . ."* In the stultifying quiet, it paused at the dominee's gleaming black shoes. *"Imithi goba ka . . ."* it sang, and came to a wary halt.

"And whose child is this, Mrs. Grace?" he asked, calm, as if inquiring about the price of squash in the vegetable shop, and oddly not cross at all.

"Oh, she's . . ." My mother stepped forward. "This one is . . . is visiting us for the day." She flicked her hand, dismissing "this one" as nothing. Less than nothing. She smiled. "Just for today."

The dominee placed his sausagey hands, one grasping the Bible, on his enormous thighs, and bent benevolently to Moliseng. He wrinkled up his nose and smiled, like an enormous, super-friendly bull, blinking down at her. "Just for today." He grinned.

Then he mustered, once again, his patience, his strength, to say, "Let us bow our heads and *pray!*" His last resort for these terrible heathens. My mother lowered her scalded cheeks and shut her eyes. The

dominee's voice rose from the bowels of the earth. First, a slow rum-
ble in consideration for all within earshot, a tremor that rounded and
grew into an earth-shattering boom with a crescendo beyond even
that to the God who made heaven, earth, and us:

> *"O Barmhartige Vader,*
> *Skepper van hemel en aarde,*
> *Ons staan voor U in ootmoed!"*

And he said the *U* meaning "you, but with highest respect," as
though someone had given him a little punch in the stomach and it
whistle-burped out, rather grandly, just like those better-than ones in
Pretoria. Then he asked for rain, if God willed it so:

> *"O Heer, as dit U behaag,*
> *Stuur tog die reen!*
> *Om Jesus wil . . . Amen!"*

Without even a breath, for those who didn't understand, and now
there were three, he raised his hands and roared out,

> *"Let us* pray!
> Pray *for the rain that will* soothe *our spirits,*
> gladden *our hearts,*
> *and* soak *our soil with the* goodness
> *of the Almighty Father!*
> *The rain that will ease our worries*
> *and answer our prayers. . . ."*

He moved himself almost to tears.

My mother knew this was not an exact translation, but more for
her benefit. It was really rather beautiful, so round, so high.

And then he said, "We pray that those among us who tempt the
serpent . . ." he looked at her through a sideways eye, "in lipstick . . .
and short skirts!" he spat out with unparalleled disgust, leering even

more through his sideways one-eye-open, at her cherry soft lips, her freckled, English, pretty, pretty, and disgusting legs! "Those who tempt the serpent thus," he continued, "will see the plague of *drought*," his eye shot up to heaven, and then slithered back down Eugenie's legs, "that their *sin* has brought upon us!" He exhaled like a spent, flat tire in a way that made you think it had to come out of one end or the other, and he'd made the discreet choice.

I sank onto the floor, thankful that on this day I was no heathen caught in Eugenie's lipsticks. In the exhausted silence, Loeska's ice-water eyes suddenly pivoted in her head, settling her gaze outside the living room window where Salamina, Iris, and Zephyr (roped in to help) were carrying an unwieldy load through our shasta daisies. My feet darted me to the window, my thoughts racing with no relief—my mattress. Every time they came to pray for rain was perplexingly, humiliatingly, the same time Salamina and Iris carted it out, not even wet! to air in the sun. Everyone turned to look. The single-file frill on the couch moved their heads as one. Their eyes fixed like cement glue on the rotting yellow stain. I stood at the window, glaring at the sun for assistance. Fix up my damned mattress, I silently screamed, wishing in the interminable quiet that just for once, I had a dress like Loeska's.

Taking their cue from the mattress, the unfortunate cherry on this unfortunate cake, the prayer brigade gathered up their Bibles and marched in a perfect column out of the front door, back down the driveway, on to new conquests.

I crawled like a hesitant insect to my mother's side out on the verandah. We watched their hats disappear behind the next sinner's bushes in the bright, beatified light of late highveld afternoon.

. .

"*I'm not having that man* in my home again." My mother stormed from the lounge and disappeared down the passage.

My father yelled back at her. She banged their door shut, and banged it back open for more shouts. I lay in my bed, still as a newborn mouse.

"I am *not* having him in my house," she shouted.

My father, who usually could calm even the devil, laughed and said, "Well, don't open the door then, Eugenie!"

"That's not funny. He saw Moliseng today. God knows what he'll do now . . . phone the police, I suppose!"

"Oh, I don't think he'll do that, Eugenie." They must have seen her before today, he said, and they've turned a blind eye. But I knew they'd never seen a "kaffir girl" running through the lounge like that.

"It's the same thing every Sunday," my mother said. "You take your bag and bloody disappear. Why don't *you* sit here like an imbecile and pray for rain?" Her outrage steamed out of every pore. "Do you know what he called me? The Roman Danger. Catholics, even those poor souls among us who've lapsed . . ." She looked up contritely, as if expecting a punishing bolt of lightning. When it didn't strike, she ventured on. "Even those of us who've lapsed are the *Roomse Gevaar*! Oh, I can't wait for him to start on the Jews." She looked at my father. "And a Jewish atheist like you . . . that'll give him *endless* fodder." Her hands made endless fodder in the air.

"Just be patient, Eugenie," he said. "Just put up with it."

"Last week, he wanted to know why we have Elizabeth at a *Catholic* school." She squelched up her eyes in disgust, the way the dominee had. *Katholic,* he'd said, as if trying to rid his mouth of rotten food. "Oh, it's because we're hoping she'll go to hell," my mother had shot back brightly, but in her mind only. Actually, she'd controlled herself, she now admitted, and had said simply, "The nuns are renowned for their educative skills, Dominee, and, frankly, we don't care if she grows up to be a bloody Hindu in a loincloth." Her voice rose again now, and Mahatma Gandhi, who had kindly visited our country and made himself the subject of fascination around dinner tables, seemed to float in a big nappy across her blue eyes, into our living room and out again. "We don't bloody *care*, as long as she's happy, and brings *joy* into the world," she foamed.

"Good God!" My father laughed, utterly delighting in her, even though her voice was that edge-of-tears one. "He must have fallen off his chair."

Actually, she didn't *say* the bloody Hindu thing, I wanted to tell from the listening post at my door.

"Well, I didn't *say* the bloody Hindu thing, but at least if you were *here,* I could escape to make tea or something." And then she added, in a brilliant, desperate remedy, "I've a good mind to go and buy the ugliest hat ever seen." *She might find one next door,* I thought. "And sit there in it next week, with my thick, crimplene dress buttoned up to my ears." She folded her hands into praying hands, like the horrible, ornamental bronze ones that sat on the dominee's desk, severed, like Zephyr's fingers. She peered out from under the supposed hideous hat, a vision of piety for the crusading dominee, who would be thrilled, victorious at last.

"I know. I'm sorry I run away, Eugenie," my father said. He looked out of the passage window much further than one could actually see. "I've had those bastards calling me a fokken *Jood* since my first day of school, when I was five years old."

That was one of the things I'd heard Prue telling very quietly when she'd visited, about when Isaac was tiny, riding with his found rabbi grandfather on their donkey cart. "Here come people!" some children rejoiced, so lonely out in the boondocks. And the mother of those children ran out of her house and said, *"Dis nie mense nie, dis Joode,"* which Prue said meant, "It's not *people,* it's Jews." Prue, also very tiny, heard it too, riding on the donkey cart that day in her faded, flowery bonnet.

"They all had their polished black shoes. And Bibles," my father said. "My feet were bare. I can't sit here and listen to it anymore."

"Where is this madness coming from, Isaac? One of your grandfathers is Afrikaans. He's a remarkable, compassionate man. . . ."

"It's not about being Afrikaans. The blacks caught in Rivonia are being defended by an Afrikaans lawyer. Bram . . . Bram Fischer. It's not about the color of your skin or what language you speak, Eugenie. It's what your father says: Good and evil live in your heart. In what you decide about it." He turned to her and joked, "Perhaps we'll all just go out on Sundays. That'll fox him!" He put his arms around her, now that she was almost calm.

"You know, Isaac, I hope to God I never go to heaven. All those bloody holy Joes up there. I'd much rather make myself useful and . . . stoke the fires in hell."

In the middle of that night, jolted from sleep to my window, I peered out under the shutter in the shining sliver where it touched the windowsill. Something was happening. Suddenly, the shutter slats lit me, lit the whole room in shadow and light like a floating zebra crossing. The scorching light vanished. Outside was black again. Still no lamps for our dirt road.

Something moved. In the stinginess of the moonless night, I could see nothing. Again, the slats shadowed, shifted. Beams of light seared in—the police van. It drove nightly up and down, some nights all night long, looking for people who were not supposed to be here.

Moliseng.

In the lights shining on the road, I saw they had somebody down. "Fokken kaffiiiiir," rang out. The words hung in the dark. I mouthed them as they were shouted. I knew those words well. He just didn't think, that man down on the road. Why had he not remembered? He was not supposed to be here. Why was he not at his home? How could he dream of coming around my house with no paper? Had he not had time to climb up into the syringa tree? Perhaps he did not know of it—in a panic I tried to whisper, to silently, secretly tell him through the window: Hide, hide yourself in the syringa tree . . . or under Salamina's bed. . . . He heard nothing. Bludgeoned to his knees, his muffled screams echoed every blow to his head, every boot into his shattering ribs. He prayed out loud for the road to swallow him. He could not hear me, and I could no longer hear him. In velvety silence, I was deaf.

I saw the door of the van slam shut, caging its bloodied prey inside. No trace remained. No sound could be heard, other than the hollow cry of a dog as the night-catching machinery made its way down other forbidden streets.

I flitted back to my gloamy resting place, my white sheets ironed by

Salamina. I perched, breathless there, stick legs dangling over the edge of the bed, in a sudden, heavy tiredness. I felt my eyes recede into dreams of falling glitter. In the intense, nothing-will-happen quiet, the wee began to run and run beneath me like a river with no end.

Far away in the night outside, a dog barked and barked. It must be Tarzan, coming to help me, I thought, before I fell away.

..

If it was Wednesday, you could sit on the kitchen floor, licking clean the empty tin of sweet condensed milk.

Morning sun burned patterns on the blue-smudge, faded linoleum. I scooped divine remains out of the bottom of the tin, with the greedy-for-sweet bee Moliseng buzzing nearby.

Mindful of Zephyr's fingers, I warned her, "You'll cut yourself on the tin!" She'd get lockjaw, and her voice would be like metal scraping a hole in the road, I said. Her seized jaw would forever be stuck in a wide-open gasp.

The bee paid no attention. She dipped into the tin, ran away, dipped in again, her pointed finger covered in a snowcap of condensed milk, then wheeled willy-nilly out of the kitchen door slap-bang into Iris, who picked her up and carted her off to the servants' rooms for a bath.

She seemed browner now. Now that she had been seen.

Flopping from side to side, I licked and licked, sugar numbed, like a windshield wiper in time to Pietros's hand. Extremely tall and rich black even in the sun, he balanced on the ladder outside with a bottle of purple Methylated Spirits and a raggedy cloth, squeaking the kitchen windows clean. I wondered if he'd heard the commotion last night. Perhaps that man on the street had been coming to visit Zephyr, or Salamina, or to sing "Nkosi Sikelel' " out at the fire.

Taut sinews glistened and rippled under Pietros's skin, as if desperate to get out. He had old cuts on his forehead where the scars had grown over like black orange rinds, sealing the pain. I swayed back and forth in sweet eating to his washing. He was much blacker than Iris. But not as black as Salamina, whose honey brown shine had made my mouth fall open with fascination when I first saw her. Iris said Pietros is much blacker than she because he's Sotho. But Iris was also Sotho, and, puzzlingly, much lighter, like a thin coffee ice cream with coir curls on top. Salamina was Xhosa. My tongue slapped in the sugary substance, "... Xho ... Xhi ... Xhoo," trying to duplicate her delicious clacket of clicks.

You were not to talk to my mother if she was counting spoons of flour and brown sugar into her mixing bowl. If she lost her place, it would be tickets.

The window jerked open, suddenly filling the kitchen with outside insect hum and the hell-deep boom of Pietros's voice, "Hello, Madam ..." My mother jumped, flying the flour into a frightened little cloud in front of her as her measuring cup clattered across the checked floor.

Outside, the cry of a crimson-throated loerie bird kindly warned the game—hunters approaching.

"I'm sorry. You gave me such a fright." Embarrassed at her shock, she bent to pick up the fallen cup. "Hello, Pietros," she said.

"How is the Madam?"

"Oh, I'm fine, thank you, Pietros." She wiped up the flour, then turned back to him and thought to add, "How are *you*?"

"Very good, Madam."

"Well, good," she said kindly, dusting herself back to her counting.

"Madam?" he said, startling her again, surprising her, really, him speaking like that without having been spoken to. Not that she minded, of course. She'd just gotten a bad fright, that's all. She ran her floury hand through a tendril of hair that tumbled hot and irritatingly into her eyes.

"Yes, Pietros?" She smiled at him again.

He leaned into the window from the ladder outside, pushing his massive upper body through it, his black shoulders wide, undeniable. "When the Madam she is going bekk to her own country?"

"I'm sorry?" said my mother, still smiling, and not quite understanding the question.

"When the Madam she is going *bekk* to her own country?" he asked, his eyes suddenly aflame with permission.

"This is my country, Pietros," she offered.

"No, the Madam she has got her *own* country, over the sea?" His muscular hand ploughed the waves as he said it, a watery path like Moses made, for Eugenie to journey back whence she'd come.

"Oh no," she said, realizing this was just a small misunderstanding. "This *is* my country, Pietros. I was *born* here . . ." she said, claiming her rightful place. She seemed relieved but cautious, as one might be in seating oneself at the dinner table with foreign guests after a silly mix-up about the chairs.

His eyes flashed.

"And my *mother* was born here," she quickly added. And then in an irrational, sudden, desperate soliciting, "*And* Miss Lizzy! *And* baby John . . . born here . . ." cheerfully offering the sweetness of us to him, like the nearest sacrifice at hand to appease an angry god.

"No, Madam," Pietros branded his words into the kitchen, his eyes bloodshot, "this one, it's *my* country. The Madam she *must* go bekk to her own country, over the sea!" His rough hands carved the way for her again, to go very, very far away. His plea was clear and certain, a prayer for help that might have sounded, in the depth of his desire, like a threat.

My mother stared, stupefied, his burning eyes, his black hands held just like the dominee's bronzed prayer hands as he said it. The loerie bird called out again. If you were a springbuck passing in the veld, you'd know—hunters. Pietros heard it. We heard it. No one blinked. I could smell his sweat, his sharp breath peeling in from outside. The rasping of insects swelled deafeningly behind him. My mother stood transfixed, flour settling on her perfect, Romanesque feet as if she were a statue grown dusty.

Pietros's eyes blazed into hers for an answer, but none came.

"Elizabeth," she said, a pinned butterfly in his stare, unable to take her eyes off him. "Elizabeth . . . go and tell Salamina to get Daddy on the phone, please." Her stone head turned suddenly to life again. She looked for me, just as riveted to the vinyl floor as she was, and suddenly shouted, *"Now, Elizabeth!"*

Her words exploded in my body. I leapt, jagged, here, there, not knowing or able to think which way to run. "Salameenaa," I howled, plummeting out into the yard. "Salameenaah . . ."

From the opposite end of the garden, an irritated Salamina, ankles swollen from the heat, came hunting for Moliseng. And there Moliseng was, running brazen as the sun out on the front lawn along the peeping-hedges.

"Jo, Moliseng," Salamina yelled. "You get *inside* the house, jhe?"

"Moliseng play *outside*," rang her elated, cheeky answer.

"Jho!" Salamina said, furious. "The dominee it's going to *see* you and phone the police."

"Outside," Moliseng insisted.

Salamina grabbed her arm and hoisted her up, feet dangling in the air.

"Jhhheeeeaahy!" Moliseng wailed, writhing like a worm in Salamina's grip.

"He's already seen her!" I shouted, forgetting about Pietros, and sick of the whole bloody thing.

"What, Monkey?" Salamina turned to me with the speck still hanging there.

"On Sunday . . . *and* this morning." I took a few steps back from Salamina's impending wrath. I'd tried to avoid telling her, but now it was out. Once again I had failed to keep the speck hidden. I quickly blamed Moliseng. "She didn't think! I was riding Loeska's bicycles and she just ran right out. But I told the dominee that she"—I showed Salamina how I had looked at Moliseng with dismissive eyes and flicked my hand just like Eugenie had done—"is visiting us for the day . . . just for today."

"Just for today," Moliseng cried.

"Sshht, Moliseng," said Salamina. She picked up the tearful speck, suddenly sorry for her anger, her frustration—sorry for her sudden hatred. "Sh sh shh," she whispered, rocking Moliseng quiet on her big hip. She looked over the peeping-hedge as if realizing in a single glance everything there is to know, the end of something, the beginning of something, the moment she dreaded. "What did he say, Monkey?"

"Nothing. He just told Loeska to get into the house and take her bicycles with her."

"Aawh . . . thank you, Monkey," she said solemnly, the way you might thank someone who has given their life for you.

She kept staring at the house next door. "Thank you, Monkey," she said again, as if a torrent of rain fell through her heart. Like a ghost revisiting old steps, she retreated with Moliseng bundled tight against her chest. She smelled her tearful cheeks, her ears, like tiny, chocolate leaves folded against her head. She inhaled Moliseng's sweet, brown smell. And still her gaze remained locked on the house next door. "Come, Moliseng," she said, so low that I heard it only because it was carried a little way in the wind.

I followed Salamina around the back of the house to the servants' rooms. Quickly she went. She laid Mollie down on the bed to sing to her, until the speck fell asleep.

I left them there. From the door of the servants' rooms at the back of our acre, I looked down toward the house and saw my mother walk calmly out of the kitchen door. She held something up to Pietros. He climbed down from his ladder to where she stood, and like a sooty giant next to her, wiped his hands on the back of his worn tan pants. Then with two quick *clap-claps* for thank you, his hands opened to take a mug of tea from her. They must have sorted the thing out.

I wandered aimlessly this way and that along the path outside Salamina's room. Feeling suddenly like not being at all in sight of the peeping-hedges, and very worried about what had just happened with Moliseng, I crept under the boiling vines. Overripe granadillas welcomed me with wrinkly smiles, like ancient dwarves who had just heard something hilarious. I sat there, peaceful and hidden, bathed in their crumpled rot. I prayed for my father to come home. Sometimes he stayed very late at his consulting rooms. Today, the wait was interminable.

After a small rest, I remembered that it was Wednesday. I scraped myself out of the vines and hurtled back into the house. Wednesday was the day of the drive-in, the day of escape! I tore past Iris in the kitchen, down the passage to find Eugenie. And yes, it was Wednesday, but we needed to wait for sunset, she said, because the drive-in does not show in the light.

When the first threads of night crossed the sky, Eugenie said we could go. With ruddy-cheeked John coddled on his pillows in the back like a chatty poached egg, and me scrubbed to shining in my nightie, a pillow to sit on for better visibility, blankets in case we got chilly, floppy-doll Anne who might like the film also, and some crayons in case of sudden boredom, we headed out of the drive.

The flickering film bathed us in stories. My mother, in her glittering weekly flight from the troubles of the boxy house and beyond to Baragwanath, smoked her cigarettes with long inhales and slow exhales. The little speaker, hooked onto our rolled-down front window, crackled faraway worlds into the car. Crickets held the night with an incessant pulsing din, interrupted every now and then by a creature or two rustling the veld leaves behind the screen. Black rhino beetles drifted lazily into the beam of light, their single horns making them seem like tiny flying devils drawn to the flicker as we were. A solitary owl hooted in the surrounding blanket of dark.

I searched the images for someone like me. No such person appeared. Only Audrey Hepburn came, who smoked just like Eugenie! And wore her hair just like Eugenie's! And people who started singing in the middle of *speaking* to someone! And Yul Brynner, who stamped, shouted, and danced with picaninn-glad feet. One day we might have television, as they did in America. But for now, out in the fresh, night veld, we watched Esther Williams slide down a fountaining staircase, then make ballet *in* the pool with flowers on her rubber hat. And swim away! And the Three Stooges, whose every cake-splatting antic delighted us to shrieks. And that cheeky doctor, Peter Sellers, who told Sophia Loren to put her tongue away, there was nothing the matter with it. And *Don't Look Now, We're Being Shot At!*, which my mother said was no joke.

Tonight, *Sammy Going South* tied his belongings in a checked hanky on a stick. With his family killed in Hitler's bombings of London, he walked south all the way across Africa, almost to where we were. Maybe he could live here and avoid anything that could kill you.

"Oh dear, what can the matter be . . . ?" he sang in the grass to himself, because everyone else was dead. But most beloved was Hayley Mills, who choked us with tears. As Pollyanna, she hurried into place as a piece of the American flag at the fair. "From sea to shining sea," she sang, standing between stripes and some stars. Her moist eyes shone.

Did they have glitter in America? I wondered. Salamina, on the mornings after the drive-in, said she'd never seen a film, and didn't know the way to America. She'd laughed at me, an embarrassed, funny laugh. She had only "fife years" of school, she said.

America, my father explained to us all, was the home of the free, and of the brave. Free and brave lived inside your heart. Laying his stethoscope on my chest in the lounge, he said if I listened very carefully, I might hear it in between the beats. I listened with all my might for them, free and braves, under the breastplate. At night I heard Zephyr's drum, beating till it seemed my heart leapt right out of my chest. And echoing in my head from my daily encounters with her, the "Rah rah rah!" of Loeska's cries pounded our hot, highveld nights into a raucous cacophony. "Free and brave, free and brave," my noisy head shot back to drown it out, once and for all.

.. .

The end of that week brought a strange quiet that echoed with Moliseng's mistake. I found myself inexplicably propelled to the fence.

"Looeskaa?" I repeatedly called. No one came. She must be busy with hats and problems like that. I wandered away from the peeping-bushes.

My mother was asleep, deeply tired again. For a while, I stood guard at her darkened bed in the early afternoon, gently patting her. Later, a Dr. Milton Bird came especially to see her, he told me at the front door when I ran to open it. He carried a black bag, just like my father's. He was neat, with gray hair, quiet hands, and bright eyes.

"Severe depression," he said in a lowered voice to my father when he finally came out of her room. "The kind that makes you want to die. It's unrelated to circumstance. We think it occurs at a deep, cellular level. Circumstance just exacerbates it. Oh, we have a pixie with ears," he said, spotting me. My father went back into the room, and while Dr. Bird smiled at me in the passage, I heard the drawer with the gun click open, and then click shut again. He came out with his jacket on, and they walked out to the driveway together, talked some more, and left. My mother would be sleeping for quite a while, he'd said.

Salamina had gone to visit her mother in Soweto for one of her two off-days—Thursday, and either Saturday or Sunday afternoon.

Moliseng, she must have quietly decided, had spent her last day with us. She would be packed up and taken to Soweto, to her old grandmother. It could not be helped. She could no longer be contained, no longer be hidden away. She would bring trouble, a fine of hundreds of rands for our family.

Salamina must have packed Moliseng's things into a tattered shopping packet. Telling no one, she dressed herself up as usual for her off-day in my mother's secondhand clothes, looking, in Eugenie's words "nicer than I do!"—a compliment that always brought a smile to Salamina's proud face. She must have squeezed her swollen feet, as always, into the Madam's old high heels. With her neat, silky-for-special doek pressing her peppercorn curls tight to her head, a bit of dark rouge on her cheeks, and some sweet violet scent, she must have heaved Moliseng up onto her back and firmly tied her into her blanket sling.

They probably walked down the driveway on Thursday morning as usual, with breakfast cleared away, me off to school, and my father headed to his consulting rooms. Everything as usual except for Moliseng leaving, and in Salamina's hand, the shopping packet of her nappies and things. No one noticed. No one had the chance to say good-bye.

They must have walked up the salty hill of Bell Street, where they would have waited, as usual, at the side of the road in the heat and interminable lines for hours, for the bus that might, or might not come. Or might not. When it finally did, Salamina would have jostled her way onto it, her sweaty feet slipping in the high shoes of the Madam, found a place to stand and, if lucky, to lean. Moliseng, asleep on Salamina's back, was driven out of Johannesburg.

Some things were allowed. And some things were not.

At the boxy house, lazy mossies chitchatted. The afternoon stood still. Incessantly still. Tomorrow, I knew Salamina would return, and on her back, under her coat and blanket, would be hidden Moliseng, as usual. Or she might be in the faded tapestry bag my mother had given to Salamina, roomy enough for Moliseng, a hiding blanket, and some old balls of yellow wool and knitting to cover her.

Lonely panic rose like a fireball in me, driving me back to the fence. I called again at the top of my voice for Loeska. Still no one came.

The next day found me adrift there again. Today, I felt certain, she would hear me. The dominee's kitchen door opened . . . my heart leapt! I caught a glimpse of Loeska in her kitchen, dressed and ready for our special games, and maybe even some rides on the silver bike. And then not Loeska, but Willery came out. She stretched clean muslin over the narrow, fruit-drying trestle tables, then vanished back into the house and closed the door tight behind her.

Loeska was not allowed to come to the fence. She'd been forbidden.

. .

Salamina was back. Her cheeks were washed. She had stayed away some extra days and explained to my mother when she returned that she had not been feeling well, and then could not find a train from Soweto with a space on it.

Not the first time that had happened. When I ran looking for Moliseng, she told me Moliseng was asleep in her servant's room, to be nice and quiet, and to not go in there. And each afternoon, she repeated the same, perhaps already thinking of bringing Moliseng back, and not wanting to worry us with it. She carried her food up to her room and ate there alone, leaving Peter Mombadi, Pietros, and Iris to eat without her in their small kitchen, or around the fire at night. Busy ironing again, she did not say or sing very much. She seemed, in the meantime, quietly uninterested in me.

By the end of the week I remembered there was indeed someone to talk to. I sped out into the yard, all the way up to the syringa tree, now hung proud and stinking with full lilac flowers. I called out to the high tree friends, and heeding the call, they rained down, tumbling from the leaves to march full force behind me around the house. Past the morning glory we went, to the studying room at the far end—used for emergencies if someone came knocking in the middle of the night. Like Mrs. Grobelaar, who'd lain in our driveway purple with asthma, her husband down on his knees in the pitch dark beside her, sobbing, "Lettie, don't leave me, oh God! Don't leave me!" His shouts for Dr. Grace to come. "She's dying!" pierced the windows of our dark house. Awakened by car lights, I'd skidded like a sleepy dervish down the passage. Find a blanket, my father had yelled to me, and bring his black bag. "Run!" he'd shouted as he tore out to her. He'd injected a muscle relaxant into her arm. She'd gasped, her blue-gray lips pulled thin and tight like chicken skin over her teeth—and then she seemed to just slip away. An ambulance arrived out of nowhere, phoned by my mother, I supposed, spotting her at her window where the light was on. Mrs. Grobelaar was driven away. The next day, Mr. Grobelaar returned our blanket. He stood on the verandah, tears streaming. "She made it, Mrs. Grace. She made it! Please thank the doctor, please thank him." Out on the verandah with him, my mother held him in her arms until he was calm.

The thousand friends had not seen Mrs. Grobelaar because those things happened in the middle of the night, and if there was nothing unusual to stand guard about in my room, they'd be folded away, asleep in the high arms of the tree. Now they strutted behind, as excited as I was. We could chat to Mabalel, the bone-swinging skeleton who lived in that room. She hovered, clattering at the slightest touch, hooked up next to my father's desk, to keep him company. The wily medical students named her after the long poem of picaninn Mabalel, who infamously had been devoured by a crocodile. Her whole village had echoed in dire warning, "Don't go near the waaahtaaar . . ."

But she waited until they were lighting the fires at nighttime, then stole down the twilight path. *"Ching ching ching . . ."* her delicate ankle bells chimed as she ran, hot with desire for the water. With just the tip of her toe, deliciously, deliriously dipped, a monstrous rush rose from beneath the dark surface. With one wild thrash the crocodile snapped her up, then slipped in eerie quiet back into the murky deep. She was gone, forever.

"Mabalel! *Mabalel!*" the poem mourned.

I gingerly pushed the door open. My thousand friends, along to bolster courage, crowded in. And there she was . . . picaninn-ghost Mabalel, a haunting specter of bones, nothing but leftover shards after she sank away into the green, night water—never to be seen again. Revoltingly, because she had no skin on her cheeks now, her lower jaw did not stick *on* to her head. Metal hooks attached her jawbone, giving it grim mobility.

From a safe distance, dying of fright, with my father's stethoscope in hand but not brave enough to touch her, I commiserated, "It must have been very sore to be eaten by that crocodile, Mabalel. But God gave you ears that don't listen. And now they've been chewn off!" I approached, an inch at a time. Her heart, somewhere in the dark hole under the breastplate, might still be beating. I might be able to save her. I lifted the stethoscope.

The air in the room moved.

Suddenly, Mabalel's cavernous jaw creaked open. With a blood-curdling yell that sent the thousand friends fleeing, I saw Eugenie standing there like a ghost.

"You little devil," she said. "I've been hunting high and low for you. Put Daddy's stethoscope down this minute. You *know* you're not supposed to touch Daddy's bones. Have you no ears? Get into the house." She ushered me out into the garden. Salamina was putting supper on the table, she sighed, and I was not even bathed yet. "If I don't do it myself, it just doesn't get done."

"Madam! Madam . . ." Salamina screamed, running up toward us from the gate. My mother stopped dead in her tracks.

"What is it, Sally? What has happened?" she asked. Salamina's terror turned the pit of our stomachs. Was it baby John? Salamina hadn't left him in the bath, had she? My mother was already running before she could finish the question, in that direction.

"Baby John it's fine!" Salamina cried out to stop her. "He's with Iris." Breathless, distraught, she said, "Madam, my cousin Dubike, he's by the gate, Madam." She pointed as if a messenger from hell stood there. "He say . . . auw, Madam, he say . . . he say Moliseng she's *gone.*"

What did she mean Moliseng was gone? My mother looked where the speck should have come running any minute. "Moliseng's here," she said.

"No, Madam, she's not here. . . . I *took* her," Salamina cried, banging her blaming hand on her chest. "I *took* her Thursday, on my day off, to my mother in Soweto, and my cousin, he say she's gone!"

"Gone where?" my mother asked.

"She's *gone,* Madam! My cousin he say she's *gone.* Jhooo!" Salamina fell to her knees, wailing, "Oh jho jhe?" as if punched in the heart. She gasped for breath, her eyes searching. Spit curdled at the corners of her mouth. I had never seen her cry, and now her eyes squeezed tight. She lifted her hand to cover them, then seemed to want to lie down in the dirt.

"Sally, I can't help you if I don't know what's happened," my mother said, reeling back a bit as if she could not think. She put her arm around Salamina to steady her—to steady herself. Iris came running with John, scooped up naked and dripping, bobbing along on her hip. She'd heard Salamina's cries, grabbed him out of the bath, and bolted like a frightened rabbit down to the street. "Iris, what has happened?" my mother asked.

"Madam," said Iris, her brittle legs shaking, "Madam, Salamina she *took* Moliseng to her mother, and now she is gone."

"But where is her mother?" Eugenie said, completely confused.

"Her mother she is at home," said Iris.

"Well then, Moliseng must be there also?"

"No, Madam," Iris said in a shaky voice, "*noh-body* can *find* Moliseng." She glanced over the no-peeping, turn-a-blind-eye fence.

"*Oh jho, oh joooo,*" Salamina howled, rocking back and forth in the sand. Her hands slapped her thighs, her chest, her stinging face, as if she alone were to blame, and now her tears ran openly.

"But what does her mother say happened?" my mother demanded.

"No, nothing, Madam." Iris shook her head, visibly frightened. She shifted John from one jutting-out, bony hip to the other. "Mm-mhmm. She doesn't know what hepphent to Moliseng."

"Well, that doesn't make any sense," my mother said. She ordered me to fetch Salamina's cousin at once, and to hurry.

I tore down to the gate, calling out, *"Dumela,"* and was stopped by the sight of the aged, black man waiting there. A dust cloud rose from him as he lifted his hat to greet me. He bowed his head. His thirsty, scratching voice answered, *"Dumela . . ."*

"You must come into the big house to talk to my mother," I said, a bit loud, because I didn't know if he spoke English.

He gathered up in his frail hands some of the length of his trouser legs to enable him to walk. They were so long, the suit so big, he had evidently given up trying to keep them folded over at the waist. He walked slowly next to me up the driveway. The dust that had risen from him followed us in a little trail. His sleeves were also too long, skimming the tips of his ragged, yellow nails.

"Hello?" my mother said tentatively.

There was not much left of Dubike. He was old and exhausted, every word a sad effort in his borrowed suit. "Good evening, Med-dem," he said, bowing his head and stepping back from her, deeply respectful. He held his disheveled brown hat in front of his chest.

"I'm sorry," said my mother. "What is your name . . . ?" Her hand flew up to cover her heart as she looked at him.

"Dubike, Meddem," he offered hoarsely, "I am Dubike." He groveled back a little further, as though he were in the presence of a queen.

"Dubike, what has happened?"

"Meddem, Moliseng she is gone. She was very tsieck, and now she is gone."

"Is she dead?" I cried, shut down at once by Eugenie's "Elizabeth, be quiet!"

Iris knelt down to hold Sally's shoulders.

"When was she sick, Dubike?" The last Eugenie had seen of Moliseng, the child was the shining picture of health. Impossible, what this man was saying.

"She drank a sour milk, Meddem. She got *very, very* tsieck." His hand trembled, showing the life running out of Moliseng.

"When? Yesterday? *Thursday?*"

"Ja, Thursday, Meddem." He clapped his palm into his other hand twice to emphasize. "We took her to the hospital," he said, as if he were carrying Moliseng right then in his arms. Then he blurted out, suddenly grief-stricken, "They told us to *go!*" He closed his eyes. He had listened, he had left her there.

"Then . . . she's in the hospital, Dubike! Salamina! She's *in* the hospital . . ." my mother said, suddenly jubilant.

"No, Meddem," he interrupted. "We went there *again*. Moliseng she is *not* there, Meddem. She's gone, Meddem."

The world went silent—every bird, every cricket, every sighing thing seemed sucked away. Finally my mother said, "What did they tell you, Dubike? At the hospital, what did they tell you?"

"No, *nothing* Meddem. We went there again. We walk the whole day, a *long* way . . ." His hand shook out the long, angry way in front of him for Eugenie to see, as if his caked, worn shoes, his burden of a suit so respectfully borrowed for this announcement, and the sorrowful dust shroud he carried himself in, as if those were not enough for her to know his journey of unimaginable miles.

Fearing it might be Baragwanath, she asked which hospital. "Yes, Meddem, Baragwanath." He closed his eyes, shutting away the hopelessness, where need outweighed anything it could provide, where people lay for endless hours on cold corridor floors, waiting for help.

My mother looked at him, then turned away as if she felt guilty for her suspicion, her fear. Was this a trick? Why had he really come? Salamina keened in shocked emptiness. Sand streaked with tears stuck to her cheeks. My mother hesitated. She looked at her watch as if the answer might be there, and again, as if she'd forgotten what she'd seen there a second before. She looked at the crumpled heap of Salamina. It was almost dark, so there would be no bus to the station in town, no train for Salamina into the township until the following day. And then it would be packed, with no guarantee of a seat or even standing room. Salamina could not return to Soweto tonight. My mother looked at her rocking back and forth, her stabbing cries wishing she had never packed up her speck, never sent her away.

"Iris . . . Iris, is Peter Mombadi here tonight?" my mother suddenly asked.

"*Yes*, Madam," Iris said, quite confident, and now that she knew when to come and when to go, impatient that Eugenie didn't seem to know what day it was, or who was where. "It's *Friday*, Madam. He's here!" she blurted out.

"Iris, I want you to go and put baby John in his cot, and then would you please tell Peter to warm up the car?"

My mother patted the empty pocket of her chiffon dress for her money, her purse. She looked at Dubike, shifting and ragged, and added, "And, Iris, I don't want Mombadi in his uniform, please." She would need to be as inconspicuous as possible. A white lady in the township at night with a driver. Better that she have him wear his ordinary clothes, she was thinking out loud. Not looking too smart, no cap. "Yes, no uniform," she said. She turned back, but Iris had vanished. "Iris, Iris, wait!" my mother cried. Iris came running back, completely confused.

"Iris," my mother said as calmly as she could, "please lock up the house, and give Miss Elizabeth and John their supper, and if you can, stay with them, please. The Master will be *very late* tonight, he's *operating*." She emphasized her words to be certain Iris understood. Iris stood stock-still. She was not at all sure now whether to come or to go. And a bit sorry she'd been so sure of herself a moment before.

My mother knelt down to Salamina. "Sally . . . Salamina . . ." She quietly stroked her. "Go to your room and lie down. Irissy will bring you some supper." Because it was visible in a dark pool, I knew she could feel Salamina's weeping skin under her cotton uniform, pulled tight across her heaving back as she rocked herself in disbelief, the life knocked out of her.

"Dubike? Would you come with me?" Eugenie asked.

He said loudly, "No," and inched forward. Then he said, "I will stay with Salamina."

"I'll go with you!" I volunteered. I did not wish to be at the house at night if Eugenie was not there.

"Don't be silly, Elizabeth," she said distractedly. "Go with Iris and be a good girl, please."

My head started banging inside, punctuated by loud wailing coming from Iris's hips. John had started to cry. It was quickly getting dark. He did not want my mother to leave. Unlike me, of course, *he* was frightened of the bloody night! Exasperated by his shrieks, my stick legs stiffening by the second, and beginning to feel that horrible shaky feeling, I smacked my hands over my ears to blot him out. *"I'm not going to stay here!"* I suddenly yelled.

"Elizabeth, this is no time to be impossible," my mother shouted. "Go with Iris and be a good girl, please. Now!"

Dubike edged forward to help Salamina get up. *"You are not allowed to go in there,"* I yelled again, frantic. Dubike leapt back in a puff of dust. He thought I was talking to him. I was trying to tell my mother. Confused and frustrated, I cried out at her again, "You are not allowed to go *in* there. You have to have a special paper to go in there."

"Elizabeth . . ." She knelt down, put her hand on my cheek, and said in a special, sweet secret, "I need you to be a brave girl and go with Irissy. Now, off you go." She hurried away.

I darted off behind her into the house, with that crying feeling that swamps you without warning. She just wasn't thinking. Without a special paper, she would be hauled out of the car by kicking-boot police and beaten. She would scream for me to come. I would not be able to hear her. I would not be able to find her. I would not be able to keep her alive.

I bashed out again, "You are not allowed to go in there!"

But Eugenie would not listen.

. .

Peter Mombadi reversed the car out of the garage. My mother hurried along the darkening driveway, pulling her yellow jersey over her shoulders. When she got to the car, I was already ensconced in the backseat. "I brought my jersey," I said quickly to allay her fears, "so I won't catch a cold, and my blanket for Moliseng. And some of my sweets for her . . ."

She commanded me to get out of the car. Did I have no ears? "Get into the house this minute," she said.

My legs would not move.

"Elizabeth, I'm warning you . . . you're going to get the hiding of your *life,* young lady. Now move." She stood there. She was not going to get in until I got out. Peter Mombadi, without his cap, kept the engine running. "*Move,* Elizabeth," my mother shouted, utterly maddened.

Tearful, I blurted back at her, with only one foot getting out of the car, "Well, if I go in, I have to phone Daddy because you need a special paper to go in there."

"Oh God, Peter, let's just *go,*" she said.

She slid in beside me on the cool, leather seat, closed the door, locked it, and pulled her jersey tight around her shoulders. I sat still as a mouse, not even kicking my legs, lest she change her mind.

I knew from the faded light that it must be after half past seven. We set off in silence. "Lights off, Peter," my mother requested, so as not to alert the neighbors, all the way down the driveway, out of our electric gate, until Jan Smuts Avenue. The same way, it happily dawned on me that Francesco the Clown went back to the circus after getting his ears cleaned. I strained to see out of the windshield. And there he was! Walking in front of the car to show Mombadi the way, his blue glitter ears streaming light in the dark ahead.

"We can switch the lights on now, Peter," my mother said quietly. And as if she knew the answer but was hoping it had somehow changed, she asked if it was indeed Baragwanath.

"Yes, Madam," said Peter Mombadi's still face. He glanced in the rearview mirror, looked at us in the backseat behind him, then at the road ahead, where Francesco still lit our path.

"Peter," said my mother in that very polite voice when she noticed the windows open, "Peter, would you mind, I mean, do you think you could please roll up the back windows?" And because Peter was so marvelous, they were already rolling up before she'd even said the "would you mind." She smiled at him, trusted him.

"Yes, Madam," said the quiet Mombadi.

The blue glitter ears trailed their magic light, snaking us along Jan Smuts Avenue's endless, elegant curves to Eloff Street, then Eloff Street Extension, through Booysens, and out into the night toward the small Baragwanath airport. As far as we would ever normally go. Beyond that point, where no one you knew lived, there would be no lights.

There were none. We turned onto a dusty road. I plastered my face to the window. The night had grown blacker than hell. No electricity here, never had been. There was hardly anyone at night with much more than a match. The moon was king in this place, but tonight it was hidden, leaving the roadsides menacing and grim.

We moved deeper into the township. Small candles glowed here and there, here and there the luxurious gleam of a battery lamp. Sour smells of suurpap porridge mingled with the smoke of fires long smothered—the burnt-out, finished smell. My mother's eyes, closed for all of Jan Smuts Avenue, settled anxiously on the opaque dark. Under us, the comfortingly smooth, tarred road had turned into a pot-holed, winding dirt path.

I suddenly remembered that cheeky other Peter, from the drive-in. Like a funny Indian, he'd said to Sophia Loren with her pretty cat eyes, "Put out your tongue!" Out mine went to the rude, horrible dark on the other side of the car window. "My heart goes poom-pooty-poom . . ." I sang, just like him.

"Which way are we going, Peter?" My mother's hand fidgeted with the pearls at her throat.

"We are going on the main road, Madam."

"Good. That's a very good idea, Peter. . . ." He should not see her anxious like this. She'd be in charge. She'd not show anything but polite authority. "I don't want to take any little side streets. Please, *don't* take any side streets."

"Yes, Madam," he answered, forthright, calm as always.

She suddenly panicked and leaned forward to check the gauge. "Do we have enough petrol?"

Mombadi spoke faster than he normally did, but his voice was like warm steel comforting cold hands. "Yes, Madam," he said.

I looked at the relentless dark and thought of Loeska. If you went in here, she'd said, you'd be killed. They do not *want* you in here. They kill anyone who tries to help them. She said they hacked at one another without mercy, and they would not hesitate to do the same to you. I thought of the chopped-up nun, murdered after soothing hundreds of women in labor, giving hundreds of babies safe passage into the world under the most adverse conditions. I thought of her arms and legs in different places, her hands, her head carved off, left behind a tree somewhere. But I'd already *been* in here, my mind hurled back at me with dizzying speed. I remembered the choir, the sweet cake, and Sister Josinta. "That was during the day," Loeska had insisted, "and you didn't go all the way in there because the police don't *let* you. Those nuns are stupid, and they gunna get hacked to death like you, because they won't *listen*." To make matters worse, my grandfather's brother Francis had gone to the Congo to teach everyone the Bible, and *he* had disappeared. No one ever knew what happened to him. Like our Victorian relatives, Loeska, lowering her voice to a grisly moan and licking something awful off her fingers, said, "They must have put him in a pot and eaten him!" My father had said that was utter nonsense. I suddenly preferred to think of my other uncle, Walter, who'd cleverly helped Mr. Marconi to make the radio, enabling us all to listen to that hilarious Dexter Dutton on Sunday nights after the news on the BBC. "Oh dear, what can the matter be," I cheerfully sang to my mother. She seemed to wish I'd just shut up but said nothing, coping very well with me indeed.

I saw with a bit of a shock that Francesco, with his warm face and lighting ears, must have needed to turn off somewhere. But I did not panic. Even though we would not usually be caught dead on this road, this was the very same way Salamina and Zephyr came each week, to go to their homes in Soweto. So take that, any stupids who feel scared! Like Francesco's going home to his circus, Salamina's and Zephyr's feet had walked this road, giving it the sanctity of safety.

At least a thousand syringa tree friends had come with us, piled in the boot of the car, some under the bonnet, some flying above to check our way. Haloed faces with leafy hair smiled in at us through the windows.

In a horrific screech, Mombadi hit the brakes. We skidded to a halt in obliterating dust, spattering tiny stones like bullets. My mother's hand flew out to restrain me but we'd already been flung hard against the seat back.

"My God, what *was* that?" my mother stammered. "Did we . . . ? What *was* that?" Her hand went to open the door to get out. Mombadi said sharply, "No, Madam!"

"My God, did we hit . . . ?"

"No, Madam," he said, hands locked on the wheel. "We are lucky!"

I scraped myself up to the window. "It's a dog," I cried. "A dog! You can see his bones."

"Good God!" my mother said. In the headlights, stumbling off into the dust cloud, was the tail end of a mangy dog, ribs poking like knives under his ringworm coat as he vanished into the blackness. "Running on the road as bold as brass." My mother touched her damp throat. The air seemed stuck, thick around us. "I hope we are lucky, Peter," she said, "I hope we are."

Mombadi, shaken, gathered himself to drive further. "Sorry, Madam." The car began to move slowly.

"You can *tell* how lucky you're going to be," I said quickly to calm my mother. She just needed to look at the little white spots on her nails, I assured her, and she'd know exactly. "Gifts, friends, foes . . ."

Something flashed past in the headlights. I whirled around in the backseat, and then another flash—a corroded blue sign, like an old goat on a hill with one leg shorter than the other, stood on the bank of the road. I read "Ba . . . ra" as we passed. "Baragwanath hospital!" I shrieked out, in case no one else had seen it.

As we approached the light in the distance, my mother asked Peter to please wait with our car at the front door. Yes, she thought it would be safer if he waited, right there, at the front door.

Baragwanath sprawled in long, cream-brick bungalows under red tin roofs, its windows bright with harsh fluorescents. Built during the war, it was the first teaching hospital in Africa, my mother told me rather proudly as we drove in, as if she felt she'd learned something marvelous there herself. It unfolded its many legs on the huge property. In what little space had not been claimed for wards, quiet lawns, threadbare but still there, blanketed the dark grounds. It seethed with the pain and impossibility of its surroundings, the streets of Soweto. My mother pulled her jersey over her shoulders again. Even here, in the only glow of electric light for miles, the night looked daunting.

Mombadi, who always did exactly as he was asked, stopped at the glass door of the original brick building. The exhaust of the car steamed into the blackness. I tumbled barefoot out of the backseat. Mombadi, without his cap on, waited. As we walked toward the entrance, we heard his car doors click, and lock.

My mother knew the way, even though she'd never been here at night. Isaac, she once told Prue, only ever took her to Bara during the day. With no nursing experience, she'd stitched in the glare of long fluorescent bulbs that glowed all day, and, we now saw, all night. She'd been in casualty with him, but I'd heard her telling Prue that she'd occasionally gone in to see the children, most with diarrhea, tuberculosis, or malnutrition. And she'd found it extraordinary when Isaac told her that for malnutrition there was no massive dose of vitamins required, no medication, just a normal ward diet. Within a week, they'd be cured. Food. All they needed was food.

We pattered down the first passage past a stack of ghoulish, used-but-empty glass blood bottles. At the far end of the corridor we spotted Matron Lanning heading our way like an ocean liner in full sail. By all accounts, she ran as tight a ship as humanly possible under the circumstances. "Good Lord, Mrs. Grace," she said, stunned to see us. She glanced down at the silver nurse's watch pinned to her vast bosom, making her prickly, ruddy chin triple, then disappear. "What are you doing here, at this time of *night?*" she asked, as if we'd landed on Mars.

She sent us down the long corridor, where green and vanilla paint, now scrubbed thin, cracked on the cold cement walls. We walked among a sea of bodies sleeping on bare, concrete floors. An acrid stench of illness rose from them like mist over a battlefield. Many cried in quiet, plaintive tones as if they had given up hope that anyone would hear.

Like Snakes and Ladders, porters pulled occupied beds in thin paths between the sleeping forms, from one end of the long corridors to the other, as needed. Skilled, wonderful old porters at Baragwanath, my father often said. Patients lucky enough to be in the beds that lined the ward walls lay on bare mattresses, each with a thin, hospital-issue dark gray blanket. The stench rose up again, mixed with sharp disinfectant. My stomach heaved. "It smells funny in here," I whispered to Eugenie.

We found the doctor's office. He was tall, a young houseman, his hair short and sweaty, and under his eyes were the same night-duty-induced rings my father had. I knew he would at once give Moliseng back to us. But instead, he said he would look through all the drawers of papers. Just as we had hidden her in the cupboard, or in her tapestry bag, I supposed she was now secreted away in a drawer, nicely covered with papers to hide her. I stood next to Eugenie, clutching the blanket I'd brought from my bed in which to wrap Moliseng, and my sweets for her. Moliseng was not in the drawer.

And then she was not in the second drawer. It dawned on me that this doctor must need the papers like a map, to find her. "Mo-li-seng," I articulated carefully to help him, "Moliseng Eleseebett. That's Eeelizabeth," to make sure he knew she was mine, with the same name, and I added "Mashlope" to be extra sure. He returned his maps to the drawers.

We were off and hunting. We looked in every bed, in every room. I ran beside my mother, standing high on my toes to check into each cot, to see who it was that lay there. In every bed, in every room we searched—until we came to what the young doctor quietly said would be the very last bed. That's where she'd be! Because it was the last bed. Delighted, I ran to her, my blanket, my sweets at the ready, to scoop her up and bring her home. I stopped dead. It was not Moliseng.

In the terrible, scorched odor that emanated from that bed, I instantly wished I had never seen the baby that lay there, with burned arms and legs, its tiny, weeping face in suppurating bandages. Eugenie put her hand to her mouth and stood very still.

"Perhaps we missed something in the records, Mrs. Grace," the doctor said. His eyes lingered on that baby, as though he wished she'd take him.

He looked down at me. I was not at all sure what was happening.

"Come," he said, holding out his hand. He had to say something, so he said, "Come, come, let's go and take another look."

And that meant looking again through the drawers of papers. Not maps, but records, he called them now—records of all the children that lay at Baragwanath that night; records of all the children who had been discharged and had gone home; records of all the children who died there.

. .

I lay in my sheets listening, the dawn light outside relentless, insisting.

"It was an idiotic decision," my father yelled in the passage outside my door. "You jeopardized Elizabeth's life! *And* your own!"

"Would you just *listen* for a second," my mother said.

But in a seething rage fueled by the terrible fright he'd gotten, he would not. He had come home near midnight to find us gone. And the car missing. And Mombadi gone! And Iris asleep on the floor in the lounge, with John falling out of her arms, having screamed himself to sleep, his puffed-up, exhausted face red-hot and angry. And Iris, incoherent in the heart-pounding panic of her sudden waking, stuttering something about Moliseng and a hospital.

He'd been on the phone all bloody night, calling every fucking hospital in the northern suburbs he could think of, he was shouting— never in his direst dreams thinking of Soweto. And when he'd run out the back to the servants' room, he'd found Dubike, a stranger to him, confused, unconscious with exhaustion, passed out like a ghost on Salamina's bed, and Salamina nowhere to be found.

"You jeopardized Elizabeth's life, and your own."

"Just *listen* for a second—"

"You *know* what happens on those streets at night."

"Well, *you're* out there!" she shot back.

"Eugenie," he turned on her, furious, "I understand your concern for Salamina's child, believe me, but to make a *stupid* decision like that, an absolutely dangerous, stupid thing to do, driving through the township in the middle of the bloody night, with our child in the car! Why didn't you phone me?"

"You were operating, it's impossible ever to *find* you."

"Why the hell didn't you phone Baragwanath?" he demanded.

"You know as well as I do," she said, angry as a stifled snake. "I had to go there myself. It's impossible ever to make any sense of anything on the phone, and if Dubike and the mother had already been *told* there was no such child there, how on earth would that have helped? She's just *disappeared.*"

"It was a stupid thing to do," he yelled into her face, outraged that she would offer any justification. "Rash and stupid, Eugenie!"

"All right, it was stupid," her edge-of-tears voice burgeoned into a weeping shout. "I'm stupid. Is that what you want to hear?" She pushed him away. "I'm stupid, stupid, *stupid!*" she cried, bashing her chest with her fist. "This *whole bloody place* is stupid!" She took a few steps back. "I did all I could think of to do, and she's missing, vanished into thin bloody air. Calling me stupid isn't going to find her." Tears started to course down her face.

My father stared at her. "I'll call Johnston," he finally said.

"We looked through Johnston's records, Isaac. There's nothing in there, not a bloody thing. How is this possible? How can this have happened?"

From my door, I saw my mother in the dim light at the end of the passage, small and spent, like someone who'd run a great distance and lost their way at the very end.

"How can this have happened?" she asked again.

My father stood at the window. His eyes drifted over the quiet dawn shadows of the no-peeping-hedges. "God only knows," he said. Just as the dominee and the Afrikaners suspected and feared us, we had begun to suspect and fear them.

I climbed back into my bed. Seeping daylight drenched the shutters. Like us, the sun had gone all the way around the world and back again. Heavy with the warm, agitated drumming of morning insects, I thought about the curl of Moliseng's lip, and the sweet smile that now was nowhere.

. .

Mud-thick silence shrouded the house for two days, the only sound the quickly quieted creak of ropes as I climbed onto the swing. And the weep of berries under the syringa tree, covering the grieving mound of Salamina in a rocking quilt of yellow gold.

I knew I would find her there. Of all the spirits that had fled into the boughs over its hundred years, now enfolded in its leaves, its berries, its aching purple flowers, one might be Moliseng. I knew Salamina would be listening for her.

My mother stayed in her bed. For two days now, I whispered on my swing to the thousand friends, she had slept and slept.

Iris sat with John in her servant's room. The house was unbearably, irredeemably quiet.

Salamina would not come inside. She stayed under the syringa tree, rocking and rocking, the way she had always rocked Moliseng to sleep.

I tried to sing to her, the sleeping song she often sang to fly me deeply away into the night—the song that tells you not to worry, hush, your mother will be there in the morning. *"Thula tu . . . thula baba . . ."* I sang in her Xhosa from my swing, to tell her, "Hush, don't cry . . ." I sang as sweetly as I could. But my voice was small, not mellow like hers. It seemed to flutter away, to hang above us in the leaves.

She never stopped rocking, even when the syringa berries fell down on her, their soft *plip . . . plip* like dew dripping off the leaves to the earth. Then quiet again.

Iris tiptoed to the circle of shade and knelt there to leave a bowl of pumpkin with melting butter, and hot tea. She set it quietly down, and slipped away again. She did not talk to Salamina. I tried to tell her it was there. "Iris has left some soft pumpkin for you," I whispered from my perch, "with some butter and hot *teeea for you . . .*" I softly sang. She could not hear me. She never stopped rocking.

The whole world was suspended in a slow, silent fall.

. .

The phone shrilled the darkened house awake. I grabbed the receiver to pat it down, stop the noise. In a stern whisper, I told whoever was too stupid to know, "My mom is sleeping!" Could I please tell my father an urgent message, a man said, regarding the child of our servant?

I pulled a 4 and 6 and 7610 out of a foggy place in my head where I must have stowed them after my father made me repeat them just in case. I hunted them down on the black phone, one by one, until I heard ringing, and the calming wash of Bekka's voice. Bekka was my father's consulting room nurse—Sesotho—amusing us always by speaking clipped Queen's English. She'd had the unusual chance of an education, and always joked she was "more white than white!"

"Oh, your Deddy Doktah tohld me, if *you* phone, Miss Elizabeth, to put you right through!"

Racked stiff with urgency, I told my father the man's name, Dr. Zwicker. His voice grew quiet, cracked in his throat. "Thank you, my love," he said, as if it was the end of something. "I'll be home in ten minutes. And you must *not* tell Salamina."

I tore up to the syringa tree. The covered heap of her lay deep in its shade, rocking almost imperceptibly now. Through the carpet of berries, I saw glimpses of Zephyr's ragged blanket over her, the one he always wore at the fire to sing his prayer song, the forbidden song. He must have put it over her in the night. Hundreds of berries lay strewn in the folds of her skirt. The comfortless, sinking light of late afternoon streamed through the long-leaf fingers of the thousand silent friends.

..

I flew up the passage behind my father. At my mother's door, I peered into the somber room.

He quietly opened the shutters, then lifted the sash windows, letting the shadows of the almond trees creep in and twine themselves on the floor like tangling ropes come to pull you away. The last of the sun streamed in above my mother's bed, tiny glitter-lights floating in on the dust to help her.

Her hair was damp against the pillow, her sad mouth fallen open in her deep sleep, as if, when her crying ceased, she'd fled to a better place.

"Eugenie," my father said, trying gently to wake her. She did not stir. "Eugenie, wake up, get dressed." He slid his hand under her, lifting her shoulders. Her head fell back, her lips still parted in the deep breaths of sleep. Slowly, her eyelids flickered open to find him there. "Get dressed," he said urgently, "Zwicker has an unidentified child at Tembisa."

"Where's Tembisa . . . ?" she managed.

"It's a brand-new hospital they're building for blacks, out past Edenvale."

"Oh God, Isaac," she started to cry. "It's not her. Did you tell him Baragwanath?"

"Zwicker says this child is under three. He put the word out for us—the doctors have been searching. He said at night now they send the overload from Bara to Tembisa, even though it's not officially open yet, and they're already behind on the paperwork." He sat next to her. "There are no papers . . . no one has claimed her. It could be her."

"Oh God, Isaac," she said, sinking back into his arms, "what if it's not her?"

"I've told Elizabeth *not* to tell Salamina." He looked pointedly to where I hovered in their doorway. He turned back to her and said barely in a whisper, but I heard, "Zwicker says they had three infant deaths at Bara on Thursday, two from dehydration."

He helped her to sit up on the edge of her bed. With the tenderness one might have toward a sleepy child, he managed to guide her into her dress. He knelt beside her to slip her shoes, abandoned like unwanted friends, onto her pallid feet. He pulled her dress straight around her soft, white knees. "Where is your cardigan, Eugenie?" he asked, suddenly impatient. I knew where it was. I looked to the chair where it lay. I'd set it there when I tucked her in.

He picked it up, slipped it around her shoulders, and stood her to her feet like a paper doll that might waft away. "Button your top button, Eugenie," he said. "It's nippy out there."

The sun had gone by the time they walked down the passage. I raced to my room. I grabbed my small pile of sweets to feed Moliseng in case she was starving, with rickets or kwashiorkor, when we found her. I ripped the blanket off my bed in case she was cold, and sped down the passage, out of the kitchen door into the dusk to see the taillights of the car heading out of the gate. I ran down the driveway after them, calling out, but to no avail. The lights of the car were going, going, and the gate closed. I thought my stomach was going to vomit itself out. I pinched between my legs so I wouldn't wet, and all I could hope was that my dad had that special paper. I whimpered back into the house, up the passage to my room, climbed onto my bed, and from some deep and tired place, began to cry. I would not be there to guard them. They would be beaten by the police, chopped into pieces by tsotsis. I knew I would never see them again.

..

At midnight, Iris came in to check on me. My bed was empty. She said she got such a fright her heart jumped right out of her throat. Feeling in my sheets for some part of me, she began to scream, hurtling away from the side of the bed. The stealthy spirit that had stolen Moliseng, and now me, was here. She screamed her way right out of the house, where she caught sudden sight of me, asleep in a dark patch of grass beyond the kitchen steps. I had gone there to keep watch on the gate, waiting for them to return.

All around the patch lay empty sweet papers. Someone had eaten all Moliseng's sweets! Someone, it dawned on me, dissipating my drowsy outrage, might have been me. Someone, I concluded, ate them in their sleep, maybe.

Stiff with cold, I stared at Iris in the dark. She had become very pretty. She knelt down to carry me to my bed and was suddenly lit up in a bright glow from feet to hair, like a shining brown candle in the night. It was the lights of the car!—waiting for the gate to open.

I jumped up. Iris caught me hard by the shoulders. "Wait, Monkey. You wait here with Irissy, jhe?" she said, her sad eyes wide.

Down at the gate the headlights went out. In the pitch dark I heard tires on the dirt driveway. Then silence. I strained against Iris's grip to see through the thick blackness. You could hear only night frogs and crickets now.

There was a momentary flash of light, then dark again. Like rain on the veld—so sweet that sound—I heard my father's polished brown shoes walking around the back of the car. He opened the door. The inside car light shone on my mother's hair. They were alive, and safe.

"Wait, Monkey." Iris caught me again, pressed me to the front of her shaking legs with both arms. "You stay here with Irissy, Monkey."

Their shadows melted away, past the prayerful frangipani, all the way up to the back of the acre, to the syringa tree. Iris, with me, was pulled like a magnet toward them. They vanished into the black again. Iris held her face away.

Still covered in berries, Salamina's rocking had ceased. She had poured her tears into the ground and listened day and night to the branches above for the spirit of Moliseng, for her few, curly lip words. Perhaps as Zephyr had said, Moliseng was waiting there to be carved out and reborn. Iris knew, Zephyr knew, Mombadi and I knew, Salamina felt every berry that fell. Comfort from Moliseng.

My mother knelt down to her. Salamina lifted her head. There in the darkness, wrapped in Eugenie's cardigan, was a small, hidden face—the special, brown face of Moliseng.

Salamina did not move. She stared through her swollen eyes as if she might be dreaming, and then all of a sudden, her mourning cloak of berries lifted into the air like confetti. She leapt up. "Oh, jho . . . Moliseng!" she gasped from the pit of her stomach. Staggering on her feet, she took what was left of her into her arms.

Moliseng was painfully thin, ashen, and too weak to move. Her head fell back in plaintive sobs that made us all feel as though our own tears were coming. And then they did.

"Oh, jho, Moliseng, jhe." Salamina tried to breathe warmth into her, kissing her small cheeks, smelling her over and over just as she had done at her birth. Moliseng had no strength at all. She lay in Salamina's arms like a little bag of bones and skin, her face streaked with exhaustion.

Overcome with joy, I jumped to say hello. "*Dumela*, Moliseng!"

"Be very gentle with her, Elizabeth," my father said, "she's been quite ill. She's still not eating properly and I promised Zwicker I'd watch her."

"Come," said my mother, wiping her eyes, laughing, and chilly because Moliseng was in her jersey. "Let's go inside, it's freezing out here."

Salamina called out to me to stay a bit. Perhaps she had felt me at the swing after all, heard my songs to her after all. I raced back.

"Eleseebett . . ." she said in utter disbelief, with tears of joy at having that tiny picaninn in her arms. "Moliseng, jhe!" She bent down to give me a better view of the lovely, naughty face.

"*Dumela*, Moliseng," I leapt to say again. "*Dumela!*"

Salamina exploded into an ecstatic rhapsody, a frenzied, foot-stamping dance of unbridled gratitude. "Moliseeaang!" she cried. "Moliseng Eleseebett Mashlope!" Once again, Moliseng's name rang out. This time, the sky was dark. This time, it was a prayer of thanks that against all odds, her baby had come home. With wet, wet tears Salamina's eyes blazed with new fire, her feet played on the earth, Moliseng again at her heart.

. .

Luckily, Moliseng was still too sick to eat her sweets. I had demolished them all.

She stayed with us in the big house. Too risky, my father felt, for her to be in Salamina's room, where she might stop breathing at night. A few critical seconds might make all the difference. Instead, she lay in a special cot at the end of my father's bed, where he and my mother took turns watching her overnight. My mother made special porridge for her, with none of the dreaded sour milk that had caused the problem in the first place.

Moliseng seemed bewildered. She did not respond to anyone.

In the mornings, Salamina would come to bring her milk, and would cup her hands to laugh at the sight of her black picaninn tucked into the white Madam's bed, in the crook of the Madam's arm. "Jho, Meddem!" she'd laugh, embarrassed.

My father rigorously examined Mollie every morning and gave her, what I deemed by the sound of her shrieks, painful injections. We blocked our ears to pat it out. She screamed blue bloody murder.

Sometimes during the day she lay in a floppy pile on the blanket under the mimosa trees. Her glistening eyes stared out of deep, sad hollows. Still, she did not respond. It seemed she had forgotten who we were, forgotten who she was. At lunchtime, over jam sandwiches and tea in the shade, Salamina would sing her name in a voice as soft as the yellow pollen sprinkling the highveld air. But she just stared, as though she heard nothing.

"Moliseng," I warned her from time to time, "if you don't eat your spaghetti, the wind will come and pick you up, and carry you far, far away, through the purple flowers of the jacaranda trees, into the yellow clouds of dust over the gold mines, right out over the Indian Ocean, all the way up . . . past the moon, and you will *never* be seen again."

When she was newly up on her tiny feet again, and a bit stronger each day, her legs jumping a bit, Salamina held her little hands and said, "Come, dance with Salamina, Moliseng, jhe? Moli-seng . . . Moli-seng!" she sang. But the speck was too weak, and crumpled down in tears. "Auwh . . ." said Salamina, scooping her up into her arms, dancing with her anyway. Moliseng was comforted by the rocking, by the sound of Salamina's honey voice so near.

"And me, too," I cried. "Uppy, uppy me!"

Salamina looked at me, her arms already full with Moliseng. "Okay, come, you climb up!" she said, bending for me to clamber up onto her back. "Jho, you are too fat, Monkey!" She laughed, heaving the three of us up straight again. "Moliseng, Moliseng Eleseebett Mashlope!" we sang.

The cheek was quickly back in Moliseng. Within six weeks, she was fat, round, shiny, and brown again. She'd begun to giggle and torment, and was even trying to bloemin' climb up the syringa tree behind me.

"Monkey too fat!" she relentlessly teased.

"I'm not fat, Moliseng, *you* are *fat.*"

We were all on the mend. Each morning found me at my self-appointed post, the bedroom shutters, checking the wind to see if it was coming to blow her away again.

PART THREE

. . . .

CHAPTER SEVEN

LAST TOUCH

◎◎

In the two years that followed, we were safe and sound. No one went missing. None of *us,* that is.

Bram Fischer, the Afrikaans lawyer who had defended the Rivonia men, had gone underground. He was facing sentencing on charges of treason for his efforts on their behalf. Before he vanished, he wrote to the magistrate who was to sentence him that he did not fear punishment but that he would not obey inhumane laws. Within a short eleven months, by November 1965, he had been caught and re-arrested. My father spoke sometimes at the dinner table of these Rivonia men, including Walter Sisulu; Mandela, who had worn skins at his first trial; Dennis Goldberg; James Kantor; and Elias Motsoaledi, all rendered missing by the government. The whites among them were imprisoned in Pretoria, the blacks banished for life to a small dot of land off Cape Town, Robben Island, from where, only if you were shlana, as Sala-mina would say, only if you wished to be eaten by sharks or battered to death against the rocks by vicious Cape seas, only if you were com-pletely shlana, you might attempt to swim to the mainland. Robben Island, where the face, the touch of a loved one, would be like a flake of snow in the Sahara.

Some daily newspapers, the *Rand Daily Mail,* the *Sunday Times,* and a few others tried to report on those who had been rendered silent, and were rendered silent themselves. One newspaper had blas-phemously dared publish the names of top Broederbond members, including the name of an official in Parliament. Their offices were ran-sacked by night, and by day their editors faced serious charges. Editors continued their jockeying with the government, trying to squeeze in-formation to the public in low-key, ambiguous articles tucked deep in their publications. Other editors, who now safely and secretly belonged to the Broederbond, championed the government's new, stringent censorship laws, citing, my father joked with my mother, the safety of the people. Better that we did not know, they felt. Faces of those under arrest sometimes stared out of our newspapers. Tortured for trying to overthrow the government, they fell in a mysterious, mangled parade from the seventh floor of police headquarters at John Vorster Square in Johannesburg onto the city street below. So distressed these prison-ers were, police said, at their own betrayals, they'd flung themselves from the windows, committing suicide. "*Allegedly,*" said my father, whose mood altered for weeks each time it happened. Money still changed hands at night under the syringa tree at the back of our acre, small efforts at safe passage out of the country for dissenting voices, so they could bring their words, their tears, their hopes, to the world out-side. But I did not know that. When I asked my father one night what the money in those envelopes changing hands at the fire some nights was for, he looked away and said, "For food, Elizabeth."

At the boxy house, John had grown into a spindly fellow with a sweet face, and an even sweeter nature. He no longer spat porridge.

He and Moliseng climbed the tree faster than I could. We perched up there like monkeys, eating stolen peaches from the dominee's yard, passed through to us by wry Zephyr, until we were sick. Occasionally in the mornings, the ground below would be strewn with berries.

Even Loeska had mellowed, followed surprisingly in her whim by the dominee. He'd been apprised of the near loss of Salamina's baby by Willery, tearful and unable to get through her work the day it happened. His softening was gauged by the fact that Loeska ventured to the fence again, and sometimes even over it to my side, albeit for precious, brief minutes at a time. Probably because of Moliseng's ordeal, and Loeska's own horrible brush with the death monkey, Loeska no longer seemed to notice the backyard blot of Moliseng, who could, by Loeska's decree, play nearby but who was not allowed to touch the bikes—silver or red. Moliseng now knew well the dangers of being sent back to Soweto, and never ran into the front yard or near the street. Like a well-trained little dog who had never tasted delicious red meat, she was content with the crumbs of life in the back.

From time to time, sweating policemen knocked at our door. The black policeman still jumped from the back of the van where he rode to run up the driveway. Element of surprise, they called it. He still dealt politely with whomever he found in the back, if he or she presented a pass. If not, his truncheon came out and they were soon *knopkierie* beaten into the police van. Moliseng became accustomed to being slipped and scraped here and there—under fences, into bushes, once between the lavatory cistern and the bathroom wall in the servants' rooms, and covered with a dirty, wet towel by wily Iris. A tiny ghost, she appeared and disappeared, her whisper, "Hide away, hide away, Moliseng hide away . . ." often the last murmur from her on the wind, until the danger had passed.

Best of all, in tandem with Moliseng's recovery, my mother bloomed once more. Our boxy house gradually filled with better furniture as my father's practice grew. A few nice things arrived for all of us, including, early one morning, a bike for me (out went my tongue! over the bushes to the still-sleeping Loeska) and two tricycles, one maroon, for John, and one for Moliseng, silver! We rolled around in the back like kings, tinkling our bells. We examined ants, sang, and covered ourselves in mud till the moon came up.

At night, we stole out to the fire and sometimes found my father already there, watching at a distance as Zephyr sang "Nkosi Sikelel' iAfrika" to a God he was beginning to feel had deserted him.

I knew the day was fast approaching that Moliseng would be legally obligated to go to school. And that, of course, meant Soweto. While no one spoke of it, a silent countdown continued in all our minds.

"Monkey?" I heard Salamina summon one day. "Come down. Moliseng she wants to say good-bye to you."

"Ah, but it's not Friday yet?" I argued, slithering down to the patch of shade where Moliseng stood in stiff, starched clothes for her return to Soweto. I knew it would be a Friday, the day of the most trains to the township.

"Yes, it's Friday, Miss Lizzy," Salamina said, her voice calm and final.

I stared at Moliseng in her proud, new things.

"Moliseng going to big school, in Soweto," she beamed, dancing in the dust just like the township picaninns, to show me.

"Big school in Soweto, Mollie," I said, dancing a little too, but my throat felt lumpy, and suddenly sad. "Wait," I said, trying to think of something she might need there. I turned to run and fetch it. Crayons, maybe, something from the house, to give her.

"No, Miss Lizzy." Salamina stopped me. "We are late. My mother, she is waiting for Moliseng on the train." She turned to Mollie. "Come, say good-bye to Miss Lizzy."

Moliseng stepped forward. "Good-bye, Miss Lizzy Monkey," she said. "I love you. Cover me with kisses?" She grabbed me by the ears and smothered me in loud, smacking kisses.

"I love you, Mollie. . . ." I kissed her back, jumping and dancing with her. "Don't pull anyone's hair there!" I called after her as they walked away, and then wished I could tell her a hundred more things.

Salamina had left a small, scuffed suitcase by the barren orange tree near the laundry, filled with Moliseng's belongings. She picked it up, took Mollie's hand, and they walked down the driveway. Moliseng's life with us was over. Salamina would now see her only once a week, on one of her off-days. Mollie could try to return over the weekends, but not every weekend, as that would draw attention to her comings and goings, and now that she was getting older, people might not be so willing to turn a blind eye.

"Bye, Mollie," I shouted after them. "Bye, bye . . ."

I stood at the gate, and watched until they disappeared up Bell Street, where I knew they would wait for several hours for a bus to take Moliseng home, to Soweto.

. .

In the empty days that followed, John cried because he hadn't realized Moliseng was not coming back. And I cried in my tree because my friend was gone. We both missed her.

Although Salamina said nothing, we felt the hole in her heart. On Thursday mornings, where she never had before, she would rush to leave in the hope of making a train to Soweto. And on Friday when she returned, she would say nothing and smooth our heads with her rough hands, as though we were her very own.

I did not want to think of Moliseng like the picaninns who ran after our bus in the township, with runny noses and caked-on flies. So I did not. I did not want to think of her running under the wheels of a car, with no fence at their corrugated tin shack. So I did not. I did not want to think of her trying to stay warm with no jersey, or falling into a fire on the sand floor of her hut. So I did not. And I did not want to think of sour milk, or the horrible stench of Baragwanath. So I did not.

My mother, despite her protestations, continued to assist my father from time to time, stitching heads in the township hospitals, but less frequently now. She preferred her own sewing. My father, too, had scaled back his night forays into the townships and spent his spare time at the Workers Rehabilitation Hospital in Joubert Park, attending to casualties from the mines out on the gold Reef. Grafting skin for burns and complex surgeries on crushed torsos and limbs were everyday work. His practice on Bell Street thrived. Suppers often lay late into the night on the warming plate, waiting for him, as I did, until he was safely home. He still insisted there was no God.

My mother took much more joy in us. I lay in her arms under the acacia trees in the afternoons, smoothed by her caress like a downy robin, along with John. We gorged on buttered Marie biscuits. She smiled at us, said how much she loved us, told us funny stories and sang sweet songs. She put me to bed sometimes, and sang to me then also, and I fell asleep at night not wondering, but knowing she would be there in the morning.

I was also saved over the next melancholy months without Moliseng by an unexpected visit to Clova. With ongoing shoulder pain, my grandfather needed further treatment, and when it came time for him to return to the farm again, we drove him to Joubert Park station near the center of town.

Jostled along the coal-smell platform after the final call, we hunted for his name pinned to one of the green carriages. He hopped on board in the nick of time and delighted us by pushing down the window of his sleeping compartment within seconds to wave good-bye. "Last touch!" he called down through the echoing announcements. The train hissed, its steel wheels igniting quick sparks on the rail. I reached up to his hands: "Gifts, friends, foes . . ." The train jolted and began to pull him away. His earth-rough hands were going, going . . . I leapt up to them, grasped them with all my might, and suddenly my bare feet were climbing *slap-slap* right up the side of the train *into* the window and I was off to Clova. My mother ran desperately alongside trying to retrieve me, but to no avail.

"Good Lord!" he said, staring down at me, and then waved through the window to allay my mother's fears. In the slow, beautiful sway of the train leaving the station, I realized that in my haste I had made a shameful error. "Hah . . . I forgot to put on my undies."

He leaned down, his unexpected charge barefoot and with no underpants. "Maybe Grandpa George can open the shop on the farm for you, and give you some picaninni undies?"

"Picaninni undies?" I cried. "I'm not wearing *picaninni* undies!" I pressed close to confide, "I have *Princess* undies, from Wool . . . worth's!"

At five the next morning, we rumpled out of our sleeping berth as the train stopped for early-morning bitter coffee at Soekmekaar, just as it had, my grandfather said, when he first came looking for Clova, and Clova was looking for him.

Later that day, despite my dismayed protestations as I ran along behind him, he opened the door of the shop, a mud rondawel with a smooth, mud floor, patted and caked down to perfection, under a thatched roof that smelled of burning fires.

"Picaninni undies are good enough for picaninns, they are good enough for you, my girl."

In the familiar African smell of malt, kaffircorn, and mielies, we hunted for underpants. Seeing the shop open, picaninns and natives filed in, looking for pipe cleaners, tobacco, brown bread, toilet paper, Koo jam, and matches. I climbed up onto the cool, dark-wood counter where the transistor with its long aerial fudged and crackled Spring-bok Radio news.

Meendli and Mphunie planted themselves on the hessian sacks like giant grasshoppers, their beanstalk knees jutting up around their ears. They ran their hands through the dusty, skin-matching brown barley and spat flat, white Hubbard squash pips like projectiles across the mud floor. Mphunie, given the advantage of a massive spitting gap between his front teeth, was still the cleverest, and because of the gap looked alarmingly each time as though he'd spat out an enormous tooth.

One of the Vendas stood against the counter where I sat, sharpening a series of knives used in the monthly throat-slitting of a pig or cow. Another stood at the paraffin pump quietly filling the little silver tins that lit the farm with flickering flames like a fairyland at nighttime. The glinting knives on the slippery counter shifted as he leaned, then clattered to the floor. My grandfather bent to pick them up, and handed them back to him.

"Yes, m'baas," the Venda said, and continued to sharpen. His name was Thoyo, not the same as but inspired by Thoho-ya-Ndou, the legendary leader of the Vendas, and it meant "head of an elephant." Like all the others, he was blacker than black, with wild, red eyes, and his scarred, bare chest bore a lifetime of tribal struggle. Some people said the Vendas were the stupidest of all the blacks, but when Thoyo looked into my grandfather's eyes and took the knives, I saw ancient knowing in his own.

I quickly lost interest in helping to find underpants I did not want in amongst the small, cotton dresses and shorts kept for the picaninns, and instead swirled myself in the bright blue cotton batik-cloths preferred by Gladness and Sweetness. I monkeyed up the shelves to raid the Chappies bubble-gum jar. Devouring the sweet of it, I read the inside of the wrapper to Meendli and Mphunie: "*Did you know . . .* that cannibals eat the flesh of their own kind?" No, they did not know.

"Here!" my grandfather said, triumphantly holding up a voluminous pair of white-cotton picaninn underpants. Unfortunately, there were no bloemin' small ones left in his shop, only size large—and they were stretchy. He held them up against me like a flopped parachute.

"Aahg, no, man," I argued, florid with embarrassment, the waist elastic right up to my armpits.

"Come," he said, hatching some or other ghastly plan.

We carried them back to the farmhouse and announced, "We've got an underpants emergency."

Undaunted, my grandmother sewed two pieces of wide elastic onto the waistband, creating lovely straps to go over each of my shoulders, solving the falling-down problem. Actually, picaninn undies were jolly nice! Soft, comfy, and roomy. Only the picaninns thought me funny-looking, giggling their heads off when I came by, but I didn't care. In the blistering heat, I ran around in those and nothing else but my dirty hat, and even went for my last-day *goef* in them, my swim in the cow trough. My grandfather said they were practical, cool, and smart, and perfect for Africa.

I swam and swam. He lit his pipe, leaned against the tractor, and watched for signs of Mahila in the dusk now falling like a shroud over the Soutpansberg Mountains.

..

He must have stood in the foothills, looking south.

Safely tucked back in my Johannesburg bed, home from Clova for less than two weeks, I knew nothing of this man. The only person who had caught a glimpse of him said he was tall, black, and wore a stolen jacket bearing the insignia of the Rhodesian Army.

It appeared, from a rough campfire of twigs and from discarded cigarette butts, that he had made a sleeping place in the foothills. Looking south from there during the night, he would have seen rolling farmlands, under thick-flung stars, lying like dark velvet ahead of him. He may have heard the rush of the mighty Limpopo up north, and the screams of Samango monkeys leaving their summit vines for lower-lying land, where they could find water, and rest.

He had no fear. He slept where starving, ridgeback creatures like Tarzan once had, where rhino and leopards roamed the dark in search of food. Perhaps he felt himself one of them.

He was in a new land. And this was a new time.

He must have dug in the earth with his bare hands. From dried-out pieces of baobab root found there later, he must have crouched by the fire, and used the sharp knife in his jacket pocket to peel the bark away. And as he ate and looked south into the darkness from there, the farmhouse must have seemed like a tiny jewel, glowing with the last flicker of paraffin.

The Vendas on the farm lay quiet that night, and quiet the next, when at dusk, the man began to walk toward the house.

In their sleep, they would not know this man, but waking, they knew with inevitability, from hushed superstition and from their own bitter experience, that one day, one night, someone would come. Someone would want the land back.

Tarzan lay sleeping at the end of his chain. His muscles twitched in sweet remembrance.

With the stealth of a panther the man came within one hundred yards of the farmhouse, to where the blue plumbagos began lining the path to the outside lavatory. Tarzan woke, stood suddenly, and stayed standing. His old ears deaf as posts, his skin prickled alive. He did not hear the call from the crimson throat of the loerie bird. He did not know the hunter was approaching.

The clatter of the chain stopped the man in his tracks, but the ensuing silence gave permission. He would avoid the blazing-eyed old guard at the kitchen door. He made a wide berth past the aloes, pointing like spears into the night, then cut through the plumbagos. Still he had no fear. He climbed the steps up to the red, polished floor of the stoep. He must have paused there.

Then he simply walked right into the open front door of the farmhouse.

My grandfather George remarked from the bedroom that it was unusual to hear the pierce of a loerie, called out like that after dark. Down the passage, my grandmother closed the bathroom door, and in the pride-of-the-farmhouse inside bathroom, began running the water for her bath. She opened the sash window to let in the still, night air, lit the candle on the window ledge, and lowered the paraffin lamp to a glow.

The man kept walking. He went straight down the passage, past the closed bathroom door toward the bedroom. George must have been looking north out of the dark window toward the mountain, facing away from the door, as he sometimes did in the evenings. Eighty-two, and partially deaf, like Tarzan he heard nothing. With all the hatred the man's life had engendered, he lifted his knife and plunged it into George's back, shattering his brittle ribs. Before George could turn, he retrieved it, then forged it in again, puncturing the lung beneath. George fell to his knees. He called out. The man plunged the knife in again, and again. George crawled toward the bed. If he could open the trunk, if he could find the gun . . . It had never been at arm's reach. It belonged to another time, another struggle.

He slumped over the bed, gasping for air, his lungs, his mouth, filling with blood. The sheets where he kneeled turned bright red beneath him.

The man sensed the value of what lay beneath the bed. He pulled the trunk out and kicked it out of reach. He buried the knife into George, again, and again, and again. Twenty-two times, he stabbed.

In the bathroom, my grandmother picked up the paraffin lamp, thinking she'd heard a noise in the bedroom—thinking she'd heard George calling her.

She opened the bathroom door. A man stood there, in the passage, blood spattered down the front of his shirt, and a knife in his hand. In fright, she pushed the lamp at him. Towering over her, he pushed it back, smashing the glass into her face, cutting her through her eye from forehead to cheek as the boiling paraffin scalded her neck, and melted like butter the pale, soft skin of her shoulder and breast.

In searing pain, she slumped to the floor. She heard the man return to the bedroom. She heard the trunk being kicked open, things thrown to the floor. Money, he wants money, she thought. He'll find the money, he'll go. She heard nothing from George. She lay still, until she heard the man's footsteps head back toward the front door, and stop. Was he in the living room, on the stoep? What was he waiting for? Why did he not leave?

Crawling down the passage toward the phone, she suddenly saw the man through the sash window that gave out onto the stoep. He was looking toward the mountain, his knife in one hand, and George's medals for bravery clutched in the other. He moved to the right of the window, out of the moonlight, into the shadow of the Yesterday, Today, and Tomorrow.

When she could no longer see him, and had heard nothing for several minutes, she crawled further toward the phone. The operator from the post office would be long gone. She lifted the receiver . . . voices, someone on the lines . . . "Dawn . . . Thom, is that you?" she whispered. "Quickly," she said, not daring to move in case he was back in the house. "It's Beth . . . Elizabeth . . . , come quickly, we've been attacked. George needs help, *quickly* come . . . Clova."

She crawled further down the passage, trying to get to George. Suddenly again, footsteps. She pulled herself into the alcove of the linen cupboard and covered her mouth with her hand, trying not to cry out.

The man walked back up the passage, ransacked the trunk again, this time for money. Forty pounds, their life savings. He grabbed a bundle of old letters and stuffed them into his stolen jacket. She heard the click and clatter of the old rifle as he cocked it . . . cocked it again.

Then he walked out of the front door. He went down past the moonlight blue of the plumbagos. Reaching the wire gate, he began to run with his newfound wealth toward the mountain, back into the night.

The nearest farm was twenty miles away. By the time Uncle Thom started his old car and sped heart in throat through the dark to get to them, the bathwater, still running, had turned the farmhouse into a river of blood.

. .

The phone rang at nine on Monday evening. Moliseng had just left to go back to Soweto after being spirited in for a Sunday visit. We had not seen her in many months and she was a bit taller, and a lot thinner. Arriving, she'd run arms open wide to me and I to her all the way down to the gate. She'd leapt up onto me like a praying mantis, wrapping her bony legs around my waist, to smell my neck and tell me, "*Dumela! Dumela,* Monkey, *dumela!*"

We'd had a high time. We feasted on peaches, tormented one another, and covered each other with kisses at the end. Now, in the ensuing quiet, I thought myself the luckiest fish alive because my father, who was usually out saving everybody's life, was home. "Take a Disprin and go to bed!" John and I prescribed to the ringing phone, wagging our fingers in our ears. "Leave us in pieces and quiet!"

"Shh . . ." my father said, picking up the receiver. "Hello . . . yes, this is Dr. Grace." His hand went up into the air, then fell like a smothering pillow over his eyes. "Oh my God . . ." he said. "God, no."

An immediate and horrible silence blanketed the house. Iris was instructed to take John and get him to sleep. Salamina put me to bed. Now she sat with me hours later in the dark, her rough Xhosa hand on me. Her eyes looked away. Her hand kept trying to soothe me, but it, too, turned away to cover her eyes.

"What happened, Sal?" I whispered in the tomb of my bed. "What happened?"

"Go to sleep, Miss Lizzy," she said abruptly. "You go to sleep, jhe."

"But what happened?" I dared again.

"It's a terrible accident, Monkey," she said, "a very bad *accident*." As if what had happened could not possibly have been done on purpose. "You go to sleep, jhe!" She looked away again, all the way away as if to the beginning of time. "Auw, jhoah . . ." she cried, tears she did not want me to see streaming. She tried to sing to me. "Your mother will be here, *Thula baba* . . ." she began. And again, she turned away.

All night long Salamina sat by my bed. I could hear my mother running in and out of the house, searching for, then demanding the car keys. My father had them. He repeatedly refused to give them up. Was she finally running away? And then I heard it, that word—gun. My mother was looking for the gun.

Like the end of a terrible battle obliterating all worries, tiny glints of light in an endless stream floated in the dark hollow above my bed, come to lull me away from my mother's night of tears into a deep sleep.

. .

In the backseat, speeding north from Johannesburg, I stretched my hands right out of the car window into the wild, dry air, patting it down, down and away for all I was worth. Nothing would happen.

Rustled from bed in the cold dark before dawn and hurried with John in silence by my father to the car, the drone of the engine had soon seduced me back to oblivion. I had no idea we were going to Clova until I woke in my blanket on the backseat. Whatever had happened must have happened at Clova. *Godwon'tletanythinghappen.* My busy hands made sure everyone was alive, made certain no crippling spells were riding on the air. *Pat it down, pat it down.* If I did it exactly right, this day would vanish like the deer into the heat.

We drove hell for leather, my father tense and exhausted at the wheel. We tore past the gold mines, onto the Great North Road, and out into the barren veld. "Eugenie, try to sleep," my father said on the outskirts of Johannesburg, and then again two hours later, around Warmbaths. But her swollen eyes stared out of the windows, seeing nothing. She didn't answer, and he didn't try again. He just drove.

We did not stop at Warmbaths to swim in the hot pools. We did not have egg sandwiches with wilting lettuce and tea at the side of the road on the cool, stone benches of shady rest stops. Instead, the sun scorched the back of the car for hours. Like steam off a split potato, heat rose off it in waves. We ploughed straight through, and turned off at Bandelierkop onto the red, sandy road where the ancient earth lay packed flat with the pounding of Mahila's feet. I felt the tires suddenly rattle where he had run.

I leapt from my cocoon, shouting out of the rolled-down window of the car into the dust, rigid glad to see the big wire gate ahead. "Open the gate, we've arrived!" I cried. But on this day, not my grandfather in his crisply ironed, khaki shirt smelling of Sunlight soap, always relieved to see our hot faces after the long drive—not him, but a strange man in a navy serge uniform and cap loomed out of the cloud of dust that brought us to the gate. Two strange trucks, one with a blue light on top, the other a tan bakkie, were parked up at the front door of the farmhouse. No joyful picaninn chatter cheered us in. Meendli, nowhere to be seen.

I crumpled back into the sweet, confused smell of polish. "The police are here," I blurted out. My father got out of the car. He lifted the thin wire loop that latched the gate. It swung open in stinging quiet.

"As you well know," the policeman said, shaking my father's hand, "there is not a single door on this farmhouse that has a lock on it."

We walked in silence toward the house. Like all things that creep up on you in the dead of night when your guard is down, come to make everything fall down crippled, all would become clear that morning. Shadows played on the cool cracks of the stoep.

Tarzan whimpered at the kitchen door, his old eyes crusted over.

Pat it down, pat it down, in my head as we walked.

"There's a murderer out there," the policeman said, "wiff medals for courage and bravery pinned to his jacket." He was out of breath. Sweat coursed down his burnt neck when he took off his cap. They'd been out all night searching the length and breadth of the farm, and beyond into the foothills, where they'd found abandoned evidence. Ashes from a small fire, and some stripped bark. Someone had been there. Someone had been sleeping in the mountain.

Around the front of the house, picaninns stood in abject quiet, huddled under the thorn tree. Vendas stood like black marble, still as the night, eyes streaming.

Thoyo was up on the stoep, sitting on the top stair, elbows on his long, black legs, oblivious as police walked in and out of the farmhouse. His cracked hands cradled his head. Gladness, who could barely speak through her tears, told us that Thoyo was the only one who had heard something. He had suddenly risen from his sleeping mat down at the kraal, thinking for a moment it was just a loerie, and then fallen back to sleep. But then, he thought he heard the cry of old Master George.

Thoyo had grabbed his knives, his beautifully sharpened knives, and run toward the farmhouse.

He was too late. He found my grandfather kneeling over the bed, bleeding profusely. He cradled George and lifted him in his sinewy arms up off the floor and onto the bed. "Yes, my baas, my Master, my baas," Thoyo had tried to comfort him. Then Thoyo ran from the farmhouse, searching, his eyes blurred. But the one who had come to take the land had fled.

Smeared with George Waltham's blood and carrying sharp knives, police thought Thoyo had done this, until my grandmother said firmly, "No, the man was not one of ours."

Now Thoyo, like Tarzan, sat in grief and shame, enraged at himself that he had not heard the feet of this thief, had not seen the deadly glow of his eyes in the dark, had not been swift enough to track him and take his life for the cowardice of his deed.

My grandfather was dead, his body already quietly taken from the farm. My grandmother lay at Elim hospital, miles away—Elim, where my mother had been born.

As the light faded into evening, we sat on the stoep in cold silence, and tears that would not stop. No faraway sound of Meendli's mouth harp. Meendli was still nowhere to be found. We heard only the screams in the hills that night, of Thoyo, hurling his grief, and ours, into the wind.

. .

When we buried my grandfather, my grandmother sat very quiet and still. The skin on her face, neck, and much of her shoulder still wept with burns. It was as if she saw and heard nothing. In the hospital, she had repeatedly asked, "What did they want, Dr. Winston, what did they want? Did you know, they took his medals, his war medals from the trunk under our bed. They *took* them." Then she sat on the end of the hospital bed, staring ahead as though she could see whoever he was running through the hills soaked in blood, sporting the medals of the man he had murdered. Her hand inadvertently folded and re-folded the edge of the hospital sheet, pleating her life back into place.

My mother had had to be restrained when we first arrived at Clova, when Sergeant Potgieter said, "We believe he was a freedom fighter from Rhodesia, who slipped across the border at nighttime, at Beit Bridge, you know. Ja, there by Beit Bridge, we think." Beit Bridge was a hundred miles north of Clova, on the Rhodesian border.

"What does murdering people have to do with freedom?" my mother screamed, and seemed to want to run into the hills herself to find this man, to demand that he answer her. My father held her arms down to her sides, then carried her crying like a child, to lie down.

Now we stood, huddled around a hole in the earth at the small, bleak cemetery on the outskirts of Louis Trichardt, forty minutes by car to the east of Clova. The wind swirled around us in a lonely wail. It lifted the dust at our feet and curled it over the edges of the grave, softening the dark pit, making it seem kinder.

"Let us pray," Father Montford said into our grief.

"*... our life, our sweetness, and our hope.*
To thee do we cry,
poor banished children of Eve ..."

I looked up and saw, across the veld, a tall Venda slowly approaching. I saw another, then another, then several more. They must have walked for hours, many all the way from Clova, many from the farms around us. Soon a column of Vendas, led by Thoyo, wound toward us through the windswept, graveyard veld. Many I had never seen before: those from Last Post, Uncle Thom's farm; from Ladybrand; from Edenvale farm; and from Golden Hill. Like an army of men, they walked in silent unison, shoulders gleaming in the sad light, their tearstained women following, wrapped in black batik-cloths. And quietly behind them, the Clova picaninns, all wearing white shirts from my grandfather's shop.

Father Montford waited until they had gathered, a wall of comfort, around us. Then slowly, he resumed.

"To thee, do we send up our sighs,
Mourning and weeping in this vale of tears. . . ."

My grandfather was lowered down into the ground. I thought of his hands. I thought of gifts. I thought of friends—how he had been mine. I wondered if he could ever have imagined a hundred Vendas come to say good-bye.

And I thought of foes.

Even as I wanted to pat him down into a rose-brown blanket of earth, where he would be safe and warm, I could not think about leaving him there. Father Montford continued his soft-spoken Irish words:

"Turn then, most gracious advocate,
thine eyes of mercy towards us, and after this exile . . ."

When it was over, we walked away. The Vendas stayed by George Waltham's grave to mourn him into the night. We left him tucked deep into the dark soil close to the place he loved, close to the land no one had wanted, where, trying to forget, trying to redeem himself, he had brought barren earth back to life.

..

We returned to Johannesburg after finding my gran Elizabeth a new place to live on the outskirts of Louis Trichardt. The deep scar across her still violet blue eyes lay stamped into her face as a reminder. She would feel strange, she'd said, in a big city like Joburg, and would rather be close to friends, to the land, and to the place where George lay buried. It was really George she could not leave, she finally said.

Her small new flat smelled of fresh white paint. Her furniture, scaled down for its new home, seemed lost and out of place. She'd brought the sideboard that housed the Spode china with those pretty green birds on the cups. The clock that had kept us all in time at Clova seemed loud, its ticking slow, clanging, in the quiet.

From the kitchen fireplace at the farm, she'd brought a hand-painted fire screen depicting English boats in full sail for her modest new fireplace, and a comfortable button-tufted chair or two from the front room. A neat pile of linen tablecloths lay folded and put away with their memories in a new drawer.

Her dresses hung lonely in the cupboard, and her few glass dressing-table bottles, which had once glittered with the simple, poor elegance of candlelight at Clova, now seemed like a small collection of dusty figures on a faded doily. Her land and life were reduced to a few chosen objects and the solitary ticking of a clock. We left her there, brave and smiling, waving good-bye to us as we drove away.

No one said, "Last touch."

No one wanted to return to Clova. No one spoke of it. We did not turn off at Bandelierkop, or come to the wire gate to say good-bye. We headed south.

When my mother arrived in Johannesburg, depression over-whelmed her. Whatever courage she'd found the night we drove through the dark into Soweto to search for Moliseng, and whatever pride she'd felt in finding her against impossible odds, now seemed to evaporate. She took to her bed for long periods of time. John and I were left to our own devices, which meant a few heated word battles at the fence with Loeska, and many hours of taking solace in the leaves of the syringa tree.

Moliseng came twice more, but nothing was quite the same. She seemed thinner each time I saw her, her skin a bit rough and a bit ashy, although she had no flies and seemed to be well. My father gave Salamina vitamins for her, with strict instructions for her grandmother in Soweto not to forget to administer them, and to do so correctly. Moliseng stayed for fewer hours, Salamina anxious about getting her back and causing us no further problem.

Salamina was not the same. I tried walking around her, to steal into her gaze from the other side, but each time, she would cover her eyes with her hand and look away. What had I done to so displease her? One day I asked her with a lump in my throat, "Sal, why are you cross? Are you cross with us?"

"Jho, Miss Lizzy," she said. A huge tear streamed down her cheek, and then another. She covered her whole face and said very quietly, "No, Miss Lizzy . . ."

A few weeks later, when she didn't bring the tea in the morning, did not, with her carefully starched cotton doek on her head and her morning-skin smelling sweet, set it as usual quietly down beside our beds as we slept, we realized she must be sick. It was not yet light. With the box of Hulett's sugar from the kitchen cupboard and a few nice biscuits to fix her ailment, John and I, still in pajamas, scampered out of the kitchen door to find her. We raced over early lawn still sharp with dew, past the granadilla vines, past the frangipani, along the still-sleeping cricket grove, down to her servant's room to clamber with wet-grass feet up onto her high bed.

Everything was gone.

All that remained was the bed up on bricks and the dank, sweet scent of her—lingering like a punishment.

In terror, we shouted for my mother, who, still in her nightie, managed to get herself down to the servants' rooms to see what had happened.

Iris, with the saddest face, said she knew nothing. And Peter

Mombadi knew nothing. They, too, had woken to find Salamina gone. My mother, tears starting to run again, stood in disbelief at Salamina's door, staring at the empty room where Moliseng had been born, and said quietly, "You take them in, treat them as one of your own, and they disappear without a word, in the middle of the night." She extended her hand, as if to retrieve something from the cold, hollow space in front of us. "Moliseng . . ."

It dawned on me in hideous slow motion that Salamina was gone, forever. And she had taken Moliseng with her. I ran, screaming across the peeping-hedges, "Zephyr . . . Zephyr!" I called until I could see his bent silhouette moving through the fruit trees. "Zephyr," I cried, unable to breathe, "Salamina's gone!"

He knew. "She's gone, Miss Lizzy."

I stared up at him, and felt some happy thing in my heart leap. "Where is she hiding?" I smiled, realizing this was just a joke.

"She's gone, Miss Lizzy." Zephyr bent to me and said kindly, "We are going to find a new somebody for you."

"I don't want a new somebody," I said, "I want Sal, I want Salamina." I started to cry, choking sobs that came out of nowhere and shook my whole body. "Why, Zephyr, why?"

He leaned down to me, his face full in mine, his old eyes moist. "She was ashamed. Ashamed. Your grandfather, Miss Lizzy." He beat his fist into his chest. "We all of us, we carry the sin of our brother." He spat with disdain into the earth. "She was ashamed."

"Why, Zephyr? Why, why, why?" I cried, streaming with tears and fright.

He lifted his blazing eyes to the God that had denied him for so long. "We've got no answer for this place, Miss Lizzy."

He turned to go, then stopped, looked back at me. His crusty, fingerless hand wiped my face. "No more tears," he said. "No more tears."

My heart burned. Who would pick me up and call me Monkey? Who would light up at the sight of me, rock me to sleep, and keep a warm hand on me until I fell away? Who would sing my sleeping song, now that I knew my mother, in her grief, could never really be there in the morning? Why had Salamina not woken me? Why had she not said good-bye? "You must go and find her, and tell her," I sobbed, "tell her to come home."

He walked up the path ahead of me, the way Salamina always had. "Come . . . you come," he said, and like an orphan, I followed him.

..

For days I looked everywhere for Salamina. I refused to believe she would not return.

I stole out nightly to the fire, sure she would have come back. I waited day and night at the gate for her, searching as far as my eyes could see up Flora Street and beyond, where the buses came in from the townships. I watched nannies passing on our street. I might see her, I thought, in her orange doek, out on the road there, and I could call out to her to come home. Perhaps she had preferred some other children. She must have found children she loved more than us.

At supper I told my father what Zephyr had said, that Salamina was ashamed. "There are things we don't always understand, Elizabeth," he said. "Zephyr is right. Sometimes, we have no answers."

Later that night he came to sit by my bed as I tried to fall asleep, and asked me to promise I would keep a secret. I was soon going to be eleven, I reminded him, of course I could keep a secret. He said Salamina and Zephyr had been illicitly helping people, those who came through the darkness around the fire at nighttime, those who were trying to work for change.

"What does that mean?" I asked.

"There are people who are now banned for their efforts, banned by our government, Elizabeth. They are separated from their families, thrown into solitary confinement, some have been deported, some sent away to life imprisonment. It means that those who remain have to work in secret to help the blacks to have a voice."

He told me that Zephyr's prayer song was indeed a prayer for change in our country, and that Salamina had more than once hidden under her brick-high bed someone fleeing from police or carrying a message. Salamina had held in her safekeeping money, he said, in brown envelopes kept under her mattress, to help those who had to be spirited out of the country.

"Are those the people in our tree at night?" I asked him.

"Some of them, Lizzy. Some just don't have a pass, but some are trying to do something to help, and they cannot afford to be caught."

"Like the freedom fighter who killed Grandpa?"

"Not like him, Elizabeth. Freedom is hard won. What he did had nothing to do with freedom."

I wanted to tell Salamina that what had happened at Clova had nothing to do with her, and that I understood now why she could not look into my sad eyes. Each day I awoke with hope she would return, and I continued to wait for her, often until the moon rose over the veld and quieted me to sleep on the concrete step of her empty room.

. .

Over the next several years, to my great relief, I mysteriously grew into a lanky girl of sixteen, with a modicum of prettiness. I'd finally adapted to my long feet, which now seemed the right size for my body. Even my tufts metamorphosed into a thick ponytail that fell well below my shoulders. I was astonished that overnight I had indeed become something of a lady, after all. My nails were clean and shiny like my mother's. The monkey I once was had been cast off, like my mud coat, and left somewhere, like a little fallen shadow.

Of course, on the score of ladylike demeanor, Loeska outdid us all. Being older, she had applied to study at Pretoria University, the bastion of high Afrikanerdom. She would be majoring in Afrikaans Language and Culture, and learning, I supposed, to further round her High Dutch vowels and roll her *rrr*'s with the efficiency of a machine gun, elevating her already better-than self. She was a prism of pride, glowing in every direction with her own reflected goodness. She barely spoke to us, often pretending not to see us at all. But she was no longer the only possible bloemin' friend in the world. We, too, had places to go and things to do. Like Tarzan once, winding his chain out from under the marula tree to its longest, we were liking our own lives wide.

My mother rallied every now and again. She did her level best, staying up all night sometimes, devotedly helping us with complicated projects, anything to "make herself useful." My father lost himself in the demands of his busy practice, and had taken in two partners. I adored him. I longed to be like him. I still walked around our garden with him some nights, looking for the bright-burning Southern Cross anchoring the Milky Way as it painted itself like glittering snow across the African sky. I no longer searched the heavens for the space monkey I'd seen waving to me from his rocket. He, too, had floated away.

Sometimes John was out there with us, chatting about his latest school exploits. Sometimes, very late, we heard voices out in the night, and could see the glimmer of the fire. I had given up going out there. Zephyr was there infrequently now. When he was not confined by age to his servant's room next door, we could still hear his voice, his waning hope, his forbidden prayer. Without Zephyr and Salamina, the fire held little magic and even less comfort.

I no longer thought of gifts, friends, or foes. I had advanced to the next finger's nail, which spoke of lovers-to-come and journeys-to-go. Who would he be? I wondered. How would he find me? Coming home one afternoon, I discovered my gran Elizabeth standing in my room at the window staring out. "Hi, Gran," I said.

She did not hear me. Outside I saw manicured green lawn, roses lining the driveway, Pietros diligently rooting out tough eintjie weeds, and the bird-infested, ripening loquat tree. I looked back at her. Her eyes were alight with love, her smile open, as if the day had just begun. "Gran?" I gently tried again, but she was lost in a dream, intently watching something I could not see. "What are you doing in my room, Gran? What are you looking at out there?"

"Oh, Elizabeth," she gasped, shielding her scarred eye in a startled reflex.

"Sorry," I said.

"Oh," she cried softly, astonished to see me so grown. "Look at you, in your high school uniform. Oh, Lizzy!" She looked out again. "You know, I could just *see* him walking out there, the sun on his shoulders . . . to pick that first loquat."

I wanted to run from the loneliness in the room. We stood in silence. I did not know how to comfort her, what to say. She began to
cry. "I still miss him," she said, her tears suddenly angry, "so very, very
much."

I crept out to the fire that night. Four people stood under the syringa tree, low embers reflecting in their skin. Two I knew. Two I did
not. Mombadi stood side by side with Iris. There was no Zephyr
tonight. Word had it that a British group of anti-apartheid activists
had been infiltrated by the secret police, destroying their plot to rescue
Mandela from Robben Island. Anyone found working for change was
now deemed to be engaging in communist, terrorist activities and
charged with high treason. Banning orders persisted, and saboteurs
were prohibited from communicating with one another. At eighteen,
young white men of all denominations were being drafted into compulsory military service for two years, to defend the policies of our
government at our borders with Mozambique, Rhodesia, and Angola.
The government flexed enormous military might. The Afrikaans Nationalist Party ruled with a majority of the white vote, and wor-
shipped, as they continued to do in collared and stockinged droves
next door, at the pews of their Dutch Reformed Church, giving
thanks each Sunday for safety engendered by the wisdom of their
God-given policies. A feeling of resignation fell like a net all around
us. And it began to feel normal. Like the flies I knew would settle on
Moliseng when she left our house for big school in Soweto, I did not
want to think of these things. I did not want to listen to talk of it at
the dinner table. The coals under the tree burned lower. Tonight, there
would be no song.

I had dreamed of marrying around the fire, full-bloom white
frangipani flowers like angels in flight, the sweet, seductive smell of
night, the hiss and crackle of the fire I so loved. Zephyr would be
there, and Salamina! Where was she? I asked the night. She'd promised
me my wedding song. Now she would not even be with me. Older
now, I accepted it. But deep down, despite all the understanding I
could muster, I was furious, grief-stricken that she had not just said
good-bye.

I watched Mombadi and Iris walk to the servants' rooms. The two men I did not know melted away into the night. Like an old ghost of the tiny self I had been, lured by Zephyr's drum when I first stole out to the fire, I moved to where they had been standing. I sat down alone under the tree in the lost, finished smell of ash. In the dark of the syringa leaves above me, I heard the low sigh of the wind, and Salamina—I thought I heard Salamina, her voice deep as malt and comforting as the smell of your own pillow. "Jho, Miss Lizzy!" she seemed to sing from far away. *"Iquira lendlela nguqonqothwane, Iquira lendlela . . ."* Her voice clicked and rose in the song of the dung beetle, for young maidens on their wedding day. "Do you know your way home?" Sitting there in the dark, I was finally able to believe she would never return. Salamina, like Clova, was gone.

CHAPTER EIGHT

I AM PART OF THIS EARTH

◎◎

The streets of Soweto exploded.

It was June 1976, and I was immersed at the University of the Witwatersrand in our anthropological beginnings and in daily debate with my friend Etta. Within minutes of the first furtive reports, word spread across campus. The day of reckoning had dawned—Soweto was burning.

By the time I'd run down to the student quad, huge numbers had gathered. Loudspeakers blared instructions for protesters, already galvanized, brazen and ready to march against apartheid through the city streets of Johannesburg. Many students avoided the scene, hurrying home, fearful of being caught in the midst of what they knew could only end in police violence. Some carried on regardless with whatever they were doing, persuaded that these were just the same shenanigans by the usual communist agitators to rile everyone up when in truth, everyone knew there was nothing to be done. The military might of the government was well known. Punishment for engaging in subversive activities was hardly a secret among students, many of whom had been dogged and arrested by the secret police, now openly a frightening arm of a government that held itself accountable to no one. Many students had been served with banning orders, making it illegal for them to confer or work with others. Some had been thrown into long terms of solitary confinement. Continuing accounts of violent, mysterious deaths while in such confinement haunted those, black and white, daring to work for change. These punishments were meted out for high crimes such as refusing to join the army, and, as in the case of my friend Etta, lesser insults like working to assist black unions in their struggle to have a voice and rights. Or for trying to create a syllabus for black students that included their own languages. Wits University, peopled mostly by English and Jewish students, and some renegade Afrikaners like Etta, was a bastion of liberalism, and unlike Loeska's University in Pretoria, it housed what the government deemed to be dangerous subversives. Still, some students didn't want to know. Some had never heard the name of Mandela.

We stood on the steps of the Great Hall. News had filtered out of the black townships—the police were shooting to kill anyone who defied their orders. *Oh no nothing will happen God won't let anything happen.*

God was not listening on that day. The police moved massive artillery into the townships. Children ran wild in the confusion, drinking free-flowing liquor, setting their schools on fire and arming themselves with bottles and rocks in newfound defiance.

Coming to us in bits and pieces, and as yet officially unreported, on the day before, June 16, almost five thousand black students marched peacefully down Vilikazi Street in Soweto. They no longer wished to study in Afrikaans, a language they found difficult and impractical because it was not their own. They'd planned to march, sing, and return home. It was to be a day of celebration, we'd heard, a day of pride in their own languages, a day to release tensions and at all times to remain peaceful.

When ordered to disperse by the police, the crowd refused, stating again their intention to sing and remain peaceful. The police responded with tear gas. In the ensuing panic, without warning, they began to fire live ammunition. People were shot and killed as they were running away.

Johannesburg lay in a pall of smoke billowing out of the townships. You could smell it everywhere. Everywhere. We waited for some semblance of reporting, whatever slivers journalists were allowed to publish, broadcast on radio and on brand-new-to-Africa television.

Tires were burned, school and church windows shattered, homes looted. Police roamed the black townships like wolves.

A week vanished in a haze of smoke and violence. When it seemed to subside, we returned to our lives. Standing at the notice board in the quad, I read a list put up by our student union, a closely watched, defiant group long deemed by the government to be dangerous.

"News that will not appear in your newspaper," it read. Fatalities—lives lost in ensuing minor disturbances:

Christopher Mzuma   16
Peggy Ditwe   18
Pietros Mseddi   24
Dora M'twetwe   14
Moliseng Mashlope   14

I read it again, and again. Our Moliseng was only twelve. No, she must be thirteen, almost fourteen? The name would not recede. It would not go away.

I ran to the phones, dialed my father at his consulting rooms. I hung up. I dialed the house. John answered. "Where's Dad?" I asked. He was operating and would be late, John said. "Promise me you won't say anything, John, promise you won't tell either of them? Where's Mom?"

John promised. He was the only person I could trust to send Mombadi without questions or an argument. "I don't know if it's her," I said. My father would forbid us to go into the township, and irrationally, having no idea where Salamina was or had been since she'd left us, I had to find her. Ambulances screamed past on Jan Smuts Avenue. "I'll go down to Jorrisson . . . tell Mombadi, and be careful."

They kill you if you go in there.

They don't want you in there.

I waited for twenty minutes. Mombadi had never denied a request, but when I got into the car, he said, "Miss Lizzy, they are not going to allow us. I must take you home." John was pale as a sheet.

"Just please go, Peter," I told him, knowing as well as he did the roads into the townships had been closed for days.

We came to the outskirts of Soweto, where police with tanks and loaded guns lay like deadly snakes in sealing lines at every entry point. We got out at the barricade.

"I need to find someone," I said, "my nanny, her child . . . my nanny Salamina." There were others looking for someone they knew.

"Move away!" the police warned repeatedly.

I imagined I could slip in past their eyes, their guns. I could run in and someone would know, someone would help us find Salamina. The rough arms of a policeman shoved me aside. "Get back," he yelled. "What are you, bloody stupitt?" Again, they ordered the crowd to leave immediately. I felt Mombadi, like a blanket, put his arm around my shoulders.

"Come," he said, "it is *not* safe here, Miss Lizzy. It is *not* safe."

. .

All around Johannesburg, in every surrounding black township, and in black townships around other cities, mothers, fathers, brothers, strangers, lifted dead children from the streets. In Guguletu they carried them, in Soweto, in Alexandra, in Mamelodi they carried them, and in Bonteheuwel they carried them, home.

The lists read like a nightmare—shot in back, shot in back of head, shot in chest, died of gunshot wounds, bullet wound to abdomen, multiple injuries, shot through side of head, reported missing, justifiable homicide, shot by police, gunshot wound to heart. In the continuing township chaos, migrant mine workers and tsotsis began killing one another using petrol bombs and knives. Baragwanath became once again a war hospital, but this time, central to the war zone. Doctors leaving each morning after a night in the casualty wards covered their eyes, their mouths, when they tried to describe what they had seen. One child after another, they could not save.

It was not immediately clear what occurred on that day, almost a week after police first opened fire on Vilikazi Street. The accounts coming out of the townships were varying and horrible. I supposed that like many other children, if it was indeed Moliseng, she must have been swept into a surge of pride. I kept hoping, praying, wondering if she was alive. I knew she could not have expected to die. She would not be so reckless, trained as she was to hide away at the mere mention of police. What could she have been thinking, standing face-to-face with them? Why did she not hear our long-ago words: *Turn back, Moliseng, run for your life. Climb up into the syringa tree, under Salamina's bed, hide away, Moliseng, hide away.*

Sworn to secrecy, Peter Mombadi returned from another foray to Soweto to get news for John and me. Salamina was nowhere to be found, he said. The tin hut where Salamina's mother had lived with Moliseng was vacant, pieces of the roof blown away by the wind. A young man was there now, Mombadi said, trying to make a home for himself and his family. He told Mombadi he'd found it empty. No one would be returning, he'd heard, because the child of that house had run in the streets, shouting at police that she was part of this earth. That child was now dead.

I lay awake. I would not tell my parents about Moliseng, not ever—my father, whose hands had lifted her into the air the night she was born, my mother, who found her when she was lost. I would never tell them. I would make John promise the same.

I threw my clothes into an old suitcase. I would do as my father advised when I was a child. I would not make this place my home.

In the morning, I said I was leaving because nothing changes.

"But, Lizzy," my father tried to reason, "*we* change things, Lizzy. *We* change them." For the first time, I knew that I had been right to worry about him. "Why didn't you tell me what you were doing?" I asked him, angry for no reason I could justify. "I did nothing, Elizabeth," he said, "except what little I could, whatever was in front of me, but I had you, my love, and John and your mother . . ." Much as I loved him, I would never be like him. I had no medals for courage or bravery, stolen or deserved, pinned to my jacket. Zephyr had been right. There were no answers for this place.

"We don't change a damned thing," I said to my father, who just stood there, looking at me with sadness. I ran out of the house, up the path to the syringa tree. Like a fool, I was too old to climb, too sad, and so much wanting the comfort of the high, lonely place I had known as a child. In the fading afternoon shadows, I sat alone under the tree for hours, trying to hear again the soft song of Moliseng. Perhaps, as Zephyr had always warned, she had flown into the leaves, the berries and the bark. Perhaps she was *in* the tree, waiting for me, as she had done so many times. I wished for her smiling face smeared sweet with peaches and full of cheek. I wished for the tumble of her naughtiness, her teasing, dark eyes hiding in the glistening leaves, her song. I wished for anything.

Suddenly, I was climbing into the branches, scratching my hands and legs, until I found my old nest. I sat in it, felt the arms of the tree around me, and began to cry.

In an impotent rage at Salamina, I counted eight, almost nine years since she'd left us. I wished for her rough hand on me, wished I could put my hand on her. I felt hatred for the police. I felt unseemly, and part of it. No words, no water, no baptism, no Irissy to hose me down. No soothing mud coat—this could not be washed off. I vowed I would never need anything from this place.

With my mother drifting farther and farther away, I was frightened to tell her about Moliseng. Even my father, who understood all things—I could not imagine looking into his eyes. I had no words to tell him.

I must have fallen asleep. I dreamed about the lively letters between that man Darwin, who oddly looked like a monkey, and my great-grandfather—discarded, having no value to the man who stole them from the trunk. I dreamed about them blowing in the wind across the foothills of the Soutpansberg Mountains, where people sang and wept with the beauty of the place long before we ever set foot there.

When I woke it was dark, the quiet moon above. The tree still held me, and in the silence I heard the berries falling, one by one. They would speckle the ground in the morning. They would tell us something had happened. I listened, and remembered in my waking that Moliseng was gone. Free, and brave, like the drum that beats in the night, free and brave. And dead, at fourteen.

..

Two weeks later, I stood with a suitcase in hand at Jan Smuts airport. Early that morning, I had stolen up to my swing to say good-bye, and to my tree, to say thank you. I would carry my secret to the land of the free and the brave, the sparkling place that had so thrilled me as a child at the drive-in.

"You'd better bloody phone us from time to time," John said.

My mother had put on a beautiful blue dress, brought plenty of tissues, and kept asking me to stay.

My father comforted her with a smile. "Wellington has to do what Wellington has to do, Eugenie."

"But, Lizzy, how will you cope?" she said. "You don't know anyone. There's no one to look after you there."

"I love you, Momsy. I'll be fine." I wiped her cheeks dry. She seemed young somehow, more childlike than ever, holding on to my father as they stood there, trying to say good-bye.

"You know we're always here, Lizzy," my father said. "If you need to come back, my love . . . we'll be here."

"Not me," said John. "The day I finish matric I'm buggering off. Won't catch me in their bloody army." With military service compulsory now, John would face two years in the army and then three months every year after that. My father had spoken recently of boys brought into his consulting rooms by distraught mothers—young men returning from Angola and other fronts, with sad, staring eyes, sores on their skin, and post-traumatic shock. Most were unable to speak of what they had witnessed, much less what they had done, defending our country for the Nationalist government. Many were being smuggled out of the country by their families, to Israel, England, Australia, and America, for "holidays" from which they never returned.

"Well, don't come banging *my* door down, I'm trying to get away from you," I said to him, not meaning it. John hugged me, his young eyes wet. "Silly billy," I said, holding him. He squeezed my hand to let me know he understood. He would never tell.

Then we were separated by the thick glass security wall dividing those leaving from those staying. I saw my father finding a place in the crowd for them, at the glass wall that ran all the way along the final walk, covered with fingerprints, shadows, and smears where people kissed through the glass and tried to think of the last thing they needed to say.

"I love you . . . don't forget me," I said, cheerful and feeling quite brave. I could still smell the sweetness of my mother's hair against my cheek, still feel the shoulders of my father's jacket, that nice, brown wool. "I love you," I called to them huddled there.

Cool evening washed over me as I walked out onto the runway. I breathed the air as deeply as I could, sweet, dusty, filled with everything I loved and everything I wanted to forget. I heard a faint echo of my father's voice, walking with him in the sinking light under the lilac flowers of the syringa tree. Turning back toward the airport building, I could see him through the windows fronting the tarmac. He was saying, "I love you, my Lizzy . . . missing you already, my love."

I waved, turned, and kept going, listening for free and brave between the beats of my heart, the way he had taught me. I heard nothing. Nothing changes, I thought. No matter how we dream of how it could be.

We pulled high into the night sky. I drifted away, hoping to find somewhere to belong.

PART FOUR

. . . .

CHAPTER NINE

JOURNEYS TO GO

◎◎

Thirteen years later, the man who had demanded the police call him mister rose like Lazarus from his tomb, out of prison. Now everyone knew his name. He was Mr. Nelson Mandela. Four years after that, I stood at the mailbox on our Pasadena street, opening a weekly letter from my father.

"My dearest Elizabeth," he wrote, jubilant. "Look! Things *do* change. Front page!" I unfolded the once heavily censored newspaper and read in sweeping, full letters: VOTE, THE BELOVED COUNTRY.

"Lizzy!" he had written across the page, "did you ever think this day would dawn? All of us, voting together."

He'd stood side by side, he wrote in his letter, with ragged men whose eyes were wet with hope. Women with babies on their backs held in their hands not a pass, but a ballot, to give a rightful place to their children. From first light, in city after city, they had cast their votes until the sun set, leaving the land and the faces of all, new. "Much of the life you knew here, Elizabeth, will now be lost, but so much more, for so many more, will now be gained."

I thought suddenly of the beauty of the veld, the gorgeous, painful smell of the air.

"You can come *home* now, Elizabeth! You can come home, my love! Love to John, if you hear from him. I miss you both, Dad."

Had Salamina lived to see it? Where was John? We had not heard from John in two years. Month after month went by with no letter, no call. How could I ever go back there? Oh God, I missed it. I missed the smell of it. Those sudden highveld thunderstorms that made the whole world grow dark at four in the afternoon, the lightning and thunder rolling the sky like four million drums, the pouring sheets of water—Africa still had no water.

I read my father's letter again and again, hearing somewhere far in my mind the sound of the train at Clova, its wailing whistle and chug in the distant foothills, a leaving sound that had always made me feel like I lived nowhere. And I realized, I was really somewhere then.

"Every place is part of you, my Lizzy," my old dad had written, "and you're part of every place. We are all just part of the earth. And we carry one another with us, wherever we go—for all time."

I knew I could not go. Even now, I could not need anything from that place. I would carry it with me, but I could not go back.

. .

Sometimes a simple thing will take you miles. A lazy fly in the heat of a Pasadena evening can carry you from your bed on gauzy wings across oceans and time to the cool, red, polished floor of a porch.

In the tinkling of spoons on saucers, the gentle clattering of afternoon tea, the cool promise of African night not too far away, familiar shadows melt across the red floor of the sheltering stoep. Tea, with milk, of course, and an unspoken prayer for rain. No one ever prays aloud unless it's an emergency. . . .

There would be no shadows now, no hot tea, no Meendli on her thin, tall-for-a-picaninn legs, cracking the flies on the verandah. I'd gone there for a moment, the fly buzzing fatly as I tried to nap, battering himself against the glass pane—even though I'd left the door open for him. You can do that in places in America.

Jangled awake by the ringing phone, I must have been asleep for an hour at least, mouth spit-wet, my face damp against the pillow in the sweltering end of another Pasadena summer, where lonely palms make that swishing sound that tricks you into thinking it's rain.

"Hello?"

"Elizabeth, my love?"

"Dad."

"Yes, it's your old dad, my Lizzy. When are you coming home?"

I tried to picture my father in Knysna in the Cape Province, in a farmhouse I'd never seen. It's surrounded by lavender, he promised, with towering lanes of oak trees planted with all the hopes of those who arrived there three hundred years ago and were met with the gawking stares and anxious hearts of those who came before. Like a silent prayer reaching into the vast blue, all those trees.

"I'll have the lawn perfect for you, Elizabeth. We're being outfoxed by a couple of determined moles at the moment, but it'll all be fixed by the time you come!" In my drowsy head I repositioned him in Knysna, on that southern shore. It will be the Cape of Good Hope forever, even though now it's just another place to go when you retire, when everything you urgently had to do in Johannesburg is done. They probably call him Dr. Grace, those who wouldn't know him as Isaac. "How's the practice, Dad?" I asked him.

"Oh, you can't really call it that anymore, Lizzy. I just patch up whoever knocks at the door, you know, whoever needs me. You'll see when you come!"

I tried to picture him without my mother, who, like Salamina, could not say good-bye. She quietly decided one evening to end her sadness—forgetting John, me, the light at dawn, the blur of gray-brown mossie wings lifting into the sky, forgetting the taste of sugar and the smell of rain. Her overdose left her nonfunctional, still in this world—everything forgotten.

After months of wrestling with his conscience, my father put her into a home to receive the best possible care. I tried now to imagine him alone, but she wandered into every room I placed him in in her pretty green-and-yellow dress—"making herself useful," she always used to say.

He told me he visits her every Sunday, that she is in a marvelous place. He told me not to worry. In the quick break in his voice, he said he whispers in her ears that I am soon coming home to her.

I listened to the sounds of my small Spanish house, the quiet hum of the freeway in the distance, Andrew's tread on the wooden floors, different when he's carrying George. I noticed the soft smells, the comforter, lemon balm in the kitchen, a house with a baby in it. I knew, from watching it a thousand times, the last light of evening had chased itself across the hills that surround us.

The click of a handle anchored the dark—Andrew, closing the door to George's room.

There is not a single door on this farmhouse that has a lock on it. . . .

He will have rocked George to sleep. He will have sung to him. I distracted myself thinking of the crease in Andrew's cheek when he smiles, the permanence of it. I closed my eyes to sleep.

George will not know the great-grandfather for whom he has been named, and he won't have Clova. He won't ever think of it, or have to forget it, because, lucky fish, he did not know it. And now, despite myself, I was sitting cross-legged in the middle of the steering wheel on my grandfather's tractor, windblown in my filthy cotton hat worn only under dire threat of the crows picking off my ears. The African earth cracked open in furrows beneath us. It will be rose-brown, he was telling me, in the lucky places.

..

Andrew had not met my father, but they were old friends on the phone. In the year that passed since the first-ever inclusive election, he gracefully fielded my father's questions and invitations, gave kind, evasive answers, not knowing the reasons I refused to go home, but knowing they ran unseen like a night river eroding its banks. "Go for a week or two, Elizabeth," he said, "your father wants you to come home." Until the day before, my mind was quiet on the subject, those thoughts like a faded, linen cloth in a cupboard, its patterns, sounds, faces, once gathered around, put away. That's what forgetting means, I reminded myself. Quiet, until Andrew came running out of the house to find me, his tone urgent, uncharacteristic. "Elizabeth, your father's on the phone . . . come quickly, it's about Salamina." My heart banged up into my throat, burning with old tears now run dry.

Andrew said her name as if he knew her.

"Is she dead?" I blurted out.

"She's been found. She's alive, Elizabeth." He seemed suddenly foreign to me, the Pasadena earth under my feet strange. I stumbled to the phone. "Dad . . . ?"

"Elizabeth, Lizzy, your old dad knows. John has come home. John has told me about Moliseng. You mustn't be angry with him, Elizabeth. Lizzy, *listen* to me. . . . I'm glad he told me, Elizabeth, and I'm glad Eugenie can no longer hear it." I could hear him struggling not to cry. I was trying to listen, to hear what he was trying to say. "It was extraordinary, Elizabeth. After John came, we walked and talked for miles along the lagoon, through the forest and far out into the veld. I thought Salamina had fallen off the face of the earth, blown away in the wind. I'd had all my old patients combing Johannesburg for her, black, white, and in between. They all came up with the same answer. And then I went down to have scones and tea at that little place under the oak trees." He laughed. "Yes, we actually have a tea room down here! Karel asked that woman if her maid was better. 'We didn't have to take her to the doctor after all, Salamina's fine now,' she said. Salamina? I thought I must be dreaming, you know? Wishful thinking. But no, there I'd been searching the length and breadth of Johannesburg up north, and there's a Salamina up the road! Well, I all but attacked the poor woman for information." Her name was Mrs. Biggs, he was saying now, Mr. and Mrs. Biggs. They'd asked Salamina to come down to Knysna with them when they retired. She'd been in Parkmore with them since she left us, and she works for them to this day. Parkmore? Parkmore was fifteen minutes from where we lived. Salamina had been fifteen minutes away, all those years that I waited for her, counted every bus that came up Bell Street—she was fifteen minutes away?

"I want you to go and see her, Elizabeth. Go and see her."

I was not looking for Salamina anymore. I had made no preparation for this news, not longed for it, even, that I knew of. I did not want to think of Salamina now, her brown arms, her Xhosa smell, the high king's ride on her warm back, that place of comfort from where the whole world might be surveyed. Her tongue clicked, like the soft clatter of rain on a tin roof. She called me her picaninn. She was my Salamina. My small heels dug into her belly, my stiff legs wrapped around her waist. For dear life I held on.

Shaking, I hung up and walked outside with Andrew. I told him when Salamina didn't bring the tea one morning, we thought she was sick. I told him we'd raced out over dew-sharp lawn, past the granadilla vines, the frangipani, to climb with wet-grass feet up onto her high bed. Everything was gone, just the bed up on bricks, and the smell of her. "She left without saying good-bye," I said. "It's not possible for me to go. George is too small to make that long journey."

"He's five months, Elizabeth. Go," he said. Andrew knew nothing of Moliseng. Why could I not speak just her name to him? Perhaps the stone in my heart would move now, dislodge a little. I hated the hardness in myself and I could not be without it. I knew better than to stand at the edge of a well. I felt my chest rise, painfully full, but the stone would not move. Like some stupid Sisyphus, I will be busy with it forever.

Andrew ran his hand through my hair as I tried to fall asleep. "Sometimes, Andrew," I dared to say into the warmth of him next to me, "I dream that I'm there. The heat, the throb of Africa all round me, in me, and I know I'm there. I dream I'm climbing in the mimosa trees, the thorn trees, the syringa trees, looking for someone . . . always looking for someone." I could feel the rush of the branches as I told him, scratching thorns against my skin, sun streaming through leaf after leaf, my search endless. And fruitless always.

"I'll go there in my dream, Andrew. I don't think I can go there."

As I faded to sleep under Andrew's smoothing hand, my childish tears ran into the pillow, and for the first time I allowed myself to know it was Salamina I had been looking for. I had been looking for her since she disappeared, looking for her through morning eyes glued shut with sleep and salt from crying, looking for her till the moon rose over the veld, till I fell asleep in her empty room. I had been looking for her, even now, a world away, in my sleep.

. .

Lifting into the night sky above New York, the great city's lights streamed away behind us in the glistening wet winter of North America.

I thought of Etta my friend—straw-blond, Afrikaans, and a rebel. After the riots, she had gone underground. I knew she had long been dogged by the secret police for trying to implement black languages in the Soweto schools. "It's Elizabeth. Do you remember me, Etta?" I practiced in my mind, as if speaking a foreign language. She must be there still. I could not imagine her anywhere else, her soul part of the bush, its sounds and secrets living in her the way birds inhabit a tree. Would she look on me now as a stranger? I wondered.

"Why don't you phone Etta?" Andrew had asked before we left.

"Etta will not remember me."

George was asleep, his tiny face unimaginably sweet to me every time I looked at him. The cabin lights dimmed for the long night ahead. I would tell Andrew about Moliseng sometime before sunrise. I would tell him that her name meant "protect her." And that it had been my special job.

The black face of the steward loomed out of the night, a moving piece of it, he was so dark. "I'm sorry," I whispered, "would you have another pillow?"

"Of course," he said quietly, moving back down the aisle of the sleeping plane. He did not call me Madam or Miess. The fact that I noticed filled me with an odd, jaunty feeling of hope, and underneath, panic that I'd noticed such a thing. Was he Sotho? Xhosa, maybe? Definitely not Zulu. I could not tell in the dark. I probably couldn't tell in the broad light of day, either, I'd been away so long, an amateur now at my own life.

The steward was back, confident, kind. "What is your name?" I asked him, wanting to let him know how much I appreciated my pillow, his attentiveness, his presence, the surprise of his black face.

"Mdeduze," he said, warrior proud. "Mdeduze, Miess."

"It's a beautiful name. What does it mean?"

His chest puffed out sweetly with his name badge. In a grown man the innocence of his pride was startling. "It means . . . comfort, Miess. Comfort." He smiled again.

I wondered if the mother who gave him that name had lived to see his smart uniform, his life above the clouds over the place of his birth—the luck of his survival.

I had no right to grieve, for God's sake. Nothing was done to me. I felt immediately inept, angry. Better to change the subject—*pat it down, pat it down*. I was still running. I was ridiculous. Andrew would tell me that protecting Moliseng was my special job as a child, that I did it well, that what happened to her that horrendous day was not my fault.

"Is the Miess all right?" Mdeduze was there again.

"I'm fine, thank you . . ."

"Only ten more hours," he told me quietly, "and we are ett home. In Jwannisbeck."

Johannesburg.

Did he not think me American?

I wanted to tell him that I was glad to be traveling back there that night with him. "Do you know your way home?" the cowherds teased the dung beetle in Salamina's song. Mdeduze wandered back into the dark. I tried again to sleep.

We began our descent into Johannesburg as the sun was setting, sealing the red-rimmed sky with the fiery fragrance of African smoke and earth. As we walked down the steps of the plane, I filled my lungs with it almost to crying. Now I knew, I said, laughing at myself, to Andrew, why exiles kiss the earth upon their return.

In the distance, the city gleamed, golden.

. .

Rushing to transfer to the Knysna flight, I looked up to see a strange yet deeply familiar silhouette moving toward us in the crowd. My old dad, stooping a bit, was running to us as fast as his age would permit. "My busy, busy Lizzy!" His jacket, his cheek against mine.

"Why didn't you wait in Knysna for us? You shouldn't have come all this way," I said, shocked to find him there.

"Oh, it's a short hop, Elizabeth. Thought I'd brave the madness of Johannesburg. See for myself, you know, all the changes . . ." Seeing the damp in his eyes, I knew he had come because he could not wait, could not believe we were coming.

"How is Mom?" I asked.

"She's doing fine, Elizabeth," he said with gusto. "I whispered in her ears when I saw her on Sunday that you were coming home!" Then he said, "She won't know you, Elizabeth. She doesn't know anyone anymore." He took my hand. "But she's in a marvelous place, Lizzy . . . it's for the best, you'll see."

"I know," I said, welling up, remembering the years of patting it all down. "I know."

"And you must be Andrew," he said, and embraced him as if he'd known him a hundred years. And George, in Andrew's arms. "Look at your little American," I said.

"Hello, George," my father said gently, opening his arms to take him from Andrew. He lifted the baby aloft for all to see. "Hello!" He cradled him again, then grew quiet. "He has Eugenie's eyes, Elizabeth, as blue . . ." He moved away from Andrew and me in a dream, a dance from long ago with the love of his life.

"Welcome, my boy, welcome to these shores," we heard him say. "You have your great-grandfather's name, George. Welcome, my boy. Welcome to you!"

..

John asked to go with me to Salamina. His years of running away had aged him a bit. He was still gentle, but strong and voraciously tall, a pip-squeak who had quite outstripped me. He kept trying to apologize for breaking his word and telling my father about Moliseng. He had battled, he said, feeling responsible. "Like Salamina's shame," he said to me, picking up George like a tiny present, "like we did something to cause this, like we could have done something to prevent it. Like we were part of it. We were, and we weren't. Fucked up. We ran, Lizzy, the way Salamina did."

My father's home was just as he said it would be, a beautiful old farmhouse, creamy and cool with a green tin roof, surrounded by hills of lavender and a grove of hundred-year-old oak trees on the outskirts of Knysna. We sat on the verandah at night looking out over the sea through the Heads, two monumental, staggered cliff faces that make a door of rock to the ocean. They enclose the lagoon on Featherbed Beach, where exhausted sailors, ravaged by storms, once laid their lucky heads on the sand to sleep.

Up on the hill in the near distance, the ever-growing shantytowns known as squatter camps were spreading themselves out and taking root. Thousands of people from surrounding countries, drawn south by the optimistic promises of the new government, now lived there in tents and shacks, joining those already there. Massive unemployment and high crime were still the rule of the day. The familiar smell of their fires hung low and heavy in the night sky. But now they had hope. Now, they were fueled by possibility, however remote, a palpable excitement in the air like unexpected rain, sweet, no matter what.

Small remnants of our life were all over my father's house; jasmine, my mother's favorite, newly planted around the verandah, as though to please her when she came home.

Mabalel, the skeleton, stood guard at my father's desk.

And sweetest of all, I found Iris in the kitchen. She had helped me to pack for America all those years ago, covered her eyes and cried when I left. I knew she had begged my father to take her with him to the Cape when he retired, and there she was, older, still wide-eyed but running the house like a champion.

We sat on the verandah at night. The soft clicking of sandals on the wooden floor inside made it seem as though my mother might appear at any moment. But it was Iris, clearing the dinner table.

Old Dieter from across the hill stopped by with a gift—a lettuce he'd grown himself on his small plot of land.

"Aag, shame, Isaac," he said, "so nice to have the kids home, hey?" His, like so many others, had left.

"Dieter had a beautiful farm," my father said, "up north of here in the Little Karoo."

"Won't live out there now," Dieter said. "Poor buggers, they just walk off the main road. Broke into Lewis's farmhouse last month, opened every tin of food and just sat, y'know, right in his kitchen there on the floor, eating tinned dog food, dry porridge, whole blocks of butter. Gorged until they couldn't anymore. Some of them are bloody starving—kill you for a bite of food." He held the lettuce like flowers in his hands.

My father had something to show me, he said. I followed him out to the back of his farmhouse. In a small well in the soil, he'd planted a young sapling, no more than five feet tall and dwarfed by giant oaks, a syringa tree. "It's almost impossible to buy them now," he said. "Hennie up the road found this one for me. They're uprooting them in all the public areas. They want only indigenous trees and plants, Lizzy. These cause terrible ecological damage. They're invaders, you know. They deplete the soil of water and nutrients. So I'll water it myself every day. But I couldn't resist. So jolly pretty. I think of you, my love, every morning when I come out here." I stood there, his arm around me, thinking of my tree, of how it must have opened its sacred boughs to release the spirits within. One by one, with each vote cast, they must have emerged into the light of the pleasant place they had once found.

. .

The following morning, John, baby George, and I got into the car to drive to the Biggs family farm, to visit Salamina. Andrew decided to stay at home with my father, feeling that John and I should go to her alone.

I hadn't slept much the night before. The early-morning sun streaming through the car windows felt kind on my skin.

Through the Outeniqua Pass we went, and after half an hour turned onto a sandy farm road that divided the hills. Everywhere, fynbos, that beautiful, rare combination of proteas, heather, and wild grasses spiked the fragrant air. Ferns taller than men and a million years old graced the roadside in shaded groves. The painterly lilac smudges of fynbos gave way to immaculate vineyards, and a smooth, white-gabled Cape Dutch farmstead.

A petite lady stood at the porch, ready to summon Salamina the moment we arrived. Seeing dust at the far gate, she ran up the porch steps calling for her to come. "They're here," we heard, as she came running back down.

Mrs. Biggs, her platinum hair as soft as candy floss in a gentle bun, in her turquoise cashmere twinset over a misty tweed skirt, stood in the long driveway like a tiny Christmas fairy, breathless with excitement. She tottered back up the steps. "Salamina, come out, they're here." After a long silence, we heard her say, "Oh, you look *fine. Come, they're here!*" She hastened back down to welcome us.

"Hello," I said, my legs suddenly shaking beneath me. "Mrs. Biggs? I'm Elizabeth . . ." I looked to the porch, to the massive, oak-front door, but no one came. "Thank you so much for having us here," I said, "to your home. It's such a beautiful farm. . . ." All around us, the land, a blanket of peace. I introduced John as my very tall little brother, and then my baby, George.

Still, no one came.

"Sorry," I said, suddenly a bit tearful and trying to stay calm. "I'm so nervous . . . is she here?"

At the cool entry to the house, I saw a quiet figure, bent, much smaller than I'd remembered, hover for a moment by the door, and then slowly move onto the porch, hesitant. "Miss Lizzy . . . ?" I heard, almost inaudibly, and then, "Miss Lizzy?" She extended her hand, her Xhosa hand toward me. "Monkey . . . ?" she said. "Monkey!" She ran to me and I to her, into each other's arms, and oh, the beloved smell of her. "You're just the same, Sal." I laughed through blurred eyes. "You're just the same. . . ."

"No, Miss Lizzy," she said, looking down. She covered her cheek with her hand. "I am old, I am too old!" In her crisp pink uniform her eyes were darker, more receding than I'd remembered, clouded by a soft film of age, her cheeks, so honey brown, so sweet, fallen.

"Oh! jho," she said shyly, catching sight of John. "You are married, Miss Lizzy!"

"Yes, I'm married, Sal, almost ten years now," I said, suddenly wanting to ask why she had left without saying good-bye, why she had not been there to sing her wedding song. "Oh! This is . . . " I said instead, "my husband is Andrew . . . this is . . . you don't recognize John?"

Both hands flew to her mouth. She looked up at him standing there with baby George, and in utter disbelief exclaimed, "Aouw, Master John? Jhoooo, you are too tall!"

"How are you, Sal?" He laughed. "What's this uniform? I thought I'd find you running the country!"

"No, Master John." She laughed with him, quietly smoothed the shoulder of her maid's uniform, and said with simple dignity and unmistakable pride, "This one it's *my* wekk."

We stood in silence, staring at one another.

"Salamina is absolutely marvelous," said Mrs. Biggs, rescuing us like a chirpy bird. "We are so lucky to have her. But of course, you all know that."

Salamina could not take her eyes off John. She lowered her hand to indicate the size of him when she'd left, and then closed her eyes and began to sway in remembrance, a picaninn dance with John, perhaps three, perhaps four. "Master John." She smiled, caught in an old dream. "Oh jhe . . . oh jhe . . ." Then, "And *this* one?" she said, looking at baby George the way we might have looked at the space monkey had he landed in our midst. "This one, it's your picaninni?" she asked John.

"Well, I wish he was my picaninni," John said, "this fat boy! Yeees!" George stared back at him. "But you're Elizabeth's, aren't you? Here, go to Salamina . . ."

Salamina said suddenly, "No, Master John." She stepped back, quietly crossing her arms in front of her lap. She looked away. She could not hold a child.

I did not know whether to speak or remain silent. Mrs. Biggs stepped forward. "Why don't we all go inside? I'm sure you'd all love a nice cup of tea. Salamina and I have been making wonderful scones for you. High jinks in the kitchen!" She looked to her, but Salamina had walked away.

"Come," Mrs. Biggs tried cheerfully, "why don't we all just go in?"

I wanted to run after Salamina, to say I was sorry we'd come, sorry we had distressed her, sorry for George being alive with her child dead, sorry for everything I could think of. "What a beautiful farmhouse, Mrs. Biggs," John was saying, going up the cool steps with George making sweet sounds. "Georgie seems to love it here, Elizabeth," I vaguely heard him call.

But I was not there. I was drawn to Salamina despite myself, despite knowing she needed to be alone. I followed her through the long vineyard to a grove of trees lining the dirt farm road leading away from the back of the house. She stopped under the trees.

"Sal . . . ?" flew out of my mouth before I could silence it. She turned.

"Sal . . ."

We looked at each other. I was so known to her, beautiful in her eyes as she looked at me. Look, I was thinking, your picaninni has grown. And then I remembered that I was not her picaninni.

"I brought you some things from America," I said, trying hard to smile. "They're in the car." I put my hand into the pocket of my cotton dress. "And I brought you this . . ." I took out a small gift wrapped in tissue paper. "It's from my house in America, from the tree at my house. . . . Berries from the tree . . ." I held them out to her.

"Moliseng . . . Mollie . . ." I tried to say.

Salamina extended her hand. She scooped the berries into her palm and deeply smelled them, then raised them to her forehead and fell to her knees. "Oh jho, oh jho . . ." she keened.

I must have fallen beside her. I felt her warm hand on my back, and grief that had no end.

Salamina put her arms around me.

"Oh jho, jhe, Eleseebett, jhe?" She held me, rocking me the way she had always rocked Moliseng to sleep.

"You must not cry for Moliseng, Eleseebett," she said, trying to comfort me. "Moliseng she is *with* us. Jhey, Monkey? When the wind it blows, when we walk under the trees, Moliseng she is with us, calling to us in the wind, Eleseebett, to be *proud*! To open our heart with *joy*." Tears glittered in her fading eyes. "We are free . . . we are free. Moliseng . . . she is with us forever, Miss Lizzy . . . jhe, Monkey? For ever and *ever*."

We rocked in silence, listening for any soft call, any whisper in the leaves above.

"Eh, Monkey?" I heard her say again, and then, remembering, I suppose, the smelly, long-footed child who leapt like a locust, full of sugar and a deep longing for a friend, she began to laugh. "Jhe, Monkey! Monkey, Monkey!"

"Come, *uppy*," she said, struggling to her feet, "uppy, Monkey." She helped me to stand. She looked out beyond the trees, to the highest part of the sky, and began to smile, as if indeed, she could hear the soft song.

. .

In the weeks that followed, I visited Salamina several times.

When she felt able, she told me how Moliseng had died.

A stranger, she said, a ragged old thing, had carried her child through the township until someone told him where she belonged. This stranger had carried her to her grandmother's shanty and, there, set her down on the floor next to the fire. Salamina said he had come all the way into Johannesburg the next day on the trains, to find her at her place of work in Parkmore, so that she would hear it from him.

This man told of how her child had stepped forward in the face of guns, and of what she had said. He spoke of how a small girl, who could not have felt very brave, but who spoke anyway, had shamed him for his silence, and burst his heart with pride and grief in a solitary moment.

Moliseng's feet had played in the twilight dust, picaninni feet dancing with pride, flicking up the stones behind her as she flew with the crowd toward the front lines of riot police. With a brick in her hand, she led her small, defiant gang with their flies and runny noses. Feverish with excitement, she'd dared them to run with her. They gathered their weapons along the way, broken bottles and sticks. Salamina said she knew these friends—Elifas, small and bony like Moliseng; Themba, wise beyond his twelve years; pretty Sara; Lindiwe, tall and reed-thin; and even small Moses, who had wanted to stay home. They laughed and teased. They called out as they approached the police, but were suddenly too afraid to throw anything—mesmerized in an instant by the line of tanks one hundred yards away, soldiers and police in full camouflage, weapons aimed at the crowd. Disheveled men, women, and children stood facing them, silenced by the racing of their own hearts.

Then, like a spring bud opening too soon, Moliseng stepped forward in the kicked-up dust. With her brick poised behind her back, she spoke. "Your bullet cannot kill me. . . ." she said, and retreated a little. Then again, she stepped forward, "I am Moliseng . . . Moliseng Eleseebett Mashlope . . ." She pointed at the ground where she stood. "I stand with you on this street. This, it's my street. My corner. My country. This, it's my place. I am *in* my place!" Her feet dug themselves into the dirt as if she'd sprung up from the ground like clay. Her dress fell ragged around her small body, her tiny, new breasts—she was almost fourteen.

Seeming to take strength from the crowd's astonishment, she dug in deeper. "I am part of this earth," she said, "but I will not lie down like mud to disappear. I am the mountain that rises up to spit in your face."

With the click of a rifle, the police shifted.

Moliseng blazed. In a surge of fearless, strident joy, she cried out, "I am Moliseng! I will not walk down the road of my mother, bow my shoulders, hide my head in shame! *I* will stand *up*. . . ." Like a smiling dream she danced before their eyes.

"I stand up!" she cried, then, not quite so sure, "Your bullet cannot kill me. . . ." She hesitated, found her voice again, and called out, "You will see me forever in your dreams, running in the fire of freedom! You will not sleep. You will hear my heart beating, beating, beating," she dared in joy, her fist bashing her heartbeat on her chest, "speaking in my own tongue!" She raised the brick and shouted the ringing call for freedom, *"Amandla!"*

A bullet pierced her lung. Her body lifted like a fluttering bird, and in a soft cloud of dust, fell back to the earth. The policeman released his finger on the damp trigger. Her brick lay in the sand beside her.

No army rallied to her cry.

Themba, Elifas, pretty Sara, Lindiwe, and Moses stood motionless in shock. The crowd screamed and ran in confusion, sweeping Lindiwe and Moses with them. And then, silence—Moliseng's special, brown face in the dirt, her bright, young blood filling her mouth. Her eyes searched for Lindiwe, for Elifas, Themba, maybe, her eyes still burning with the celebration of being seen.

No one helped her get up. Her blood trickled from under her lip. She tried to understand. She looked to any face around her. Still no one moved.

Themba, shaking, stood forward. Themba, tall and strong, and pretty Sara also, stood forward. Moliseng smiled at them. She knew them. "Cover me . . ." she said, lifting her head, "cover me . . . with kisses," trying to take some breath from them. Themba fell down to her.

A loudspeaker crackled orders to disperse. Someone pulled Themba away. The last of the crowd receded, vanishing into a familiar mist of pain.

Then this old man, Salamina said, black as the sad night, walked to where Moliseng lay. He did not know her.

"Move back," the police shouted in a ringing echo—then silence.

He scooped his arms under her, raised her to his chest, then struggled to his feet. He stood there, refusing to move, with somebody's child cradled in his arms. He cried out for the life he could not give back to her. He cried out for all he had tolerated, for all he had not said, all he had failed to do. He cried out for the sweet surprise of her, the words he had heard her say, the pride of her spirit. He cried for a place where someone's child lay dead in the arms of a stranger, and for a mother, who on that terrible night, if she could be found, would receive this broken sparrow in lieu of her child.

Salamina told me she had buried Moliseng in a simple box, dressed in her school uniform, clean white socks on her small feet, her shoes polished, her special, brown face immaculate. It had rained that day, settling the dust. The aching sounds, tears and singing, continued long into the night and for many days thereafter. There were many children lost, she said. So many.

"Jhe . . . my Moliseng . . ." she said.

We sat together in silence for a long while. I told her that I had searched for her during those terrible weeks. I told her that I'd run away.

"If you could see my heart," she said simply about my having come to see her, about being found after all these years, "my heart, Eleseebett, it is white as snow that you are here with me."

I never told her I wished she'd said good-bye. My grief in the face of hers was meaningless.

I had only two things left to do. I had to say good-bye to my mother. And I had to go to Clova, if for nothing more than to see what was left there.

CHAPTER TEN

FINDING ONE ANOTHER

◎◎

"*If you don't come, I'll bloody kill you!*" my old friend Etta said in her thick Afrikaans accent on the phone. She was living in Johannesburg, in Rivonia, building clinics for AIDS orphans, and shelter for those who had nowhere to go. "If you bugger off to America without seeing me, I'll bloody kill you!" she said again.

Etta's house was not the self-sacrificing hut I expected, but a beautiful home in the northern suburbs where she entertained diplomats from around the world to support her ongoing work. She herself had not changed much, other than her straw-blond hair, now more practical, cut short around her still-astounding face. She still swore like a trooper, and cared about nothing but helping anyone she could, wherever and whenever she could. And I couldn't help noticing, she wore underwear now.

"You put me to shame, Etta," I said, watching her walk outside with a shaky little black fellow, no more than two, his face dripping with sweat from the simple act of taking a few steps—orphaned, and himself ravaged by the disease.

"Shame's a waste of time, Elizabeth. We can sit on our arses blaming ourselves, and worse, blaming someone else, or we can get up every day and bloody well do something. Look," she smiled, glancing at the boy walking valiantly beside her, "look, on he goes . . . No one to blame. No point. Just important that he goes on." She picked him up and carried him for the rest of the walk, wiping his streaming face with her sleeve.

"So, you sure you want to go alone?" she said.

I was sure.

The following night, Andrew and George stayed on with Etta, and I began the journey I had made so many times as a child.

From Joubert Park station, the train headed out past the gold mines, through the smell of smoke for so long called Soweto, now lit in patches with electric light, and then out, alongside the Great North Road. I did not long to stop at Warmbaths to swim in hot pools. I was in a rush, and for the first time that I could remember, I did not feel afraid. As the train rumbled and picked up speed, I saw the dark veld illuminated ahead, as if Francesco himself were lighting the way.

From what I'd heard, Clova had lain fallow for several years, in the care of the government while a buyer was sought. Once again, no one wanted it. The bloodshed there seemed to stain the land the way Mahila had ravaged it. It was finally purchased by a family who never lived there. Instead, they'd ceded it back to the government when the Bantustans were developed, official homelands created for the thousands of squatters descending over the borders of Angola, Zimbabwe, and Mozambique, seeking work and food. These homelands now edged the borders of Clova and the surrounding farms.

After bitter morning coffee at Soekmekaar, I followed the slanting sun through the train window along the first foothills of the Sout-pansberg Mountains, waiting like old friends, certain you will return.

At Louis Trichardt, I picked up a car and drove the last miles, turning off onto the red, sandy road where the rabbits had run across at nighttime. I came to a long dirt path that brought me to the old wire gate.

I turned off the engine and waited there in silence.

I had expected to find nothing, and I found not much more than that. No one came to the gate. I walked along the tiny stones that still lined the driveway.

"Last touch," I heard my grandfather say.

There was nothing much left of the house. It had been ransacked. Not a single belonging remained. Even the bricks that once had made the smooth, creamy walls had been removed one by one, stolen, so that all that stood were varying degrees of half walls. I felt oddly distant, as if looking at a painting of a ruin, until I noticed the cracked floor of cement, the red, polished floor of the stoep. I sat down on it.

No Vendas stood proud and dark in the distance, no sjambok whip cracked.

I did not enter the half walls of the house. I did not wish to see the pride of the farmhouse, the inside bath. I did not want to walk down the passage.

Out on the verandah, I listened to the quiet, the audible, lazy haze of the heat. The Yesterday, Today, and Tomorrow seemed unchanged, in full bloom, flourishing as if it had noticed nothing. I could smell the sweetness of the blue plumbagos milked into the air by the sun, and the dryness of the windblown, long grass that now covered the farm as far as the eye could see. If I closed my eyes, I thought, it might rain.

Just as my father had warned, my mother had not known me when I went to see her. Like a tiny bird in her bed, her once beautiful hands thin and pale on her blanket, she stared vacantly into the room. The eyes I remembered, as blue as English violets, her pretty, pretty eyes, seemed washed and dull—empty. Her hair, neatly brushed by the nursing staff, fell in a small halo around her face. I sat at the foot of the bed hoping for a sign, a movement of her hand, maybe, to tell me she knew I was there.

None came.

After a while, I'd lifted the blankets from her feet. I smoothed and smoothed them, keeping my hands soft as I could. I gently patted, patted it all down and away as I had always done for her, hoping the warmth of my hand would let her know that I loved her.

And then I crept away.

She'd left a note that night. I knew it by heart. "My darling Elizabeth, my good girl. I ask simply that you know I did my very best. Look after your wonderful dad, and John. They are lucky fish to have you. I love you."

I stumbled off the verandah in a haze. I wanted to run into the fields of lucerne. They were gone. I wanted to run down to the kraal to find Sweetness and Gladness. They were gone. I wanted to run into the hills like Thoyo, to scream my grief to the wind. Instead, I ran through miles of tall, scratching grass, the sun beating down on my streaming face, until I lost my shoes and felt my feet plunge into the rose-brown earth.

I stood there, panting, all around me the wind folding the grass in waves. And in the shimmer of the foothills, I thought I saw a dark shadow, moving quickly at first then stopping, as if it had noticed me. It moved again, along the rim of the horizon, a mirage in the heat. A man? A dog . . . Tarzan . . . the man with the medals?

As the haze in my eyes subsided, I saw that it was indeed a young man. He was tall, black, extremely thin, in a dark suit with a white shirt. He seemed to walk straight out of the mountain. He walked with a sense of purpose.

"Hey!" I called out, waving.

He stopped, as if he'd heard something on the wind. The scent of smoke and sour porridge from the Bantustans was starting to claim the evening air.

"Hello!" I called again.

We began to walk toward each other. He stared at me as if he'd never seen another human. And, I suppose, I at him.

In his hand, he carried crumpled papers, maps of some kind. "Hello . . ." I extended my hand.

"Miess!" he said, shaking my hand, palm-thumb-palm, the African way. "What are you doing here?" His question stunned me. I did not know what to say.

"Who are you?" I asked politely.

"Minton," he said, putting his hand on his chest. "I am Minton."

I instantly knew him to be Venda from the coal black of his skin, the gentleness in his face. But he had no scars.

"Do I know you, Minton?"

"I don't know you, Miess," he said simply.

"Oh, I'm sorry, I'm Elizabeth," I said. "What are you doing here, Minton?"

"I have come to claim the land," he said. "I am trying to buy this land from the government." He looked off into the distance at the fading Soutpansberg. They seemed to have crept nearer in the dusk.

"Claim the land?" I said, almost inaudibly. My heart started to race.

He was an attorney, he said. He came here as often as he could, he said. He wanted the land for the memory of his mother, who had lived here as a child, and had told him of this place. Her name was Meendli.

He did not wait for me to ask. He told me that Meendli had been shipped away to the homelands, where he was born. She spoke often to him, as they scratched and scraped the barren earth for food, about a place called Clova, an old baas called George, who gave her strawberry jam. He made as if he were holding something in his arms, a child, meaning the way George had held the land.

"Meendli . . ." I tried to say. Minton, I suddenly remembered, was the name of a porcelain factory in England, the name under some of the cups in the kitchen at Clova.

Meendli had died of starvation in that homeland, he said. After years of drought and no food, "many, many" had died. He had come now to find this place of plenty called Clova, where his mother had been born.

He began with the first light of each morning, in the mountain, he told me, so that he could walk the land with his maps and look over it, stretching before him, at nightfall.

He invited me to walk with him. He showed me where the farm began and where it ended, according to his drawings.

And I told him some of where it began for me.

Before I turned to go, I wished him well. He extended both his hands to me. They were strong.

"Last touch," I said.

"Xchuse me, Miess?" he said, puzzled.

"I'm glad you are here," I said.

I saw Meendli in his face, beautifully imprinted there, the last light catching a copper glow in his hair. I wished for the sound of her mouth harp as I walked away. I cannot say that I heard it. I was distracted by the glint of hundreds of tiny wings, like moving pieces of twilight.

Butterflies.

I don't mean the majestic kind. I just mean the ordinary kind, bobbing about, the kind that come and go, and stun you with their beauty just the same. And you never forget the bright, momentary blur of them.

GLOSSARY

......

batho ba Modimo	Xhosa, *oh my God*
biltong	dried meat, like beef jerky
blerrie	Afrikaans pronunciation of *bloody*
broeks	shorts, or pants
boerewors	Afrikaans, farmer sausage
Broederbond	Dutch, Band of Brothers
broeders	Dutch, brothers
cozzie	swimsuit or swimming costume
doek	head scarf
dominee	pastor of an Afrikaans church
Dumela, dumela aghe	African, Hello, hello, how are you?
eintjie	vigorous weed
fokken	Afrikaans pronunciation of *fucking*
goef	South African English, slang for *swim*
hessian	sackcloth
Imithi goba kahle	Zulu traditional song: Everything will be all right
impi	Zulu warrior
kafee	small general store
kaffir	derogatory name for black person
kaffir-boeties	brother of kaffirs
kielie	Afrikaans, tickle
kinderkrans	Afrikaans children's Bible group
knopkierie	truncheon carved of wood
koeksister	Afrikaans, a sweet, baked pastry

kom binne	Afrikaans, come in
kraal	group of hut dwellings
kya	mud hut
laager	circle of wagons
laapa	Zulu, *over there*
Mabalel	poem of the same title by Eugene Marais, 1871–1936
Mevrou	Afrikaans, Mrs.
mielie	Afrikaans, corn
morgen	unit of land equal to 2.116 acres
mossies	common gray sparrow
my skattie	Afrikaans, my darling
niksgewoonds	Afrikaans, people used to nothing
"Nkosi Sikelel' iAfrika"	Zulu, "God Bless Africa"
picaninn	term of endearment for black child
rondawel	round mud hut with thatched roof
riempie	a thin rope made of animal hide
shongololo	common pitch-black garden worm
sies	Afrikaans, expression of disgust
sjambok	usually single-strand whip made of animal hide
spruit	Afrikaans, stream
stoep	verandah, or porch
sourmilk	traditional African / Xhosa food
suurpap	Afrikaans, porridge made with sourmilk
tannie	Afrikaans, aunt
thula baba	Xhosa, hush, baby
tickey/tiekie	tiny coin, threepenny bit
Tickets!	British derivation indicating ruin or dire consequences
Tokolosh	diminutive African folklore devil
tsotsi	violent black gang member
veld	open farmland, or countryside
veldskoens	Afrikaans, shoes made of buckskin
Venda	an African tribe

vieslike skande	Afrikaans, terrible scandal
volkspele	Afrikaans folk dancing
Voortrekkers	early Boer settlers, 1800s
vuilgoed	Afrikaans, filthy rubbish
vygie	succulent plant with bright flowers
Xhosa	an African tribe

ACKNOWLEDGMENTS

......

My deepest gratitude to Daniel Menaker for the skill and beauty of his editing, and the grace of his spirit. I am profoundly honored to work with him.

Heartfelt thanks and respect to Gina Centrello, and to the excellent people at Random House, especially Stephanie Higgs, Dennis Ambrose, Tom Perry, Karen Richardson, Barbara Fillon, Gabrielle Bordwin, Barbara Bachman, and Matt Kellogg.

Heather Schroder at ICM is a magnificent human being. I am grateful beyond words to know and work with her.

Margot Meyers for her passion, Martin Kooij for unlimited wisdom, and Sam Cohn for his immense care.

My profound thanks forever to Matt Salinger for the gift of his friendship, for reading, for his keen mind, for saving me from despair and exulting in my joy, and for his deep love of this story. Jayne Brook for being a true friend, and for her superb literary insight. Larry Moss, who first gave me the courage, and the best of himself, to begin an extraordinary journey. Louise Horvitz for wisdom and love beyond words. Sunya Currie, Jeff McCracken, Pat King, Peter Terry, and Jim Milio, who grace me with life-sustaining friendship.

My gratitude always to Howard Schultz and Dan Levitan, and thanks to John Kelly, Howard Rosenstone, Ron Gwiazda, and Dramatists Play Service, Inc.

For a thousand acts of kindness and so much more, Richard Baskin, Jason Alexander, Julie Harris, Jimi Kaufer, Mame Hunt, Mannie Manim, Fred Orner, Jeremy Taylor, George Joseph, Ledoux

Kessel, Guy Webster, Rory and Ginny O'Farrell, Constance Wiseman, Clare Martin, Patience Daniel, Lesley Harris, Jennifer Butler, Robin Rohr, Jean-Louis Rodrigue, Simon Willson, Penny Charteris, Fahiem Stellenboom, Caryl and the girls, and the Salinger family. To Caroline, Sally, Antoinette, Pamela, little Monica, Sharon, and Gwyneth—you are always in my heart. Derek and Kathleen Ralphs and family, especially Mary, little Clare, and Alan, the Hough family, and Srs. Imelda and Evangelist for indelible kindness. Isaac and Shirley Gien, Sjoerd Schaaff, Tsidii le Loka, Tsepo Mokone, Tish Goldberg Hill, and Paul Potgieter for generous research.

Gracie, Sylvia, Cam, Royd, Pete, Lol, Tony, Ian, and my family one and all, you are everything to me. Most of all, Kevin, Claire, and Megan, for caring so deeply and giving so much. And, immeasurably, to my beloved father and mother, Isaac and Shirley, for their deep love, generosity, and compassion. I am always on that walk with you.

To children of South Africa, old and young, near and far—I am grateful every moment.

ABOUT THE TYPE

This book was set in Caslon, a typeface first designed
in 1722 by William Caslon. Its widespread use by most
English printers in the early eighteenth century soon
supplanted the Dutch typefaces that had formerly prevailed.
The roman is considered a "workhorse" typeface
due to its pleasant, open appearance,
while the italic is exceedingly decorative.